By the same author

Dark Lantern
A Very Civil War
Out of the Shadows
The Widow
The House on the Hill

Three Sisters

CAROLINE ELKINGTON

Copyright © 2021 Caroline Elkington
All rights reserved
www.carolineelkington.net

For Nicki, Christina, Claire and Anna — the Backup Sisters.
With love.

One

The sight that met the gentleman's coldly critical gaze, as his carriage turned the last corner before the village, was not at all what he had anticipated. He had been looking forward in a desultory fashion to being back in the countryside after a brief sojourn in London on unavoidable business matters and had always enjoyed the final part of the journey as they climbed the long wooded hill to his ancestral home near the summit. Although, being a smoothly rounded Cotswold hill, he felt it barely merited the title of summit, which sounded as though it should be graced with a peak and a cairn of stones. His hill was more like the shoulder of a well-rounded female.

He let down the glass and poked his head out of the window to see what all the noise was about.

The area of grass, wishfully given the grand name of The Village Green, was barely long or wide enough to keep anything but some very narrow, well-behaved cattle or some small sheep, as long as they remained single file at all times.

There was a rusting water pump, a horse pool, which was home to three white ducks, and an apple tree, which, as it was May, was in full bloom, a pale pink carpet of fallen petals circling its elderly trunk like a forgotten petticoat. Its apples were sour and usually left to rot unless fed to livestock, but no one had the heart to chop it down and replace it. There were also the village stocks, which had long since fallen into disrepair and had not been used in earnest since the previous century.

Until now.

He banged on the carriage ceiling with his silver topped cane and bellowed at the coach driver to stop, which the fellow did, pulling up the horses with no thought for their delicate mouths, obviously imagining it to be an emergency worthy of such an overly dramatic response. The only occupant of the carriage swore roundly and jumped down onto the lane.

With a furious word to his driver, he strode across the green, cutting a swathe though the small knot of onlookers, wielding his cane like a small-sword.

The surprised recipients of sharp blows to their backs or shoulders, jumped smartly out of his path and had the grace to look a little shamefaced, before the more cowardly of them slunk away hoping not to be recognised.

"What is this!" snarled the gentleman to the remaining few, as he came up to the old stocks and looked down from his great height at the outraged occupant of the medieval instrument of public humiliation.

She looked back at him, her face streaked with mud and tears, which he suspected, quite correctly, were tears of anger rather than self-pity. He observed with a frown the last of the village boys making themselves scarce and noted his estate steward's son retreating figure and the youngest child of the innkeeper but having registered their frightened faces, he turned his attention back to the object of their persecution.

He quickly prised open the heavy iron bar, which thankfully had not been padlocked and lifted the wooden plank up so that the imprisoned creature could escape.

This she did, with more haste than dignity, and flushed with indignation, she pulled her voluminous skirts down around her bony ankles.

"*Oh!*" she growled, and it was indeed a growl as she sounded like a maddened wild animal. "*OH!* I am *incensed!* I shall murder them all! Every one! The *varlets!* The *slipgibbets!* You *scullions! Rampallians! Fustilarians!*" she shouted after the departing miscreants.

"I believe it would be prudent to stop there," interrupted her rescuer, as she paused briefly to take a breath, "Before you betray the full and shocking depth of your knowledge of thieves' cant and Shakespearean insults! Where a young lady such as yourself managed to acquire such a grasp on the language of the underworld, I cannot begin to think. I would tell you that I was much impressed were I not so afraid of attracting your ire!"

The girl snapped her mouth shut and scowled up at him. "You know Shakespeare?" she asked in a more reasonable voice.

"Not personally, no, but I was forced to read a good many of his works by my tutor."

"*Forced!* But, why did you have to be *forced?* You must surely realise that he was a *genius!*"

"So I've been told. You clearly have a keen regard for his words."

She smiled through the smears of mud, "Oh, yes indeed!" she sighed, "He had a way of making words into the prettiest things imaginable! So delightful when spoken — "

"Or bellowed so vociferously."

The smile widened into a bucktoothed grin, "I'm not sure what that means but it's a lovely word!"

"It means forcefully. As in you were shouting very loudly."

She cocked her head at him, "That's interesting. You're not talking down to me," she observed in some wonderment. "And you haven't yet told me that little girls should mind their manners and be seen but not heard!"

He laughed, "No, indeed! Why should I? You already seem to have an adequate, albeit rather scandalous vocabulary, so who am I to carp? Why shouldn't you show an interest in learning what is, in comparison, an inoffensive word. It's obviously a keen interest of yours."

"Cursing?"

"Well, that too, I suppose! But I meant language in general. Shakespeare, more specifically."

"I *adore* Shakespeare! Although I'm not supposed to read it really. According to Aunt Euphemia, it will spoil my mind and make me unsuitable for matrimony. *Marriage!* I'm only fourteen!"

Recalling his manners, the gentleman rescuer put out a hand, "We haven't been formally introduced, Miss — ?"

She wiped her filthy hand on her skirts and grasped his firmly, "Pennington. Miss *Pandora* Pennington."

He bowed elegantly over her still grimy hand, "Miss Pennington, Marcus Denby, at your service."

"Oh! I've *heard* of *you!* You're the gentleman who lives at Cuckoopen Manor. I heard all about — " she faltered for the first time, "Oh, I — I'm sorry! I would *never* gossip! Augusta wouldn't approve!"

"It seems my reputation unfortunately precedes me. I am indeed that gentleman. I dread to think what you have heard. No! Please don't feel you have to enlighten me! I must assume Augusta is your very strict ?"

Miss Pandora Pennington laughed at this, "Oh, gracious no! She's my eldest sister."

"She sounds as though she's rather stern."

This was greeted with a resigned sigh, "She is a trifle serious sometimes. But it is only because her life is one of endless toil and misery!"

"Oh, dear. That is most unfortunate."

"She does it all for the sake of the family, you know! Suffers so."

Sir Marcus Denby hid his amusement well, "I'm sorry to hear it. Is there nothing that can be done to rescue her from a lifetime of drudgery?"

"No, she says it's her lot and she is perfectly happy with it."

Thinking the sister sounded like a strait-laced old maid, he changed the subject and said, "I noticed that you emphasised your name rather deliberately."

She pursed her lips and scuffed the toe of one satin sandal on the grass, its ribbon dangling dangerously, "Well, yes, that's very noticing of you, Sir! I am in the habit of doing that because even though the name Pandora is utterly ridiculous, I'm generally called — *Dora* — and I particularly dislike having such a humdrum name. A name can say all the wrong things about one, do you not think? You see, you're called

Marcus — a very fine Roman name and Shakespeare used it too — although — " she paused, her good manners finally getting the better of her.

"*Although*, if my very poor memory serves, did not Marcus Brutus stab Caesar?"

"He *did!* But he was *much* goaded!"

"Was he? I'm not sure my classics master would have agreed."

"Well, your classics master sounds like a perfect nincompoop!"

Miss Pennington saw his dark brows go up and she reddened beneath the muddy signs of battle, "I'm so sorry, I shouldn't have said that. Sometimes my tongue runs away with me, and it gets me into no end of trouble."

"I can see that it might. But now, to more important matters, Miss Pennington, if I may? Those nasty little boys? Why had they put you in the stocks? It seems an odd thing to do to such a cultured female."

She couldn't quite meet his searching gaze and looked down with great interest at the grass stains on her sandals. "I shall be in Augusta's black books."

"Why is that? Because of the boys?"

"No, because I *begged* for satin slippers even though I knew we couldn't afford them — and *look* at them — they are ruined on their very first outing! And she will tell me over and *over* how very *expensive* they were, and I shall probably have to scrub floors and eat gruel as penance."

She missed the vexed look that crossed Marcus Denby's severe features, "Would you like me to have a word with her — to explain how you came to be in such a predicament? Perhaps she might relent."

Her eyes flew to his, wide and anxious, "Dear me, please don't! She would be so very cross that I had once again brought — ig — igno — "

"Ignominy?"

"Yes, *that!* She's always worrying about it. She thinks it will ruin us."

He glanced around and seeing the driver holding the restless horses steady, he came to a sudden decision.

"Where do you live, Miss Pennington? I don't think I've heard your name before — so I don't believe you can be local — "

"We *are!* Now. I mean, you're correct, we weren't to begin with — we were from Cheltenham, but we had no choice but to come here — or we might have sunk further into penury and ended our days in the poorhouse!"

"Is that so? I'm exceedingly sorry to hear that. So, perhaps if you tell me your direction, I can take you home in my carriage."

Miss Pennington considered him carefully for a moment and then looked longingly at the extremely smart travelling carriage with his coat of arms emblazoned on the side in scrolled and gilded lettering. It was too tempting! How could anyone resist! Such a dilemma was unfair for a girl whose head was stuffed with romantic notions and adventure!

"That would be — *as fine as fivepence!* The girls will all be so envious — but — Augusta wouldn't like it. She would say that I should never get into a stranger's carriage! Of course, you're *not* a stranger anymore! We have been introduced! And after all you rescued me — although I must tell you that I had a *splendid* plan of escape and didn't really *need* rescue!"

"Of course not. I merely assisted you. If you could show me where you live — no one need see you in your present state of — disarray."

She glanced down at her clothes indifferently, "I suppose it would save Augusta from becoming *overwhelmed* with shame. All right, I'll accept your kind offer," she said, inclining her head graciously, "And anyway, they'll be so *green* with envy when they see me ride up behind such *prime-goers!*"

Sir Marcus choked back a laugh and taking her hand guided her around the stocks and across the rough green to his much-admired equipage. He handed her into the carriage and saw her settled before having a word with his driver.

"Aye, Sir. I know where that one does live. She's forever getting herself into scrapes! A regular little hoyden by all accounts."

His master instructed him to take them there before heading home to the Manor. The driver touched his forehead and grumbled a bit, but seeing his employer's expression, he jumped back onto his box, waited until everyone was seated and then he drove right through the village and along the lane that led to the church before turning into a short driveway and passing through some dilapidated wooden gates.

Looking out of the window with interest, Sir Marcus asked Miss Pennington if she was sure they were going in the right direction.

"Oh, yes, Sir Marcus. This is where I live."

"Good God," murmured her rescuer, "You are from the Seminary?"

"Why do you say it like *that?*"

He looked out of the window at the house as they approached it. An ugly mishmash of architecture, none of it of any merit; not a mansion by any means but a good-sized rambling house that appeared to have arrived there by some terrible accident, to form an entirely forgettable building that no man would own to designing. He shuddered and wondered who would consign their daughters to such a place; surely no one with any sense or enough money to send them to a renowned boarding school or to hire excellent tutors for them at home.

At this point his small companion stuck her head out of the window and shouted a very creditable view-halloo that made him wince.

The carriage drew to a halt in front of the house and the main door opened to reveal a small group of girls, a very tiny elderly lady, who instantly reminded him of a heron, and they were followed out by a very pretty stout girl with a worried expression and then another, older female with shining chestnut hair and a high bridged, long nose. She was dressed in severe dark grey crape as though in mourning and she had the distinct air of one who was braced for a fight.

She eased her way through the overawed girls and tripped lightly down the steps to greet the visitors.

Sir Marcus handed his companion from the carriage onto the gravel drive and turned to acknowledge the female who he surmised might be the elder sister.

"Miss Pennington?" he said but got no further because he was interrupted.

"*Gussie!* This is Sir Marcus Denby from Cuckoopen Manor! He brought me home in his *carriage!*"

"I can see that, Dora," replied Augusta Pennington in her softly modulated voice, "What have I said about — ?"

"Well, I *told* him you'd say that! But you see — I had no choice!"

"No choice?" repeated her sister with some asperity, "No choice! Pray tell me exactly why you now resemble a ragamuffin when, last I saw you, you were neat as a new pin?"

"Perhaps, I might provide an explanation," offered the gentleman, "I did rather insist that she came with me — "

"*Did* you indeed! When I have spent the last decade telling her on no account to go off with strangers, which she is so very inclined to do!"

"I can only apologise Miss Pennington. At the time I thought it was probably for the best, to save her from walking through the village looking like a — ragamuffin."

There was a moment's silence and then, "I do beg your pardon, Sir. I am a little agitated after spending a good hour searching for her, we are all weary and anxious." She turned to her small sister, "How on earth did you come to get so — *grubby?*"

Dora Pennington shrugged, "It was Silas and Roger and the others — they were throwing stones at the ducks on the horse pond and so I threw a pebble at them and hit Silas on the cheek — which I have to say was a very *lucky* shot — but he practically had a *seizure* and chased after me and I would have escaped, but I tripped over my slipper riband and they caught me and put me in the stocks and threw *mud* at me and that's when Sir Marcus came along in his fine carriage and chased them away — "

"Dora! Are you hurt? Are the ducks all right? Oh, you poor thing!"

The younger Miss Pennington had the grace to look somewhat abashed and cast an apologetic glance at her rescuer, hoping he would understand that her sister was not always this compassionate where she was concerned. She was pleased to see his answering nod and she was able to reassure her sister that she and the ducks had all escaped unscathed. Although, she said, conspiratorially, Silas had bled quite badly and would probably have a permanent scar!

Augusta Pennington sighed, "I shall have to pay his mother a visit tomorrow at the inn. Oh, dear me, and she's such a dragon where he's concerned and believes him always to be innocent of all charges!"

"Would you like me to intervene, ma'am?" asked Sir Marcus.

"Gracious no! I am very used to dealing with her and shall get it sorted in a trice! But thank you for offering and for bringing Dora home safely."

"It was a great pleasure and very — educational," responded Sir Marcus blandly.

Miss Augusta Pennington flinched slightly, "Oh heavens, has she been quoting at you? I do beg your pardon — she has yet to understand that not everyone is as bookish as she! She's of an age where she believes everyone should have their minds improved and is quite determined to do so whether they want it or not."

Sir Marcus caught the swift sidelong look from the younger sister and decided not to allude to her actual choice of words, "The quotes were exceedingly apt," he said with a polite smile, "I have to admit that I was impressed, as it's a rare thing to find a female with an aptitude for reciting Shakespeare."

"It was used to incense her father."

His eyes slid to the darkly unfashionable gown, "Your father? Is he — ?"

"Long since," she replied shortly. "Thrown while out hunting."

He looked suitably sympathetic and gestured at the ill-favoured building behind her, "I'm sorry to hear that. You have been here long? I had not realised that the Seminary had changed hands."

She shot a glance at the elderly lady beside her, "It hasn't really changed hands, Sir Marcus. Allow me to introduce you to Miss Beauchamp, an aunt of mine — and the proprietor of this establishment."

The little lady, all in shades of light blueish grey with quantities of lace about her shoulders and in her silver hair, and an abundance of pearls, stepped forward and peered short-sightedly up at him, "How do you do, Sir Marcus — what a pleasure it is to finally meet you."

He gallantly kissed her proffered hand, very much in the old style and admired the pronounced twinkle in her harebell-blue eyes, "Miss Beauchamp, it's an honour. I have of course, heard of your establishment."

The elderly lady smiled merrily up at him, "My sister and I began the school twenty years ago, but she is now bed-ridden, and I cannot run it by myself. It is so very fortuitous that Augusta and her sisters were able to join us because otherwise we would have had to close down, and I cannot imagine this horrid old place without the sound of our girls running amok within its walls! The sounds of joy can change the complexion of an ugly pile such as this."

Augusta Pennington gently urged the other lady forward; she had been lurking at the back of the little gaggle of girls with a disapproving frown marring her remarkably pretty face, "And this is my middle sister, Miss Flora."

He bowed, she bobbed a curtsy and pleasantries were exchanged, but he was given the very marked impression that he did not meet with her approval. "Three sisters? No brothers?"

Miss Flora Pennington curled her lip, "Thankfully no. Three sisters are quite enough — there's seldom any peace to be had as it is. Imagine if there were boys too!"

"Not all boys are the same. I was not in the least disruptive as a child. I doubt you would have even noticed me," remarked Sir Marcus.

"You are a rarity then!" declared Flora with undisguised disdain.

Her elder sister, seeking to change the subject before things became too heated, said, "May I offer you refreshments, Sir Marcus? We shouldn't have kept you standing out here all this time. Unless, of course, you have more important matters to attend?"

He took the not-very-subtle hint and politely declined, and bowing, bid farewell to the curious assembly, said something polite and unmemorable to Miss Beauchamp, nodded to Miss Flora and as he was offered Miss Dora's grubby hand, shook it firmly and hoped that she would soon recover from her nasty experience.

"Oh, *pooh!*" said that young lady wrinkling her nose, "If you hadn't happened along, I would have routed them in a moment!" Then on seeing her elder sister's admonishing expression, remembered her much neglected manners, "But, *thank you* very much for releasing me from the stocks. I wasn't sure if I'd be able to reach the metal bar or lift that heavy plank — so you were *quite* useful after all!" She saw the light in his eyes, "And I truly *adored* riding in your carriage! It'll be a real feather in my cap!"

"I am delighted that I could be of service. Perhaps you will allow me to take you for a longer drive one day to see the orchards blossoming?"

"Oh, yes, that would be most acceptable!" said Miss Pandora Pennington earnestly.

He acknowledged them all and then climbed back into the elegant carriage and they watched until it had disappeared through the gates and was heard clattering up the long hill.

A short but meaningful silence ensued.

Dora glanced at Augusta anxiously, biting her lip.

Miss Beauchamp sighed lustily, "Well, you may now be in something of a fix Dora, but it was well worth it for a glimpse of that Adonis!"

"Adonis?" scoffed Flora, "He was hardly that! He wouldn't have looked out of place in an undertaker's parlour! What a solemn countenance and cold eyes! No wonder his wife — "

"Flora! That's quite enough, thank you!" said Augusta in her most quelling voice, "And, Dora, you had better go and get Jennet to help you out of those disgraceful clothes! And do try not to get mud everywhere! Oh, look at your slippers! They are quite ruined."

Dora rolled her eyes and turned to stamp mutinously up the steps. She stopped at the top and looked back at her sisters, "He knows Shakespeare! And he said I had a very good vocabulary!" and with that parting shot, she disappeared into the house, followed by an equally sullen Flora.

Augusta took a deep breath and met her aunt's mischievous eyes, with her own concerned hazel ones, "It's all very well, dearest Aunt Ida but it will not do! She cannot just vanish when she pleases and return in the company of someone we know very little about apart from some very salacious gossip! If word gets out, we shall be ostracised, and the school will suffer!"

Miss Ida Beauchamp gave a little chuckle, "I think, as usual, you are making a mountain out of a molehill, my love. Apart from being an unusually burly sort of fellow, he seemed to be otherwise most unexceptional — one would never guess that he had such an interesting history! One should not be tempted to judge anyone by their outward appearance — be they Hephaestus or Adonis. Appearances can be surprisingly deceiving. It is quite possible that our apparently notorious new neighbour is as mild as milk beneath that arresting exterior."

Augusta frowned, "You do not *really* think him an Adonis, Aunt?"

Miss Beauchamp gave her a pitying look, "*Beauty is bought by the judgement of the eye.*"

"Shakespeare," said her niece with a shake of her head and no small amount of resignation. "I thought him more like Hephaestus, so very — ugly — well, no not ugly precisely, but — sinister looking!"

"Do you not think that perhaps his past is to answer for that? Are we not merely the sum of what has happened to us? He has clearly suffered a good deal in his life, and it shows. One would never guess looking at me now, but before all our trials and tribulations, I was once considered a great beauty!"

Augusta couldn't help but laugh as she had inherited her aunt's likeness including the dreadful Beauchamp nose and something of her plainness. Sadly, she had not her *joie de vivre* and ability to find the good in everyone and everything. Augusta feared she was much more like Aunt Euphemia who lay abed upstairs and was probably, at that very moment, ringing crossly for her tea!

Reading her face, Aunt Ida put her delicate hand upon Augusta's arm, "You are nothing at all like Phemie! She was utterly spoiled by Papa because of her inestimable beauty and was ruined by the empty admiration of those who so unhelpfully worshipped at her feet. She was never made to consider using her brain. It's just fortunate that she excelled at watercolours and sewing! Poor thing. You and I, however, are made of sterner stuff and if you'd just allow it your life could be very different. Along with an impressive nose, you have our much-despised streak of Beauchamp impulsiveness — it has been the cause of many of our ordeals. But sadly, *your* past has weighed you down with more responsibility than you would like, and you have forgotten how to enjoy yourself, preferring to hide yourself away in case you are made to endure any discomfort or humiliation."

"Oh! Well, that's certainly a damning description! I had not realised I had become so very commonplace! How galling."

"Augusta Pennington! You know very well that you are far from commonplace! Who else would have taken on a boarding school like this with no complaints and at a moment's notice! You are quite an extraordinary young lady and if it hadn't been for you, we would have lost our little school and would be living under a hedge!"

"Nonsense! *We* were in a much worse predicament, and you rescued *us!* Once Papa was no longer around, we were bound for the poorhouse, but your wonderful letter came just at the right moment — I could say at the *last* minute! The house had been sold and the new owners were practically banging on the door and moving their trunks in!"

"It was serendipity."

"Yes, I suppose it was. Now all we have to do is save the school!" !"

Two

Approaching Cuckoopen Manor, the glossy black carriage slowed and took the turning to the stables, the driver well aware that his master disliked being put down at the front of the house.

Sir Marcus jumped down, thanked both driver and groom and went into the house by way of the kitchens. Luckily the staff had heard the sound of the wheels crunching on the long drive and had all leapt to their various tasks just as though they had been toiling ceaselessly since the day he left.

They may as well not have troubled themselves because the Lord of the Manor marched past them with only the most cursory of nods in greeting, apart from when he spied his butler loitering in the hall.

"Beecher! There you are. I should have sent warning, but I was overcome with a sudden desire to be back in my own place and not amongst strangers and had not either the time nor the inclination to compose a letter or send a messenger," he said brusquely.

"No, of course not, Sir Marcus. Everything is ready anyway so it would have been wasted effort, we are always prepared for your arrival," said Beecher in his habitually enervated tones.

"Naturally, I know I can always depend upon you. Anything to report — of any urgency? I have no desire to know about damned molehills or any such nonsense."

"There is a quantity of correspondence on your desk, Sir."

"That sounds ominous," reflected Sir Marcus, "Nothing else?"

"Nothing, Sir."

His master strode away towards his study but stopped on the threshold and looked back at his butler, who had not yet moved, anticipating such an occurrence.

"The Boarding School run by the Misses Beauchamp?"

"Yes, Sir?"

"What do you know about it?"

"Very little. I have heard however that recently they had been failing to attract any more boarders and were in danger of closing. Also, that some young ladies have come from Cheltenham to live there — the nieces I understand. I believe, although I would not swear to it, that the elder Miss Beauchamp has taken to her bed making it impossible for her sister to continue with the running of the school alone."

"Ah, those will be the ladies I just encountered. The Penningtons. And I was introduced to Miss Ida Beauchamp — a rather superior lady. Any other gossip, Beecher?"

His butler sniffed in a deeply offended manner, "*Gossip*, Sir! I do not listen to *gossip*. I merely happened to bump into Miss Beauchamp in church a few weeks ago and she informed me of the changes. Was there anything else, Sir Marcus?"

"No, you may go!"

"Very well, Sir," said Beecher unhappily and he left the hall, his back rigid with offence.

Smiling to himself, Sir Marcus went into his study and closed the door. He leant upon it for a moment and breathed in the scent of leather-bound books, an applewood fire, lit candles and his horrid dog, Quince.

That creature had, on hearing his lord and master in the hall, jumped down from the forbidden sofa and placed himself in readiness by the door, so that he was able to hinder his master's entrance into the room to greater effect, by being forced to back away as the door opened, wag his tail and jump up at the same time, therefore creating a sort of animated barricade, which first had to be overcome in order to gain access to the study.

After the initial greetings were out of the way and the feverish whining and fawning had ceased, Sir Marcus instructed him firmly to return to his bed. Quince cast a longing glance at the still-warm, fur-covered sofa and slumped desolately into his cold and unwelcoming basket. He hauled himself upright again turned around and around, trying to find the perfect spot to settle and then collapsed once more, this time with a long-suffering sigh. Lying one paw across his nose, he returned to his dreams of chasing squirrels in the woods.

His master eyed him with disfavour and wondered why on earth he had allowed his brother to foist such an unruly beast upon him and then he turned reluctantly to the pile of correspondence that awaited him. He began to sort through the letters, discarding some and putting others into a separate pile. His actions slowed and he gazed out of the casement at the Manor's extensive grounds and allowed his mind to wander.

Dora Pennington and her odd sisters came to the fore and he thought idly about the school and began to consider why it might be failing. Times were changing and a seminary run by two elderly, old-fashioned ladies was bound to have lost its allure when there were now so many other establishments in competition with it. Education for females was becoming quite the fashion apparently. He had no doubt that their syllabus would have been an unedifying mixture of etiquette, dancing, sewing and possibly Italian, if they were lucky. Nothing out of the ordinary to entice the new, increasingly wealthy, middling sort of folk to their door. Now that it was considered acceptable to educate one's daughters, new schools were springing up all over the country. The Beauchamp Seminary would find itself very much out of step with the newcomers and would more than likely be forced out of business. He imagined, from just her outward appearance, that Miss Augusta Pennington was probably of the same mind as her aunts and would eschew any sudden changes to the syllabus and any innovative advances would be rejected out of hand.

He shrugged. Well, more fool her! The only way to succeed nowadays was to modernise — or be left behind to bob helplessly in the backwash as the innovators sailed away with what should have been your earnings.

He returned his attention to the sheaf of envelopes and papers in his hand.

Shaking his head, he opened the first letter of interest with an ivory knife and wondered why he was even bothering to waste his energy thinking about such trivial things as education for females. It was none of his damned business what they did with their school. He paused and considered why he had been moved to show an interest in the first place.

Miss Dora Pennington — or should it be Pandora! There had been something about the way she had conducted herself when under heavy fire and thoroughly outgunned and outnumbered. She showed no fear and despite the obvious dangers of her situation, she had remained sanguine about her chances of escape and when released had issued forth a volley of pithy insults that had shocked and impressed him. He realised that he'd forgotten to ask where she had encountered Shakespeare's works — he doubted the elder sister would approve of such ripe language. She had the look of a typical schoolmistress — starchy and humourless.

"I have a feeling that I shall be seeing Miss Pandora Pennington again whether I want to or not," he said to Quince, who was moved only to twitch a whiskery eyebrow in response.

"Her sisters seem to be wholly unexceptional. In fact — which one was it — yes, Flora — although undoubtedly a very pretty girl, she looked ill-humoured, and the elder sister was — *what* was she?" He pulled his mouth down as he thought and decided he hadn't been left with much of an impression at all. She seemed a little insipid but had not, thankfully, appeared to be the ogress that Dora Pennington had described so vividly. She had shown proper concern for her sister's welfare and no hint of there being imminent punishment for the mud-spattered runaway. Few gentlemen would look twice at her; she had her aunt's features but not her sparkle. Her clothes were obviously chosen in an effort to make her look matronly and as though she were capable of running a school. It hadn't worked. She merely looked unapproachable and uninspiring.

"It's rather peculiar that only the youngest sibling should be so lively and engaging. The difference is quite marked and unusual." But the dog remained unmoved by his ruminations. His attention returned to the letter he held, the direction on the front written in a very familiar, lavishly curlicued hand.

"Forget the school and its inmates! This letter can only mean one thing — and it cannot be good."

He was right.

He read the contents and his expression darkened dramatically until the point at which his staff, who knew his moods well, would have run for cover.

It was at this point that Beecher scratched on the door and quietly entered the study, saw his master's thunderous face and backed out again on tiptoe. Dinner would have to wait, he thought.

The letter was crushed to an unreadable ball and thrown into the fire. It hit the firebricks at the back and bounced out again, landing on the Persian rug where it burst merrily into flames.

Sir Marcus leapt to his feet and kicked the letter into the hearth where he quickly stamped out the fire whilst cursing roundly. Once it had cooled, he picked up the now singed missive and spread it out, charred flakes drifting to the floor and his hands turning black from the soot.

He reread it, his already grim mouth, clenched into a thin straight line.

"Hell and damnation!" he uttered with some violence.

The butler hovered outside the study waiting for the sounds of wrath to die down before he dared to venture back in to announce dinner and ask if Sir Marcus would be requiring the covers to be laid in the dining room as it was just him supping.

Beecher was devoted to his master, but not blindly so. He had learnt, over the many years he had served him so faithfully, just when to remain out of sight and when to make his presence known. If one happened upon Sir Marcus when he was in low spirits, one was very likely to have one's head bitten off and then stamped on. It wasn't even the abundant amounts of wine or brandy that were consumed, it was the fact that he imbibed alone that caused Beecher's concern. Drinking alone was never a good notion — particularly for someone as morose and hot-headed as Sir Marcus. The day after an immoderate bout, his master was generally not fit for anything apart from sitting with his head in his hands and complaining about the infernal noise of the dog breathing and the blinding light of the candles. Everyone stayed in the servants' quarters and kept their heads down. It was a foolish hireling indeed who put their head above the parapet because, despite his deplorable condition, he was still a remarkably fine shot! His tongue was notoriously sharp-edged and, when in his cups, he was inclined to dismiss servants without thought. Beecher would have to calm their shattered nerves and re-hire them the following morning and Sir Marcus never seemed to notice that they remained in his employ.

He wondered what was in the letter that had triggered this outburst. He had an unpleasant suspicion that it might be the usual ghost from his master's past and, if it turned out to be that, it would very likely end in *several* servants being dismissed and he could even envisage his own untimely heave-ho from the Manor — although, when it had on occasion happened before, he had taken no notice and carried on as though nothing untoward had occurred. Sir Marcus had said nothing, when daylight eventually dawned, to torment him, and normal life had quietly and inexorably been resumed with no acknowledgement of the unspeakable deeds committed on the night of excess.

Beecher pondered his master's strange enquiry about the Misses Beauchamp's Boarding School — it had been entirely unexpected as he had never heard the place mentioned before. He wondered what had suddenly prompted an interest in such a thing. No gentleman in his right mind would take any notice of a school for ladies, least of all his employer. As he plodded glumly back to the kitchens, Beecher made a mental note to make enquiries in the village. He was not going to be caught napping again! Preparation was the key to staying in control of his domain.

* * *

In the rather chilly parlour of the Misses Beauchamp's Boarding School, Augusta Pennington was wearing her sternest expression and frowning at her youngest sister with a kind of weary resignation. She was optimistically hoping to impress upon the wayward child the importance of paying attention to sensible advice. It was met by resolutely dry eyes and a mouth held so tightly shut that a wafer could not have passed between her lips.

"Dora, I cannot allow your behaviour to go unpunished! Otherwise, how would that look to the other boarders? They would believe I have one rule for you and another for them! One cannot govern the school like that. They would write to their parents and complain about unfair treatment. No, it really will not do! I'm afraid you must make reparation for being so wilful. I am very sorry, but I must confiscate your Shakespeare."

"*No!*" cried the delinquent child, tearing at her hair in anguish, "*Anything* but that! That's too *cruel!* I *promise* I will behave! I will study all day and help the other girls, even the ones I don't like, and I will *even* sit with Aunt Euphemia — just *please* don't take my books!"

Inwardly wavering, Augusta tried hard to stand to her guns with a show of courage that was all pretence. But her sister was gifted in the art of wearing down her opponent with relentless rejoinders until she would forget the reasons for the admonishment and would give in almost without realising what had happened.

Augusta was determined that this was the moment to make a stand and ensure that the frequently wayward Dora would not endanger herself or bring shame upon her family again. Since their father had died so tragically and so unnecessarily, she had let things slip because she had more pressing matters on her mind — like keeping a roof over their heads and food upon the table. Also, it was easier to ignore the tantrums and strange fancies than to face up to endlessly having to chastise or cajole.

She was ashamed to say that during those bleak early days when so little made sense, Flora had seen that her younger sister was getting away with some exceedingly poor behaviour and she stepped in and took over the disciplining and Augusta had been truly grateful. She was glad to have one less concern and failed to notice that as a consequence of her inability to govern, both her sisters were suffering. It was ironic that she had had to take charge of the school and was expected to save the establishment from imminent collapse. Everyone depended upon it. Everyone was depending upon *her,* and she could depend upon no one.

Her sisters were, on the whole, far too young and inexperienced to be reliable and her aunts — well, one was very amusing and a fount of wisdom, but she was becoming quite frail, although she would never admit to it, and the other — the other was really quite tiresome with her constant demands and the forgetfulness that had come upon her recently. Aunt Euphemia was not good at managing her anxiety, so she had taken to her bed in order to have some control over her environs. It may only be her bedchamber, but it was to quickly become her own personal queendom and she ruled it by being as taxing as she could be.

Augusta felt sorry for Dora but knew she must stand her ground in this battle or lose the war.

"You will please bring me all your volumes of Shakespeare and I will keep them for a fortnight."

This was met with silent outrage when Augusta had expected a fit of hysterics and she was for a moment, taken aback, and then she saw the marshal glint in her sister's pale blue eyes.

"If you do not, Dora, I shall be forced to take steps."

Dora tossed her head and shrugged carelessly.

Augusta clenched her jaw, "I will seize all your books and keep them for a month!"

"You wouldn't *do* that! *Nobody* could be that wicked!"

"I can and I will. Now please, go and fetch them and don't even think of hiding any — I know precisely what you have on your shelf."

"*Oh!*" exclaimed Dora in disbelief, "*OH!* I shall *never* forgive you!"

And she ran from the parlour and slammed the door behind her, leaving her sister shaking with both fury and anxiety. She put a trembling hand to her mouth and tried to steady herself. She had always hated arguments and any show of anger usually had her scurrying for safety. Her father had been much given to losing his temper for no good reason and it had meant that she now did her level best to quash any tantrums before they began. It didn't always succeed, but until now she had managed to deflect most of the girls' youthful passions into something more constructive; some form of exercise generally helped Dora, and in Flora's case she had noticed that a nice slice of bread and butter calmed her. Flora was not given to rages; she sulked and glowered and fretted. Augusta was very much afraid that Flora's temperament was more like Aunt Euphemia's than was altogether comfortable.

The door was suddenly flung open, and Dora thundered back in and dropped a stack of some eight or so volumes of Shakespeare's plays and sonnets onto the table.

"There!" she said furiously, "I hope you're *happy* now!"

Augusta sighed, "You know very well that I am not happy! How *can* I be when you are so miserable and when you refuse to listen to advice? You must consider that you may very well have been seriously hurt, Dora! What if those dreadful boys had, God forbid, left you in the stocks for hours and someone in the village had seen you in such a predicament? It would have made a dreadful scandal and we would have been ruined!"

"That's all you ever care about! Scandal! You don't care about us!" said Dora in a deceptively quiet voice. "I cannot think why you should be so obsessed with such things. Nobody cares!"

"I have my reasons and I can assure you that Polite Society *does* care and will make anyone who does not conform to their rules pay the price and they will be ostracised. That means that you and Flora could find it difficult to meet acceptable suitors and you may never have the chance to marry."

"Oh, pooh! What do I care for marriage! I hope I never have to marry! Anyway, y*ou* are still a spinster!"

Augusta winced at the word — it always made her think of a spider crouching in its web, waiting and waiting for a fly to come along. But no fly comes. "Honestly, you cannot use me as a gauge — I have no desire to marry — "

"Then why should *I?*" cried Dora plaintively. "I can see why you'd want Flora to wed because she'd have to move away! That would be a blessing for everyone — except her unfortunate husband!"

Augusta shook her head in despair, "I do wish that you wouldn't talk about your sister in that way — it's not kind and it does not show you in a good light either. She cannot help the way she is, any more than you can help the way *you* are!"

"So, I need not change then!" declared Dora in triumph.

"You know that's not what I meant," replied Augusta stiffly. "I mean that none of us can help our temperaments, but that does not mean to say that one cannot at least try to modify them in some way in order to fit into society."

"I do not *want* to fit into society! I want to be an author or an explorer and travel the world looking for undiscovered wild animals and plants. I most certainly do *not* want to sit about painting Grecian urns! What a dreadful prospect!"

"You do not want to have children and the security of a comfortable husband who will care for you and a home of your own? You would rather travel the world in great discomfort and probably die of some dreadful foreign disease in Constantinople?"

She received an old-fashioned look, "I could die of some dreadful disease in *England!* And we don't exactly live in great comfort as it is."

"Dora! This house may not be the epitome of style but at least it's a roof over our heads and provides a respectable means of supporting ourselves."

Dora sighed theatrically, "You're right, I know, but — it's all so — *dull!* Why does everything have to be so dull! Why cannot I live like a Shakespearean character and dress as a man and fight with swords?"

"I have no clue, my dear. You are not the only one who wishes for something more, you know! If you think that I am content with the way my life is then you'd be very much mistaken. I would like to be someone who confronts her problems fearlessly, instead of cowering hopelessly in the corner. I would like to be able to get through just one day without some frightful calamity. Or the constant fear that the school will fail, or Aunt Ida or Aunt Euphemia might die. I cannot sleep at night for worrying."

Dora dashed to her sister's side, her face a picture of contrition, "Oh, Gussie! I'm *so* sorry! I sometimes forget that you have to bear all of this — and shoulder the responsibility for all of us! It's unfair and I am *horridly* inconsiderate and *deserve* to have my books taken away!"

Augusta recognising genuine remorse, took her in her arms and embraced her and they both allowed the strain of the argument to evaporate, and Dora was able to come to terms with losing access to her beloved books for a very long fortnight because she saw that her contrition and obedience might make one less thing for Augusta to fret about.

Also, although it was not yet fully hatched, she had a splendid plan.

* * *

Flora politely scratched on the bedchamber door and not expecting a reply, as her aunt was a little hard of hearing, she entered the room. It was unbearably hot, the fire stoked and giving off both unwanted heat and a haze of smoke and the windows and curtains firmly closed. There was a strong smell of some overly fragrant potpourri, which made her nose itch and the unbearable smell of the small lapdog — some sort of terrier bitch with pointy ears, a rough coat and an unsteady temper.

She approached the monumental bed and peered nervously through the gloom to try to locate where the choleric little beast might be hiding. Having been attacked so many times, it had considerably sharpened her instincts for self-preservation, but as long as she kept her wits about her she was usually able to avoid the needle-sharp teeth and her limbs remained intact.

"Who is there?" asked a tremulous voice from the depths of the bed.

"It's me," replied Flora, eyeing a small mound on the counterpane with suspicion.

"That's a singularly unsatisfactory response!"

"It's Flora. Your great niece."

"Come closer, I cannot see you. I do not understand why it's so very dark in here. Is it night-time? I don't recall having my supper."

"No, it's only early evening but the sun has gone down, and you do have all the curtains closed."

"I cannot think why!"

"Because you say the light hurts your eyes."

"And it is quite so. I am exceedingly delicate, you know. I always was. Not like Ida, she's sturdy and built for manual work — I always thought she was really more suited to being a farmer's wife. I could have married. I had offers. There was this one gentleman — oh, but he was so handsome, it took your breath away!"

The old lady stirred amongst the profusion of pillows and shawls, lace hankies and bottles of smelling salts. Somewhere in the shadows, as yet unseen, something growled long and low, incensed at being disturbed.

Flora cautiously leant towards her and was not in the least surprised when her aunt said petulantly, "Oh, it's *you*. The fat one. Where are the others? The plain one and the impertinent one with the teeth."

"Augusta is supervising the girls' supper and Dora is still in everyone's black books after getting into a scrape earlier."

Her aunt gestured for her to move closer still and then whispered, "They all want me dead, you know! They want my money. They know I've hidden it somewhere and are just waiting for me to die so that they can search for it. I once had a Duke ask for my hand — he was as ugly as sin, so I refused him. Otherwise, I would be a Duchess!"

Flora, who had heard all of this a hundred times before and took no notice, made the appropriate noises and then asked her aunt what she'd like for her supper.

"A baked egg — with bread and butter. Salt on the egg and no crusts on the bread."

"Yes, Aunt Euphemia, just as you always have it then." Flora had no idea why they bothered to ask because recently she always asked for the same things to eat. Dora said if she consumed any more eggs she'd start clucking! Flora couldn't help snorting at the thought, but something in her demeanour seemed to antagonise the dog even more and the vile beast rose rapidly to its feet and jumped stiff-legged across the bed, its yellow teeth bared, hackles raised and yapping in falsetto tones. Flora threw herself backwards and out of reach of the snapping teeth.

Euphemia grabbed the terrier by its spiky tail and dragged its back, crooning sweet words at her little treasure, "Bonny! Darling Bonny! Don't take on so! I'll not let the nasty girl hurt you!"

Flora caught the malevolent look on the dog's face and with a cursory farewell she sped from the room, her magnificent bosom heaving and sweat beading her brow.

Three

There were eight students in all, counting Dora. The girls' ages ranged from just eight to fourteen and their families mostly lived within the county, apart from one child, whose merchant father lived and worked in Bristol. Their numbers were dwindling rather rapidly. They were about to say goodbye to yet another boarder whose doting parents had found a more suitable school closer to their home and a prospective suitor for her.

Miss Ida and Miss Euphemia, when she'd been well, taught etiquette, watercolours and singing, Augusta gave lessons in reading, writing and basic arithmetic, while Flora helped the teachers and taught sewing, at which she excelled, and an exuberant female named Mrs Priscilla Winkworth schooled the girls in dancing. But even the teachers had decreased in numbers recently and they were now left with only one male tutor, the Reverend Owen Cheadle, who was a regular contributor to their lessons. He taught Scripture and Morals and seemed not to notice that no one paid his lessons any attention whatsoever. He talked on and on in a nasal monotone as though punctuation and breathing were not required. He lectured them on how any immoral behaviour would mean that they would not gain access to the Kingdom of Heaven and would, more than likely, spend eternity in Hell, in torment. Only Dora put up her hand to ask *precisely* what he meant by *torment?* Would it mean there would be no books or cake? She privately thought it would mean that Reverend Cheadle would be hired to lecture them ceaselessly, even though they begged for mercy and pleaded with him for forgiveness. She spent most of his lessons staring blindly out of the window and longing for the bell to ring.

"Pandora! Kindly pay attention! What did I just say?" demanded Reverend Cheadle banging his hand rather half-heartedly on his desk.

Dora swung her gaze back to him, "You *said*, 'Kindly pay attention!'"

"Do not be insolent! You know very well what I meant. What parable was I reciting?"

"It was about a man scattering seed on the ground," replied Dora without energy.

"Well, do you not see? It's what I am trying to do! I am scattering the seeds of knowledge so that they may sprout in you and grow and ripen!"

She looked at him with marked dislike, "So that you can harvest me with a sickle? That sounds perfectly *beastly*. I cannot think why you would want to do that."

She knew immediately that she'd gone too far and waited for the axe to fall. She had no idea why she couldn't manage to control her tongue — it seemed to have a mind of its own and she sometimes wished she were more like Augusta who always kept a tight rein on her emotions and never did anything out of character or allowed her common sense to be overruled. But Reverend Cheadle prosing on and on made Dora so irritable that it was a constant battle not to answer back. And now she had allowed herself that small hollow victory, which was bound to bring more punishment and even worse, Augusta's deep disappointment.

"Miss Pandora! How many times do I have to remind you to be seen and not heard? It is not becoming in a young lady to be so forthright with their opinions. You must learn to keep your thoughts to yourself and perhaps to try not to have those thoughts in the first place. I shall be having a word with your sister — again!"

Dora got to her feet and meekly hung her head, her hands folded neatly and she somehow managed to force two large tears out and they trickled down her penitent face.

"I — I'm *desperately* sorry Reverend, I don't know what came over me. I know that I am a constant source of exasperation to everyone, especially you, sir, and I can only apologise and beg your forgiveness and pray that you won't bother Augusta with tales of my wickedness because she has so many much more serious worries at the moment."

She could see the Reverend falter and she began to hope.

"Well, it's certainly an improvement that you have so readily asked for forgiveness and that you are showing some concern for someone other than yourself! I shall refrain this time from consulting with your sister because I realise that she is overset with concerns about the future of the school." He considered the headstrong creature in front of him and thought she looked properly ashamed of her behaviour for once. "You can make amends by helping me distribute food to the poor and needy in the village. That might make you more aware of the sorry plight of those who are less fortunate than yourself."

Dora was silently rejoicing because of her narrow escape. She mumbled her grateful thanks and said she would do her very best to reform and promised faithfully that she would serve the Deserving Poor and learn from her mistakes.

Reverend Cheadle was very well satisfied and continued the lesson looking rather pleased with himself.

Dora immediately began to wonder how she could avoid the Deserving Poor and put her splendid plan into action.

* * *

As Reverend Cheadle left the premises at the end of the school day, he hovered with obvious intent, first in the narrow dark hall and when it stubbornly refused to bear fruit, he loitered on the front steps for a while, looking hopeful, but he sadly suffered yet more disappointment and then, grimly determined, he had a final fling of hovering in the garden but to no great effect, before expelling a profound sigh and admitting defeat. Then, out of the corner of his eager eye he saw a slight movement and saw, to his baffled delight, his quarry in the distance, making her way back to the house.

If I pursue her, he thought, I shall look foolish and if I shout out, I will need an excuse for arresting her progress. He considered merely waving in greeting but could not be sure that he'd been noticed as he was right on the other side of the garden. Whilst pondering his awful dilemma, the object of his immoral desires was unaware of his ardent presence and fast disappearing around the corner of the house, and it was too late for him to do anything at all apart from mourn his indecision.

Reverend Cheadle stood welded to the spot for a moment and acknowledged that he would have to say extra prayers that night for almost giving in to his contemptibly weak-minded cravings. He would have to learn to curb his carnal appetites and decided that he would go without his supper to show just how penitent he was. The fact that his housekeeper would have already made a delicious evening meal for him, which would be a sin to waste and that she would be wounded to the quick if he refused what she had laboured over, did not concern him — it was the thought that counted and, on a particularly shameful thought entering his head unbidden, he added a few more prayers to his evening devotions.

* * *

Augusta heard nothing that day about her sister's contretemps with the Reverend and was able to concentrate upon the dreaded visit to Mrs Millicent Crouch at The Wheatsheaf Inn the following afternoon. She had come up against Mrs Crouch several times before when Dora had somehow managed to best Silas and his brother in a war of words, or when she'd finally given into her rage and retaliated after having her hair violently pulled. It seems that Silas Crouch brought out the worst in Dora and it was to be a never-ending battle with his terrifying mother.

The first time she'd had to beard the Gorgon in its lair, she had had some notion that her position at the Seminary might give her the edge, but her hopes were to be quickly dashed. Mrs Crouch took no prisoners. Her sons were, as far as she was concerned, without fault and anyone accusing them of anything other than being angelic, would be chased from her premises with any weapon she happened to have to hand.

Augusta had, on the first occasion, worn her best straw hat, on hair dressed rather higher than usual to give her some authority and she wore her best closed gown of woven grey silk, which although a little outmoded, had been cleverly modified to disguise the original style. Augusta had enlisted Flora's nimble fingers to help her with the adjustments and had been well satisfied by the results as Flora was surprisingly deft considering her plump little hands, which moved with impressive speed and skill. She just seemed to know what she was about, and it had always been that way since the first day she'd picked up some coloured silks; she had a natural affinity with dressmaking and embroidery that was so far beyond the average female that it was almost uncanny. With the addition of a lacy muslin tippet, Augusta thought that she looked quite respectable, if a little matronly.

It had absolutely failed to impress Mrs Crouch. She had spent a decade as landlady of The Wheatsheaf, and nothing daunted her. She had fought off robbers and inebriated rapscallions with her bare hands and quelled debauched lords with a dangerous sneer.

Augusta, dressed with just as much care and, for the sake of propriety, accompanied by Hannah, the housemaid, very nearly lost her nerve as she approached the inn, but gathered herself with a sharp word and marched into the alehouse with her head held high, although her heart was beating the retreat inside her chest.

The saloon was empty apart from a middle-aged man behind the bar, who looked up as she entered with an insolent look in his dark beady eyes.

"Good day, Mr Crouch," said Augusta and was pleased her voice came out without quavering, "I am here to see Mrs

Crouch. Would you be so kind as to summon her for me please?"

Mr Crouch knew which side his bread was buttered and he nodded with an ingratiating smile and disappeared into the back room, where she could quite clearly hear him bellowing for his wife, followed by the sound of heels clattering on the stairs, a sharp-tongued admonishment and the arrival of Mrs Millicent Crouch in full sail.

Augusta braced herself and tried hard not to show on the outside the terror she was feeling on the inside.

Mrs Crouch was small and wiry and bristling with self-assurance, something Augusta had always had to feign.

"Mrs Crouch," she began with a confidence she didn't feel, "I have come — " but that was as far as she got because Mrs Crouch came out from behind the bar with her face wreathed in alarming smiles.

Not entirely sure what was happening, Augusta tried to speak, "I have come to — "

"No, no! Do not say another *word!*" cried Mrs Crouch in shrill tones, "I am most humbled and honoured that you should visit our low abode! Indeed, I am quite overcome! Please, be seated Miss Pennington. Allow me to offer you some ale! No? Then, here take this chair — rest your weary feet! No? Then, pray tell me what I can do for you?"

With her head spinning, Augusta searched for some words that might make sense, "I have come to talk to you of my sister's unfortunate — "

Mrs Crouch held up a work-reddened hand and interrupted her, "There's no need, Miss Pennington, no need at all! I gather that there was a slight misunderstanding, and the result was that my boy learnt a lesson he won't never forget! I have to tell you that he's had his hide tanned into the bargain by his Pa! Well deserved. Well deserved! Little varmint. He's mucking out the stables as we speak. Serves him right."

Opening her mouth to try to get a word in edgewise, Augusta managed to say, "I don't quite follow — "

Mrs Crouch pursed her thin lips together and held out her hands in a supplicating gesture, "There's no need to say no more! The whole thing's been explained and — " here she winked at Augusta in rather a vulgar manner, "It's all signed and sealed, and all parties are most gratified! A nod to a blind horse is as good as a wink!"

"I'm afraid I have absolutely no idea what you're talking about, Mrs Crouch!" said Augusta, mystified and becoming increasingly anxious by the odd confrontation.

Mrs Crouch shook her head, "Oh, there's no need to concern yourself! I won't say a thing! My lips are sealed! I'll take it to the grave! No one will hear it from me!"

"Hear what, precisely?" asked Augusta faintly.

"It's all been nicely seen to, Miss Pennington! Not a word, I swear!"

"Not a word about *what*, Mrs Crouch?"

"About your gentleman friend. Anyone can see you're no light-skirt — no, indeed, one only has to see the way you trick yourself out to know that you're a well-respected schoolmistress!"

Augusta wasn't sure what to be more insulted by: the fact that she had been compared to a light-skirt, or the fact that despite wearing her very best clothes she still was considered frumpish — she might just as well not have bothered to deck herself out in all her finery because it made no difference. As her father had once told her, "You cannot make a silk purse from a sow's ear."

She fixed Mrs Crouch with a penetrating stare, "Are you telling me that — someone has — talked to you about — the incident on the Green?"

"No! I'm telling you that *someone* has *seen me right* over said fuss on the Green! It's a good man that has deep pockets and isn't afraid to dip his hand into them!"

Augusta tried desperately not to panic, "Which gentleman are we talking about?"

"Why, the Lord of the Manor, no less! Not to everyone's taste, I can tell you! But generous!"

"Oh, my God!" breathed Augusta. "Do you mean to tell me that Sir Marcus Denby came here to the inn and gave you a payment to — to forget that your son put my sister in the stocks and pelted her with mud?"

Mrs Crouch looked a bit put out, "No! Well, yes. He said Silas should be brought to account for his bad behaviour and then he would see his way to greasing my palm, although he didn't use those exact words — but he made it very clear that I should not mention it again."

"Oh, my God," repeated Augusta, feeling that if the earth should open up and swallow her that she'd be eternally grateful. She had turned quite pale and Hannah, who happened to be loitering in the hall, watching the encounter with interest, saw the obvious distress upon her mistress's face and went quickly to her side.

"Miss? Are you all right? P'raps we'd better get you home now!"

Augusta looked at her as though she'd never seen her before, "I — I am feeling rather peculiar."

"Come on, Miss, let's leave!" as she helped Augusta to her feet. "It smells bad in here," she whispered, "And you look like you're going to swoon. You'll feel better with a nice cup of tea in you," and she led Augusta out of the alehouse and into the bright sunlight in the lane outside.

Augusta took a moment to just breathe the fresh air and get her bearings and then they began to walk slowly back to the school. Augusta on very shaky legs, which didn't seem to want to do her bidding.

"Miss Augusta? Would you like to sit down on the bank for a moment, you look awful queer!"

"I do feel rather unwell," murmured Augusta and allowed herself to be steered to the grassy bank where they both sat down in the shade of an elm tree.

Hannah took off her hat and fanned her mistress with it.

"We really shouldn't have gone into The Wheatsheaf — it's not a place for ladies to be seen," she said, looking up and down the lane for any sign of assistance. There was no one about.

"Do you think that if we rest here for a few minutes that you'll be able to walk back to the school, Miss?"

Augusta nodded, but when, after sitting for a short while, she tried to stand, she became dizzy, and Hannah made her sit down again.

"Oh, dear, I really don't think I'm quite ready. It was all so dreadful — " said Augusta in failing accents.

"Oh, *please* don't faint, Miss! What shall I do!"

She fanned Augusta harder with the hat and said a silent prayer.

Her prayer was answered.

The sound of a carriage travelling very fast assailed her ears and she looked up hopefully to see a tip-top curricle career around the corner. It was pulled by two perfectly matched horses, galloping at full tilt, hooves sending stones and dust flying and the carriage bouncing along behind as though being chased by the very Devil himself. Holding the reins was a very fine gentleman indeed, handsome as any Hannah had ever seen and she only stopped gawping like a simpleton at him when it had nearly drawn level and she realised that it wasn't going to stop. She leapt to her feet and jumped into the lane to wave her hat at the driver, whilst fervently hoping that she may not be killed.

Seeing her almost too late, the gentleman hauled valiantly on the reins and drew the horses to a shuddering halt a little way past the now quaking Hannah.

She uncovered her eyes and dared to look up, realising that she hadn't been trampled to death by the temperamental-looking animals. The young gentleman had jumped down to calm his precious horses and another fellow, she hadn't at first noticed, was striding towards her, his face thunderous.

"In God's name, what were you thinking! To jump into the lane like that — you could have killed us all! Are you totally deranged?"

"No, indeed, Sir! But I was desperate! It's my mistress! She's unwell and I didn't know what to do for the best. I couldn't leave her, you see?"

The gentleman's hard eyes focused on the limp form lying on the bank and he immediately went to her and kneeling down, chafed her hands in his.

He called over his shoulder to his friend, "Charles! We need water and smelling salts at once! See if they have them at the inn."

"Dash it, but I must look to my horses — they're still in quite a state!"

Hannah stepped forward and picking up her mistress's fallen reticule, delved into it and pulled out a small bottle of smelling salts, "She always keeps them by her for her sister, who often has convulsions!" she explained.

He took them and waved the bottle under Augusta's impressively long nose. She stirred and pushed it away with a shaking hand and opening her eyes, gazed up at the gentleman beside her.

"*You!*" she uttered in tones of deep exasperation.

"Yes, 'tis I. Are you feeling better, Miss Pennington? What on earth brought on such a strong reaction?" asked Sir Marcus.

Augusta struggled to sit up so that she could face him eye to eye, but he had to assist her, which slightly defeated her noble purpose. She shook away his helpful hands and straightened her hat crossly.

"*You* did!"

"I, Madam? Are you sure? Perhaps you are still feeling unwell? I am very sure that I have done nothing to bring on so dramatic a condition. What is it that you think I have done?"

Augusta was no longer pale, her cheeks now flushed with indignation, "I have just been to see Mrs Crouch — "

Sir Marcus inclined his head slightly, acknowledging the hit, "You need say no more! Think nothing of it. I was merely doing what I could to ease the situation. There's no need to thank me," he said blandly.

"*Thank* you? Have you taken leave of your senses? I was not going to *thank* you!"

"Quite right too! How very sensible of you when there is not the smallest need. So, you were overcome by the heat of the alehouse? It can be intolerable when combined with the stench of stale beer and boiled cabbage."

Augusta made an explosively angry sound and tried to stand. She failed, her impractical shoes slipping upon the grass. She gave up and subsided once more onto the bank, feeling not unlike a beetle stuck on its back, helplessly waving its little legs in the air.

Sir Marcus got to his feet in one lithe and easy movement, despite his bulk, and held out his hand to her, "Allow me to assist you before you injure yourself further ma'am," he suggested with a soundless laugh.

"Oh!" exclaimed Augusta, ignoring his hand, "How *dare* you! Leave me be! You — you — provoking, meddling, *odious* man! Mrs Crouch — that *awful* woman — she thought — she believes that I am — that *we* are — oh, I cannot *tolerate* the way she looked at me! As though I were — as *though* — ! If this gets out — if the parents hear rumours — the school will be *finished! You* have done this! It's insufferable!"

"Ah, I begin to see daylight," observed Sir Marcus silkily, "Well, there's no need to make such a fuss, my dear girl! It's nothing but a storm in a glass of water. Take no notice. I'm sure that you have enough cachet in the village to quash any unfounded insinuations. Besides, The Wheatsheaf is only frequented by ne'er-do-wells and cutpurses."

"Is that all you can say! My name will be bandied about by just such people — I will be a laughing-stock!"

"Thank you! I'm deeply flattered, ma'am," he said wryly.

"It's all right for *you!* You're a man — it will just add more allure to your notoriety! I may well lose my means of making a living!"

"Allure? That's an interesting view."

Augusta searched for something cutting to say, "I am not saying that *I* find it alluring! Quite the opposite. I cannot abide those who foist dishonour upon the innocent because of their irresponsible behaviour! It disgusts me."

At this fortuitous moment the other gentleman, having at last calmed his highly-strung animals, came to see what was going on, "Marcus, we shall have to be on our way before the horses get chilled. What has happened here?"

Sir Marcus eyed the dashing young man with a wry smile, "Head out of clouds for a moment, dear boy! We have other things to consider. May I introduce my younger brother, Charles, Miss Pennington? He has absolutely nothing to recommend him apart from his skills as a carriage driver! In that he is, without doubt, a *nonpareil* — otherwise he would have run down your maid."

"How do you do, Miss Pennington," said Charles Denby, bowing over Augusta's prostrate figure. "Is there anything I can do to help?"

"Thank you, but as you can see, I am very much at a disadvantage down here — I would like to be standing again — I think I'm no longer in danger of fainting. If you could give me your hand, I think I shall manage to right myself."

Charles Denby did as instructed and in a trice had Miss Pennington on her feet. He steadied her until she'd regained her balance and helped her from the bank onto the level ground of the lane.

Augusta dusted herself down and turned to thank her rescuer, "I'm very grateful to you, I was beginning to think I may be stuck there for good!"

"I could have quite easily assisted you," said Sir Marcus cordially.

"I would rather have been helped by a serpent," responded Augusta in withering accents.

Sir Marcus bowed ironically and smiled, "You are too kind ma'am," he murmured.

"Miss Pennington? Where do you live? If you care to brave my driving, I could take you in my curricle?" said Charles Denby cheerfully.

"That's exceedingly kind of you, Mr Denby! I should like that very much, but will not your brother then have to walk?" She sent a triumphant look at his impassive brother.

"Well, a walk will do Marcus good. He's been in a devilish temper all day for some reason!"

And so, after taking her reticule from Hannah and thanking the maid for her courageous part in the rescue, Charles helped Augusta up into the fancy racing vehicle, and then jumped up himself, cracked his whip and they took off so violently that she was forced to cling to the sides and just had time to glimpse the irksome fellow grinning after them, before they were bowling along the lane in what Augusta considered an unnecessarily reckless manner.

A still smiling Sir Marcus was left to escort Hannah back to the school and as they strolled along the lane, he encouraged her to talk about working at the school and obliquely prompted her to tell him about her employers. She was more than willing to chatter, having had such a trying afternoon and he was a surprisingly good listener.

Four

Thoroughly shaken by the speed of the short journey back to the school, Augusta was barely able to express coherent thanks to Mr Denby and found herself stammering her gratitude in the most gauche manner imaginable.

"I was delighted to be of assistance, Miss Pennington. To be perfectly frank, I was having to endure a lecture from my brother about my expenditure and was glad of the distraction! He is in charge of my finances, and I have to answer to him. Head of the family, you know!" He gallantly offered his arm and led her up the steps to the front door. "So, this is the famous Seminary for Young Ladies? I had no idea it was here on my brother's doorstep until he mentioned its existence for the first time this very morning. Imagine that! It's astonishing what one can overlook when one is not paying attention! My charming brother will tell you that I *never* pay attention, but do you know that I have never yet had a carriage accident! He's a fine one to tell me that I must attend to my affairs when he — no! I must learn to keep my own counsel or else I shall be in trouble again. Anyway, this looks like a splendid sort of place — if a little cheerless. I'm sure the young ladies must be thrilled to be here."

Finally able to collect herself, Augusta shook her head, "I'm afraid we're losing our students almost monthly. It appears that the fashion for educating girls waxes and wanes and because we're not in the city and able to provide the highest quality surroundings and tutors, the parents are choosing to look elsewhere. But, still, that's neither here nor there. Would you care to come in for a dish of tea?"

Charles Denby was just about to decline the gracious offer because he found everything about schools and education a bit of a bore, when the door opened, and a young girl dashed out to greet them. She was wearing a rather unattractive cotton gown covered in a plain apron and her brown hair was decidedly dishevelled. She grinned at them, showing her prominent front teeth and her laughing blue eyes to advantage.

"Oh, *there* you are! At last! You must come *quickly* Gussie! We are in such a state!"

"What on earth is wrong?" demanded Augusta, much alarmed.

Suddenly aware that there was a visitor, Dora explained, with one eye on the elegantly attired stranger, "The chimney sweep came, and the blockhead didn't think to ask about the kink in the kitchen chimney and he only put a *goose* up! And now it's quite wedged and cook wants to relight the fire and *burn* it out and the sweep won't hear of it and the goose is honking loudly and there's soot *everywhere* and there'll be no dinner unless something is done *quickly*! Where have you been? You've been away an absolute *age*! We must go, right *now!*"

Augusta opened her mouth to ask why such a cruel custom was deemed acceptable but didn't get the chance as Charles Denby stepped forward, *"Lead on, Macduff, and damn'd be him that first cries, 'Hold, enough!'"*

Dora stopped in her tracks and stared in admiration, "Macbeth! Oh, how splendidly fitting! Although you misquoted — it's *"Lay on, Macduff!"* But never mind that now! This way, *quickly!*" and she raced off, followed by Mr Denby, who threw his hat and gloves down on a table in the hallway and disappeared through the door at the far end, leaving Augusta standing with her mouth still slightly open.

In the kitchen Mr Denby found a scene from a Hogarth engraving and let out a delighted bark of laughter as he surveyed the pandemonium all about him. This was more like it! He suddenly had a feeling that being rusticated this time would not be so tedious after all! Trinity term may have been curtailed for harmlessly firing a gun over the head of the tradesman who kept relentlessly dunning him, but an enforced summer spent kicking his heels in the countryside, was definitely looking up!

The cook was armed with a rolling pin and a lit candle and behind her cowered a very large, sobbing housemaid, whose face and person was covered in soot and feathers. The flagstones were littered with more of the same and amongst the debris was a small terrier of some description who was devouring a half-cooked leg of some farmyard beast once destined for the table and growling all the while to keep away anyone who might be tempted to take it from her. From the chimney came sounds of the distressed and enraged goose, and black clouds swirled, feathers fluttered and cook bellowed. The sweep seemed much goaded and was standing in front of the fireplace his muscular arms akimbo and a dangerous look in his eye. He too was blackened with soot, but it looked as though it had been that way for months, so engrained into his skin was it. His hat had come off, leaving a curiously pale strip of skin at his hairline and that hair was plastered down with sweat and he was telling cook in a loud voice, meant for yelling at small boys up chimneys, that no one was going to cook his precious goose!

Mr Denby viewed the scene with the utmost delight and taking off his coat, threw it carelessly down on a nearby chair. He then rolled up the sleeves of his pristine white shirt and approached the chimney sweep with an air of one who was not used to being denied.

The sweep eyed him belligerently and put up his ham-like fists. He was slightly taken-aback when the elegant young man merely laughed and said in aristocratic tones, "Kindly step out of the way and I will retrieve your wretched bird from the chimney! No, I shouldn't try that if I were you! I am a champion boxer — well versed in the noble art of pugilism!"

For a tense moment, the bristling sweep faced up to the amused and horridly relaxed youth and after a brief standoff, the poor man stepped to one side and allowed Mr Denby to access the fireplace.

Thoughtfully not showing his jubilation, Charles Denby turned to the cook and asked for a piece of string which she provided instantly, recognising the voice of one who knew what he was about. Mr Denby then disappeared up the chimney until only his boots could be seen. There were sounds of a scuffle and some ripe cursing, a few more feathers fell silently into the cold embers of the fire and then Mr Denby jumped down and stood back, holding the end of the string upon which he gave a sudden and very insistent tug. The result was even more chaos, as the infuriated goose was pulled free and tumbled, flapping its massive wings, down into the mounds of ash, where it proceeded to beat those monstrous wings and make strident noises as a dire warning to anyone who might dare come too close.

Charles Denby turned to the speechless sweep, "All yours, my good fellow and I wish you the very best of luck!"

It was at this precise moment that Augusta walked into the kitchen followed soon thereafter by Hannah and Sir Marcus, who had just returned from their enforced walk from the village.

Augusta looked at the devastation: the bewildered sweep struggling with a murderous looking goose, the cook trying to wrest the mangled leg of lamb from an irate Bonny, the housemaid wailing, Dora looking, for once, innocent of any charges and Mr Charles Denby, in shirt sleeves, covered in smuts from head to toe, grinning.

She looked and for a moment contemplated joining the housemaid in a lusty bout of weeping, but after due consideration, she burst out laughing instead. She laughed until tears streamed down her face, and everyone stopped what they were doing, including the greedy lapdog, and stared at her with varying degrees of dismay. Unable to collect herself, she quickly went out of the kitchen and fled to the parlour where she indulged in a lengthy fit of hysterical giggling.

She mopped at her eyes and tried to catch her breath but to no avail.

The door opened and Sir Marcus came in, observing her with some concern, "Miss Pennington? I think you should probably sit down if you are to continue in similar vein. It would not be good for your health to swoon twice in one day!"

She squinted at him through the tears and made a valiant attempt to stop but only managed to produce some wild hiccupping before continuing unabated.

"I shall begin to worry if you do not stop this. Should I call for the doctor?" enquired Sir Marcus, eyeing her in silent appreciation.

Augusta fought for control and after several more minutes, her shoulders stopped shaking, she was able to draw in a steady breath and sink into a nearby chair.

"I — I must tell you Sir Marcus — I have had — the most *dreadful* day! As a rule, I strive to avoid situations that might make me — anxious! But today, I seem to have cannoned from one horrid crisis to the next — without a moment to gather my disordered wits. I must apologise for my rude behaviour in the village — I had allowed myself to become quite overwrought at the thought of having to face Mrs Crouch again. Last time she was quite threatening, and I was very put out that you should have gone behind my back and bribed her to keep her quiet! High-handed, indeed, Sir! The worst thing being that she *winked* at me! As though she were conspiring with us over some salacious secret! It was *humiliating!* I fear she now believes that I am a fallen woman and soon the whole county will be talking about it, and we will have no choice but to close the school!"

Sir Marcus had been watching her face as she spoke and thinking idly that when she was animated, she didn't look quite so unremarkable, and he had very much enjoyed seeing her laugh so helplessly.

He collected himself and replied, "There is no need to be concerned. That woman can say what she likes, and no one will believe her. You are a respected member of the community and anyone who matters in the slightest will trust what you say."

"But that is not the *point!* The scandalmongers will not so easily be put off and my reputation will be in tatters. You are a *man* — "

"Something I cannot help," said he, dryly.

"Oh, no — I mean — being a pampered male, you will have no notion how even the most trifling scandal can ruin a mere female — how readily people will believe the very worst of a woman with no proof other than someone's unreliable word. It can be done in an instant and her life is as good as over."

"You sound a little like a distressed damsel from one of those histrionic novels written by female authors for a purely female audience," observed Sir Marcus.

"I think you mean that to be insulting," said Augusta, "But, you know, it is a miracle that women can read and write at all — thanks to the *gentlemen* who rule our lives! Imagine not being able to read to amuse yourself or just pass the time and learn about new things and see into the minds of others. To only be encouraged to *sew* and, as my dear Dora would say, so scathingly, to paint Grecian urns! It is beyond impressive that we have still somehow managed to educate ourselves. I think men are just afraid and determined to keep women under their thumb so that we cannot rise up and take over! Oh, and I forgot the main reason we are so magnanimously allowed to grace a man's world at all — to produce an *heir!*"

Sir Marcus widened his eyes a little, he had never heard a well-bred female speak so before and had to admit to himself that he was a trifle unsettled by it. He had thought himself to be enlightened in his ideas but on hearing Miss Pennington he was rapidly having to reform his opinions.

She saw his expression change and her cheeks reddened, "Oh, I'm so sorry. I have allowed my tongue to run away with me."

He smiled, "Miss Dora has acquired that same trait from you I see."

"Oh, gracious, I do hope not! I constantly beg her to think before she speaks but it makes no odds — she just blurts out whatever comes into her mind, without thought or careful consideration. She is not in the least bit like me thankfully! She knows not my extreme caution or any form of moderation — she gives into every whim or notion that enters her head and cares not for the consequences! I, on the other hand, am inclined to much restraint in the hopes that all mortification and anguish can be safely avoided. Our mother, you understand was sadly given to recklessness and — and well, I had hoped that Dora would not be like her — " she finished lamely.

The dark brows went up, "I understand, the Misses Beauchamp are your mother's sisters?"

She nodded, "She was Viola Beauchamp, the youngest of them and they were all three brought up in Brighton. My father was used to saying that too much sunshine and the sea air had addled their brains. He became very disillusioned with the Beauchamp side in general and blamed their very distant French heritage for their peculiarities. My mother — " she began but was perhaps fortunately prevented from saying more by the door opening. It was held open by a still sooty Mr Denby so that Dora could precede him into the room.

"It's just too funny!" laughed Dora, "The goose took against Bonny and chased her around the kitchen and out into the garden! Cook has taken to the cooking brandy! The sweep is chasing his goose down the drive, Bonny has disappeared altogether, and I have brought Mr Denby through because he would like some refreshment, as the soot was very thirst-making. Hannah is preparing it and she says there are Apricot Tarts for tea!" She saw her sister's expression, "Are you quite recovered now Gussie? I'm so sorry about the mess — it all happened so suddenly. I had no chance to stop it! Mr Denby was *marvellous!* He just resolved everything in a trice. But, although he has washed his hands, he is still rather messy so I had better cover the chair before he sits or else it will be ruined!

I shall fetch a square of drab cloth from the cupboard — I won't be a moment!" and she went out in haste.

Augusta smiled warmly at Mr Denby, "Thank you so very much for saving the day. It was so fortunate you were here. I don't know what we would have done — !"

"*I* could perhaps have helped?" suggested Sir Marcus.

She looked at him in surprise, "Oh, yes, of course you could. It's just that — " she faltered, feeling a little flustered.

Understanding dawned and Sir Marcus bowed ironically, "Oh, I see! You think I am too mature to be rescuing obdurate geese?"

Augusta, who had been thinking something like that, quickly denied it, "Goodness no! Not at all!" she declared not very convincingly.

"Thank you," said the gentleman with pronounced dignity, "As you are clearly just out of the nursery yourself it must seem as though I am in my final years. I can assure you that I do not as yet suffer from any distempers, gout or dropsy brought on by my advancing years. Neither do I have any signs of rheumatism thus far, but I am not counting my chickens just yet as my best days are now behind me, and I have only decline and death to look forward to."

Augusta gasped, "Oh dear, no! I had not thought — I — was just — I did not mean — " her halting excuses ceased when she saw the gleam in his eyes, "Oh! I *see!* You are funning! Well, there's really no excuse for that kind of behaviour! I truly do not think you to be too old! It's just that your brother is so much — so — well, he seems a little younger!"

"He is very much younger, I will readily admit. He is in fact my stepbrother and some twenty-three years younger but that is hardly our fault. My father unwisely remarried late in life and Charles is the result — his mother was little more than a babe herself. It was very provoking for me at the time, but I became used to the idea eventually and have learned to tolerate my new brother."

"Gratified, indeed!" said Mr Denby, genially.

"Although, I might add, he has just been sent down from Oxford for trying to intimidate a tradesman who was foolish enough to dun him."

"I had *promised* him payment! It's hardly my fault that his coats are so dashed dear! How is one supposed to afford the everyday things of life if they are so vastly overpriced? It makes no sense at all!"

"It makes no sense to you because I have been unable to drum any understanding of finances into your head, however hard I try! Nor have you shown any kind of compassion for those less fortunate who must make their living by selling their wares."

"If you only knew how *hard* I have tried to behave as you would dear brother! I have remained alone in my chambers, night after night, and forgone all pleasure, just as you would and have even tried to emulate the lacklustre style of dress you favour, but I'm afraid I cannot derive any satisfaction from looking like a confounded parson, it just will not do! From your attire you seem as though you were cut out for the Church or some such dreary existence! I had no wish to turn into such a dull dog!"

"It is my turn to thank you, dearest Charles!" said Sir Marcus with a subtle warning glance that Augusta intercepted and read correctly.

"I think I should ring to see what has happened to the refreshments," she said quickly and was much heartened when Dora came flying into the room bearing the promised drab cloth she had finally run to ground.

"It was in the top floor linen cupboard, if you please! As though we never have call to cover the furniture! Here, I'll spread it over this chair, Mr Denby and you can sit down, at last."

Augusta saw the tension leave Sir Marcus and breathed a sigh of relief. She knew just what it was like to be driven to distraction by one's siblings and to have one so much younger must be a particular trial. As her sister flew about making room for the tea tray and Mr Denby settled himself whilst trying hard not to transfer the soot from his clothing to the furniture, she was able to take a long look at Sir Marcus and came to the conclusion that he only looked like a rather more mature gentleman when his face was in its serious mode but when he allowed himself to smile, the laughter lighting his grey eyes, he appeared a good deal younger and less forbidding. He suddenly looked up and returned her searching gaze with brows raised quizzically. Embarrassed, she averted her eyes.

Hannah arrived almost immediately bearing a large tray and it wasn't long before Mr Denby was tucking into thinly cut Bread and Butter and delicious Orange Tarts and remarking upon how hungry his unexpected adventure had made him.

"You are always hungry, Charles," said his brother.

"Yes, 'tis true! I can never get enough to eat! It's *devilish* tricky at Oxford to persuade them that what *they* consider to be enough is not *nearly* enough! I could eat these tarts all day!"

"I'm so glad," said Augusta warmly, "You certainly deserve a reward for your efforts. I wonder if the sweep has caught up with his goose yet!"

"It's no doubt had its wings clipped so that it cannot fly — he'll catch up with the vile creature eventually. I must say it's a bad day when one is induced into wishing for climbing boys to do the sweeping instead of geese!"

Augusta was rather shocked and couldn't help but say so, "Those poor children! Being forced up chimneys and made to breathe in the dreadful sooty air and risk being burnt or stuck. That's no life for a child. It should be banned — I cannot think why it is still allowed."

"But then more geese would be forced up chimneys instead," observed Mr Denby reasonably.

Dora put down her glass of lemonade with a decided snap, "Then someone should invent some way of sweeping chimneys that *doesn't* involve any kind of actual being having to suffer! There *must* be a better way."

Mr Denby looked at Miss Dora with a good deal of astonishment and not a little respect. He had never previously considered how chimneys were actually swept or had been prompted to take into account that there might be suffering involved. He was rather disturbed by the thought that he would now know this, and should he ever have the misfortune to have to request his chimney be swept, he would have to do it in the full knowledge that it would entail that either a goose or a small, probably orphaned boy would have to be ill-treated in order to do so. It was hardly fair! With this in mind he commented, "The sooner they invent a mechanical sweeper the better in my opinion!"

Dora beamed at him, "Very well said, Mr Denby! Have you ever invented anything?"

Sir Marcus interpolated, "Yes, he has — intriguing new ways to be sent down from Oxford. This is the second time but the first time apparently, although he swears it was an honest mistake, he insulted the vice-chancellor's daughter, and I had an accursed time getting him reinstated."

"She should have been flattered!" exclaimed Charles Denby in disgust.

Augusta, seeing the glint in her sister's lively eyes decided it was time to draw the conversation to a close before Dora felt compelled to start asking inappropriate questions, which she was very likely to do.

"Sir Marcus, can I offer you more tea? Another Apricot Tart?"

He cast her a comprehending glance and shook his head, "I have had, as my mother would have said, an elegant sufficiency. And really we should be on our way — we have surely delayed you long enough."

"After all you have both done today, it was the least we could do and anyway it's a Saturday so there are no lessons in the afternoon," responded Augusta roundly.

That seemed to be the signal for the end of the visit and Sir Marcus and his brother made their excuses and left in the curricle. Augusta and Dora watched it dash away down the drive and disappear.

They stood for a moment in stunned silence.

"Well," breathed Dora eventually, "What a strange day! Did you see Silas at the Wheatsheaf?"

"Thankfully, no," said Augusta, suddenly recalling the ghastly incident in the alehouse, "It was bad enough as it was! Mrs Crouch is the most appalling creature and I hope never to have to face her again. You have been warned Dora! If you cause me any more anxiety and embarrassment I shall — I shall give you to the chimney sweep to be his new apprentice!"

Laughing, they went in.

* * *

The curricle swung into the Manor's long driveway and Charles Denby cast an appraising look at his brother's stern face.

"They seem very nice, Miss Pennington and Miss Dora! I must say it made a nice change to meet a female who don't scream and have an attack of the vapours because things were going awry. Miss Dora was an absolute Trojan! Not in the least daunted by all the hullabaloo going on around her. In fact, she seemed to relish it and I must say that I too found it to be rather invigorating!"

"I'm sorry to hear you say that," said Sir Marcus calmly.

"Really, why?"

"Because it demonstrates to me that you will never be content to settle down to the mundane things of life."

"I should jolly well hope not!" said Mr Denby with considerable feeling.

"I do not think it's a good idea that you spend much time at the Beauchamp's Seminary for obvious reasons."

"What obvious reasons? I cannot think of any!"

"You know very well, Charles. I don't think that a ladies' boarding school is a fitting place for a young man to be seen — lurking."

"I was not intending to *lurk!* But I had thought that I might visit occasionally because they seem to be very pleasant and otherwise I shall die of boredom!"

"If only I could trust you — "

"You *can!*" declared Charles eagerly, "I swear that I shall behave with all propriety and will not disgrace you again. Oh, please Marcus! Months at the Manor will otherwise be Purgatory!"

"Thank you," muttered Sir Marcus bitterly.

Charles drove the curricle adeptly into the stable yard and they drew to a perfect halt so that he was able to turn and fix his sibling with the full force of his most beseeching smile, "You know I only mean that there's naught to do but ride and attend church and talk to the local gentry's unappealing wives and daughters and go hunting rabbits with Quince! It's hardly what I'm used to, living in Oxford."

"Perhaps being forced to consider your moral integrity for a while will remind you of your responsibilities and your duties to the family. I would really rather that you didn't plague Miss Pennington with your nonsense — she has enough on her plate at the moment."

"Oh? What is troubling her?"

"The imminent closure of the school."

Charles looked nonplussed, "It is to close? But surely we could help them find a way to prevent that? It wouldn't need a great deal of effort."

Sir Marcus looked askance at him, "Help them? Why on earth should we do that?"

"And you say *my* moral integrity needs attention!" remarked Charles pithily.

Five

Sir Marcus Denby put the brandy glass away from him and looked at it in disgust. He was seeing at least two glasses as he was squinting slightly, having been imbibing dangerously since the sun went down.

He was not in a very agreeable mood, his head ached, and the room was swimming before his bloodshot eyes. He had bellowed at Beecher and would have probably kicked Quince had not the animal had the good sense to remove himself to the kitchens, where he hid under the table.

Beecher quietly kept a watch over his master, observing him sink into his usual state of despond with a good deal of misgiving. He misliked the nasty look in his eye; it didn't bode well for his servants, and he wondered if he should wake Mr Charles who had retired to bed early to ask his advice although he wasn't at all sure that, being so young and inexperienced and a loose screw by all accounts, he would be of any use at all! He would more than likely just join him in the bottle of brandy and that would be most unhelpful. No, he would deal with this himself — he had done it often enough.

He guessed it was the letter. It was always a letter nowadays. In the old days, in the days of Lady Birch Denby, for a while, things had been quite pleasant. Cuckoopen Manor had been a gay sort of place then, like any other family home; there were parties and convivial evenings of cards, music and dancing and Sir Marcus had been, on the whole, quite cheerful. Beecher checked himself — no, not *cheerful* exactly but not so fixedly morose. There were days when he almost seemed like himself again and then the darkness would creep up on him once more, the brandy stocks would be depleted, and Quince would head for the kitchen with his tail between his legs.

Beecher was never quite sure what to do for the best, so he kept guard and made sure no physical harm came to his master. The day after such a bout of drinking, Sir Marcus would be unfit for company and Beecher would have to fend off any uninvited visitors at the gates to save them from a torrent of abuse and a view of Sir Marcus as drunk as an Emperor. He would never allow anyone to see him in such a state. When the Black Dog was over him and he was lost to the melancholy, there was no point in trying to prise him out of the megrims too early — it was wasted effort, one just had to be patient and gentle with him and, more importantly, impervious to insult.

He had had high hopes after his return from the drive with Mr Charles. They had both seemed in high spirits, laughing and ragging each other like brothers always do, but it had only lasted until the letter was brought out and discussed at length and Mr Charles had thoughtlessly suggested a glass of brandy before bed.

Beecher stood guard by the door ready to dodge any missile that might be hurled and prepared to keep anyone from entering the room.

Sir Marcus was mumbling into his empty glass. The butler hazarded a guess and pretended not to hear the muttered demands. It was hard to refuse someone who was paying one's salary and keeping a roof over one's head, but he didn't like to see him this way and was quietly determined not to encourage him in his misery.

The next words were clearly audible, "Miranda, *Miranda*."

"Yes, Sir Marcus, I know."

"N-no one knows — only *I* — know."

"Whatever you say, Sir."

There was no other sound for several minutes and then Sir Marcus attempted to sit up in the chair, but only succeeded in slumping a little further sideways, the glass hanging precariously from his numbed fingers.

"Shending — the girl!"

"Sir Marcus?"

"I-Imogen," explained he, unsteadily.

"Ah. Yes, of course," he muttered, blenching at the mention of Sir Marcus's daughter.

Sir Marcus looked up but was unable to locate his butler through his unfocused eyes, "She's coming."

Slightly taken aback, Beecher answered, "*Here*, Sir?"

"Yesh, here — to stay."

"That's good news," said Beecher mendaciously.

"*Is* it?"

"You are her father so I am assuming that you will be glad that she is coming to the Manor."

Sir Marcus opened one bleary eye and stared in the general direction of his butler's impassive voice, "I haven't — sheen her since — she was a baby. I — I don't know her." His chin sunk onto his chest, "What — the D-devil are we to do?"

"Well, I suppose, Sir Marcus, that we shall somehow contrive to manage just as we always do. May I enquire if Lady Birch is coming with her?"

"There's the d-damn — rub! The — child comes alone!" said Sir Marcus in tones of deep despair.

Thinking that there was something very unusual about all of this, Beecher said carefully, "That is perhaps for the best — in the circumstances, if you recall last time, Sir?"

The last time, Lady Birch had paid an unheralded visit and it had ended in shouting and tears. Accusations flew, insults were bandied, doors were slammed, and precious objects were deliberately smashed. It had been an unedifying time for all concerned and it should not at any cost be repeated.

"Yesh," agreed Sir Marcus, "'Twas very bad. V-very bad indeed."

"We shall prevail," said Beecher gravely. "When does she arrive?"

"D-day after — on — Monday."

"Excellent. I shall warn the staff and begin preparations. We shall need to find ways to occupy her I expect. A lively young lady, no doubt. Probably takes after Mr Charles."

"G-good — God! I damned well h-hope she don't take after me! Best hide the damn b-brandy!" And he laughed uproariously at his own quip and promptly fell into a stupor for which Beecher could only be profoundly grateful.

* * *

Miss Ida Beauchamp had listened with interest to Reverend Cheadle's lesson that fine Sunday morning and puzzled over the meaning of it. It was clear that there *was* some hidden meaning and that it meant something very particular to him, as he had become quite choked up in his delivery.

Miss Beauchamp knew the bible story of David and Bathsheba and felt sure, in her own mind, that Reverend Cheadle was somehow talking about his own dilemmas, and she wondered who his Bathsheba was and she determined to see if she could find out. It was perfectly clear to her that the poor man was in torment, and she thought she could probably help him. Even though he was a singularly tiresome fellow, she didn't like to see anyone suffering. She rather thought his Bathsheba might be Mrs Priscilla Winkworth, the dance mistress — she was such a vivacious lady, so filled with the joys of rhythmical movement and excessively frilly ball gowns! Every gesture she made was enough to gladden one's heart, and she often sang as she moved gracefully about the school. If one met her in a corridor, one was always left with the conviction that she had lit that dark corridor with her exuberance, like a glowing lantern.

Ida Beauchamp truly hoped that the Reverend *was* lusting after Widow Winkworth because she felt he could really do with some jollity in his sad life — he took everything far too seriously and the girls often complained that his lessons were tedious, and they were finding it difficult to stay awake!

She paid particular attention to the Reverend's surreptitious glances but couldn't gather anything from the secretive looks and sighs. Much diverted, she kept a close eye on him and watched as the congregation filed past him in the porch in order to thank him and praise his sermon even though most of them had no recollection of what he had said.

There goes Hannah and Jennet, the housemaids, she mused, and oh, dear, that dreadful Mrs Crouch from The Wheatsheaf, although what she was doing in a church, God alone knew! The Reverend was talking to Augusta now and smiling insincerely at something she was saying and there is dear little Pandora, talking non-stop as usual and now, last in the queue is poor Flora, looking blankly around her as though trying to recall where she was and why she had come. What an odd girl, she was! Rather like, in some ways, her own sister Euphemia. What a thought! Nobody would want to be like Phemie! No, indeed! Now, Flora's bobbing a polite curtsy to the Reverend and he's saying something and — oh! Oh, *dear* — oh, surely not! That cannot be so! Ah, what a *disaster!*

* * *

Flora tapped on the classroom door and when bid enter, did so. She tiptoed up to Augusta who was supervising a reading lesson with their pupils, and she passed her a note.

Augusta opened it up and read it.

Her face flushed with alarm.

"I will see him after the lesson. He will have to wait — in the withdrawing room. Make sure he has some refreshment."

Flora nodded and went out again.

She found the visitor still waiting in the hall and ushered him without ceremony into the withdrawing room as instructed.

"Augusta will be along in a minute — at the end of the lesson. You see, it's a Monday and we have lessons on a Monday," she said rather .

"Ah," said the gentleman, with ponderous care, "So it is. A Monday. I should have considered. Very thoughtless. I will await her arrival here then?"

"Yes. Would you care for some refreshment?"

"No, I thank you. I am refreshed just to be here."

Flora gave him an impatient look, "Pray be seated, then."

He moved slowly to the nearest armchair, considered it for a moment and then trod across to the other side of the room and stood looking down at another chair, he nodded, took out a handkerchief, flicked it over the chair and then carefully lowered himself into it, with a small sigh.

Flora inwardly rolled her eyes and was relieved to hear the school bell being sounded in the distance to signal the end of the lesson. She had often wondered why they bothered with a bell at all when they had so few pupils and they were all in one classroom anyway, it really didn't make much sense to her. She supposed it made the house seem more like an actual school. She heard her sister's unhurried footsteps approaching and quickly opened the door to help speed her arrival.

Augusta looked decidedly flustered with unattractive flashes of colour high on her cheekbones, and she was frowning.

"Sorry, Flora," she whispered, "I came as quickly as I could." Her anxious eyes settled upon the gentleman visitor, "Cornelius! What a pleasant surprise! I had not expected to see you so soon."

Mr Cornelius Bacon had risen to his feet and crossed the room, at his usual measured pace, to greet her, "Augusta, my dear. You are looking well. I found myself in the vicinity. Urgent matter of business with my lawyer. Lives nearby. Most auspicious. I could combine two visits. Two birds, you understand! After my last visit I will admit to being at something of a loss. I had thought — "

Augusta knew precisely what he had thought on his last visit to the school and had not, at the time, been able to find the right words to let him know her own thoughts on the matter because she had been in a state of panicked confusion and rendered briefly speechless.

Mr Bacon had entered her life by stealth. The elder brother of a previous boarder, he had had the occasion to call on them to collect or return his sister and had apparently formed some kind of one-sided attachment to Augusta without her having any knowledge of it. She had thought him to be a little strange, oddly attentive and inclined to hover. It was always a challenge to be rid of him at the end of one of his unannounced visits. He spent a good deal of unnecessary time poised on the threshold of the front door, one foot in the hall and one on the terrace, and he could stay like that for half an hour or more, talking in fractured sentences, interlaced with unwelcome, half-hearted compliments. It was almost more than Augusta could bear and she was hard-pressed not to push him down the steps and slam the door. Instead, she listened blankly and said nothing in reply — a stratagem she now realised had given him entirely the wrong impression. He now seemed to think that she was agreeable to his hesitant advances. There had probably been a moment, right at the very beginning, when she could have disabused him with just a word or a quelling look, but now she felt it was too late to say anything without extreme embarrassment on her part and the possibility of outrage on his and she could not bear a fuss or any kind of confrontation.

It was not as though he was some kind of ogre — he was perfectly pleasant. He had only ever made veiled hints about his intentions towards her, which, she realised now, she had failed to notice, and had never yet tried to seize her in any kind of ardent embrace, for which she was deeply thankful. He was not even repulsive to look at. In fact, he could be considered handsome in a lifeless fashion — his features uniform, his smile regular and every other quality he possessed would no doubt conform to the exacting standards of most ladies on the hunt for a spouse. One could be in his company for several hours whilst firmly believing him to be a more than usually well-formed gentleman but then the following day his countenance would have somehow been erased from one's memory, no matter how hard one tried to call it to mind.

"Last time you called, Cornelius, I seem to remember that it was just as the girls were leaving for home after the winter term and we were in complete turmoil. It was most unfortunate. I was unable to stop and converse with you for very long as I couldn't spare the time — there were parents and relations to talk with and forgotten items to be found and goodbyes to be said. By the time we had finished, and all was quiet again, you had left without saying a word."

A tiny frown marred the smooth expanse of his forehead, "I had come specifically to ask you something. I saw you only in the distance. I waited."

"I am so sorry, Cornelius, but you must have noticed that I run a school! There are certain aspects of being a school governor that precludes that person from being able to conduct life in a normal manner. The girls must always come first."

"That would, of course, have to change," said Mr Bacon obliquely.

"Change? I am afraid that cannot change while I still have a school to manage."

"When we are married. I will not allow it. No, 'tis not fitting. In a wife."

"*Married! Who* are you marrying?" asked Augusta turning pale.

"Why, you of course," replied Mr Bacon with a bemused expression. "Who else? I was pleased to inform you last time."

"Inform me? *Inform* me? I do not recall you saying anything of the sort! I would have remembered something as serious as that!"

"I said to you, 'Do you not think we would deal admirably together?' You replied, 'I do indeed!'"

She stared at him in confusion, "You *said* — but if I heard you at all, I had no idea what you were talking about! What was I doing at the time?"

He considered for a moment, his finger to his chin, "You were tying on a small whining girl's bonnet. She was complaining that she'd lost her gloves. Her mother was there. And a nursemaid. They were late for an appointment. You must remember as it was such a momentous occasion!"

"Ah, yes, I do remember — that was Lady Latimer and her daughter Mabel. She's a very highly-strung child and had become quite overwrought about her gloves and had tied her bonnet on crookedly and Lady Latimer was urging her to bestir herself because they were expected elsewhere, and she was delaying them, and her father would be angry as he had urgent business to attend — being a highly regarded magistrate. And the nanny was fussing about a mark on the child's gown and wondering if green really became Mabel as well as blue." She took a breath, "It seems to me that it was hardly an auspicious moment to mention something that might have an appreciable effect upon both of us!"

Mr Bacon looked affronted, "When was I *supposed* to do it then?"

"Perhaps when I was able to understand the significance of your words and make some intelligent response! Perhaps when I had a moment to myself and was not in the middle of a crisis! It was very thoughtless of you."

"Thoughtless? I had thought a good deal about it. I had not come to the decision lightly. My father objects prodigiously to the notion. He thinks schools for ladies an abomination and the females who run them to be below the salt," said Mr Bacon candidly.

"An — an *abomination!* Below the salt? Why, I am most *gratified* by your father's opinion of me and my school! Oh! I wish you would tell him on my behalf that if it weren't for men like *him* the world would not be in such a backward state! Women would be educated in all the subjects men are allowed to choose and *unlike* those idle wastrels who squander their time and their parent's resources at university, most females would be *glad* of the chance to improve themselves!"

Mr Bacon looked as though his favourite dog had just been eaten by a bear. Augusta had never seen his bland face register so much emotion. She opened her mouth to say something more but was halted by a polite cough from somewhere behind her and, recalled to her senses, remembered that Flora was still in the room acting as chaperone.

"I think, Cornelius that you had better leave. I have another class in a few moments and cannot be late for it. I, unlike your father I suspect, am a firm believer in teaching by example and they shall not see me shirking my duties. So, I will say, out of inherent politeness, thank you very much for calling upon us and I bid you good day!" And she crossed the room and held open the door for him.

Mr Bacon eyed her with steadily growing disappointment but sensing that she was not in the mood to listen to reason, he nodded to Flora, whose mouth was slightly agape, and passed Augusta as though sidestepping a nest of adders and made his way delicately to the front door. He paused on the threshold as was his wont and looked back at her.

"We will discuss this in a less heated manner next time," and he went out.

"*Next* time!" exclaimed Augusta with some asperity, "There will be no *next* time!" But he didn't attend her, and she watched as his retreating figure, proceeded stiffly down the steps, mounted his horse and rode away.

She turned to Flora, "I have never — *never* been so provoked in my life! What a pompous numbskull! How could he think that I would ever *consider* him — I have *never* thought of him — I thought what a dreary man he was! Below the salt indeed! How *dare* he! Oh, I am so *incensed!*"

"Yes, that is perfectly obvious," remarked Flora, "Your face is rather overheated and it's not at all becoming."

As her sister's colour then deepened considerably, she decided to remove herself post-haste for the sake of her own well-being.

* * *

Unusually, the travelling carriage came to a halt in front of the Manor and, as no one had noticed it arriving, there was a moment of confusion as the footman quickly changed his direction and dashed to the front door to greet the guests. Beecher glowered ominously as he passed the poor fellow and muttered that in order for the house to run smoothly one should always be vigilant or one would find oneself scrubbing pots in the scullery! The footman wiped the nervous sweat from his upper lip with his sleeve and stood rigidly to attention.

Beecher, who had been expecting the new arrivals to arrive that day, proceeded solemnly down the steps to welcome them. There was no sign of his master who had been properly top-heavy the night before and was now nursing a well-deserved headache, so Beecher had his excuses prepared.

The gentleman alighting from the carriage was well-known to him and, as he never caused him any bother, he had no reason to be put out by his appearance at the Manor. He handed down a young girl and then an abigail of some sort.

The butler bowed and his master's cousin, Mr Jonathan Frost, turned to acknowledge him, "Beecher! You haven't changed one jot! Still as well-turned out as a Duke! We're here at last! The road out of Burford was blocked by a toppled coach and we stopped to assist and then waited until fresh horses were brought and the passengers — an apothecary and his wife had been sent on their way again. It took over an hour and delayed our journey I'm afraid. The wife was much distressed and loath to return to travelling so soon after such a calamity. Luckily no one was badly hurt apart from a manservant riding with the driver, and he was thrown clear but damaged his ankle slightly in the fall. Poor fellow! Anyway, we're here now and this is my cousin, Miss Imogen Denby-Birch and her maid, Faith. I fear that Miss Imogen has had a rather tiresome journey — we have discovered that she does not travel well! She is feeling a trifle indisposed and would probably appreciate being shown straight to her bedchamber! The roads were particularly bumpy, and the coach seemed especially unstable! We stopped at inns several times on the way in order to give Miss Imogen a chance to recover and found that sipping lemonade had a beneficial effect upon her queasiness. Did we not, Imogen?"

Miss Imogen Denby-Birch, who was the colour of parchment, looked up at him from large watery eyes and made no comment.

Beecher, who had never met the child before and on the whole was not in favour of children at all, suffered a shudder of alarm as he noted the overall lack of any animation coming from the small creature. She was, he supposed, not having a great deal of reference on the subject, a taking little thing, pretty in a washed-out sort of way, but — remembering her mother only too well — he wondered how his master and the vivacious Lady Birch had managed to spawn such an unprepossessing child. He tried smiling guardedly at her, but got no response, not even a flicker, so he beckoned to the housekeeper, who was awaiting instructions in the hall.

"Mrs Primrose, this is Miss Imogen and Faith. Would you be good enough to escort them both to their chambers and make sure they have everything they need. Miss Imogen is feeling unwell. Apparently, some lemonade would be very much appreciated. And perhaps some of Monsieur Baudin's Lemon Wafers? They might help?"

The housekeeper who was every bit as cheerful as her name, greeted the child with reassuring warmth and led her and the maid inside.

Mr Frost watched them go and heaved a relieved sigh. His job was done. It had been an arduous journey and his apprehensive charge had been violently ill several times, which had taxed his usually fathomless well of patience. He had only accepted the onerous role of guardian because he was some sort of cousin to the child and had felt obliged when her mother had tasked him to escort her daughter across country to Cuckoopen Manor. He was overdue a visit to see Marcus anyway so had accepted the challenge without giving it much thought. Only a few miles into the journey he had begun to wish he'd given it more careful consideration and perhaps even had the gumption to politely refuse. He was not, he felt, very knowledgeable about the care of children, as a rule happy only seeing them in the far distance and he had not had siblings of his own to practice upon. It had come as a rude shock to him that the pale, listless and rather harmless looking girl, who had been abandoned so imprudently into his care, would in fact turn out to be such a great trial. The journey had turned very quickly into the most dreadful ordeal for all of them and even though Faith had done her utmost to comfort Miss Imogen, there seemed very little anyone could do to stop her being so ill. At first, he had felt sorry for her, but then he had just prayed for the trip to end. It was like a bad dream and his only desire was to wake up from it and hopefully enjoy a large brandy with his cousin.

On that thought he stopped Beecher in his tracks as he was calmly organising the unloading of the trunks, "Where is Sir Marcus, Beecher? I hope he is — well!"

Understanding the implied meaning Beecher replied, "As well as can be expected, Mr Frost."

"Ah, I see. Where will I find him? In his study or is he still abed?"

"He was, when last I saw him, exactly where I was forced to leave him last night, sir. In the study — insensible. Mr Charles is away for a few days, so I was unable to get him to bed without causing injury to us both and did not care to call for help, when he was in such a parlous state."

"And do we have any clue why he has succumbed once more?"

"Yes, sir. I think the reason is unfortunately all too obvious and is only likely to get more pronounced in the next few days."

"I see," said Mr Frost thoughtfully, "I shall beard him in his den. You had better wish me luck!"

"I do, most assuredly, sir and I shall be in the hall should you need assistance."

"Thank you, Beecher! *There are few die well that die in battle!*"

"My sentiments exactly, sir."

* * *

The study was in darkness and reeked of strong liquor and the fire was nought but cold ashes. Mr Frost made his way cautiously to the windows and threw back the curtains to let some light in. He heard a groan behind him from the depths of the sofa and turned to inspect the grim results of too much brandy and a perverse nature. Blue devilled as usual, he thought to himself, and was glad to see Beecher arrive with a tankard of the famous Denby remedy for sobering those who were worse for wear. All he knew was that it contained eggs and spices and possibly that renowned cure, the hair of the dog. With the butler's help, they manhandled Sir Marcus into partaking of the foul brew and were without sympathy when he choked and tried to refuse it.

"There you are dear cousin! Just a few more mouthfuls please! It'll make you feel more yourself — whatever that may be!"

After a short tussle, they won the battle and were able to successfully sit him up and allow the magic elixir to do its work. Another twenty minutes saw him able to string a faltering sentence together and although it was interlarded with cursing and threats to their persons, they were eventually able to assist him upstairs to wash and change his clothes.

Six

Looking very much more the thing, Sir Marcus cautiously consumed some chicken boiled with rice, followed by baked ox cheeks with a side dish of asparagus, a pie of mutton and potatoes, poached eggs and spinach and finished with an orange jelly. He was abstemious with the wine because his cousin had pointedly reminded him he had duties to perform and was expected to at least pretend to put on a good front for his daughter.

Finally, he sat back in his chair and glowered darkly at his companion.

His cousin, who knew his ways well, remained unmoved, "Feeling better, Marcus?"

"No thanks to your meddling."

Mr Frost chuckled and poured himself another tankard of ale, "No, I am quite sure that Beecher knows precisely how to deal with you when you're in your cups! Honestly, I would have thought it time you had grown out of such youthful practices. 'Tis hardly befitting a father of a small daughter. Or is it *because* of your small daughter?"

Sir Marcus regarded him with disfavour, "Do not tax yourself trying to understand the reasons, Jonathan. Let it be enough that an unexpected letter from Lady Birch will oft set the cat among the pigeons. You were recently with the charming Lord and Lady Birch — how do they do?"

"The same as ever. They both seem miserable. He is in town a good deal where he haunts the gaming hells, I'm told — as I understand it, he is something of an authority on losing prodigious amounts at the tables! He entertains his set of friends at Birch House while Miranda plays hostess and flirts outrageously with every "gentleman" there! It's not a sight anyone would wish to see let alone a close relation and 'tis best the child is away from it, in my opinion, although she evidently spends most of her days shut away in the nursery with a dreary old nanny. I must admit that I begin to feel sorry for her — it's no life for a child, even an odd fish like Imogen. Her mother ain't precisely maternal! And her stepfather is — well, vastly wealthy and surprisingly immature and almost as volatile as his wife. Needless to say, their marriage is stormy — as you can imagine and, in the tumult, they forget all about the child, which I have to say is probably a good thing as they are not the best example to her. She's brought out for inspection on rare occasions and performs like a trained monkey! I unfortunately witnessed it at the Christmas ball they gave and although I know nothing of children *per se* I think I know an unhappy pet when I see one!"

Sir Marcus put his head in his hands and emitted a groan that could have been mistaken for an indication of intense pain.

"That damned woman! She's done nothing but make my life a misery and now she must pass on her — dubious legacy to the unfortunate child — "

"Your *daughter*," commented Mr Frost, "Your *only* daughter."

"I do not need reminding for God's sake! Did Miranda happen to mention why she was sending her to me and for how long?"

Jonathan Frost's eyes flickered, and he twitched his shoulders uncomfortably as though his jacket had become suddenly constricting, "I — I'm not sure really — she wasn't very forthcoming when I asked. She was — otherwise engaged and barely spared a moment to wave goodbye to Imogen."

Sir Marcus eyed him with suspicion, "But you have an inkling, do you not?"

His cousin shrugged, "'Tis only conjecture but I must say she has sent a great many trunks of clothes and possessions with her. Imogen certainly don't want for nought in *that* way

— so I have an idea it may be for some while. Did she not say in the letter?"

"No, she wrote mostly of herself and how they now move amongst the *haut ton*. She seems to have found her true level at last. She barely mentioned the child apart from to mention that she would be arriving today and that you would be escorting her. She gave me no time to write back and refuse." Sir Marcus saw the expression of distaste upon his cousin's generous face and grimaced himself, "It's no good looking at me like that! I cannot pretend to be something I am not, Jonathan! What do I know of children? Thanks to Miranda, I do not know this — my daughter at all. We are strangers."

"Imagine how *she* must feel, being sent so far away to a place she has never seen before, to a father who wants nothing to do with her! Hardly an auspicious beginning!"

"I do not know what is expected of me," said Sir Marcus with a gesture of impatience.

"'Tis simple, dear cousin, you are required to be a father to your daughter. I would have thought even a blockhead like you could work that out!"

"A father? I last saw her when she was just a babe in arms and since then have had no word of her. How does a father act? I had a rather poor example."

"There's no use asking me! I am not even married! I have no experience in this and therefore can be of no use to you — however, I would have thought that it was rather obvious — she will need reassurance, guidance, stability and love. What else is there?"

"So, you're telling me I just have to treat her as I would a new dog?"

Jonathan laughed, "No! I am *not!* She'll need more than food and a warm place to sleep! Ah, that's got me thinking though! She's a female!"

"You astonish me."

"I mean to say — she must have some female companionship. Not just a couple of elderly male relations and Beecher."

"She has her maid," said Sir Marcus, looking a little bemused.

"Her maid? That won't do! Faith was only sent at the last minute because I suggested a young girl should have a female companion of some sort on such a long journey. Now she should have some friends her own age and perhaps a nursemaid?"

Sir Marcus considered this for a moment and then shrugged, "We can find her a suitable nursemaid from the village I expect. I daresay Beecher will know of someone. He has never yet let me down."

When he was consulted, Beecher was secretly astounded and filled with a creeping alarm. He had never in his whole career been asked for advice about children and certainly had never had to contemplate what might constitute an acceptable nursemaid. He was wifeless and without issue so had no experience at all to bring to bear upon the matter. He thought for the briefest moment about telling his master that it was beyond his capabilities but knowing how Sir Marcus was likely to react he decided against it.

It would cause him a long sleepless night of soul-searching.

* * *

Miss Imogen Denby-Birch sat on the edge of her bed and looked about her. Faith was unpacking her things and putting them away in the linen press and the chest at the end of the bed. The bedchamber was nowhere near as grand as her own room at Birch House, but she thought it was quite pleasantly cosy. Her feet didn't quite touch the floor and she was still wearing her bonnet and cloak.

"Shall I remove my outdoor clothes, Faith?" she asked in her faint little voice.

Faith looked around at her and sighed, "I'll help in just a moment, Miss Imogen. I'll just finish putting your petticoats away."

"Yes," said Imogen, "And my stockings."

Faith sighed again and wondered if perhaps Miss Imogen had been friendless for so long that she'd forgotten how to converse. It was like talking with a particularly dull farmyard animal, only you'd probably get more response from a sheep or a goose.

"I shall be twelve years of age soon," mused the child.

Faith politely agreed.

"Perhaps I shall be allowed to have a friend of my own."

"I don't see why not, Miss. It's only natural to want a friend of your own."

"I miss Nanny."

Faith closed the door of the press and went to her charge, "Of course you do. She's all you've ever known! But she was far too old to make such a journey! It would have killed her."

"Yes, Mama told me so."

"Right let me help you take off that bonnet," said Faith firmly, wondering why people bothered to have children when they never saw them until they were old enough to quit the nursery by which time it was far too late to undo the damage. She thought that Miss Imogen's spirit had been crushed by the years shut away from her family with only Nanny for company — an old woman who, although perfectly nice, was old-fashioned and unnecessarily strict. And it seemed to Faith that Miss Imogen never did anything mischievous, which seemed unnatural in such a young girl.

She took off the bonnet, leaving just the huge white frilly indoor cap to cover her lacklustre hair. She divested her of her short white velvet cloak and tidied everything away. She was just wondering what to do next when there came a welcome scratching on the door, and she let in a housemaid bearing a tray of very welcome refreshments. After the maid had gone out again, Faith sat Miss Imogen down at the small table and encouraged her to eat the Lemon Wafers and sip the Lemonade. She assured the child that it would make her feel better and after a short while this was confirmed.

"I do feel a good deal less sick," said Miss Imogen.

'That will be because we are no longer bouncing along in that awful coach, but also because Wafers are just the thing for when you are indisposed. My mother used to bake me Ginger Biscuits when I was feeling ill. Had me as right as a trivet in a moment."

Miss Imogen looked at her blankly, "Your mother *bakes?*"

Faith laughed, "Well, of *course* she does! She's a very good cook."

"How — strange," reflected the child in some bewilderment, "I cannot imagine my mother cooking. Or even going anywhere near a kitchen."

"Our mothers are very different, Miss. Lady Birch is — well, she's more — decorative. Mine has always worked hard. She has seven children, so she has no choice."

"Nanny said Mama is a Great Beauty and much admired and does not have to do anything but smile to get what she wants."

"That is probably very true. She is certainly beautiful and always the centre of attention."

"I think I'd rather have had your mother, Faith," murmured Miss Imogen sadly.

"I can see that you might! But never mind, you have your father now!"

This was greeted with a look of consternation, "My father? Should I call him Papa? Or Father? Or Sir Marcus?"

Dumbfounded, Faith shook her head, "I should think you could call him Papa! I would never call my Ma Mrs Keckwick — not to her face anyway. She'd cuff me round the ear!" She eyed the child sympathetically, "Come along! Let us get you changed out of that mucky frock and into something a bit more suitable to meet your Father!"

Miss Imogen looked at the maid with a slight frown, "What is 'right as a trivet'?"

* * *

After Sir Marcus had dined and was feeling more able to face up to his new responsibilities, he and Jonathan Frost waited in the withdrawing room for Miss Imogen to arrive.

Sir Marcus stood before the fire, which despite the early May warmth was blazing away, crackling and snapping busily and Mr Frost was comfortably ensconced in an armchair nearby and Quince was snoring gently in his bed.

Eventually Beecher came in and announced their visitor. Miss Imogen Denby-Birch came in hesitantly and hovered by the door as though poised for flight, Faith stood just behind her and looked much calmer than her charge. She was used to putting on a brave face in front of her employers.

"Ah, Imogen, dear child, I suppose I should introduce myself as we have not seen each other since you were a baby! I am, of course, your father — do please call me Papa, if you find that acceptable. Come in and make yourself at home and let us get to know one another. Sit here in this chair. There you are, is that not an excellent place to sit?" asked Sir Marcus in such alarmingly cheerful tones he received a despairing glare from his cousin for his pains and wondered what he had done wrong.

Imogen sat on the very edge of the chair, perched like a small, underfed bird, her tiny hands clasped together so tightly, her fingers were white, the knuckles gleaming brightly. She tried not to look at the large scruffy dog lying so dangerously still; he looked like he might spring up at any moment and devour her!

Her father stood and stared down at her, thinking how very small she was for her age and wondering what he should say next. He bid the maid to sit on the little sofa at the back of the room and turned back to the inanimate child.

"Well, this is certainly quite a surprise, is it not! I don't doubt that you are equally as astonished as I. It seems that your mother has, without warning, decided that it would be good idea for us to get to know each other. It's rather late in the day but it's never too late to start afresh. I must admit that I have very little experience in the guardianship of children —

or anyone else for that matter. This is all very new to me — as it must be for you too. We must somehow find a way to be — comfortable with each other, do you not agree?"

Realising that some response was expected of her, Imogen nodded listlessly.

"I think you will like it here at Cuckoopen Manor. You can ride my brother's old pony and play in the grounds and take Quince for walks — " Her face, already colourless, froze into a lifeless mask, "Oh, you do not ride?"

Imogen shook her head and surreptitiously peered out of the corner of her eye at the Evil Beast lurking in the corner.

"Well, that can soon be remedied. We can have you on a horse and galloping about the place before you can say Jack Robinson!"

At this Imogen looked as though she would surely faint away, so Mr Frost decided enough was enough, "Imogen, you do not have to immediately leap on a horse so do not worry. But, if you should wish to learn how to ride, it can be easily accomplished, but only when and *if* you wish it. Also, I have a feeling that you are not keen on dogs, are you?"

She shook her head again and pressed her lips firmly together.

"You have no need at all to be frightened of Quince — he is undoubtedly large but as gentle as a lamb. He can be a bit of a rascal, but he will do you no harm, I swear! But again, there is no need for you to be concerned, no one will make you walk him unless you wish to."

Sir Marcus was listening to his cousin and beginning to realise that he had hidden depths, he had had no idea he could be so solicitous or knew how to speak to a child in such a reassuring manner. It came as something of a shock to him and he looked upon Jonathan with dawning respect.

Imogen, on hearing she was not to be forced to confront any kind of Savage Beast, began to visibly relax. That is to say, her fingers unclenched enough to regain some colour and her breathing became not quite so constricted.

It was an awkward meeting for everyone and after she and her maid had left to have their supper and go to bed, Sir Marcus would probably have turned to a bottle of brandy had he not had so disapproving a witness.

The next few days were no improvement on the first. He said the wrong things, either showed too much enthusiasm or too little, made the child flinch like a startled deer and her enormous eyes fill with unshed tears and generally showed himself to be a poor example of a parent.

Jonathan found him slumped gloomily in his chair late one night and tried to suggest that he took a different stance, but his cousin was not in the mood to listen to his good advice.

"Perhaps you could just ask her what she would like to do, instead of trying to force her to do things that clearly terrify her. She is not like any other child I have seen, even from a distance! She is timid and a little spiritless and everything seems to make her shyness worse. I fear that her mother and stepfather have brought her to this. How can we expect her to be anything more when she has known only Nanny and the nursery? She has not come into contact with other children or animals or even anyone who showed an interest in her and what she thinks. It's tantamount to cruelty really. You wouldn't treat a dog like that. She's had no siblings to protect her. The poor strange child has been almost entirely alone her whole life — it's no wonder that all that's left is this washed-out limp rag of a creature."

Sir Marcus looked thoughtful, "I was just thinking of a young lady I met the other day. They could not be more dissimilar. Miss Pandora Pennington… her sisters and aunts run the Ladies Seminary in the village. She is all fire and sparks, while Imogen is all — grey mist."

"That's a little unfair, Marcus! This other female, this Miss Pennington? How did you meet her and where is she now? Does she appeal to you?"

"Good God no! Not in the way you are suggesting! She's only just fourteen! And I met her, purely by chance, when I rescued her from the clutches of a gang of small boys, although she said she was in need of no rescue. Charles was here — he met them the sisters and one of the aunts at the school and helped out when a goose became stuck in their chimney. He'll be back tomorrow thankfully. I'm hoping he might be able to talk to Imogen — I suppose he's some sort of uncle to her, but as he's so much younger than me, it's just possible that they may have something in common." He pondered this for a moment, "Although I cannot see anyone, not even Charles, having much in common with such a dreary little thing."

"Ah, you are too harsh, Marcus! Give the child a chance. These sisters, what ages are they?"

"As I said Miss Dora is fourteen and the middle sister, Miss Flora is, I believe, nineteen and the elder one, Miss Augusta Pennington, is anything from thirty to perhaps forty! She is the quintessential school mistress. A little unmemorable and old-fashioned. She takes offence for no reason and angers easily and yet — she laughs like a free-spirited child, which is rather disconcerting — she absolutely collapses with laughter. It was — unexpected."

Mr Frost, interested to hear more of this "unmemorable" female said, "Nothing to look at then?"

"Nothing at all. 'Tis a pity she's not more like her aunt, Miss Ida Beauchamp, who has a good deal of character and sparkle, but Miss Pennington has very little to recommend her. Although her hair is a striking shade of reddish brown and very shiny and her eyes are a remarkable golden sort of hazel."

Jonathan Frost nodded, "She sounds very dull indeed," he agreed.

* * *

Charles had arrived back on Tuesday full of his adventures with his friend from Oxford and informed his brother he'd purchased an absolute prince of a horse. But as this was met with glowering disapproval, he quickly stopped talking about it and set to wondering why Marcus was in such ill-humour. It wasn't long before he had worked out the reason and come to the conclusion that something would have to be done about it because otherwise it made life at Cuckoopen Manor intolerable and he had no desire to spend his entire summer having to avoid being in the same room as his brother — he was looking forward to having a little fun and now he had his new acquisition in the stables, he was keen to spend some time riding and showing off his knowledge of horseflesh.

But first, he had to sort out his brother.

* * *

Step-uncle met step-niece and there was not precisely a meeting of minds but something about Charles's benign high-spirits made Imogen forget to be quite so frightened and although the difference in her was hardly marked enough to see, she watched her uncle's antics with what might almost be called interest.

It was not until the following week however that a brilliant idea came to Charles as he idly observed Imogen sitting alone on a stone bench in the garden watching one of the gardeners skimming debris from the fishpond and he realised that he could solve everyone's problems at one fell swoop. He just had to bring all the relevant loose threads together and his idyllic summer would be safe and there would be other beneficiaries into the bargain. He stroked Quince's tufted head and began to work out the knots in his scheme whilst bearing in mind the proverb that advises honey catches more flies than vinegar. As luck would have it, Fate had a similar idea, but found a more serpentine way of delivering the same result.

* * *

Dora and Flora were picking elderflower blossoms so that Cook could make Elderflower Cordial; Flora being the taller of the two had a shepherd's crook and was pulling the branches down for Dora to cut the flowers. They already had a good basketful and were just picking the last ones when there was the sound of loud barking and distressed chickens.

"That doesn't sound very good," remarked Flora irritably.

Dora put down the basket and picking up her skirts, ran swiftly across the lawn and around the house to the kitchen garden where they kept a small flock of hens. The sight that met her eyes made her slightly falter in her headlong charge, but as one of their precious birds was about to be assaulted by a huge disreputable looking dog, she continued at speed and swooping in, scooped up the distraught chicken and threw herself into the hen enclosure, tugging the gate shut behind her. She looked in anguish at the dreadful marauder, which was now on the other side of the fence and wondered how long it would take it to realise that the fence could be easily jumped.

She put the hen back in its house and firmly wedged the door. She then eyed the dog suspiciously and was just about to yell for help when she noticed that the creature, far from baying and snarling at her like a wolf, seemed to be whining happily and wagging its untidy tail, its narrow hindquarters in constant movement and its expression ingratiating.

Dora approached it slowly and spoke in a soothing voice, "Good Morning to you! I must say that you don't look very fierce, but you *were* about to ravage one of our hens — although, I suppose you *might* have just been playing! Ah, I see that there might be something in my notion!" The dog was making excited high-pitched sounds that seemed to be trying to convey some sort of affable message. "I believe you might possibly be just looking for company!" said Dora, holding out a tentative hand over the fence.

The dog licked her fingers in ecstasy and reassured about its intentions, she patted its bony head and admired its characterful eyebrows, which gave it a quizzical expression that convinced her, perhaps unwisely, that the creature meant no harm.

"I wonder who you belong to? I've never seen you about in the village. I think I'd have noticed a handsome creature like you! Have you escaped your owner?" She cast her eye around and spotted a bundle of twine in a wooden pail, which she quickly availed herself of, unwound and after some encouraging words persuaded the dog to allow itself to be collared and tied to the fence.

Flora arrived bearing the overflowing basket of elderflowers, "You just ran off! What is *that!*" she demanded looking with revulsion at the panting hound. "You can't leave that there!"

Dora was already feeling rather protective of this new addition to the school, "It's just rather boisterous but I am absolutely certain it means no harm. The chickens are all quite safe and unhurt. I'm going to find out where it's come from and return it to its owner — they must be missing it dreadfully. Although, I quite fancy keeping it for myself! Look at its dear little eyebrows and happy smile! I think it's very intelligent."

"I think you can safely call it a he, Dora."

"Oh," said Dora, much impressed, "How *clever* of you to know!" She smiled at the expectant hound, "You're a gentleman! Although I must say that you don't behave like one! I wonder who might know where he comes from?"

"Why don't you ask Arthur Sippence? He knows everyone in the village."

Dora beamed at her, "Oh, you are so right, Flora! I shall go at once — he's probably in the stables!"

And with that she raced away leaving Flora looking disparagingly at the dog and the dog looking hopefully at Flora.

As she had correctly surmised, Dora found Arthur Sippence working in the stables; an elderly fellow hired to do all the repairs around the school, he could turn his hand to just about anything.

He looked up from what he was doing and smiled at Dora, "Miss Dora Pennington, as I live! An' what be you doin' back here in the stables? Come to bother me for somethin' no doubt!"

Dora laughed, "Indeed I have, Mr Sippence! I have need of your wisdom. There's a dog — a *big* dog — it was around the henhouse, and I've tied it up, but I need to know who he belongs to."

Arthur Sippence got to his feet, "I'll come and take a look then Miss," he told her cheerily and together they went to examine the trespasser.

The dog greeted this newcomer as though they'd been friends for life, fawning in the most embarrassing fashion and grinning slavishly.

Mr Sippence took one look at him and nodded knowledgeably, "That be the dog from the Manor. No doubt about it — seen him with Sir Marcus on occasion, running alongside when he's out riding. Never seen 'im out by 'imself though."

"Oh," said Dora, doing some busy reckoning in her head, "I shall walk him home straight away. I'll just fetch my straw hat."

Mr Sippence gave her a shrewd look, "Perhaps you should take Hannah with you," he suggested, "Those folk at the Manor — "

"Oh, I don't think that will be necessary," said Dora blithely, but encountering a frown from her sister, she rolled her eyes, "Oh, all right," she sighed, "I'll take Hannah but — "

Flora made an angry little snort that Dora knew well, and Dora gave in, knowing she couldn't win the argument.

She untied the dog and thanking Mr Sippence dashed off to find her sunhat.

Flora and Mr Sippence exchanged an eloquent glance, he doffed his cap and made his way back to the stables relieved that Miss Dora wasn't really his concern.

Seven

Dora led the now ecstatically faithful hound up the lane, trailed by Hannah, who was delighted to get out of her usual duties, although she wasn't at all sure that Miss Dora should be roaming about the countryside with an untamed beast on a piece of string. The dog seemed to recognise the route they were taking and jumped up and down just in front of her, gazing up into her face excitedly all the way up the long hill, which Dora told him was a sad waste of his energy and besides that, he was hampering her progress. The dog took no notice.

They arrived at the Manor and after a moment's consideration, went to the front door, Dora believing that the dog *must* be a beloved member of their family and would therefore be welcomed home with open arms by Sir Marcus himself.

She knocked and a footman opened the door and looked down at them as though they were tinkers selling their wares.

"Good afternoon. I am Miss Dora Pennington from the Ladies Seminary and I believe this is your dog!"

The footman looked at the animal and thought what a pity that it had been recovered; it was such a nuisance around the house and had no manners whatsoever.

"It is, Miss. I shall inform Sir Marcus. He's been out looking for him since this morning. Will you wait in the hall?"

"Yes, thank you, that would be splendid. What is the name of the dog, please?"

"He is called Quince, Miss," he replied disapprovingly, and he went to find his master.

"*Quince!*" exclaimed Dora happily, "Shakespeare! Oh, it suits you well. I shall miss you, you terrible creature!"

"Why would anyone miss that appalling excuse for a dog?" asked Sir Marcus coming into the hall, followed by Charles and Jonathan.

Quince, recognising his master's deep tones, went into a frenzy of delight, dancing and bowing, fawning at his feet then jumping up and pedalling his huge paws in the air. Sir Marcus bent to greet the disreputable animal, scratching his ears and telling him that they'd wasted most of the morning looking for him.

"Good afternoon to you Miss Pennington, may I introduce my cousin, Mr Frost and my brother, you've already had the misfortune to meet. Where did you find Quince?"

Dora smiled at him, pleased to see her rescuer again, "He was distressing one of our hens — she had somehow escaped her enclosure and was running free. He did no damage and was easy to capture, putting up no resistance at all."

"I'm very sorry to hear that one of your hens has been bothered. I hope she recovers from the shock. Quince is usually quite restrained around farm animals, and I am at a loss to know how he managed to escape. Thank you for returning him to us. Now that you are here perhaps you would care for some lemonade? It's quite hot out today, is it not?"

"It is, but I wore my sunhat so shall thankfully not get freckles!" announced Dora with a bucktoothed grin.

She and Hannah were ushered into the withdrawing room and made comfortable. Beecher arrived and quickly dispatched a footman for refreshments.

Quince, delighted to be home, after making sure that his master was as overjoyed as he was, finally stretched out on the rug in a patch of sunlight and fell into an exhausted sleep.

"He's a very fine dog," said Dora admiringly.

"My brother is not of the same opinion, I'm afraid," admitted Charles, "When I couldn't manage Quince in Oxford — far too many carriages and noisy things to chase — I gave him to Marcus believing that the country would be the best place for him, but I'm sorry to say he's just as unruly here as in town. Marcus would have been happier with a pug or a small lapdog!"

"Oh, do not say that!" cried Dora, "My Aunt Euphemia has just such a dog, called Bonny, and she's thoroughly evil! You met her, Sir Marcus, in the kitchen — she was eating Cook's leg of lamb! A more revolting creature you'd be hard pressed to find! I would have thought that Quince was *precisely* the dog for you!"

Sir Marcus shook his head, "In that case I'm not at all sure what you must think of me, Miss Dora."

"Oh, I think very well of you," declared Dora artlessly, "I was only telling Augusta the other day, how very heroic you were in the face of such a bloodthirsty mob that day on The Green."

Mr Frost made a choking sound and sent his cousin a look of profound respect, "You haven't mentioned this, Marcus! Hiding your light under a bushel?"

Sir Marcus didn't dignify this comment with a response.

Charles was watching Dora's lively countenance as she listened to the conversation and suddenly looked as though he had discovered something monumentally interesting. Making his excuses, he left the room in a rush.

Sir Marcus and Mr Frost exchanged resigned glances.

"Do you have a dog of your own, Miss Dora?" enquired Jonathan.

"No, indeed, I do not! Apart from Bonny there are only the chickens and an exceedingly old, one-eyed cat who is supposed to keep the mice at bay but cannot even cross the kitchen without bumping into the furniture! I do not think I would ever be allowed to own a dog. Flora is not keen on animals and Augusta would think it a distraction."

"Well, I give you my full permission to borrow this vile creature anytime you have a fancy to be dragged headlong across the fields. He could do with more exercise, to tire him out and make him more biddable."

"Oh, *thank* you!" breathed Dora.

A moment later Charles returned bringing with him a wide-eyed Imogen, who had been prised from her bedchamber, like a limpet from a rock, and despite a whispered protest, which wasn't heard, she was bustled unceremoniously downstairs.

Charles wore a look of decided triumph, "Here look! I have brought my step-niece to meet you, Miss Dora! Miss Pandora Pennington, may I introduce to you, Miss Imogen Denby-Birch! Is this not the best notion ever?"

The two girls gazed at each other, guardedly on Imogen's part and with great interest and friendliness on Dora's.

"Imogen? What a *pretty* name, you lucky thing! I am saddled with Dora, which does not suit me at all!" said Dora cheerfully. "I think I would have been a much better Titania or Valeria. Do you not think it would be better if the child could choose her *own* name?"

Imogen blinked at this loquacious individual and wondered if an answer was expected of her. She could think of no suitable reply so kept quiet. When she realised that the girl was looking at her expectantly, she nodded cautiously.

Dora smiled her toothy smile and said comfortably, "Augusta, my eldest sister, says I talk far too much, so I expect you are trying to get a word in. I would very much like it if you showed me around, Imogen. Would that be possible? I have never been to the Manor before — oh, of course, I have seen it from the *outside* in the distance and have heard tell of its magnificence but never thought I'd have a chance to see it for myself! So, this is very exciting, and you must know all the nooks and crannies so are probably the very best person to show me around your home."

As Imogen had not until that moment considered Cuckoopen Manor to be anything but a temporary lodging, she was slightly taken aback and the idea that this might now be her "home" made her wonder if she would ever have to return to Birch House. For a brief moment she reflected on where she might actually belong.

Dora turned confidently to Sir Marcus, "Would it be all right if Imogen and I went to explore the house, Sir? I promise I will *try* not to get into any more scrapes!"

"Rescuing Quince is hardly a scrape, Miss Dora. It's more a heroic act. But I should be delighted for Imogen to show you around. You had better take your maid with you — the only caveat would be that the woods are best avoided as there are sometimes poachers in them and the gamekeeper shooting at squirrels — as gamekeepers are wont to do," advised Sir Marcus.

Dora agreed to do as he said and then with a nod to the others in the room, she took Imogen's cold little hand in hers and drew her to the door. Charles opened it and bowed them through.

After the door had closed behind them there was an awe-inspired silence, then Jonathan Frost chuckled appreciatively and Sir Marcus said, "Charles, my boy! I begin to suspect that I have been very much mistaken in you! Did you, by any chance, *plan* this?"

Charles looked a little smug, "Well, I must admit dear brother, that the thought had crossed my mind."

"'Tis pure genius," said Mr Frost with the greatest respect.

"Yes, I thought it might answer. I must say that Miss Dora is a very engaging female. She seemed to see immediately what was needed and read Imogen like a book! Clever girl."

Sir Marcus stroked his chin thoughtfully, "I am not at all sure what the sister will say about her fraternising with the enemy! We didn't get off to a very auspicious start and I think she considers me a reprobate. From something Miss Dora let slip, I think some part, if not all, of my history might be known. She buttoned her lip as quickly as a monkey steals a nut, but I fear the truth is out and, in her eyes, I am an unprincipled person. It didn't help that Mrs Crouch winked at her! Quite set her hackles up."

Jonathan was bewildered, "Mrs Crouch? Winking? What is this nonsense, Marcus? We all know that you are on the whole, a rogue, but you do have a few redeeming qualities!"

"Oh? And what might they be?"

Jonathan laughed, "I'll admit, I cannot think of any offhand! But tell me about this Mrs Crouch!"

Sir Marcus briefly explained the ordeal that Miss Augusta Pennington had suffered at the innkeeper's hands and that it had been mostly his fault.

"I can see why Miss Pennington despaired of you," said his cousin, "She was justified. Winking indeed, the temerity!" and he laughed again with his usual enjoyment of the ridiculous.

"I believe Miss Pennington feared her hard-won respectability would be forever impaired just for being acquainted with me, let alone having the charming Mrs Crouch convinced that Miss Pennington was my er…light o' love."

"Is she very much respectable, this Miss Pennington? Her sister seems blessed with quite a mischievous character. Is the sister so very different?"

Charles was listening to this with brotherly curiosity and interrupted, a vague idea in the back of his devious mind, "She could be nothing other than a school mistress! Is that not right, Marcus? She's perfectly pleasant, but I would say, perhaps a trifle commonplace."

His elder brother cast him a disparaging look, "As you no doubt recall, on our second meeting she showed considerable spirit and rang a fine peal over me, leaving me in no doubt of her opinion of me."

"I'm delighted to hear it. You sometimes forget to be obliging and people are driven to give you the cold shoulder and avoid you after they've met you just once!"

"I'm overwhelmed by your good opinion, dear brother. I do not think I am yet excluded from Polite Circles and even though Miss Pennington may think me very low, I can, in fact, still gain entrance to the drawing rooms of the *haut ton* or Boodle's if I so wished." He grimaced, "Which, of course, I do not, under *any* circumstances! I have had more than enough of their ludicrous pretensions. Let them think what they will, I really do not give tuppence for their approbation! I can live without such sycophants."

"You only say that because you no longer have a wife who demands that you and she circulate amongst the highest ranks of society! You are free of all constraints now and may do as you please!"

"I have always been able to do as I pleased," growled Sir Marcus, his mouth thinning to a forbidding line.

"Oh, no, don't come so haughty with me! I may still have been in long coats when Miranda was beginning to cut capers but it don't mean that I didn't hear things and notice things!"

"I believe you were a mere seven or eight when she took Imogen away," said his brother in calmer tones.

"I was unnaturally perspicacious!" declared Charles gleefully.

"You were unnaturally *obnoxious!*" said Jonathan, "And still are, for the most part."

"So, dear boy, you believe me to be beyond redemption?"

"Certainly *not!* Anyone can be reformed — even a scoundrel like you!"

"Again, I must thank you. You have some clandestine scheme for my daughter then?"

"I do and Miss Dora is a small part of it."

"Will you let us in on this plan or are you determined to keep it a secret?"

"I will share it with you when I'm good and ready and not before."

"Stubborn and guileful like your dear father."

"He was *your* father too."

"Do not remind me!"

* * *

Imogen was not at all sure which way to turn. She had spent the last week mostly in seclusion in her bedchamber just as she had at Birch House and had only ventured downstairs for meals and for the occasional uncomfortable interview with her father. Her step-uncle was kind to her and had taken her for walks around the garden in the sunshine, but she had not really seen much of the house. She now had this strange girl holding her hand, which was a vastly curious sensation, and she was asking her what they should explore first. She had no idea but didn't know how to voice her uncertainty.

Miss Dora Pennington smiled at her in the warmest manner and said conspiratorially, "I really only suggested exploring because I thought it might be nicer for us to be away from all those tiresome gentlemen! They look at one as though one might explode or do something quite outrageous! It's amusing, but I find I tire of them quite quickly. Why don't we just find somewhere to sit in peace and quiet — away from all the grown-ups."

Imogen cast around desperately for somewhere that might do and suddenly remembered the stone bench under the weeping willow by the fishpond. With a good deal of shyness and hesitant broken sentences, she led Dora out into the garden to what she would from that moment on think of as "her spot".

While Hannah tactfully wandered down to the pond, the two girls sat for a moment and pretended that they were enjoying the view, as the sun glinted on the water and the fronds of the willow moved gently about them like a pale green waterfall.

They were very different in appearance, the one very slight and delicate and remarkably short for her age and possessed of an inherent stillness born of a strong desire to remain unnoticed. The other was tall and gangly like a colt, with an expressive face and expansive gestures; she emanated a liveliness of spirit that was hard for anyone not to find delightfully contagious.

Dora was very much just an artless young girl who, throughout her life, would always hurtle from one escapade to the next. It was just her nature to think she could master any kind of situation without asking for assistance from anyone. It would, in the years to come, lead her into many a tight spot and adventure, but also, eventually, to sheer unadulterated happiness.

At that moment she was only concerned with the wraith-like child beside her. She had never met someone so nearly not there — she had felt when she held her hand that she was trying to hold onto morning mist. It was bewildering and fascinating. She had seen in an instant that the gentlemen, although very charming, were overwhelming for her and making her want to disappear and Dora had immediately wanted to rescue her.

Imogen sat very still, while Dora kicked her heels and fidgeted.

"I think," began Dora after a little thought, "That we could be very good friends. I am never wrong about this sort of thing."

Imogen looked up at her blankly and wondered if she were mad. If she *were* mad and they became friends, it would probably end badly and she, Imogen, would end up all alone while Miss Dora Pennington was put in a home for the deranged. *If*, however, by some miracle, she happened to be quite *sane*, then she, Imogen, if she did nothing, might miss out on her very first real friendship and spend the rest of her life alone.

It was a dreadful dilemma.

Dora, sensing that there was some kind of battle going on within Imogen's fragile mind, took her hand and gave it a reassuring squeeze, "I want you to know that you'd be doing me a *very* great favour! I have two sisters — one much older and extremely strict and the other, well, she despairs of me — we couldn't be more different. If you were to agree to be my friend, I would be so very overjoyed!"

Imogen's huge eyes shone, "I — I w-would like that very much," she whispered, astonished at her own bravery.

Dora gave her a quick hug and tried not to mind that Imogen shrank a little in her embrace, "What a *day* I'm having! First I find Quince and then because of his trying to make friends with one of our hens, I found *you!* Is that not absolutely *splendid?*"

Imogen thought about this for a moment and, after due consideration and taking all the possible and probable dangers into account, she nodded.

It was all Dora could do not to dance around the fishpond. She felt she'd won the first skirmish and with that little victory tucked under her belt she felt that things could only improve.

She hadn't yet put her true plan into action but meant to try before she left the Manor.

"I live at the Ladies Seminary just outside the village, you know! It's really nice and if you'd like I could take you there one day to show you." She saw Imogen stiffen and realised she must not try to push her too far too fast. A little at a time and she would hopefully be able to win her trust. Dora decided it must be a little like having a ghost for a friend or a handful of smoke.

"Do you read?" she enquired, changing the subject.

She was rather perturbed when Imogen shook her head but was careful not to show her dismay.

Holding onto smoke was already proving to be quite tricky!

"Oh, I don't suppose that you've ever had the chance?"

"My — mother thinks it's — not necessary for a female to read," murmured Imogen apologetically.

Not *necessary,* thought Dora indignantly, trying to imagine a life without books, which then reminded her that she was not to have her books returned for another *week.* She knew that she had deserved the punishment, but it didn't take the sting out of it.

"Well, it's really just a matter of finding the *right* kind of book. I particularly like Shakespeare, but he wouldn't suit everyone. I shall look through my books and see if I can find you something."

Imogen sat very still, hardly daring to breathe.

Dora, sensing that she had said something that had thrown her new friend into something of a quandary, cocked her head and smiled warmly at her, "You know, if we are to be friends then you must learn to say what's on your mind, or we shall be forever at cross-purposes. Did I say something thoughtless?"

Imogen swallowed nervously and thought that her life was becoming ever more complicated and difficult to bear.

"I — I cannot — read. I — have never been taught," she faltered.

Dora was fully aware that girls were often left deliberately uneducated, fit only for marriage and endless child-bearing and little else — while having herself been reared in a family where the females had been routinely put into the hands of a ferocious Scottish governess who believed, quite radically, that girls needed every advantage in order to survive in a world run almost entirely by men and who, despite having to stand her ground and risk being dismissed, ensured that all three girls in her charge were given as good an education as she could possibly give them. Which, thought Dora, was just as well, as they'd ended up in the Seminary! Miss Agnes Murray had not taught them much besides reading and writing with a little history and literature thrown in for good measure, but it had been an excellent start for them to begin their own educational endeavours.

"Oh, I shouldn't be downhearted about *that!* My sister Augusta will be able to help you, I am sure! I think if you were able to come to the school and I explained to Augusta — "

If it were possible, Miss Denby-Birch turned a little paler, "Oh, no! I — I do not think — not to the school! Mama would not approve!"

"Well, it's *most* fortunate that your mother is not here then and cannot see what you are doing! I think it's perfectly *beastly* to deprive anyone of the joy of reading! Let us agree that the minute I have persuaded my sister to help us, we shall begin some lessons and in no time at all you and I shall be able to discuss the books we are reading! Imagine that!"

Imogen tried very hard to imagine it but failed miserably. She had not been blessed with a vivid imagination like Dora's and having been kept in seclusion for most of her short life meant that she was very restricted in her ideas. After accidentally overhearing her mother and stepfather discussing what should be done with her, and hearing mention of a convent, she had thought briefly that she might as well be a nun but after a little consideration had decided that she didn't like the notion of being imprisoned with so many other strangers. And anyway, as far as she knew, she wasn't the right religion to join a convent, although she didn't really know what religion she was. But the deciding factor had been that, as far as she understood it, nuns were forced to wear ugly black gowns and veils and she thought that sounded depressing. She may not have any friends or be able to read, but she had some exceedingly pretty gowns and took a good deal of interest in them. She had already noted that Dora's gown was not at all modish and was made to last rather than for its beauty.

"I like gowns," she said apropos of nothing.

Dora recognised this as an opening of sorts and pounced upon it, "Oh, I do *too!* But because of our *circumstances* I must wear what Augusta describes as *serviceable* gowns and be thankful! It means I only have one gown for best, which I wear to church on Sunday and the others are in various shades of grey so that they don't show the dirt!"

"Dirt?" queried Imogen in confusion.

Dora laughed, "Why yes, *dirt!* Augusta says I attract it like a sheep's fleece attracts sticky burrs!"

As Imogen had no clue what a sticky burr was, she was none the wiser. But she was very certain that she did not want to emulate Dora and get her gowns dirty. She was unable to contemplate just how you would do that anyway. It would surely mean having to do unspeakable things.

Seeing Imogen's bewildered expression, Dora sighed inwardly and reminded herself that Rome was not built in a day and therefore she would have to be uncharacteristically patient in order to rescue this particular waif.

She stood up and called Hannah away from her contemplation of the fish in the pond, "I had better go home before Augusta finds out where I am! She will read me the

Riot Act as it is, but I must just have a word with your father before I go."

They walked around the house and into the hall, where Dora decided not to wait for Imogen to take the lead and she marched up to the withdrawing room door and after a sharp tap on it let herself in and as the idea was already in her head, she began talking immediately.

"Sir Marcus! I really must be off now, but before I go, I just wanted to ask you an *enormous* favour. I know from our first encounter that you like Shakespeare and therefore I have surmised that you *must* be in possession of some books — perhaps even a whole *library?*"

Slightly startled by this unexpected onslaught, Sir Marcus could only agree and wait for clarification.

Dora beamed at him, "I am wondering, in that case, if you would mind *awfully* if I were to come and avail myself of your books?"

Sir Marcus was puzzled, "Of course, Miss Dora, my library is at your disposal. Please borrow any books you want."

"Oh, I am *very* much obliged to you, Sir! But would it be all right if I came and read *here?*"

Sir Marcus, with light rapidly dawning and his eyes gleaming, bowed, "That would be most agreeable. You could call on Imogen at the same time you are making use of the library. May I ask how long your own books have been confiscated for?"

Dora, realising that she may well have met her match looked suitably abashed, but nonetheless grinned up at him, "You are *very* clever! I have another week of torture to go. But I do feel that as long as I don't take your books home with me that I am not *really* flouting the rules, am I?"

Sir Marcus, foreseeing trouble ahead, could only hope that the deception would never be discovered.

Eight

Naturally, Augusta heard about the escaped dog and the hen incident from a much-nettled Flora who was also keen to inform her elder sister about Dora's expedition to the Manor with the stray creature. Augusta had listened in silence but inwardly despaired about her youngest sister's inability to curb the immoderate side of her nature. She understood that Dora did everything in good faith and that if challenged before the event, she would realise that her proposed actions were not acceptable for a number of perfectly sensible reasons. She was a clever and resourceful girl, but not inclined to much careful deliberation or judicious thought. She would rush headlong into each scrape and only stop to consider the consequences of her actions when it was too late, and the damage had already been done.

Augusta was quietly distraught that Dora had gone to the Manor, even if she'd had the good sense to take Hannah with her. Although Augusta had met Sir Marcus and, against her best judgement, rather liked him, she had no wish to see someone as young and innocent as Dora getting embroiled with a gentleman who had earned such an infamous reputation. Augusta knew that Dora would only see what was right in front of her and not take time to consider that he might not be a suitable companion. Dora knew nothing of his unspeakable past. Augusta was forced to check herself and admit frankly that she had no idea why his past was spoken of in hushed tones and never mentioned in front of the children, only knowing for sure that he had, at some point in his misbegotten life, become the subject of local scandalmongers. Reverend Cheadle refused to even speak his name in front of the ladies of the parish, which of course only increased everyone's fascination with him and that disreputable history.

Augusta had been astonished to hear Cook declaring that she knew the reason for his notoriety and had been forced to intervene when the reason was divulged. Augusta had had to very firmly quash the notion that Sir Marcus had killed his wife's lover, saying, quite truthfully, that as Lady Birch was still married to her second husband, this particular version of the story could not possibly be accurate. To say that Cook was deeply disappointed would have been an understatement.

Miss Ida Beauchamp discovered what had been going on from Augusta, who had related the sorry tale through clenched teeth and was staggered when her aunt merely chuckled and shook her head saying, "*Dear* Augusta! If you only knew the mischief I got up to when I was a girl, you would be scandalised, I am quite sure!"

"I cannot believe that you did anything as shocking, Aunt Ida! Dora is incorrigible and seems never to learn from her mistakes. I fear it will all end in disaster, and she'll be snubbed by Polite Society, and she'll never achieve a suitable marriage."

"Well, I'm quite certain that she'd be delighted to hear that! She is not a *usual* girl at all and has not, as yet, developed an interest in matrimony or an overriding need to be accepted by anyone other than her loved ones and, even then, I feel sure she's only paying lip service. She will ultimately find some kind of harmony within herself and begin to understand what is required to secure the life she desires by being a little more circumspect. I believe her greatest virtue is that she always tells you what she has done, *eventually*. We must be grateful that once she realises her mistake she willingly owns up and faces the consequences without too much argument."

Augusta heaved a sigh, "I know I am too hard on her sometimes, but I am so afraid that she will be like her father."

"There is absolutely no likelihood of that Augusta! Dora is thankfully nothing like her father. He had no redeeming qualities at all and was devoid of all finer feelings. You must not compare them! Comparisons are odious. It is wholly unfair on that poor girl. All three of you take after the Beauchamp side and that is why he was so very hostile to any signs of — our more eccentric characteristics rearing their head. He thought us quite freakish." She paused to consider for a moment, "Of course, Viola *was* a little unconventional and Phemie is, shall we say, — *outré* —, but they were neither of them nearly as bad as he made out. I would hazard a guess that, being insecure himself, he constantly found fault in order to reassure himself that he was still in charge of his little kingdom."

Augusta smiled then, "You always find a way to make my concerns seem so — trivial or misguided! I agree with you about Papa — he was a tyrant in his own home and deserves no sympathy whatsoever. Mama must have driven him quite mad with frustration! Flora, I am very much afraid, takes after Aunt Euphemia but that cannot be helped. She has her good points, which must be acknowledged. She is far less woeful and doesn't suffer from the same kind of anguish that plagues Aunt Euphemia, but she is certainly a martyr to her unsteady temper."

"We all have our faults, Augusta," remarked Ida Beauchamp with a decided twinkle in her blue eyes.

Augusta couldn't help but laugh, "You are saying that I too am flawed? I don't know how you can intimate such a thing when I am so obviously perfect!" She frowned suddenly, "All joking aside though, what on earth are we to do about Dora and her newfound friends? We cannot allow it to continue! If word got out that we permit her to frequent the abode of such a notorious person — not only might the school suffer but Dora might find herself vilified for her nonchalant attitude towards Sir Marcus and his family. I don't think she has any idea of the scandal linked to his name, but to be perfectly frank, I do not think she'd care one jot even if she did! We cannot allow her reputation to be ruined by such a close acquaintanceship with them. I do not think the gossips will take into account the fact that she is only fourteen either and they will lay most of the blame, quite rightly, at our door!"

For a moment Miss Ida Beauchamp regarded her great niece with a teasing smile, "I think you should have a quiet word with the gentleman in question and perhaps find out the truth about his historical peccadilloes and allow him to defend himself against the charges. Then at least we would know where we stand."

Augusta looked appalled, "Gracious! I could not *talk* to him about it! Oh, the very thought puts me to blush! What a dreadful notion!"

"How else will you discover if he is going to ruin us all by mere association? How will you be able to warn Dora to take care if you don't know the truth about him? You cannot, surely, just take the word of some malicious busybodies? That is not like you Augusta, my dearest child! You are usually, above everything, even with your strait-laced ways, inclined to be fair-minded in your dealings. Did not Sir Marcus rescue Dora? And his brother come to your assistance and solved the goose problem. They seem, on the surface, to be rather pleasant fellows. I understand from Dora that there is also a cousin, Mr Frost, whom she seems to think is a stout-hearted sort of chap. She does however seem very concerned about Miss Denby-Birch's state of mind and, more particularly, her lack of reading skills, which she is determined shall be improved forthwith! I believe it will be good for her to have a project outside the school to keep her out of mischief."

"You must be deluded, Aunt if you think anything will keep her out of mischief! I will talk with her and try to decide what to do about it. Now I really must go and make sure Jennet has brought the washing in in case it rains this afternoon. She sometimes forgets and it makes so much more work!"

"And I must tend my sister, she must be desperate to complain to someone by now!"

* * *

On the days when there were dancing lessons, the thumping sound of un-fairy-like feet on wooden boards and the insistent and slightly tuneless twinkling sound of the hugely inferior harpsichord, which had been donated by a local merchant whose daughter had once attended the school, filled the air to the exclusion of every other sound. Mrs Priscilla Winkworth was inclined to be rather too enthusiastic in her playing as she was in everything she did, and the melodies suffered a good deal. Miss Euphemia protested vociferously about the disturbance and banged on the floor with her walking stick, which just added to the general din. And Bonny barked continuously as though she thought the house were being attacked by something monstrous.

Augusta would retire to her study and try to block out the cacophony and if she couldn't concentrate, she went into the garden and pulled up weeds with excessive violence.

After lessons finished and the girls were allowed out to get some fresh air and stroll about to cool down, Augusta was chatting to Mr Sippence about a shrub she was a little worried about and out of the corner of her eye she caught a glimpse of Dora slipping out of the gate and turning up the lane in the direction of the Manor.

She lost the thread of what she was saying to Arthur Sippence and wondered where her sister was off to in such a stealthy manner. She quickly apologised and left the caretaker looking amused by all the intrigue at the school.

Augusta dashed inside and snatched up her sunhat and shawl and flew after her sister, hoping to stop her before she reached the Manor. She had not taken into account just how fast Dora could be when she had some particular purpose in mind.

Augusta, not thinking very clearly, tried to keep pace but all she could see was the occasional flitter of skirts ahead of her and was so intent on keeping up with her quarry that she failed to question her own actions and in consequence she arrived at the Manor completely out of breath and very pink in the face. As she stole around the hedged drive towards the main house, she cannoned straight into a tall and exceedingly solid impediment to her progress.

"Miss Pennington! What on earth brings you to my door and in such haste too?" asked Sir Marcus sounding infuriatingly amused.

She looked up at him in dismay. Of all the people to bump into! She wished she were anywhere but there and cursed herself for having rushed into such a madcap venture just as thoughtlessly as Dora would.

Furious with herself she gasped and stammered, "I — I did not expect to see *you* — "

He glowered suddenly, "That does not surprise me! I would have thought you would wish to give me a wide berth after everything that has occurred. Mrs Crouch and the winking incident for instance, which was, I'll freely admit, my fault."

Feeling utterly foolish Augusta adjusted the ribbons on her hat and tried to recover her composure.

"I thought I saw my sister coming this way and — "

"And you wished to stop her before she became blighted by my shocking reputation?"

"Oh, no — of course not — I was merely concerned because she left the house without taking Hannah with her and I have *expressly* told her that she must always be accompanied even if she is just going to the village!"

"And does she usually obey?"

"Never! She is sadly bereft of any kind of circumspection and as you have already seen for yourself is much more drawn to doing as she pleases and falling into scrapes. I fear — " she hesitated and bit her lip.

"You fear she has fallen into a much worse one now?"

"You keep interrupting me!"

He laughed, "I am afraid you will never finish your sentence and I have an impatient nature."

"So I see! I was going to say that she should not be pestering you and your family — she will run you all ragged!"

"I can assure you that my daughter will be delighted to see her, as will be my disreputable dog! I must apologise for the behaviour of said hound, by the bye — I understand he disgraced himself by assaulting one of your hens?"

"Oh, dear, no! He did not damage her at all — not a feather out of place! According to Dora he was just curious about the chicken and wanted to play. Mr Sippence has made sure that the pen is more secure now."

"Good for Mr Sippence. Although, I must warn you that a fence does not usually stop Quince! Anyway, you have no need to worry about Miss Dora pestering us. The house is large, and she and Imogen find things to occupy them that keep them mostly out of our way. Charles and my cousin Jonathan have taken to her, and I must say that it makes a change to hear laughter about the place."

Augusta narrowed her eyes, "Exactly *how* many times has she visited the Manor, Sir?"

Sir Marcus raised his brows, "Ah, an unfortunate slip of the tongue. Can we forget I mentioned it?"

"No, we cannot! Has she been before this? I mean, after the dog rescue?"

"Once or twice," hedged Sir Marcus.

"Well, which is it — once or twice?"

"I wasn't counting but perhaps three times?"

"Good gracious! I am entirely at a loss for words!"

"*Are* you?" he queried, wryly.

Augusta made an explosive huffing sound, "I believe I should like to speak with my sister, Sir Marcus and then take her home with me!"

"By all means," he replied cordially and led the way into the house.

The two girls were found in the withdrawing room, sitting together on the window seat and Dora was explaining something to her friend with expressive hand gestures but as the door opened and her sister unexpectedly walked in, her hands froze in mid-air and her expression went from animated to guilty in a moment.

"*Augusta!*"

"Yes, 'tis I, dearest! I cannot think why you should look so mortified! You must be here with Aunt Ida's permission, no? Or perhaps you asked Aunt Euphemia!"

Colour stole across Dora's cheeks and as she stood up to face Augusta, her chin sank onto her chest, and she pressed her lips together over the words that wanted to spill out. She knew this was not the time to make excuses, but she wondered exactly how much trouble she was in and cast Sir Marcus a quick questioning glance, which was answered with the slightest shake of his head, and she breathed again — he had not told Augusta about the library! What a *Paladin!*

"Miss Pennington, may I introduce my daughter to you, Miss Imogen Denby-Birch. She has just recently come to stay at the Manor and was in sore need of some female company. Your sister has been invaluable, and Imogen very much looks forward to her visits."

Dora peered apprehensively at her sister's unsmiling face and her heart, usually so impervious to censure, quailed a little.

Imogen, feeling that something was required of her made a little curtsy, "Miss Pennington, I — I have heard so much about you from Dora."

"I have no doubt!" said Augusta tartly and then immediately regretting her tone she added, "I am so very delighted that Dora has found a friend so close by. It is all very well living in a school full of girls, but they come and go, and poor Dora can never really count on them as true friends."

There was a sudden burst of noise from the hall and the sound of cheerful male voices exchanging good-natured banter and Sir Marcus opened the door and beckoned them into the withdrawing room, feeling that Miss Pennington's ire might be diluted by his relations' high spirits.

The two young men came in and Mr Frost was introduced to Augusta. They explained that they had been out for a ride, to put Charles's spanking new horse through his paces and see how it compared with one of his brother's finest animals. He was happy to report that he had not wasted his money!

"He's a regular sweet-stepper!" he declared, "Is he not, Jonathan?"

His cousin readily agreed, and they went on to eagerly discuss, in deadly dull detail, the horse's finer points, with little regard for the ladies present.

Sir Marcus caught Augusta's quick glance and his smoky grey eyes glittered so much with laughter that she couldn't help relaxing her shoulders a bit and returning his smile.

"Charles, may I suggest that this is not the time to dissect your latest purchase!" admonished his brother, "Perhaps instead we could be talking about things Miss Pennington might take pleasure in?"

Brought swiftly back to his senses, Charles apologised profusely, "Please forgive me, Miss Pennington! Marcus will tell you that I tend to get carried away and particularly when it comes to horseflesh, a subject my brother takes little interest in, despite his stables overflowing with prime goers!"

Sir Marcus shook his head, "And we're back to talking horses once more! We cannot win." He rang the bell to summon Beecher and begged Augusta to stay awhile and partake of some tea or lemonade. She didn't feel able to refuse as the two other gentlemen added their voices to the invitation.

Jonathan Frost had been observing the elder Miss Pennington with interest and thought that she seemed to be an odd sort of female; dressed as though she were some twenty years older and with nothing in the way of beauty to recommend her, but there was a certain something about her, a hint of some undiscovered depths that she seemed at pains to keep hidden. He found it rather fascinating and because he was fairly certain that his cousin found her of some interest, he was keen to find out more about her.

"Miss Pennington, Charles and I were discussing your Seminary and wondering if you took only ladies who board?" he said.

"At the moment we have no girls who come in daily, but there used to be a few local pupils who lived with their families. That was when the school was doing well."

Charles and Jonathan exchanged a look, "And do you have room for any more pupils, I wonder, or are you already at capacity?"

Augusta, wondering why she was being interrogated about their numbers replied frankly, "We have not been at capacity for some while, Mr Frost. It seems that parents would rather send their daughters to an Academy, not just a lowly school, and some of the more discerning are not partial to their beloved and pampered children rubbing their well-bred shoulders with the offspring of mere merchants! We have sadly become the victim of social conceits and then, to crown it all, one of my aunts took to her bed and Aunt Ida could not manage on her own. They were losing pupils at breakneck speed, and my sisters and I have failed to halt the exodus I'm afraid."

"Have you thought to advertise?" asked Charles.

"It has thankfully not yet come to that!" said Augusta.

"'Tis surely a trifle short-sighted to dismiss such an infallible method of selling one's wares?"

Augusta visibly stiffened, "My aunts have always relied purely on word of mouth and recommendations. They would rather the school foundered than advertise!"

"I have heard that one only needs an endorsement from The Lady Magazine — a perfectly respectable publication — to win the very best clientele. Do not ask me where I heard it, for I cannot remember!" grinned Jonathan Frost.

"If Miss Pennington does not wish to advertise, that is surely her prerogative," commented Sir Marcus, "Ah, Beecher! You have come just in the nick of time."

There was a welcome break in the conversation and Augusta hoped that there would be no more references to advertising.

Tea was poured and cakes handed around. Augusta tried to catch Dora's eye as her greedy sibling helped herself to several slices of Seed Cake and a handful of Dutch Biscuits, as though she were starved of food.

"A child with a healthy appetite!" remarked Sir Marcus blandly. "Who does not like a cake!"

"Certainly, Dora has a very sweet tooth, and I will admit that I was not above bribing her when she was younger and harder to manage. I am ashamed of it now as I see how she has become addicted to sweetmeats and such tempting things."

"I wonder if you are so easily bribed, Miss Pennington?" murmured her host.

"No, I am not! I seldom change my opinion on anything so am not susceptible to bribery!"

He raised an eyebrow, "Then I am damned for certain. I had hoped that if I offered you some sweetmeats — "

She looked at him, puzzled, "I do not follow — "

"I think you are probably aware of the local gossip and as I have already fallen from grace in your eyes — "

"Fallen from grace!" exclaimed Augusta, "In order to *fall* from grace you would have to have been in my good graces to start with!"

He gave a shout of laughter and Charles looked at him curiously, having not heard his brother laugh like that for some time.

"Fair point, Miss Pennington!" conceded Sir Marcus.

Augusta, at once ashamed for having spoken her mind, and strangely elated that she had made Sir Marcus laugh, didn't quite know what to do with herself. She had lived with her parents and sisters and then with a clutch of female boarders and teachers with the one male exception, Reverend Cheadle. To be, as she was at that moment, surrounded by gentlemen, was an unknown occurrence for her and she was finding it exceedingly unsettling. She wanted to just gather Dora up and run away from the Manor leaving behind all the Denby family members who had no understanding of how much she loathed being the centre of attention. She sometimes felt that she had been allowed no choices in her life and had just had to submit to other people's whims. She would not have denied her aunts because she loved them, even Aunt Euphemia, but she did wonder if things had been different — if her father hadn't been so unbearable and died so senselessly, whether she may have had a chance at a conventional life that any female might have wished for. She checked herself, perhaps she wasn't a *conventional* female, perhaps that was part of the problem.

Sir Marcus Denby, observing Augusta's face, wondered what had made her look so melancholy. He suddenly had a curious desire to erase the desolate expression from her face.

They finished their tea and enjoyed some desultory conversation about innocuous topics like the weather and the state of the roads and then Charles and Jonathan took the two girls and Quince outside for a game of cricket on the velvety lawn.

Sir Marcus and Augusta followed at a more sedate pace and found a bench to sit upon and watch the uneven contest in relative safety.

They sat in silence for a few minutes, listening to the gentlemen trying to impress upon Dora that following the guidelines was necessary for the success of the game; she was not easily convinced and proceeded to play by her own set of imaginative rules, which ensured there was much laughter and frustration in almost equal measure.

The silence between Augusta and her companion grew until she began to feel a little awkward. She wanted to break it but didn't know what to say that might not be misconstrued in some way. She wished she could assure him that whatever gossip she might have heard, she took not the slightest bit of notice of it, but that would mean acknowledging the existence of his rumoured misconduct, which would be embarrassing and would mean lying, as she had been undisguisedly dismayed on hearing some of the gossip.

He, on the other hand, was wondering whether to suggest to her that she take on his daughter as a pupil at the Seminary and teach her how to read and write and perhaps give the poor neglected child a new lease on life. He had no idea what else to do with her and was beginning to realise that he could not solely rely on Dora to release Imogen from her self-imposed seclusion.

In the end they both turned to each other at the same time to say what was on their minds and spoke in unison. They both then stopped, tried to speak again and clashing once more, stopped and smiled at each other and then laughed.

The low evening sun was glancing off the cricketers as they ran back and forth and their shouts rang out across the grounds, along with the echoing sound of ball hitting their heavy wooden bats. Quince, thinking the game was being played entirely for his benefit, chased after the players, hampering them as best he could by running off with the ball and losing it in the undergrowth or by gambolling in frenzied circles just in front of them as they tried to take a run. Eventually even he ran out of energy and had to lie down, right across the wicket, so they had to leap over him in order to make their ground.

"God, I feel old," reflected Sir Marcus despondently.

"How old *are* you? asked Augusta before she could stop herself.

"I am absolutely ancient — two and forty," he replied.

"Oh, I don't think you look a day over — forty!" said Augusta.

He glanced down at her, and his gaze held hers for a moment, "I think Miss Pennington, that you are coming out of your shell and I'm not at all sure that I approve."

She turned her face away and pretended that she was watching the cricket match to allow the heat in her cheeks to fade without notice.

She heard him laugh softly and it was like a musical note being plucked and vibrating inside her chest; for a baffling moment she wondered what was happening and then Dora tripped over Quince and landed shrieking in a heap of skirts and petticoats and startled dog and Augusta was able to go to her rescue in order to cover her own confusion.

Laughing, Dora scrambled to her feet, in a most unladylike fashion and Augusta, sensing that the excitement was likely to make her forget how to behave with even a modicum of decorum, said in tones that brooked no argument, that it was long past time they returned to the school as the girls would soon be sitting down to dinner. She saw the look of disappointment on her sister's flushed face but quelled her with one of her famous looks. Dora heaved a frustrated sigh but remembered to make at least a pretence at being polite; she thanked everyone and told Imogen that they'd see each other soon.

Imogen, who had been dubious about playing wild games in the first place, as though she were some lawless ragamuffin, had not been able to conceal the fact that she'd hugely enjoyed herself and even she, so usually pale, had some colour in her cheeks.

"That was — very different — a-and — surprisingly nice," she said in her faint little voice.

"We shall find endless different things to do this summer!" announced Dora confidently, "We shall have *such* adventures!"

Imogen frowned. She was quite happy to play in the garden but wasn't sure that she was ready for adventures — they sounded dangerous and unseemly! But she was now so reluctant to lose Dora that she weakly agreed.

As Augusta made her way across the lawn, with Dora, who was expecting a good scolding on the way home, trailing reluctantly after her, she found Sir Marcus walking beside her and looked up at him in some puzzlement.

"I shall, with your permission, walk you back to the school," he said almost apologetically.

Inwardly rather pleased, she nonetheless said, "Oh, there's really no need! It's not very far and I am quite used to fending for myself."

"I am sure you are, but I must insist that it is never advisable for any female to be without an escort. Highwaymen, you know."

She laughed, "Very well, Sir Marcus, I cannot argue with that! Thank you. Come along Dora!"

Dora said her exuberant farewells and skipped after them, brimming with a mixture of heady excitement at the excellence of her newfound friends and a creeping anxiety that her books might be in danger of further confiscation.

Nine

They walked slowly down the long, gently sloping hill, beneath the avenue of beech trees, the evening shadows deepening as the sun edged closer to the horizon. Augusta shivered as the air cooled and realised that she'd left her shawl at the Manor. She'd have to remember to fetch it another day, as it was a favourite.

"I must thank you for taking Dora in — I know she can be a nuisance sometimes, but she means well. You must say though, if she becomes too much."

He glanced down at her as they strolled along, "I should be thanking you. You see, Imogen was — foisted upon me, by her mother, Lady Birch, without warning and without explanation. To be frank, I have no clue how to deal with any girl, let alone one who has been so repressed. Compared with Dora, she seems a little — vacant and I wonder if it's too late to undo the damage or if perhaps this is how she would have been anyway."

Touched that he should take her into his confidence, Augusta felt able to tell him what she had discerned from her first meeting with Imogen, "Oh, I don't think you need concern yourself too much! She is, as you say, somewhat restrained in her ways, but I think that is just a shield that she's been forced to erect to protect herself. You could see that she shrank from joining in with the cricket to start with, but it didn't take much persuasion from Dora to overcome her reticence and then I do believe she was truly able to enjoy herself even though it was so very clearly not something she would normally have appreciated."

"You give me hope, Miss Pennington. I find I am quite keen to improve her life. As I have your attention may I ask what you think about another concern I have?"

"Of course. I hope it's not something Dora has done!"

"No, you will be astonished to hear that she is perfectly well behaved. It's to do with Imogen and her want of education that has me wondering if you might be able to help. I realise it would be a huge imposition and you may not be able to see your way past the Denby notoriety but, on the other hand, you would be helping an innocent babe who will otherwise be consigned to a lifetime of ignorance!"

Augusta couldn't help smiling a little, "Oh, very nicely done, Sir! How can I now refuse without seeming callous! You have set me up to look heartless if I should deny your request! Abominable conduct!"

"I suspect you would expect nothing less from such as I!" He came to a halt and looked quizzically at her, "*Would* you have refused?"

"How will we ever know now that you have loaded the dice!"

"You may add yet another transgression to the long list!"

"I still am in the dark as to the nature of the request, Sir Marcus."

He glanced back at Dora who was picking wildflowers from the verge and humming to herself, "Miss Dora can read and write, and she has asked me, quite rightly, why my own daughter is unable to do the same. I was at a loss as to how to answer, having had to relinquish all rights to Imogen's upbringing in order to avoid yet another damaging scandal and probably hurting the child in the process."

Augusta was startled, "You *fought* for Imogen?" she enquired abruptly.

His face darkened, "I did. Although, I had only to see what trouble that fight might have brought upon everyone had I continued with it, to bring me to my senses. I would have lost the case anyway. My wife had already poisoned the waters so that I stood no chance of gaining custody of my child. Lord

Birch had a good deal of influence and threatened to make Imogen's life a misery, so I let it drop and forgot about it. You look shocked, Miss Pennington."

"I suppose I am. I had no idea — I thought — "

"You believed the gossip? Well, why wouldn't you? My reputation was already mired in half-truths and outright lies, and I was the subject of some very unsavoury rumours — some of which, I readily admit, are true. Let us just say I had a misspent youth and very much enjoyed all that entailed. One only learns regret when it is too late to alter things — history is precisely that, the past and therefore immutable. I occasionally look back and feel mildly contrite, but that is the best I can do, I'm afraid."

"But you *can* alter the future," mused Augusta. "You are perhaps hoping to make up for lost time with Imogen?"

"You make me sound a paragon, which, I can assure you, I am not! I aim only to tidy up a few loose ends and maybe leave everything a little neater."

"How long is Imogen to stay with you?"

"There's the rub. I have no idea. Miranda did not feel it necessary to tell me — or our daughter for that matter and although I have written to her to ask what her plans are, I do not expect to hear from her as she has never been inclined to think ahead. She lives for the moment and woe betide anyone who gets in her way!"

They had reached the gates of the school and they stopped and waited for Dora to catch up.

"Lady Birch sounds as though she is rather original."

He laughed without humour, "Oh, she certainly is that. Rules mean nothing to her, and if anything or anyone interfered with her schemes, then they were thrown overboard."

"Poor Imogen," said Augusta softly.

"Indeed, she bore the brunt I expect, which is why — "

"All right. I will take her on. She can come to the school on a daily basis, and we shall see what we can do to help."

Sir Marcus looked baffled, "What folly is this, Miss Pennington? No arguments? I am worried."

She smiled, "There is no need. I have made up my mind. It is through no fault of her own that she has such neglectful parents so I must and *will* tuck her under my wing! Dora! Come, we are so late. Thank you, Sir Marcus, for a lovely afternoon, it was most unexpected, and I shall look forward to seeing Miss Denby-Birch here at seven in the morning for her first lesson."

"Seven!" uttered he, in some astonishment, "I shall have to get Beecher to deliver her! Seven! That is barbaric!"

"It is perfectly usual, Sir! Thank you for walking us home," she said through a chuckle and following a dancing Dora, she marched up the short drive to the school, knowing that he stood watching her go.

* * *

Augusta didn't have time to mull over the afternoon spent at the Manor because there was always so much to do for the efficient running of the school. There were letters to answer and bills to pay, staff to advise and girls to soothe, menus to approve and sisters to be chastised. It was perhaps fortunate that she was too busy to think about Sir Marcus and what he had told her. If she had been able to spare the time she might have idly wondered about his misspent youth and those unsavoury rumours! She was not entirely innocent and knew from things she had overheard that gentlemen were much given to very poor behaviour where women were concerned. She also knew that there were different types of female, some who would not have batted an eyelid at the thought of assisting a young man with the unsavoury part of those rumours! She was, on the whole, rather prudish and did not approve of immoral behaviour; she had had quite enough of that during her early years — her father had been much given to flaunting his conquests in public, and in order to tease his wife, who was much given to jealous rages, he had made sure that she knew about every indiscretion. Augusta was fully aware that some of her mother's primness had rubbed off on her but was glad that it was the only quality she had inherited from Viola Beauchamp. It would have been hard to bear if she had also been endowed with some of her other less admirable traits. Flora had adopted a few, none of them good, but Dora had sidestepped them and even though she had not seen much of her father in her more impressionable years, she had managed somehow to inherit his reckless attitude. Nature, thought Augusta crossly, had a good deal to answer for!

* * *

Miss Imogen Denby-Birch arrived promptly at seven o'clock the following morning and declared that she had never seen her father up so early!

"Oh?" said Augusta mildly, "Did Sir Marcus escort you?"

"He did. Complaining all the while. He brought me in the carriage as he said I shouldn't get my slippers covered in dust, especially not on the first day." She looked round her, at the rather grim corridors and dull paintwork, "This is very nice," she declared as one who had not been privileged to see anything quite so lacking in style or luxury. "What interesting furniture."

Augusta whisked her past all the battered, heavy and second-hand items that she had previously not really taken much notice of but could now appreciate were hideous.

"We shall take the class in my study, Miss Imogen. I shall be giving you your lessons myself as, of course, our other teachers will be busy with the pupils. Later in the day, there will be dance classes and music, where you can join the other girls and also painting. Do you like to paint?"

Imogen considered this carefully, "I do not think I have ever painted. Mama thought it a messy occupation and was fearful for my gowns."

"Good gracious! Well, here you will be provided with a wrap-around apron, which will protect that rather unsuitable dress you are wearing. Perhaps tomorrow you might like to choose something a little less elegant to wear."

Imogen looked down at her white silk gown, "This is my oldest and least modish gown. It is a *robe a l'anglaise*," she explained disparagingly.

"Ah, you speak French!"

"No, I don't," said Imogen.

Augusta sighed; it was going to be a long morning.

* * *

Flora was sitting with her Aunt Euphemia and listening to that lady talk of the long distant past and how she had once been considered a diamond of the first water. Flora had no idea what this meant and had no interest in finding out. She used her visits to her aunt to do nothing; it cost her very little to sit and let Euphemia's nonsense just wash over her while she sat staring into space, not heeding a word the old lady said.

"None of you girls have inherited my beauty — more's the pity. You are probably the least unattractive of them, but you are very fat. You could go on a reducing diet — gruel and vinegar. Vinegar is very good for weight loss I am told. Of course, I never had to diet — my figure has always been perfect, and it hasn't changed since I was a girl. Yes, vinegar. You have quite a pretty face — if a little ordinary. Milkmaid prettiness, I call it. Your skin is good, smooth and pink. Your hair is thick and quite a good colour — gold, I suppose you could call it. I have gold, you know! No one shall find it. Ida's just waiting for me to die so that she can have it for herself. Your eyes are not very exciting — hazel, like your father's. They should be blue if you are to have queues of suitors like I did. Oh, *Bonny! Must* you chew everything? Is that my kid glove you have there?"

And so it went on, Euphemia with her constant flow of words and Flora with her inattentiveness.

"Your father was a lesson to us all. He was so very handsome and yet so very unreliable. Darling Viola could not see it — would *not* be told — she tumbled into love with his *beaux yeux* and his glib words. Darling Viola was a ninnyhammer. Bonny! That *is* my glove! Oh, you *naughty* beast! You've chewed the thumb right off!"

Flora stirred herself and quickly snatched the carcass of the glove away from the snarling lapdog. She held it up and examined it, "It's quite dead, Aunt Euphemia and sadly beyond repair, I'm afraid. Shall I throw it out?"

Miss Beauchamp picked up a periodical, rolled it up and swatted her precious Bonny with it. Growling, the dog slid away and hid under the bed.

"There's nothing to be done. Throw it away! What a dreadful waste. You should have been keeping an eye on her! What use are you if you just sit there like a fat sheep?"

Flora fixed her aunt with a look of mild contempt, "Perhaps you would rather I didn't come and sit with you at all, Aunt Euphemia."

There was the briefest silence before the old lady put a trembling hand to her head, closed her eyes and wailed, "I have a migraine coming on! You have made me ill with your hurtful words! Call for Ida! I must have my ginger water at once! And my lavender oil."

"Yes, Aunt Euphemia," said Flora eyeing her aunt with distaste and ringing the bell at the same time. "You know, I cannot understand why you insist on being so objectionable all the time. You catch more flies with honey than vinegar — anyone knows that!"

Miss Beauchamp sniffed affectingly into a lacy handkerchief and told Flora to go away. Flora was more than happy to oblige and was quitting the hatefully overheated bedchamber just as Hannah arrived. She asked the maid to fetch Miss Ida Beauchamp and went out into the cool of the corridor where she surprised herself by bursting into tears.

* * *

The lessons with Imogen were going well and Augusta felt it was as though the child had been held back by a dam; the water had been rushing into the reservoir and given only the slightest encouragement it had burst its banks and the dam could no longer hold back the flood. Imogen, as always, sat very still in her lessons but, like a sponge, she soaked up all the knowledge offered and although she asked no questions and made very little effort to communicate in any way, Augusta found a way of teaching her that produced good results. Dora was a splendid help in encouraging her friend and making her feel that being uneducated was nothing to be ashamed about. She assured her that at one time most of the females in the country had no education, but that at last things were improving in leaps and bounds.

Every day, Sir Marcus arrived early in the morning to drop his daughter at the front door and every day Augusta found a thoroughly plausible excuse not to be there to greet them.

She had a thousand things to do. She could not afford the time to exchange pleasantries with every parent. There was more important business to be attended. And it was bad enough that Sir Marcus was darkening their door at all without her being spotted chatting merrily to him every morning. It would do their reputation as a respectable establishment no good at all. Either Charles or Jonathan would collect her in the afternoon, and they'd take Dora back with them for tea.

Then one afternoon Augusta was passing carelessly through the hall while Imogen was struggling to get the ribbons on her hat tied neatly. Augusta went quickly to help her, and the door suddenly opened and there was Sir Marcus on the top step, a dark shadow against the light and she squinted up at him in confusion and tried to concentrate on tying the big blue bow under Imogen's small chin with slightly shaky hands.

"Ah, there you are," said Sir Marcus affably. "If it hadn't been for Imogen relating every tiny detail of your lessons, I would have thought that you had left the country and were not just avoiding me."

"I am *not* avoiding you!" declared Augusta sharply. "I am very busy with school matters!"

"Of course you are."

"Well, I *am!* You have no notion how much work is involved — "

"I think I might have a fair idea."

Augusta opened her mouth to say something cutting but saw the extremely pronounced glint in his eye.

"I'll thank you not to tease me, Sir! I cannot be at the door to greet everyone — it would take most of my day!"

"Rehearsed," said he, infuriatingly but accurately. "You do not want to be seen talking with such a scoundrel because you think it will do the school no good."

"I have no time for this!" muttered Augusta wishing she had not risen to his bait.

"No, indeed. I was hoping to find you at home. In a moment of madness, I offered to take Miss Dora for a drive to see the last of the apple blossom and of course Imogen would like to go, and I was wondering if you would care to accompany us?"

"I cannot spare the time to go jaunting about the county!"

Imogen stepped a little closer, "Oh, please, Miss Pennington, it would be so nice if you came too."

Weakening slightly at such an earnest plea, Augusta sighed, "I wish I could come too, my dear, but truly, I have too much to do."

"It will be on Sunday afternoon after church so you will be free and as it's a day of rest, you shouldn't be working anyway," said Sir Marcus unhelpfully.

She just stood and stared at him, her face speaking volumes.

"Quite so," he remarked, his eyes alight with amusement and not just a little triumph. "We shall take you up after church, perhaps not from outside the church as that might set tongues wagging, but we shall meet you here, if that is acceptable to you?"

An angry puff of air escaped from between Augusta's tightly clamped lips, "You know it isn't!" she hissed with as much dignity as she could muster but, seeing Imogen's eyes widen anxiously, she bit back some other choice words,

"However, I would be *delighted* to accompany you, Sir Marcus. I shall not forget your kind invitation!"

"No, I don't suppose you will," said that gentleman with a mocking bow.

* * *

Sunday arrived and much to Augusta's disappointment there was no Biblical deluge; in fact, she'd never seen the sky so brilliantly blue and cloudless. It was as though she were being ridiculed by Nature for even thinking some rain might save her.

Dora, naturally, was beside herself with excitement, but openly wishing that she had a fitting gown to wear on such a momentous occasion. Flora took pity upon her and found a bright pink satin ribbon and replaced the old white one on her straw hat so that it looked much refreshed. Dora was ecstatic and actually embraced her sister.

With four of them to accommodate on the trip, Sir Marcus had no other choice but to take the lumbering road coach and apologised for it being hard to see out, but no one seemed to mind as he promised they would stop at regular intervals to view the blossom. He also promised a picnic, which prompted Dora to ask if there would be cake.

They had left the church after the service and returned to the school, Dora with light skipping steps and Augusta with a heavy heart and a good deal of dread. She tried to analyse her feelings on the matter, wondering why she was so dead set against a harmless trip into the countryside to see the last of the blossom. It made no sense at all. She thought it was probably the thought of Sir Marcus's scandalous history that was making her reluctant to be seen in his company. *However* — the more she examined her reasoning, the more she realised that it was not so much his past that was bothering her but more his present!

She winced at the intrusive thought and chided herself, a little embarrassed to be thinking about him at all, especially as he was the father of one of her pupils.

She had dressed with special care for church that day, making sure that she looked the part of the prim and proper schoolteacher, wearing her best gown, a sober grey as always and her hat suddenly featherless and now only adorned with a pleated silver-grey ribbon, as she had ruthlessly removed the frivolous bow as well.

There was a slight stir at the rear of the church after she had found their pew and seated herself, nodded to various friends and acquaintances, exchanging whispered greetings, and asked after relations who were in poor health. A ripple of what could only be described as excitement, went through the congregation and she couldn't help but turn to see what had caused it.

She discreetly twisted her head this way and that to see past the Sunday best hats and finally saw the instigator of the curious reaction.

There, with no sign of any shame, was Sir Marcus Denby, his daughter Imogen, half-hidden beneath an enormous beribboned hat, Mr Charles Denby and Mr Jonathan Frost! The entire family in fact.

This was an entirely unknown occurrence, and it was small wonder that the faces around them were looking both shocked and intrigued. She heard someone whisper loudly enough for several rows of worshippers to hear, "What on earth has finally brought *him* to his knees I wonder?"

Augusta quickly snapped her head back to face the pulpit and told Dora sharply to do the same, as her sister was trying very hard to catch Imogen's eye and wave to her.

The service went all too fast, and it seemed like just moments before they were all gathering outside in the sunshine once more and exchanging meaningless pleasantries. Out of the corner of her eye she watched with consternation as the Denby family made their inexorable way across the grass towards the Pennington and Beauchamp corner, where Reverend Cheadle was lingering rather hopelessly, having long ago run out of things to say. He was just about to move on when he saw the three gentlemen from Cuckoopen Manor advancing towards their party and felt obliged to stay there and defend the innocent females in his care. He watched in horror as his Miss Flora was introduced to the invading Denby clan and saw how Mr Frost smiled at her and then so slyly bowed over her hand, making her frown and snatch her hand away. And he decided in that moment that he would have to make his offer as soon as maybe or else risk losing her.

Miss Ida Beauchamp was, as usual, observing the developments with a strong appreciation of the ridiculous together with a growing sense of alarm. She could plainly see trouble ahead on more than one front.

Reverend Cheadle was doing his obsequious best to move the Denby family on, informing them eagerly that several highly esteemed persons would like to talk with them, but his insistent and patently false words fell on stony ground and no notice was taken of his suggestion. He then tried to usher Miss Flora and Miss Beauchamp away to greet old friends, but it was like trying to move mountains! He could tempt no one to budge an inch and he was becoming quite desperate. He didn't like the look of Mr Frost, who was a hearty sort of fellow — robust and solidly built. Reverend Cheadle was just astute enough to realise that this interloper made him look underfed and a little weakly and he did not like the comparison. He was much relieved to see that Miss Flora was taking no notice of the gentleman, which showed good sound sense on her part. She was glaring crossly at the grass.

Flora was thinking that she would rather be back at the school, away from these strangers and their handsome faces and presumptuous manners. She had no wish to stand in the bright sunshine pretending to be grateful for their condescension. Sir Marcus Denby's cousin was laughing loudly at something Dora had just said and Flora thought him rather oafish. She could see that Reverend Cheadle was hovering nearby and in some distress about something, but she couldn't think what could be bothering him so, unless he had heard about Sir Marcus's disgraceful reputation. The

Reverend was wringing his hands and opening and closing his mouth like a fish. He really was a silly little man.

Eventually the small gathering began to disperse and the Penningtons and Beauchamps made their way through the churchyard, under the lychgate and into the lane beyond. Mr Denby and Mr Frost said their jovial goodbyes and made their back through the village towards the Manor while Sir Marcus and Imogen followed the Penningtons, a little way behind so as not to cause any consternation.

Flora, hailed by a friend just by the gate, was therefore a little delayed and was forced to trail after at some distance. This was unfortunate because it gave Reverend Cheadle the perfect opportunity to scamper after her and fall into step, saying untruthfully that he had some errands to run in the village.

Flora said nothing, being slightly embarrassed by his excessively eager manner. She walked briskly and was dismayed when he kept pace with her, making little galloping steps to keep up. She could hear he was out of breath, so slowed down again, thinking it would be dreadful if he dropped dead from a heart attack and everyone concluded that it was her fault!

"Miss Flora! Miss Flora!"

She stopped in her tracks, "Yes, Reverend Cheadle?" She looked down at him with withering pity.

He licked his lips nervously, "I have been thinking a good deal."

"That's because you're a clergyman. It's what clergymen do."

"Yes, yes! I must tell you that my thoughts have begun to stray to my future — I find myself not content with my life as it is."

"I'm sorry to hear that," said Flora, not in the least bit sorry and wishing heartily that he would go away.

"I have been recently forced to consider changes — to my present situation."

"Oh, are you leaving the parish?" asked Flora rather too keenly.

He looked affronted, "No, of course not! Leave my living? No, no! Being rector is a lifelong commitment. I would never think of quitting my parish — it is unthinkable."

"Then, I'm not sure that I understand, Reverend."

He laid a hand on her arm, and she looked down at it as though a poisonous insect had landed there. "I have been considering matrimony!" he declared.

"Well, that's nice," she replied vaguely.

"If I take a wife, she will be able to help me with my pastoral work and will enjoy some of the comforts of living in such a fine rectory as Church Rise. Imagine being allowed to reside in such a property! And I only answer to the diocesan bishop — I am the incumbent for *life!* I have glebe land, but of course I rent it to a local farmer, and we share the produce. It is a perfect solution. I am comfortably off and the work is not arduous."

Flora scowled at him, "I cannot think why you should be telling me all this, Reverend Cheadle!"

"Well, I would have thought it perfectly obvious!" uttered that fellow in amazement.

"I can assure you that it's not!"

"I am proposing to you!"

Flora very nearly fell over her own feet as they suddenly ceased to work in the accepted manner, and she turned to stare open-mouthed at him.

"Proposing!" she exclaimed, "Proposing *marriage?* To *me!* Here? Have you taken leave of your senses?"

Reverend Cheadle blenched and held up his hands defensively, "I had thought — I had hoped you might be receptive — you always seem so — I was sure that you would be amenable — " he faltered.

"Good God!" said Flora, "I had never even *considered* such a thing! A rector's wife! *Me!*" She fixed him with a steely glare, "I have no desire whatsoever to be married to you — or anyone! Why on earth would you choose me of all people!"

"I think you would make an excellent partner in my endeavours."

"How romantic!" scoffed Flora. "So, you're not desperately in love with me then?"

Finding himself under unexpected attack, he floundered, "I — I well, I have thought of you — I am very much — attracted to your — generous — lines!"

"Generous lines! You mean you are drawn to buxom females? Oh, gracious! What a fine hobble! Well, I never! Who'd have thought!" She looked at him appraisingly and then thought for a moment of Aunt Euphemia.

She laughed bitterly.

"Oh, all right then! I suppose it's better than dying a wretched old maid!" And she took herself off after her family at great speed, leaving Reverend Cheadle standing abandoned in the middle of the lane, thinking that his offer of marriage hadn't gone precisely as he had planned.

Ten

Flora caught up with the others, somewhat out of breath, as they were clambering up into a glossy black coach that sat impressively in their drive. Her laughter had quickly died, and she was now quite serious.

As she went by the coach, Sir Marcus was handing Augusta up the steps. She stopped for a moment and said bluntly, "Reverend Cheadle has made me an offer and I've accepted," and then before anyone could say anything she marched on into the house.

"*What* did she say?" demanded Dora from within the coach.

Augusta had paused in her ascent and was staring at the front door.

"I believe she said she was going to marry Reverend Cheadle," she replied, mystified.

"She did," said Sir Marcus taking Augusta suddenly by the hips and hoisting her without more ado into the coach.

"Oh!" she exclaimed as she tumbled in an undignified fashion onto the seat.

"You appeared to be stuck," he explained.

"I wasn't stuck! I was thinking!"

"Well do it with more speed."

"You are very ill-mannered, Sir!"

"I know, ma'am — it's one of my besetting sins. I make no apologies."

Dora and Imogen had been watching this and saying nothing, but they exchanged a wide-eyed look and Dora whispered into Imogen's limp curls, "I don't think they like each other very much!"

Once everyone was settled, Sir Marcus instructed the coachman, and they were off. When they reached the main road out of the village the ride proved to be quite bumpy, and Sir Marcus apologised for any discomfort they might be suffering.

"No, I am sure it's very good for one's kidneys!" remarked Augusta resentfully.

"Well, you *would* insist upon joining us!" said Sir Marcus, "Otherwise we could have gone in the curricle. It would accommodate me and the two girls easily."

"Oh!" said Augusta, and then refused to say anything else for the first part of the trip so incensed was she. When she at last cast him a fulminating glance under her eyelashes, she found her host smiling to himself and that compounded her ire, and she swore to herself that she wouldn't speak to him for the rest of the journey.

Sadly, they soon came to one of the promised stops and she was forced out of the carriage to admire the orchards full of pale pink blossom. The sight was so very beautiful that she was unable to hold her tongue and allowed an exclamation of delight to escape her.

"I thought you wouldn't speak to me for the whole day after our inauspicious start," murmured Sir Marcus.

She stiffened and stuck her chin out, "I am not so infantile, Sir!"

"No, of course not. I would never dream of accusing you of such a thing, but I was a trifle concerned in case the trip turned out to be a little quiet. I see now that I was mistaken — you would not allow a slight misunderstanding to ruin the girls' day out. It would be too shabby."

They were standing on a grassy bank, looking down over a vale that was frothed with blushing blossom and her eye roamed over the acres of apple trees with much appreciation whilst she struggled with a strong desire to speak her mind. Years of having to contain her feelings was hard to overcome and the struggle was soon won by her natural moderation. She was finding, however, that she could easily be driven to distraction by the right person — or was it the *wrong* person. She wasn't quite sure.

Dora turned a rapturous face to her sister, "Is it not the best thing you have *ever* seen, Gussie?"

Augusta nodded.

Sir Marcus pointed out a flock of geese ambling amongst the cow parsley that frilled like petticoats around the trees. "They should be pink geese," he said, "That *would* be memorable."

"Now, you're being foolish."

"Quite giddy," said Sir Marcus, "I think the coach has jolted my brain."

"Too much sun," suggested Augusta.

"Very possibly, or it might be the company."

"Oh? You are partial to the company of schoolgirls? Somehow that does not surprise me in the least."

Sir Marcus gave a low laugh and flicked her cheek with a careless finger, "Miss Pennington, are you trying to goad me? Because if you are, I can assure you that it will take more than insults — my hide is as thick as a rhinoceros's."

"Of that I have no doubt. After years of shameless behaviour, you must eventually become inured to all kinds of defamation," she muttered.

"The blossom is, I think, rather good this year as we have not suffered from drought or the usual gales," said Sir Marcus casually as Dora came bouncing up to them.

"Is this not *pretty?* Flora could make me a gown from the blossoms, and I could go to a ball! Oh, I *wish* I had a gown like that! What did Flora say as she went by? I *thought* she said she had had an offer! I must have misheard. That *cannot* be right! I mean, *Flora!* She's always as cross as two sticks! Imagine someone wanting to be married to her!"

"Dora Pennington, that is not only horridly rude but also unkind! Have you forgotten that Flora put a new ribbon on your hat?"

Chastened, Dora made a face, "No, but you will admit that it's very unlikely that someone should — " seeing her sister's face, she swallowed her words and went back to Imogen who was laughing and pointing at the geese.

"Look how pompous they look, Dora! Just like Beecher when someone has offended him!"

At the third place they stopped, Sir Marcus instructed the footman and the coachman to take the basket and rugs down to a small stream at the bottom of the meadow. When this had been accomplished and everything set out, they made their way down the grassy path and whilst the girls raced up and down the riverbank, exclaiming shrilly at what they could see and frightening the wildlife away, Sir Marcus made sure that Augusta was comfortably arranged and out of the sun beneath a small knot of aspens.

She looked up at him, "You do not feel the urge to throw me at the ground, Sir? I commend you for your restraint!"

For a moment he returned her gaze steadily, "Well, until you mentioned it, it had not crossed my mind, but now I cannot help but be a little diverted by the thought."

The heat that flooded Miss Pennington's cheeks fled just as quickly and was replaced by shocked pallor. She was unable to speak.

He smiled, "As you have no doubt already heard, ma'am, I am utterly beyond redemption."

"If you are, it's nothing to be so puffed up about!" said Augusta with feeling.

"Puffed up? I cannot think that I was ever called 'puffed up' before. Can I pass you a glass of lemonade and a pastry?"

Augusta choked on a laugh and bit her lip, "Really, you are incorrigible." She looked up at the girls who were now picking meadow flowers, "Do not go too near the water. It may look harmless, but the currents might be strong!" she called out.

"The same could be said about you," murmured Sir Marcus with an arrested expression in his eyes.

"I beg your pardon?" said Augusta, not having heard him clearly.

"Oh, nothing. I was merely talking to myself," he reflected.

"I think I would like one of those little meat patties please. If Monsieur Boudin made them I am quite sure they'll be delicious."

"Your wish is my command," said Sir Marcus and filled a plate with dainty pasties and other delicacies.

The girls, seeing the food coming out, dashed across the meadow and threw themselves down on the rugs and while chattering like a pair of noisy finches they helped themselves to the delights and ate without much thought for their manners or anything other than the excitement of a day away from the school.

After a while, Dora snatched up a large wedge of gingerbread and she and Imogen raced off across the meadow, giggling.

Silence fell. The gently soporific sound of the stream and somewhere a song thrush, grasshoppers and the buzzing of insects filled the air and on hearing a sharp call high above their heads, Augusta squinted up into the bright sky to see if she could see what was making the distinctive sound.

"There," observed Sir Marcus shielding his eyes and pointing, "A buzzard."

Augusta saw the tiny dark scribble against the blue and nodded.

He picked a daisy and began to make a daisy chain. Augusta watched.

His fingers were surprisingly deft considering the general bulk of him. She was fascinated and found it soothing. Her eyelids drooped. The sound of the stream grew louder and then softer and faded away. She heard the cry of the buzzard again, so very very far off. The heat of the day was gentle but insistent and she wished she could take her shoes off and wriggle her toes in the soft grass. She wished….

She heard the sound of girls laughing. And a man's voice. And thought for a moment that she was at the Seminary. She opened her eyes and saw the tall grasses and cow parsley steepled over her head. She closed her eyes again.

Suddenly awake, she sat up in such a rush that she felt a little dizzy.

Looking around she saw that the picnic had been cleared away and that down by the stream, Sir Marcus, Imogen and her sister were sitting on the bank, fishing for imaginary fish, with makeshift rods. She put up a hand and found her hat had been removed and she was wearing a daisy chain in her hair. She attempted to straighten the skirts of her gown and found her feet were bare. She pulled them swiftly out of sight and tucked her gown around them as though someone might see them and be scandalised. She glanced around and saw her shoes standing neatly together, each one with a stocking folded carefully into the toe.

For a moment she was indignant.

She wiggled her toes.

She wondered.

With difficulty she got to her feet, her *bare* feet, and then feeling like a naughty child, she tiptoed down to the riverbank, the long grass silky against her legs and she had to dismiss a sudden urge to dance.

Dora saw her and waved, shouting something about catching fish for supper.

Sir Marcus glanced up from casting his willow rod and she saw his eyes flicker to her feet, so she brazenly pointed her bare toes out from beneath her petticoats.

As she drew nearer, she could see a disquieting glint in his eye.

"Hoyden" he said severely. "Are you not afraid someone will see?"

"What out here — miles from anywhere?" she grinned, "It's funny, I was thinking earlier that I'd like to take my shoes off."

"Yes, you nodded off whilst mumbling about it."

"Oh, no! How embarrassing."

Dora expertly flicked her rod over her head and Imogen stared at Augusta.

"You have daisies in your hair, Miss Pennington," she said a little critically.

"Yes, I have no idea how they got there," said Miss Augusta Pennington.

"Sir Marcus put them there!" announced Dora, "I saw him, while you were asleep! And he took your stockings off too!"

"You talk in your sleep," said that scoundrel heartlessly.

"I didn't say anything — ?"

"Incriminating? No, ma'am, sadly you did not. You merely muttered incoherently about your shoes, and I was able to determine your wishes. I did check first that the servants were out of sight though. I am exceedingly interested to discover what you fear you may have given away in your sleep though. Is it so very damning? Have you dark secrets you cannot share with anyone?"

"I do not."

"So, confidently said. I must believe you then."

"Not everyone is like you Sir Marcus, concealing an unspeakable past."

"Concealing? I am not concealing anything. What do you want to know? I will tell you right now, here in this field. Daisies become you, by the way. Should you ever wed, do not consider any of the more exotic flowers, you must wear daisies in your hair. They seem to say something about you. Miranda was fond of lilies. I loathed the smell of them."

Dora looked at them with brows knit, "Augusta will never marry — she has the school to think of! And Flora *cannot* marry Reverend Cheadle! Only consider, he would be my *brother-in-law!* It would be too dreadful! She must have gone mad!"

Augusta, knowing that her middle sister had recently been even more morose than usual, asked herself if they had perhaps been ignoring some hidden suffering. It was hard to tell because Flora covered her feelings with ill-humour, and everyone had become used to seeing her disappointed face and hearing the sound of her feet stamping sullenly across the wooden floors. She had been born frowning, thought Augusta, remembering the scrunched up little face her mother had presented to her. She wondered if something had particularly upset her and driven her to this extreme response. As she had always shown a pronounced disdain for Reverend Cheadle, it seemed an odd thing to do and so very inconsistent with what one would expect.

"Flora can marry whomever she likes, Dora. Perhaps she sees something in Reverend Cheadle that we are unable to appreciate."

"She said he reminded her of an emaciated beetle."

Augusta heard their host's cough and suspected it had started out as a laugh. She sent him one of her famous quelling looks and he turned away, but she could still see his shoulders were shaking.

"It really isn't polite to repeat what people say, Dora — or, for that matter, to encourage poor behaviour in the young by showing just how little one knows about discipline and moderation!"

The guilty party turned a now serious face to her, "Oh, I know nothing of moderation, Miss Pennington, and discipline is best kept for the schoolroom, so if you are hoping that I shall turn overnight into the perfect example of a parent, I fear you are going to be exceedingly disappointed."

"Again, it's nothing to be so puffed up about! It's yet another blot on your character. It's a wonder that you can bear to look at yourself in the glass!"

"I came to the conclusion, many years ago, that there are some souls not worth the effort of saving. Mine included."

She regarded him gravely, "That is a dreadful thing to say. There is no soul, however blackened, that is not worth saving. I think that you have been left too much alone with your thoughts, Sir Marcus, and in your bleakest moments have been tempted into believing the worthless opinions of others."

"And I think, Miss Pennington, that under that impenetrable exterior of primness that you are in fact a warrior for the persecuted degenerates of this world."

"*Are* you a degenerate?"

"Most probably, I think, yes."

"*Am* I prim?" queried Augusta, a little downcast.

"I believe that you wear a mantle of primness, but I do not think it goes deeper than that. I have seen quite hopeful signs."

"You are hopeful of what exactly? That I am not really prim?"

"That you might be worth the effort of saving."

Startled, she blinked at him, "I do not *need* saving, Sir Marcus!"

"But surely, my dear girl, we all need saving in some way."

"I think you're talking nonsense again. You should wear your hat to keep the sun from your head!"

"I don't think it would help, in my case. It's too late."

"Aunt Ida says it's never too late."

He raised his brows, "Then perhaps, as I believe her to be one of the very few thoroughly sound females, I shall endeavour to be more optimistic."

Augusta watched the two girls as they span in circles, skirts flying, and getting dizzy they fell giggling into the grass.

"I never wanted to be prim," she mused.

He fixed her with a long look, "I had no intention of offending you, Miss Pennington. I had supposed that you probably knew already."

She tried to smile, "Yes, I had my suspicions but 'tis sometimes hard to acknowledge one's own imperfections, is it not?"

"I don't find it so. Although, it is essential for the curtailment of one's self-esteem to have them regularly pointed out."

She laughed at that, "You only have yourself to blame, Sir!"

"Yes, I suppose I do. Being a foolhardy youth should quite rightly haunt one for the rest of one's days."

Impulsively Augusta reached out to him and put her fingers on his arm, "Oh no, do not say that! Imagine doing something rash as a boy and it must be forever thrown in one's face, even into old age!"

"Thank you, but I am not quite in my dotage yet!"

"I didn't mean *you!* You are not very old at all! Oh, dear, it would be better if I didn't speak!"

He covered her fingers with his and she flinched slightly, feeling a surge of some unknown emotion course through her. She rather briskly withdrew her hand and tucked it under her other arm, out of sight and out of reach and was careful not to look him in the eye.

"You're very kind, ma'am, but as I'm old enough to be your father, I think you're right in what you say."

"You would have still been at school when I was born! I am five and twenty!" she exclaimed.

"God, you're just a child!" groaned Sir Marcus, putting his head in his hands. "I am further gone than even I had thought."

Augusta frowned at him, "I don't understand. What do you mean 'further gone'?"

He raised his head and stared into the distance, "I think I mean that my optimism was fleeting."

"You're talking in riddles."

He didn't respond.

"You said you'd tell me about your — unspeakable past — " she ventured, feeling suddenly audacious.

He sighed, "I did, rather rashly, didn't I? Are you sure the truth is what you want to hear?"

"It makes no odds to me in the end, but all I know is what I have overheard — I have been told nothing directly and would rather hear it from — "

" — the best authority."

"It makes perfect sense surely."

"I only hesitate because I have a strange fancy to have at least one person regard me as though I were not the Devil incarnate."

"I hope I shall not so easily change my opinion — it would be pigeon-hearted. I would not care to think that I was a *craven* female! I am supposed to favour the Beauchamps, who are, on the whole, rather resolute individuals."

"I can see that. All right, but I will notice if you cut me dead in the street or skirt around me after church as though I might be contaminated."

"I swear, I shall not do anything of the kind!" retorted Augusta, laughing.

"Then I must, in order to set the scene, take you back a little way to explain a bit about my father. He was not, I suppose, a typical parent although he had the excuse that he was of his age. He, Sir Leopold, was utterly without morals and had no hesitation in pleasing himself with no thought for anyone else. My mother was an insipid society beauty, who died of neglect and loneliness before she was out of her twenties. I do not remember her. My father married again, choosing a biddable child from the schoolroom and eventually, after losing two other infants, they had Charles, which is the only good thing that ever came out of either of his marriages. Charles has a good heart and the morals of a saint. I have no idea where he gets it from. My stepmother, Gertrude, is an inveterate social climber but otherwise harmless, although she regrettably allowed my father to do just as he pleased. He was seldom at home even for his second wife and not long after I was breeched, he had decided that I was to be his little accomplice in all things. It amused him to take me to places where no gentleman should ever be, let alone a child — but no one dared challenge him and I became a kind of talisman for his set of debauched friends and was a regular at all his clubs and gaming hells. I was tolerated by the proprietors and staff because his intimates were legion, and they had too much to lose if they were to bar him from their establishments.

For me it became commonplace — it was where I grew up. It was where I learnt my code of conduct and where I met those who would influence my adult life. His circle became mine and as I reached maturity, I was shown even more depravity and learnt that everyone can be bought for a price."

He paused for a moment to study her face but found it to be as tranquil as before, so he continued, "You will not have heard of a place called the Hellfire Club thankfully, but it was as its name a den of vice, and it became my second home. It was there that I met a certain nobleman, an elder statesman, who took pity upon me in a small way and tried to save the small amount of good still left in me. He took me to his home to keep me away from the horrors of that place — and I repaid him well. Without a qualm, I seduced his wife, a much older lady, and ruined her in the eyes of society. She unfortunately, having been much neglected, fixated upon me and thought herself lost to love. The compassionate nobleman tried unsuccessfully to kill me in a duel and then cast her out of his house and a scandal ensued that shook the Establishment to its foundations. I suppose things may have eventually righted themselves, but the lady in question decided that life was not worth living and brought hers to a dramatic end and I was forced to flee to France, where all good scoundrels go to make their fortunes, which I did, at the tables. And there I met my own dear wife, Miranda — another mistake I have paid for dearly. Over there, dancing by the stream, you see the only good thing that came from that particular liaison. You would think I had learnt my lesson, but I must be a slow learner."

"Yet you married Lady Birch!"

His laugh was mirthless, "Yes, I was neatly tricked into it. It was before I decided to officially acknowledge our — liaison. In the end, it turned out I'd been duped. It was nothing more than a timely deception to keep me in line — and more fool me, I believed her. Inevitably, after we married, that lie was uncovered — then eventually Imogen arrived. It was too late for me by then. On hearing the good news, I decided it was high time to make some changes and naively thought that Imogen's arrival would herald a new era of contentment. But my oh-so-dear wife had other plans and I can hardly blame her. She had already met Fabian Birch.

Thinking that the child should not be exposed to her mother's excesses — yes, I do see how ironic that is — and hoping that the poor little creature might be my salvation, I began to fight for her. However, I soon realised that the mess and scandal that it would create would do no one any good. We divorced and that was, in itself, a minor scandal, but was sooner forgotten than my earlier transgressions. I had given myself up to life on the continent and was vaguely content with my lot — and then my father thoughtlessly died, and I felt honour-bound to brave the disgrace and return home to take up my responsibilities as his son and heir. It was a half-baked attempt to make amends, but no amount of good intentions will ever make up for the fact that I have ruined lives. I will never be allowed to forget it."

He was observing his daughter through narrowed eyes, squinting a little as the sun slid down the sky, gilding the willows and striking sparks on the surface of the water.

Augusta was thinking about what he'd told her and wondering how she felt about it. There was the prim part of her that was repulsed by his story and wanted to have nothing more to do with him in case he tarnished her family and then there was the maternal part that just wanted to pull the small boy to her bosom and stroke his hair until he felt better. There was another part of her though, which she wasn't so keen to acknowledge — a part that she had no business being in possession of and was heartily ashamed of. That part she would keep hidden and hope the unexpected wanton in her would never be revealed.

He turned to look directly into her eyes and, infuriatingly, she found herself blushing.

"I've shocked you," he said quietly.

She took a deep breath, "Yes, you have. It would be a lie to say otherwise. I would not be human if I were not profoundly dismayed — and yes, shocked by the story I have just heard! As you say I have a puritanical streak and that side of me is appalled that there is a world of such wickedness out there and that anyone could willingly corrupt a small boy in such a way. Yes, I *am* shocked. But I also understand that you held no sway over your father and that it was he who should have protected you and kept you unsullied. Not only that but he actively sought to debase you until you were at his level. It was his solemn duty, as a father, to shield you and he failed in that and so many other ways. I cannot blame you — nor should anyone, who knows the full story. You were a child, an innocent child. In my opinion there is nothing worse than abusing the trust of a child. I must say I thought my own father a philanderer and worse, but I am beginning to see that his crimes were trifling in comparison."

"*The sins of the father are to be laid upon the children.*"

"The Bible *and* Shakespeare at one fell swoop," murmured Augusta, in a voice charged with heartache.

"Ah, no, don't be sorry for me, Augusta. That will not do at all! You must cast me out. Tell me to never dare darken your door. Damn me to Hell. And do not look at me like that either! God, I should have kept quiet. I am no longer that young boy and I do not need anyone's sympathy."

"No, I'm sure you don't. I expect that you are entirely self-sufficient and a regular care-for-no-one! You are deadened to all joy and emotion because, of course, 'tis easier that way. You are inured to censure and cannot be wounded because you are like the tortoise and have a hard shell to protect you."

"A tortoise?"

"Or do I mean an armadillo? No, it's a tortoise!"

She saw his eyes gleaming and pressed her lips together to stop herself saying anything more.

"I think you might be surprised if you knew how — " he reflected but didn't finish his sentence as Dora hurtled towards them, followed by Imogen with grasses in her hair and her skirts bunched up in her fists so they wouldn't impede her progress.

They threw themselves down onto the rugs and gabbled happily about what they'd been doing, which didn't amount to very much but seemed to have amused them a good deal.

"I could stay here *forever!*" sighed Dora. "We could build a house just up there and this could be our garden and we could all live here together! Wouldn't that be blissful?"

Augusta, not liking the turn the conversation was taking, snatched up her stockings and, as secretly as she could, began to pull them on, followed by her shoes.

Sir Marcus watched her efforts with unabashed interest and Augusta, perceiving his scrutiny, buckled her shoes in haste and pulled her skirts down over her ankles.

"Too late," he remarked affably.

"If I *was* witless enough to feel sorry for you, I find it is now withering on the vine!" she snapped, and gathering her scattered senses, she scrambled to her feet, "I'm delighted you two girls had such a splendid time, but I do think we ought to be going home now or they will think we have been abducted!"

"Abducted! By *highwaymen?* Oh, famous! Imagine! They would be very dashing and brave, with feathers in their hats and silver-mounted pistols and they'd take all our jewellery and demand that we give them all our golden guineas! It would be *such* fun!"

Augusta could see that Imogen was not quite so enamoured at the thought of being held up by dastardly highwaymen, so she called a halt to her sister's flights of fancy and picked up her hat and resolutely set off up the hill.

Sir Marcus observed her sudden retreat and the smile slowly died from his eyes and rising in a leisurely fashion, he began to gather up the rugs.

Eleven

Later that night, whilst safely tucked up in her bed, Augusta mulled over the day and came to the conclusion that a good deal had changed since that morning. She had hugely enjoyed the outing and knew that the girls had too, and she was glad that she'd been persuaded, much against her better judgement, to join them. She was even glad that Sir Marcus had taken her into his confidence and told her something of his past. Knowing what he had been forced to endure, through no fault of his own, made her realise that it was very possible that he did have a soul worth saving.

However, there were moments during the day when she really hadn't been sure what was happening; he was inclined to say things that she couldn't understand, almost as though talking to himself, or if she did understand them, she immediately felt that she'd been mistaken in her interpretation of his meaning.

There had been several times when she had been thoroughly at a loss to know how to respond. When he'd brazenly stared at her ankles! Well, that was beyond anything! Although, he had of course done worse and actually removed her stockings and shoes while she'd been asleep! That was unforgivable. She had kept the daisy chain and laid it carefully on the table beside her bed.

She knew that his upbringing, if one could call it that when there had been no discernible child-rearing at all in any traditional sense, had twisted his views and given him a jaundiced outlook on both life and humanity in general. She couldn't even imagine how it must have crushed the poor child's innocence and given him such a warped and bitter perspective. She was filled with a violent desire to go back to his childhood and rescue him, to gather him to her and drag him out of the clutches of those fiends who would, so casually, ruin him. He may now be at peace with the consequences of his past, but she was absolutely certain that that was just a convenient truth to cover his suffering. Augusta had a fair notion that the young Marcus Denby had been wrenched from his true path and set instead upon a very different one and, from that moment on, he had been adrift.

Somewhere in the back of her mind was the germ of an idea; a conviction that she could rescue him because she alone could see his true worth. For a while she lay staring up at the canopy above her bed and pondered this.

Why she was so sure of his virtues when others found them hard to see, she could not quite fathom. He had, by telling her about his early years, risked her fleeing in disgust, but had persisted in sharing the sickening account with her. He knew her to be a prim and prudish schoolmistress and had several times goaded her about her strait-laced character. She found him infuriating and fascinating in equal measure. He made her laugh when she really ought not and surprised her at every turn — not always in a good way! But today he had trusted her with something that had made her feel, on one hand, like weeping, and on the other, had forced her to confront the rather more bloodthirsty side of her nature. She would have liked to have killed Sir Leopold and his cronies with her bare hands but, realising that this wasn't something any lady should admit to, she swore to keep it to herself. Until that moment, she had no notion that her thoughts could so readily turn murderous.

Her father had always told her that she was destined for a bad end, but as he had already gone so far down the path to damnation himself, she had ignored him, confident in her own virtuousness.

Now, she was having doubts and thinking that perhaps he had been right. She had only to meet someone with intense grey eyes and an infectious smile and she was already willing to commit murder for him! Gracious, she was as bad as Dora with her wild imagination and ridiculous yearnings! Or even worse, Aunt Euphemia!

"I have a school to manage! I cannot allow myself to be distracted from my true purpose. I simply must stop being so shatter-brained." And she pummelled her pillows as though they were the enemy and, settling down with a heartfelt sigh, she tried to go to sleep.

But that night sleep eluded her.

* * *

Dora awoke with a sinking feeling in her stomach. She remembered immediately why that was and pulled the counterpane over her head. She heard her sister come into the bedchamber and buried herself deeper into the feathery softness.

"It's gone six o'clock, Dora!" announced Flora. "He'll be here at seven and you have to have breakfast before you go."

Dora's muffled dissent fell on deaf ears. The covers were ruthlessly removed, and she had no choice but to sit up and face the day.

"*Torment*, that's what this is! I cannot see how rising at this time will make any difference! It matters not *when* they receive their parcels. They can eat whenever they choose — it doesn't *have* to be in the morning. It could be supper! Poor people eat supper don't they!"

"I think you should consider someone other than yourself, Dora. The sooner they have their supplies the sooner they can stop worrying about where the next meal will be coming from. It's selfish in you to want to stay in bed instead of assisting Reverend Cheadle in his worthy endeavours."

"You're only saying that because you *have* to! You can't malign your own betrothed! That would be hugely indelicate! Oh, pooh, Flora, you're not *really* going to marry him, are you? I mean, *Reverend Cheadle!* He's such a beetle-head!"

"Dora!"

"Well, it was you that said he was like an emaciated beetle in the first place!" She swung her feet to the floor, "And it's no use looking daggers at me! You're the one who's lost your mind and forgotten how much you despised the Reverend and now you've accepted his offer of marriage! It's *madness!*"

Flora said nothing but handed her sister her underclothes.

"*Why*, Flora? Why would do you such a thing?" She waited while her stockings were found and watched her sister's clenched face.

"Well, if you must know — I don't want to end my days caring for Aunt Euphemia! She is so poisonous! I really cannot bear it any longer."

Staggered by this emotional admission, Dora flew across the bedchamber and hugged her sister fiercely, "I'm so *sorry!* I didn't mean to tease you! I know that you're the one who bears the brunt of her spitefulness. And I know the kind of things she says. She's mean. But she can't help it. She's trapped in that bed and has nothing else to do but make mischief."

"I know but somehow she knows just what to say to make the deepest cuts. She may have been a great beauty in her time, but I can tell you some young beau had a narrow escape!" said Flora bitterly. "Now get dressed! He'll be incensed if you keep him waiting!"

"I think this is almost as bad a punishment as having my books confiscated!" grumbled Dora.

* * *

Reverend Cheadle was at his most condescending and instructed Dora on how she should behave when helping the Deserving Poor. Dora felt it entirely unnecessary advice as she knew very well that one treated everyone just as you would wish to be treated yourself. It was so obvious it was ridiculous. But she managed to button her lip and suffer his lecture with insincere good grace. To her profound consternation she discovered they were to travel in his battered old gig. Since Dora had been driven in Sir Marcus's carriage, she had acquired a taste for more sophisticated modes of travel and looked upon this contraption with scorn. He had handed her one heavy basket to put at her feet and another to hold upon her lap and then he climbed up into the cart, making it bounce about and Dora had to clutch tightly to the basket to stop it sliding off her lap and spilling its contents all over the drive.

As they drove sedately into the village, Reverend Cheadle kept up an unremitting homily on how Dora could improve her morals and learn to be a better person. Dora paid no attention and instead admired the countryside, which was looking at its colourful best and waved to the occasional villager she saw.

Just outside the village they turned down a narrow rutted lane, which bumped its way down a hill and into a sheltered combe where a small, shabby farmhouse crouched. There was one elderly cow leaning against a wall and some scrawny chickens scratching half-heartedly in the dirt. Dora thought it looked otherwise deserted and glanced up at her companion for guidance.

"Farmer Bramfield. Lives alone. He can be a little irascible on a bad day. You can take his parcel to him but don't expect to be thanked."

They drew up in front of the building and Dora handed the Reverend her basket and taking a large parcel from it, she hopped down and trod warily up to what she thought might be the front door. It was hard to tell as most of the house had been engulfed by ivy. She pushed her way through the trailing tangle of vines to a very insecure looking entrance and knocked on the rotting wood. No sound came from within, and she turned to look at Reverend Cheadle who flicked his hand at her dismissively, so she tried banging on the door a little harder.

She heard something, an angry shout, a banging sound and then heavy footsteps. She retreated a pace backwards and waited nervously.

The door was dragged open with some difficulty as it was warped and broken, and out of the darkness peered a face and it didn't look happy.

"Mr Bramfield? I am Miss Dora Pennington from the Seminary and I've come with Reverend Cheadle — " she got no further because her words were cut off by a roar of outrage. She jumped like a startled rabbit and held the parcel in front of her as though it might protect her.

"Cheadle! *Cheadle!*" bellowed Mr Bramfield, "That verminous ballock — that squeeze crab — that herring gutted weasel! That jaw-me-dead!"

"*Mr Bramfield?*" interrupted Dora desperately, "I *beg* you — I have brought you some — some supplies. Shall I just put them here and leave? I really don't want to make you so cross, it's not good for your health."

Farmer Bramfield seemed to suddenly see her and blinked into the light as though waking from a nightmare. "Who be you?" he snarled.

"Miss Dora Pennington from the Seminary."

"I don't want you 'ere!"

"Well, to be perfectly frank Mr Bramfield, I don't really want to be here either! But it's an unjust punishment for a misdemeanour! It was only very slight, I swear — I mean I didn't *murder* anyone!"

Farmer Bramfield was staring at her open-mouthed, "Youse bein' punished by that sly ol' devil, Cheadle?"

"Yes, and it was only for answering back in class!"

He considered her for a moment from narrowed, rheumy eyes, sucking in his already gaunt cheeks and leant towards her, searching her face, "Cheeked him did 'ee? I say well done! I say 'ee's fine b'me then! 'Ee can leave that there. I'll take it."

"Oh, that's so *very* kind of you! You see, it'll put me in his good books, and he may stop scolding me for a few minutes!"

"Glad to 'elp, Miss. Anythin' to spite that weasel-faced mangy cur!" said Mr Bramfield, "'Ee be careful, there be tinkers hereabouts — I seen 'em up by the woods. They'll kidnap 'ee and take 'ee for a bride!"

"Goodness Gracious! Do you really think they would? I'm not at all sure I'd like that! I'll keep an eye out. Thank you for the warning. I can hear Reverend Cheadle complaining so I'd better go. It was very nice to meet you though. I hope you enjoy the supplies!"

She raced back to the gig and clambered back up onto the seat unaided.

"Well, you took your time!"

"He wanted to chat," explained Dora, "He seems a very nice old man."

Reverend Cheadle, who regularly had to say additional prayers over his malicious thoughts about Farmer Bramfield, said nothing and urged the horse to get them away from there as fast as possible.

After a few more visits, Dora came to the conclusion that very few people liked their rector; some openly declaring that he was only interested in himself and that he never really listened to their problems. The more she heard, the more she worried about Flora and her impetuous decision to marry him. You'd have to be deranged to want to be tied to such a man for the rest of your life and even though Flora could be difficult at times, Dora wanted her to be happy.

It was as they were returning to the village through the woods that Dora spied a small group of people standing beside an open fire. There were two carts and a few piebald horses, a straggle of skinny dogs and some scrawny children sitting in the dirt playing with some sticks. There were two domed tents and some ragged clothing hung on a makeshift washing line between the trees.

"Oh, *look!* There are the tinkers everyone keeps mentioning!" cried Dora.

"Don't acknowledge them!" said the Reverend snapping the reins over his horse's rump.

Dora couldn't help but look at them. They were so alien to her and she was fascinated by the romantic notion of living out in the open, under trees, or even in a meadow with a stream; she found it hugely appealing.

The tinkers watched them go by. Their faces sullen and inhospitable.

"Ignore them!" commanded Reverend Cheadle. "Thieves and tricksters!"

"Oh, my *goodness!* They're just human beings!" gasped Dora. She turned her head to see them as the gig rattled away along the track.

In the tinkers' midst was a young woman; Dora thought she seemed distressed, and she drew her attention. She was holding something, something small and, whatever it was, it was hanging limply in her arms and the woman was looking to the sky in what seemed to Dora to be supplication.

"Oh! Reverend Cheadle! Stop the cart! Oh, *do* stop! We simply *must* go and see!"

"I will not stop Miss Pennington! Not for anything! They would murder us if we were to stop!"

Dora turned to him and, with some violence, ripped the reins from his hands and pulled the horse to a standstill, "We *shall* stop! We cannot just pass by! Think of your Bible, Reverend! The parable of the good Samaritan! You can just wait here if you're too afraid!" And she quickly jumped down from the gig and approached the group of tinkers. The scent of woodsmoke and horses was overpoweringly strong. She eased her way between the people, ignoring their fierce looks, and reaching the woman, realised that she was holding a baby in her arms, and, to Dora, it looked extremely unwell, if not dead. Without thought she knelt beside the woman and gently pulled back the shawl that covered the child and examined the tiny, pinched face.

The men behind her were muttering to each other in an odd language and they sounded angry and as though they might mean her harm.

And then, she heard the gig leaving.

Well, she thought, if that isn't just the *limit!* Wait until Augusta hears of this! That brought her up short as she realised that she was in yet another scrape and that Augusta was not going to be very happy about her part in it.

She reached out and touched the baby's cheek and found to her inestimable relief that there was some warmth still there and it was breathing very faintly. Looking around at the faces glowering at her, she took a deep breath, "Has the child seen a doctor?" she asked anxiously.

No one replied, but one young man stepped forward and grabbed her arm rather roughly. She tried to shake him off, but he started to pull her away.

"This lady — the *baby* — needs help! Let me go! I only want to *help!*"

The man began to speak harshly, and she knew if he wouldn't listen then she was in trouble.

"Oh, why can't you *understand!* I can fetch a doctor! *A doctor!*"

The young man stopped tugging at her arm and scowled at her, "Doctor?" he said.

"Yes, *yes!* There's a doctor in the village and my sister can help too! Oh, *please!* The baby is so ill! Why must you be so stupidly cross?"

He stared at her, "You must leave. Not welcome. Go now."

Dora, knowing that time was of the essence, put her hands on her hips and stared right back at him, with an expression her elder sister would have recognised, "No, I'm *not* going, and you can be as vexed as you like! I want to take the mother and baby to my sister. She'll know what to do. You must hitch the horse to the cart *at once!*"

The tinker stood his ground.

Dora, exasperated beyond belief, marched across the clearing and untied one of the horses from a peg in the ground and led it to the cart.

Of course, she had no idea what to do next and cast the young man a desperate look. He joined her and within minutes had harnessed the animal. Dora smiled at him and then went back to the distraught woman. She held out her arms and was quite taken aback when the woman willingly passed the infant to her. She gestured to the cart, but the woman just covered her face with her hands.

Deciding that the mother was obviously beyond being able to move or be in any way useful, she glanced at the man, and he shrugged and without a word lifted her and the baby up into the cart.

Dora had not really considered her actions and only now, as the cart bounced along the track, did she truly pay attention to the slack little bundle in her lap. It was just a baby and undernourished. She couldn't tell if it was a boy or a girl.

It took about ten minutes to reach the school and although the tinker was reluctant to drive the cart through the gates, Dora persuaded him, and they stopped in front of the house.

The man helped her down but stayed by the cart while she climbed the steps to the front door. The door was opened by Hannah, who had seen her arrive from the parlour window.

"Fetch my sisters!" commanded Dora without ceremony and Hannah went scurrying away.

Dora took the child into the parlour and with her legs feeling quite weak, she sat down in the nearest chair and waited.

The hurried sound of footsteps heralded the arrival of Augusta and very soon after, Flora.

"Dora!" cried Augusta as she entered the room, "What have you been about? Where is Reverend Cheadle and — what is that you have there?"

Dora, who had reached the end of her tether just pulled back the shawl to reveal the baby's grey countenance.

Augusta turned to Flora, "Send for Doctor Inwood at once!"

She examined the child and then gently took her from Dora's exhausted arms and laid it on the sofa.

"Dora, can you ask Aunt Ida to come please?"

Dora hauled herself out of the chair as though she were a hundred years old and without saying anything she went out.

On taking a closer look at the tiny scrap, Augusta had to fight back tears; she noted the birdlike limbs, fragile enough to be snapped by an overeager embrace and observed that the baby was a boy.

Dora arrived back with Miss Beauchamp who was looking anxious and moving with a speed that belied her years.

"Augusta! What have we here? Oh, my word! Poor little mite. Ah, let me see — a little boy — and no signs of spots or rashes — no pustules — that is at least a good sign — "

Flora returned and with her the young man she had found standing by his cart in the drive.

"I thought he should be here too," she said.

Augusta saw the strain in his face and taking him by the hand led him to the child, "Are you the father?" she asked him.

He nodded, "Yes. He's dying?"

Miss Beauchamp looked up at him, "He's very ill but the doctor has been sent for. What is his name?"

"James."

"You are from Scotland?" asked Ida Beauchamp, recognising the lilt in his voice.

He nodded, "At one time, my family came from there."

"My family came from France — a very long time ago. You are tinsmiths?"

"Aye."

"The doctor won't be long, I expect," said Flora, "I sent Jennet."

"We do not trust doctors," said the young man.

"Oh, you can trust Doctor Inwood — he's very good and always comes to help here at the school!"

He didn't look convinced, but his anxiety for his child outweighed his fears.

"I am Miss Ida Beauchamp, and this is Miss Augusta Pennington and Miss Flora, my nieces. You've already met Dora, the youngest."

"Brave girl," he said solemnly.

"Yes. She certainly is!"

"I am Robert Duncan, ma'am."

Another quarter of an hour passed, and they fell into uneasy silence, while Augusta stroked the baby's head and spoke quietly to reassure him and Mr Duncan hovered, refusing the offer of refreshment or a seat.

"I hear someone, at last!" said Flora, rushing to the door.

It was the doctor and a breathless and red-faced Jennet who wanted to see what was going on. Miss Beauchamp sent her straight away to fetch hot water, clean cloths and cordial.

Doctor Inwood nodded briefly to everyone and went immediately to the child and, whilst he was thoroughly examining him, he asked Mr Duncan questions, which the poor man answered as best he could.

Doctor Inwood had once lived in London with a lucrative practice and a large house and staff and everything a gentleman could want, but he tired of the whining ladies suffering from the vapours and languishing disorders and their husbands with attacks of gout because of the way they indulged themselves without restraint. He had a sudden yearning to do some actual good and decided to move his astonished family into the wilds of Gloucestershire, on a whim. His wife, Elizabeth, was as always understanding and, although she could never tell him how much she missed her town life, with the shops and the parties, she followed him and supported him in his desire to help wherever he could. Their three children were still young and found village life very much to their tastes, so there were no complaints from that quarter. Doctor Inwood's practice grew quickly, and he soon settled in and was discovered by Miss Ida Beauchamp and became both a benefactor and the school physician. His duties usually amounted to no more than seeing to grazes, coughs and colds and perhaps a wasp sting. He also looked after Miss Euphemia, who was something of a trial to him, but Miss Ida made up for that by being an absolute delight to converse with. There had been, over the years, a few crises but none that had been without a prompt solution. Since their nieces had arrived, he had noticed that Miss Ida was able to stand back and let them do most of the work and worrying and he was glad of that.

This was an altogether more challenging state of affairs, and he was not able to confidently predict the outcome. The child was extremely ill, and recovery looked, at first sight, unlikely. But after questioning the father, things began to make more sense and he could make a cautious diagnosis.

"I must speak with James's mother as soon as possible. I believe this to be a case of marasmus — and, from what Mr Duncan has told me, that his wife has been seriously ill for a while after a difficult birth and has been out of her mind since, I suspect she has been unable to breastfeed properly. The baby is severely underweight, but I have hopes that with the right treatment he will eventually return to health. I cannot promise a complete recovery, he may have some permanent damage, but with excellent care and good nourishment and a little luck I think he will live."

Dora burst into noisy sobs and Flora went to comfort her, drawing her into her generous bosom and stroking her hair, her own eyes tightly closed to keep the unwanted tears at bay.

Mr Duncan finally sat down, collapsing into a nearby chair and putting his head in his hands.

Jennet arrived at that moment bearing a pitcher of hot water, and a bundle of clean cloths and stood on the threshold wondering what on earth had come over everyone.

Twelve

It was decided that little James Duncan should stay at the school and be nursed there as there was plenty of assistance available and Miss Beauchamp and Augusta had a good knowledge of how to run a sickroom. Doctor Inwood went to see the mother, Mrs Duncan, and came to the conclusion that she had for some time been suffering from melancholy brought on by a traumatic childbirth, a common enough complaint, but as it had gone untreated for so long, the child had been a victim of her agitation; she been unable to breastfeed properly but was not aware that the poor child was receiving very little sustenance and in grave danger. The family had been unwilling to consult a doctor, believing all medical people to be charlatans and having no money to pay for their services anyway, and had consequently been trying to treat her themselves. Doctor Inwood was unusually sympathetic to their plight, understanding that travellers suffered a good deal of persecution under the Law and from the local people who thought them to be horse thieves and kidnappers. He was a broad-minded sort of fellow and had time for everyone as long as they behaved in a proper manner. He explained to Miss Beauchamp and Miss Augusta that this particular band of tinkers were from the highlands of Scotland, Gaelic speaking and craftsmen by trade. He said that their language was not pure Gaelic but a mixture of Scots and cant. They were known in Scotland as Summer Walkers and had been forced to come South because of persecution and the inclement weather in the North.

Mrs Duncan was taken to the small cottage hospital he had created in the house next to his own and was running with the help of some benevolent and hard-working ladies from the village. He had been thought quite mad when he had suggested such a thing, but it had quickly become an important part of life in the area and had already saved several lives and provided help and support for those in need. After learning his trade in London, he had learned advanced ideas and had seemingly infinite reserves of forbearance.

Miss Beauchamp thought very well of him and was pleased to tell everyone so; she said she knew a good man when she saw one.

It was over a week before there was any hopeful signs of improvement in the baby and his nursemaids, who had shared in his care, hung over his bed watching his every movement with anxious eyes.

"I do believe he has more colour in his cheeks," said Augusta optimistically.

"Yes, and his breathing is much easier," replied her aunt as she wiped his tiny brow with a cloth sprinkled with rose water. "And he has taken a good amount of breast milk, which will do him no end of good. It was so considerate of Doctor Inwood to think of providing a wet nurse and bless her, she's been highly beneficial for the infant. To see little James sucking so keenly! What a splendid sight! The doctor said then that the worst might be over — and it was. Now he will begin to gain some weight and he'll be as right as fivepence!"

"Oh, I do hope you're right! It is so very hard to see him too ill to even cry — it's unnatural. The last few days have been dreadful, and I pity his parents. Mr Duncan hovers outside every day and needs so much convincing to come into the house. Doctor Inwood tells me that Mrs Duncan is on the mend at last, although there is a long way to go before she can return to her normal life and take James back, and her mind is still not yet completely healed. That poor young man must have been in agonies! Both his wife and child in such peril and nowhere to turn. People can be so cruel," she sighed, thinking of Sir Marcus and his father's wickedness.

Miss Ida fixed her with one of her perceptive looks, "You are not thinking of the Duncans, are you, my dear! I feel sure that Sir Marcus has divulged part of his history to you, because you have been very much distracted since returning from your outing to see the blossom."

Augusta looked up, a little taken aback and wondered how much to tell her.

Her aunt continued, "Oh, do not feel you must share his confidences with me! It makes no odds to me anyway. I have decided that I like him very much and shall not be dissuaded from my opinion. I am a very good judge of character you know!"

Augusta smiled, "Yes, I *do* know. I have always trusted your instincts and found you to be infallible! But you do not know the truth of the matter. It is so very much worse than we thought and although I am — gratified that he should feel he can tell me — I am also deeply shocked and hardly know what to do for the best!"

"I feel sure that you have thought it over, Augusta. You are very much inclined to worry things to death before making up your mind. Has what he told you changed your opinion of him?"

"Well, my opinion wasn't very high in the first place! I had thought him to be rather stern and high-handed at first and then came to the conclusion that he was actually rather too frivolous — but now, I — really don't know! What he has endured — the life he was compelled to live — it makes his character flaws seem more understandable and I think — I think that I should try to help him."

"Ah, you pity him."

"No, indeed I do not — he would hate that. I think I understand him a little better and can see that he is someone who has just been led astray when he was too young to know better or to stand up for himself. Oh, Aunt Ida, he was a mere child when his father decided to corrupt him! I shall not tell you what occurred but needless to say, he was made to suffer quite dreadfully, which accounts for his present state, I fear."

Their tiny patient stirred in his sleep and both ladies watched him keenly for a moment, holding their breath, until he settled again.

"It's good that he's sleeping. It's a much healthier sleep than before," whispered Miss Beauchamp. "I do think I can see a little roundness in his cheeks."

"I think so too. Although, his eyes are still sunken and his skin not a proper colour yet."

"We must be patient, in *all* things, my dear. Patience is most certainly a virtue. But you must take care though not to give your heart too easily, because if he does somehow recover, and I pray to God he will, he will be leaving with his family. They are travellers and seldom stay long in one place."

Augusta, knowing her aunt well, heard the cautionary words and read their hidden meaning correctly.

"Oh, there is no danger of that, I swear!" she lied, barefaced, knowing that it was already too late and that her ridiculous heart had been stolen away by a pair of laughing grey eyes and she was doomed to a life of heartache because she'd been so careless.

"I once fell in love with a footman, when I was about ten years old," mused Miss Beauchamp, her eyes misting over a little at the memory. "He was always so neatly turned out and stood so still! Mother had him removed which made me exceedingly unhappy for a while. Girls are sadly susceptible to a handsome face."

"Well, Sir Marcus is *not* handsome — " blurted out Augusta before she had thought. She put a hand to her mouth, "Oh, I don't mean — I — I — oh, goodness gracious!"

Her aunt chuckled, "So you have said already! I, however, think he carries himself well for such a large gentleman and he has a certain air of authority and a great deal of humour, which gives him the appearance of handsomeness, do you not think?"

Slightly caught on the wrong foot, Augusta faltered, "He — is not really what I would call handsome at all, Aunt Ida! He is too — glowering."

"I quite like a man who glowers a bit."

"I cannot think why! Surely one would want a man to be cheerful and full of enthusiasm?"

Miss Beauchamp looked quite appalled, "One would quickly tire of that kind of sentimental behaviour! Only think, to always be greeted with a joyful smile! To have your lifetime companion always filled with exuberance! How swiftly one would become exhausted! No, one wants to be able to smooth away the frown of someone you love! To kiss away his ill-humour and coax him back into a good mood with your clever wiles!"

Augusta's eyebrows were practically in her hairline, "Aunt Ida! I had no idea that you are the most incorrigible romantic! Well I never!"

"Just because I never married does not mean that I am insensible to notions of love and romance. I should have liked to marry but never had the chance."

"I am all astonishment," said Augusta, looking at her aunt with new eyes.

Miss Beauchamp gave a delighted little laugh, "I like to think I can still shock people at my age!"

"How shall I ever eradicate the image of you "kissing away" some handsome gentleman's ill-humour?"

And they both fell into helpless giggles while their patient slept peacefully.

*　*　*

Mr Duncan regularly visited but always seemed reluctant to enter the house and had to be persuaded. He sat for hours beside his son's bed and said very little, just staring at the tiny creature lost amongst the snowy white bedlinen. He liked the ladies very much and soon learnt to trust them, but a lifetime of persecution had left its mark, and he was always on edge despite everyone trying to put him at his ease. He could see that James was slowly recovering but found it hard to express his gratitude. In the end after several false starts, Miss

Beauchamp put a gentle hand on his arm to stay his hesitant words.

"There is no need, Mr Duncan. We all do the best we can. We are truly glad to help. How does your wife do?"

"She spoke a little yesterday. Didn't make much sense though."

"Oh, that is good news! The sense will return, I am quite sure. Things will work out, you know. I have great faith."

He thought her a lovely lady but didn't share her faith in a perfect outcome. He had no idea how he could repay them for their kindness, and it worried at him like a ferret after a mouse. He had already asked Cook for any pots that needed mending and was in the middle of weaving a willow basket for their cat to sleep in. But it didn't seem enough.

* * *

It was not long before news of Dora's latest scrape came to the ears of Sir Marcus. He had delivered his daughter to the school every day for a week and had seen neither Augusta nor her aunt. Puzzled, he had eventually asked Imogen if anything untoward had happened.

"Oh, there's a little tinker boy staying — he's very ill and they're nursing him back to health. And Dora is not herself at all. She found him and she cannot seem to forget what happened! She barely talks. And Miss Pennington is distracted in our lessons and jumps every time the bell rings. She looks quite ill herself. It's all very strange."

"Good God," said Sir Marcus. "A tinker, you say? What has that girl been up to now!"

Imogen looked at him and thought he looked extremely serious, so said no more. She was a little peeved that Dora was not paying her enough attention. She had grown accustomed to having someone who listened to her and cared about how she was feeling. Now, Dora was always dashing away on important business or frowning into the distance as though troubled by something.

Sir Marcus immediately collared Beecher and asked him what the hell was going on at the Seminary. Beecher always knew all the gossip and was delighted to be able to recount what he had heard from, first Reverend Cheadle, then Mrs Inwood's housekeeper. He had then seen fit to question Hannah when he bumped into her in the village and was aghast at the news that Miss Beauchamp had a very small vagabond staying at the school with them! He was not surprised, however, to find that the whole debacle had been instigated by Miss Dora!

Neither was Sir Marcus. He was entirely unmoved by the fact that they had taken in some sickly child; it didn't surprise him at all. He was slightly concerned that Miss Beauchamp had come into contact with what could very possibly be someone with a contagious disease and he found that he was a little uneasy that Dora seemed downcast; it was so very unlike her.

But, and this dismayed him more than anything, he was anxious that Augusta, according to his daughter, appeared to be suffering in some way. He tried to shake off the unwonted feeling that he must immediately rush to their rescue and for a day or two he pretended a marked disinterest in anything to do with the school or those who ran it.

There was another persistent and irritating thought that occurred to him and that was that no one had apparently considered asking him for his advice or help. He began to wonder if perhaps Augusta had written him off as unfit for their acquaintance now that she knew the unadorned truth about him.

After two days of ignoring his brother's attempts to joke him out of his foul temper, he asked Beecher to bring a bottle of brandy to his study.

Beecher backed out of the room looking like a broken man. He had just begun to hope that those nights were behind them; his master had seemed so much more cheerful recently. He went straight to find Mr Frost and, although ashamed of his duplicity, he informed him of Sir Marcus's intentions. He watched in some alarm as Mr Frost went directly to the study and was closeted there for some while. Beecher could hear angry voices and after a while a long silence, followed by what sounded like a long muffled discussion.

Mr Frost eventually reappeared and told Beecher that Sir Marcus would be going for a ride in the morning. Beecher wondered if he was to be dismissed again and retreated to the kitchen to await his fate.

* * *

Sir Marcus and Mr Jonathan Frost dismounted outside the school and allowed Mr Sippence to remove their horses to the stables.

On entering the dark and dingy hall, Hannah showed them into the withdrawing room where they patiently waited.

After about fifteen long minutes Miss Flora arrived and was unable to conceal her astonishment at seeing them there.

"I am so sorry to have been so long — we are at sixes and sevens this morning! What can I do for you?" she asked rather briskly.

Sir Marcus bowed politely, "Firstly, I have not yet had the chance to offer my congratulations on your betrothal, Miss Flora. I wish you happy."

Flora's response was to frown and clench her jaw.

"And to say that Mr Frost and I have come to ask if we can be of any assistance? We have heard about Dora's latest venture."

"Oh, dash it all!" said Flora almost to herself. "There's really nothing you can do! It's all in hand."

"I am delighted to hear it but still I would like to offer our services in any way you might see fit to use them."

"Too kind, too kind," muttered Flora vaguely. "I cannot say precisely what is needed, you understand. It is such an odd situation, but I do think things are improving a little — but it has been a very trying night." She looked from one gentleman to the other, "I suppose it might be a good thing if you could entice Augusta out of the sickroom — I truly fear for her health! She has hardly slept this last week and will not leave the child's side. Dora is in lessons at the moment, but she is very down for some reason, which is not like her. My aunt is coping stoically as usual and is sitting with her sister, who has heard of our little patient and is fearful of being murdered in her sleep! By a *baby!*"

Sir Marcus considered what might be best and then said, "Could you take me to the sickroom please?"

Flora looked a little perplexed but nonetheless nodded and led the way upstairs. Jonathan Frost made himself comfortable and prepared to wait for Flora to return.

She took Sir Marcus to the child's bedchamber and, leaving him there to fend for himself, she stamped back downstairs to look after the other unwanted visitor. The day, she thought, was rapidly deteriorating into chaos.

Augusta was sitting beside the bed bathing the infant's hands very gently, her head bowed and her body limp with exhaustion. She didn't look up when he entered the room because she was expecting Flora.

He crossed to the bed and stood looking down at her.

"You could have sent for me," he said softly.

She turned suddenly and, in her eyes, for the briefest moment, he saw a glimpse of unadulterated joy, but it was quickly smothered, and her expression clouded over, and he saw just how worn out she was. Her face was colourless and her eyes dull, she had quite clearly lost weight and was unnaturally listless. His heart gave a surprising little lurch, which he took to be the shock of seeing her so beset with worry and he glowered at her as a result.

She smiled wanly up at him, "Good morning, Sir Marcus. You look cross."

"I think am — a little. To find you like this. Why is it that you cannot ask me for help?"

She put the wet cloth back in the basin and then dried the child's tiny hands.

She tried to rally herself, "There was no need! We have managed. Doctor Inwood has been absolutely marvellous. And Flora and Aunt Ida have been indispensable."

"But you, no doubt, have insisted on doing more than your fair share and now look at you!"

"Do I look a sight?" said Augusta putting a rather shaky hand to her hair, which was hanging in damp wisps about her face.

He inspected that face, "No, indeed, you do — but you look like a ghost and as though you might fade away before my eyes." He glanced at the child in the bed, "How is the patient?"

She pushed James's straggled curls back from his forehead, "Oh, he is so much better — although he may not look like it. He has had a slight fever and consequently has had a tiresome two days, but I think he's now bouncing back. The Doctor came early this morning and was much relieved to see his progress."

"And when did you last sleep, Augusta?"

She thought for a bit and shook her head, "I cannot remember."

"May I make a suggestion?"

"If you must," she said, on a sigh.

"I find that I really must — although it surprises me as much as it does you. I would like you to go to bed for a while. I will sit with the patient. And before you argue, I am perfectly capable of keeping an eye on him. You need to sleep."

Augusta looked up at him and even through her extreme exhaustion she felt an irresistible tugging sensation, just under her ribs, but she quashed it ruthlessly and opened her mouth to take umbrage. But then, thinking better of the impulse, she closed her mouth again.

"Very sensible." remarked her companion kindly.

Augusta made to stand up, but her legs were not quite steady, and she reached out a hand and had it immediately grasped by Sir Marcus.

"Do you know, I am not feeling at all the thing. I believe I will just rest here on the day bed for a while, if you don't mind. I'd rather be close by."

Still firmly holding her hand, he led her towards the little sofa against the wall, "I do not mind in the slightest. I will be glad to keep an eye on both of you."

She cast him a sleepy look from already half-closed eyes, "I am really rather tired — I had not realised — I am so sorry —"

"I have no idea why you're apologising to me. There is no need. Sit down," he instructed and when she weakly obeyed, he lifted her legs up and placed them on the sofa and tucked her skirts around her ankles. He then fetched a spare pillow from the bed and lifting her head with great care, he arranged it so that she was comfortable. He found a quilt draped over a chair and spread it over her and saw that she was already nearly asleep.

"Thank you," she murmured.

And for some inexplicable reason he bent over her and dropped a swift kiss on the top of her head.

She mumbled something and promptly fell into an unconscious state.

He stood for several minutes looking down at her with an expression of confused exasperation on his face.

"Damn it all to hell," he said, grinding his teeth.

Then he went and dutifully checked the infant in the huge bed and settled down in Augusta's recently vacated chair and felt the lingering warmth from her body seep into his. He shook his head and cursed again.

After a few minutes, he turned the chair so that he could keep an eye on both patients but discovered, to his profound dismay, that it was Augusta he was watching with the most interest.

Thirteen

Meanwhile, Flora had realised that she couldn't abandon Mr Frost in the withdrawing room, however much she may have wanted to. So, she reluctantly joined him and began to make, what she hoped was, polite conversation, which consisted of her crossly asking him how he was liking Cuckoopen Manor.

"I like it very much," he replied amiably, "It has everything one may require and is comfortable despite its ridiculous size."

"It is very big," agreed Flora, wishing she had Dora's gift for conversing with careless ease.

"Do you teach here?" he asked.

"Sewing."

"How very — useful," said he.

Oh, heavens, thought Flora, I could really eat some bread and butter!

"I like sewing," she continued, trying desperately not to think of bread and butter.

"I like horses," said Mr Frost, floundering.

"They are useful too," said Flora, grasping at straws.

"One couldn't do without them."

"No, indeed. A bit like bread and butter."

Silence fell.

Flora cleared her throat, "I don't suppose you'd like some bread and butter and some coffee, would you? Have you had breakfast?"

Mr Frost cheered up immediately, "I haven't. We didn't have time. Marcus was so keen to leave. That would be splendid — I am feeling rather famished!"

Breathing an audible sigh of relief, Flora leapt to her feet and rang the bell for Hannah, and it wasn't long before they were sitting before a tray laden with hot coffee, a plate stacked with bread and butter, a mountain of Ratafia biscuits and spiced Breakfast Cakes, still hot from the oven. There was a wedge of cheese and a dish of golden yellow butter and hot chocolate for Flora, who didn't like coffee.

"Now, this is indeed painting the lily!" exclaimed Mr Frost happily and prepared to tuck in.

"Well, I am so glad that you appreciate a hearty feast, Mr Frost! Some gentlemen just pick at their food as though they've already eaten and they turn it over with their fork, examining it, clearly not enamoured of it. I do like a man with a healthy appetite," admitted Flora.

Mr Frost looked up from the overflowing plate he'd made for himself, "But I had thought you were to marry Reverend Cheadle, Miss Flora! He surely never eats anything at all!"

Flora didn't like to hear the name of her betrothed; she had been so deeply disappointed to hear how he had behaved, leaving Dora on her own with the tinkers. He had come to the school the next day because he was teaching scripture and had tried to stop Flora in the corridor to speak with her, but she was still in the grip of sisterly fury and turned her back on him and stamped away. He had followed, skipping to keep up, and begging her to listen to his excuses for abandoning a young girl to such danger. Flora was not in the mood to forgive and turned a deaf ear. He tried to explain that he had been going for help and that he would have returned for her once he'd found assistance. Flora had eyed him just long enough to give him a withering look and then she'd spun on her heel and disappeared into the parlour, slamming the door in his pleading face.

Her hand was hovering over the plate of bread and butter and for a moment she gazed at the little triangles longingly but then withdrew her hand, "You are quite right. He does not approve of food, I think. He believes it pollutes the mind. Which, I must say, is stupidly ironic when he is so enamoured of my —" she faltered into silence and blushed fierily, realising just in time what she had been about to say.

Mr Frost was staring at her in some bewilderment, "How can one not approve of food? That is nonsensical! One needs food to live! And anyway, it's so dashed tasty! And he says he don't like it but — wait, oh, I *say!* Are you telling me — ? Oh, by Jupiter! What a gudgeon! The man's an imbecile." He took an absent-minded bite out of a buttered Breakfast Cake and looked down at it admiringly and then at Flora who was watching him in growing alarm. "No, no! I was just thinking that one should really have something in common with your spouse. I mean, it stands to reason, don't it? Do you want to spend the rest of your days tied to a fellow who don't like a bit of bread and butter — even if he is enamoured of your — ?"

Flora looked aghast, her eyes widening in dismay, "When you put it like that it does sound insupportable."

"You really should have some, you know! It's quite the best bread and butter I have ever had."

She smiled at him, wondering how she could have thought him oafish, "I do try to make sure that it is not forgotten amongst all the fancy dainties other people prefer for their tea. I could have it any time and be perfectly content with its simplicity. I think there's very little better than good, old fashioned nursery food."

"Oh, I sincerely agree. My cousin has a French chef, and very good he is too, but he is so inclined to Frenchify the food when it is already the best it can be! Sauces on *everything!* Complicating things for the sake of it." He paused and cast her a considering look, "You know, I have met Reverend Cheadle and, although I am sure he's a very fine rector, I cannot quite see that you would wish to — even if he thinks — and anyway, he's such a dried-up old stick! There, it's out! I *cannot* like him! Why on earth did you accept his offer? I know it's not polite to ask but when I heard, my first thought was that you wouldn't suit at all."

Astounded by this stream of honesty, Flora took a piece of bread and butter and nibbled at its edges thoughtfully, "I suppose you could say I'd had an epiphany. You see, I look after Aunt Euphemia and she is very much given to speaking the truth — the truth as she sees it and has no qualms about hurting people's feelings, and I suppose I should not be so sensitive but sometimes she can be so very — *cutting*. The other day was just one of those days when she felt it necessary to tell me all my faults and it just so happened that Reverend Cheadle then declared himself and I was not at all keen. In fact, as I have always loathed him, I was disgusted, but then I had this vision of Aunt Euphemia and I thought it would be better to be married to the Reverend than spend the rest of my days being insulted."

A Ratafia biscuit paused halfway to Mr Frost's mouth and hovered in the air, while he stared at Miss Flora in considerable astonishment, "You must have taken leave of your senses! I can see that one would not willingly wish to stay where one is not appreciated, but to consider Reverend Cheadle's offer when frankly, you could have anyone you choose — it sounds quite irrational."

At this Flora laughed out loud, her milkmaid prettiness suddenly becoming animated, her cheeks shining like polished apples.

Mr Frost, observing this unexpected change with interest, chewed reflectively on the Ratafia biscuit.

"*Anyone I choose!*" gasped Flora, "Oh, you are so very droll! I don't think you realise how limited most female's options are, and if you should be unfortunate to be in the least — flawed —"

"Flawed?" interrupted Mr Frost ruthlessly, "*Flawed?* I am not sure I understand! Are you suggesting that you think yourself deficient in some way?"

"I fear that if you are about to say that you think I have no imperfections, I shall never be able to believe anything you say ever again!" announced Flora, much amused.

"No, no! We all have imperfections! That is to be human. But I will admit that when I first saw you in church, I was — well, frankly, Miss Flora, quite bowled over!"

"By the sheer size of me?"

Mr Frost shook his head in confusion, "I mean to say that the sun was shining on your hair and turning it to glinting gold and I thought I'd never seen such a perfect complexion — so, smooth, so soft — perhaps I shouldn't — "

"No, *do* go on! I'm most intrigued!"

"Well, I thought you looked like a Botticelli painting!"

At this Flora finally lost her grip on her limited social graces and fell back in her chair roaring with laughter and still clutching a slice of bread and butter in her hand. "Oh, *oh!*" she gulped, "A — *Botticelli!* That is the funniest thing I've ever heard!" She put down the bread and butter on her plate and searched frantically for her handkerchief but could find none, so Mr Frost handed her his, a concerned frown upon his kind face.

"Why yes! Surely you must know? You are the spit and image of his Birth of Venus! I thought it immediately and was utterly bewitched! I cannot think why you should find it so funny!"

He watched her mop her streaming eyes and then blow her nose without any affectations at all and he thought what a refreshing change it made. He had met and been hunted by so many artful females that he had learnt to avoid them wherever possible. He was untitled but very comfortably set up, with a substantial inheritance and a fine house and that was all they seemed to need to throw their caps at him. It was all right for Sir Marcus; he was so far beyond the pale that he was now mostly ignored by the society beauties in pursuit of a husband. But this odd creature, had shown no signs of even being aware of him as a potential mate and had, in fact, shown that she wasn't interested by accepting the Reverend's hand. He had thought her so luscious, glowing softly in the morning sunshine, and had wanted to plant a lingering kiss on her dimpled hand but she had snatched it away before he could.

"I — I have never been described as a Botticelli before! Oh, it's just too ridiculous! Aunt Euphemia says I am like a fat sheep!" and she went off into a fit of the whoops again.

"A fat sheep? She must be *blind!*" exclaimed Mr Frost.

Hiccupping in an unladylike fashion, Flora raised her flushed face and reddened eyes to his, "I eat too much and am exceedingly ill-humoured," she told him frankly.

"I think your frown is rather adorable," said he.

She looked at him for a long moment, frowning, "You think — ? I fear that you must have escaped from Bedlam, Mr Frost!"

"Oh, do call me Jonathan! But please, tell me — do you *truly* wish to marry the rector and be a rector's wife?"

"I *do!*" said Flora savagely.

"Why?"

She thought about this, "Because I don't want to end up being like Aunt Euphemia. She's so bitter and lonely and full of hatred for anyone who has a better life than her, which is everyone! But I am her least favourite so must bear the brunt of her wicked tongue."

"Well, that's it then! You don't love Reverend Cheadle at all, you're just afraid for your future!"

She made a disgusted face, "*Love* him? I most certainly do not! Especially as he left Dora all by herself with the tinkers, who, of course, meant her no harm, but he was not to know that, and he *fled!*"

"I say! That's not up to snuff! It's not acceptable in anyone really, but it's somehow worse in a Man of God!"

"That's precisely what I thought. He said he was going for help, but I can tell from his expression that he feels ashamed of his cowardly actions. I cannot even look him in the face. I'd like to plant him a facer," she said without thinking.

"Plant him a — ? Boxing cant now! This is *priceless*. Miss Flora, if we can somehow find a solution to your rash decision to wed the rector, would you mind if I called upon you?"

"Called upon me? For what purpose?"

He smiled at her and passed her the plate of Ratafia biscuits, "For the purpose of wooing you, of course!"

"Bedlam must be missing you, Jonathan Frost!" said Flora popping a biscuit between her perfectly pink smiling lips.

* * *

Augusta stirred and mumbled something in her sleep and Sir Marcus thought he had spent most of their acquaintanceship watching Miss Pennington sleep. He smiled to himself. As a man who liked to be active, he found it rather surprising that he found watching her sleep strangely satisfying. She kept very still and had slept like one dead. He realised that she must have been sorely tested by the arrival of the sick child in their midst but, in her usual way, had just rolled up her sleeves and would, no doubt, have gone on until she dropped. He had never known anyone so selfless before and wondered what she would make of his previous circle of friends; they were so different, so inconsiderate and selfish and critical of anything they suspected might be provincial, which the Penningtons certainly were. They would also have made much of her dowdy clothes and unremarkable face. He gazed at her sleeping figure and contemplated the Beauchamp nose; it certainly was impressive, and she was inclined to make good use of it, looking down it with *hauteur* and making one feel quite abashed. In repose her face had lost some of its usual tension and her wide mouth was relaxed and almost seemed to smile, curling at the corners. It made her look younger, and he began to see that responsibility at such an early age had made her seem more advanced in years. He tried to imagine her dressed in the kind of gowns his mistresses wore, or those of his wife, Lady Birch, and found it difficult to picture her decked out in jewels and lace, with feathers in her hair and her face made up with paint and patches. It would be like a church mouse wearing shoes with diamond buckles, incongruous and rather unseemly. He wondered why he was even bothering to think about her. It was surely a waste of time. She had heard about his past now and that would surely be enough for any lady of quality to cast him aside.

He had seen the look in her golden eyes when he entered the sickroom, before she came to her senses and quickly covered her undisguised pleasure at seeing him. For a moment he had felt that insistent grip on his heart, but he rejected it, knowing that it could only bring trouble and disappointment for everyone concerned and he had had his fill of censure, which is why he had removed to the country in the first place. London was not the ideal environment for someone with a shameful past; the talk grew louder and more insistent until he could not enter a room without a noticeable silence falling and he had finally grown tired of being the reason that conversation died, weary of being forced to brush off casual remarks about his father's proclivities and pointed enquiries about how he had spent his time in Paris. He had, at times, wanted to shock people and tell them some of his heinous activities, but always managed to answer with restraint, not giving them any reason to clutch their daughters to them to keep them safe.

That unguarded look in Augusta's eyes had been a warning sign and he was very aware that he should tread lightly. She had clearly led a sheltered life, even if she had had her share of trials and was altered because of them. She would be vulnerable to any gallantry paid to her and he had no desire to give her entirely the wrong idea. He was not fit to be in company with his old low life friends, let alone someone as virtuous as Augusta.

She opened her eyes at that moment and stared at him as though not recognising him and then he saw light dawn and she put a hand to her hair, which had become a little more disordered and she sat up, swinging her feet to the floor and casting an anxious glance at the bed.

"All is well, he still sleeps," said Sir Marcus.

She busied herself adjusting the tippet around her shoulders, in order to take some time to recover from the oddly intimate feeling she was suffering after waking up with a gentleman in the same room, particularly *this* gentleman. She suddenly felt rather awkward and a little too warm.

"Thank you so much for staying. I hope I haven't slept too long. You must be dying to get away."

"Not in the slightest. You have been asleep for a trifle under two hours. I think it was much needed and I feel I must scold you just a little for spreading yourself too thinly. You are at breaking point my dear girl, something I know a good deal about. A short nap will not, however, be enough to prevent even more serious lassitude if you should continue in similar vein. It would be short-sighted to persist in neglecting yourself like this Augusta and to allow your own health to suffer so I am going to risk being thought high-handed and am going to suggest finding some extra help — even if only as a temporary measure."

"Well, no, really that will not be necessary, Sir Marcus — " began Augusta resolutely.

"Firstly, I do wish you would call me Marcus, as you have no doubt noticed, I have taken to calling you Augusta, despite not being invited to do so! And secondly, I shall not stand for any arguments about this. My mind is made up and I shall be finding someone to come in and assist you in the child's care. I cannot have you fading away to a veritable ghost before my eyes and not attempt to halt the decline. I am very much afraid that I am just as stubborn as you and shall win this particular skirmish."

"Oh," said Augusta limply, "I see that I have been well and truly drubbed."

"You have. There is no use fighting me. In anything."

"Tyrant."

"Very probably, but then I never had anyone to put me in my place and tell me to behave myself."

"No, that is clear — more's the pity," remarked Augusta, "But, you have us on your side now whether you want us or not and we are an opinionated collection of females and will not tolerate any kind of superior types trying to browbeat us! And we will not allow you to believe that you are unfit for society and become lost to melancholy."

He lifted one dark eyebrow and fixed her with a wry look, "You mean to be my protector?"

She managed a laugh, "I suppose I do. I think that all you lack is someone, a sister perhaps, to set you back on the right path."

The brow went a little higher, "A sister?"

She stuck her chin in the air, "Sisters are *everything!* I think that is where you went wrong in the first place! Not having sisters — which of course wasn't your fault! Well, now you have the equivalent of three! Imagine that!"

His eyes were alight with amusement, "I am trying to, ma'am!"

"I prefer it when you call me Augusta," she said, his smile reflected in her eyes.

"Well, I suppose — as we are to be siblings!"

There was something in his voice that gave her pause, but his face told her nothing, "And I shall contrive to remember to call you Marcus, if you wish."

"I do wish. I should like to hear my name on your lips," said Sir Marcus, who gazed at her mouth with evil intent and was rewarded by a look of confusion. She then jumped to her feet and went to the bed to examine James as he slept.

"He does look so much better now. It is astonishing what some nourishing food will do for a fellow!"

"Indeed. I hope that someone is feeding poor Jonathan. He suffers a good deal if not fed at regular intervals."

"I expect Flora will have seen to that. She is also very keen on her meals."

"That is fortunate."

"Oh, why?"

"Because I believe my cousin has developed a *tendre* for your sister."

Augusta looked astounded, "Good gracious! For *Flora?* Are you *sure?*"

"He has not said in so many words, but I believe I have seen telltale signs. You sound surprised."

"I am, a little. She can be very — headstrong and ill-humoured — and apart from that she's betrothed to Reverend Cheadle!"

Sir Marcus shrugged, "That would be a disastrous match. He's a regular goose-cap and she has such fervour that cannot and should not be contained. Jonathan is a similar sort of person — but relentlessly cheerful."

"I was only recently warned that a cheerful spouse would not be desirable — that one would quickly tire of it."

"Now why on earth would someone be warning you against excessive cheer, I wonder?" pondered Sir Marcus idly.

Augusta, wishing she hadn't spoken, turned away to hide the colour flooding her wan cheeks. Honestly, she thought, it's as though I've lost control of my wretched tongue!

Taking pity on her, Sir Marcus then said that he had better go and see how Mr Frost was, "He will be wondering where I am and thinking that I have abandoned him for good."

He went to the door, "It's been a pleasure — watching you sleep again, Augusta. I hope to have the chance to do it a third time, e're long! I shall be sending you a nursemaid of some sort — I will ask Beecher to arrange it as hiring female staff is not one of my strengths." He cast her a look that spoke volumes, "I have yet to discover where my strength lies," and he left the room, leaving Augusta staring at the door with her mouth open and her heart racing.

Mr James Duncan very thoughtfully chose this moment to suddenly exercise his much-improved lungs and make his presence known and Augusta was forced to abandon her ridiculous daydream and pay attention to her wailing charge.

* * *

In the withdrawing room, Sir Marcus found his cousin, who had absolutely no notion that he'd been gone for nearly two hours and, having eaten just about every morsel of food on the tray, was starting to think about his dinner but was reluctant to call a halt to an afternoon of unadulterated bliss. He had seldom been so happy and when Sir Marcus strolled in apologising for keeping him kicking his heels, he was able to say, with complete sincerity, that he hadn't noticed the time.

Sir Marcus, noting Miss Flora's heightened colour and sparkling eyes, decided that he had arrived just in the nick of time to save his cousin from rushing headlong into something that needed some judicious thought. He knew Jonathan to have romantic inclinations and although he was certainly old enough to decide for himself, he had no wish to see his cousin make a serious error of judgment. He was beginning to wonder if it was wise to allow Jonathan to remain at the Manor when he was in danger of succumbing to an admittedly pretty face and an alluring figure. There was also the problem of Reverend Cheadle to contend with and he could see a good deal of unpleasantness ahead for all of them, if things should go awry — and in his experience, things always went awry.

* * *

As they rode away, Jonathan Frost was unusually quiet and said nothing until they had reached the gates of the Manor.

Then he cast a furtive glance at his companion and rushed into speech, "I know what you're thinking! But it's not true! I am in earnest. I have never been more in earnest!"

"I am sure you are, dear boy," replied Sir Marcus with maddening calm.

"She doesn't know about Brock Hall nor does she care a fig for my social standing, my inheritance or anything else for that matter, because she doesn't know about it, so you can take that look from your face! She was entirely indifferent to me, thinking me an oaf, if you please! *Me*, with my winning smile and sophisticated manners! It's hard to fathom! Of course, now she is betrothed to that damned parson and that does present a slight problem."

"A *slight* problem? I think you underestimate the power of the Church. Have you a plan to free her from Reverend Cheadle's desperate grasp?"

Jonathan dismounted and relinquished his horse to the groom who had appeared from the stables.

"Well, if the worst comes to the worst we could always elope!"

"You shall do no such thing. I will not have you bring scandal to the Pennington and Beauchamp door. But nor will I condone you leading Miss Flora on a wild-goose chase — it would be unkind and not the behaviour of a gentleman."

"Well, what am I to do then?"

"You will bide your time and try not to disgrace us or Miss Flora."

"That's fine talk coming from you, Marcus!"

"I know, and I'm sorry to be a hypocrite but I am very serious in this. I do not want Augusta to have to shoulder any more worries at the moment. She has enough on her plate."

"Ah, I begin to see how the land lies!"

He received a dispassionate look but had, for some reason, never been in awe of his cousin's renowned temper, so he held his ground.

Sir Marcus handed his reins to the groom, "If you are insinuating something Jon, you had better just come out with it."

"I think, and do please correct me if I'm wrong, that you have shown a marked preference for Miss Augusta Pennington of late and are in a state of indecision about how to proceed."

Sir Marcus Denby turned on his heel and walked away without making any reply.

Fourteen

Life at the Seminary gradually returned to some sort of regular routine. As little Mr James Duncan regained his strength and began to show slow but encouraging signs of recovery and the delightful and extremely competent nursemaid, provided by Sir Marcus within a day of promising such a miracle, turned out to be heaven-sent, Augusta was able to return to her teaching duties, and although still suffering from the effects of too much worrying and sitting up all night, every night, for over a week, she was starting to feel a little more like herself.

The nursemaid, Mrs Maud Garth, had been recommended to Beecher by Mrs Inwood, who had made enquiries in the village and discovered that the lady who had helped her with two of her children's arrivals into the world, was still very able and more than willing to help with a sickly baby, despite being warned that he was a tinker's child. To which she replied, "Pooh! What do I care for that! We all need tinkers to mend our pots! And it matters not if the baby's father is an out and out villain — I would treat them just the same. A true Christian cannot turn a blind eye to those in need. And besides, I do so *love* a baby!"

And so, she arrived at the school in a brisk whirlwind of efficiency and soothing words and within half a day had the place running like clockwork. Augusta was able to relax her shoulders, which were so tightly knotted that her neck ached constantly, and she could not tilt her head without wincing. There was a small part of her that resented having to hand over the reins to someone else and she had briefly considered exercising her authority by telling Mrs Garth to mind her own business, but it had only taken a telling look from that lady and a pointed remark about the welfare of the child being of the utmost importance and Augusta was silenced.

As she wandered through the girls' dormitory the following night, she was able for the first time in over a week to sit on their beds and ask them how they were, to chat about everyday things and brush Mabel Latimer's wildly frizzy hair in an attempt to tame it a little. She then read Fidelia Hill's letters from her mother, because her reading skills were not keeping pace with the others and the poor child found it hard to decipher Mrs Hill's much-crossed missive, the looping letters overlapping carelessly so as to disguise the meaning, which made Fidelia much inclined to weep into her pillow, and she had to be gently coaxed out of her misery. Then there was little Lady Patience Farryer, who was just nine years old and needed singing to sleep most nights because she missed her mother and younger sister. Augusta would stroke her hair and they would sing softly together until Patience became sleepy and then Augusta would continue until the child had drifted off. It all took time and with the added burden of the sick baby, she had not had a moment to see to her usual duties and was feeling very guilty about it. She needn't have worried though because she discovered to her great joy and relief that, while she had been otherwise occupied, Flora had, of her own accord, shouldered her sister's responsibilities and had made sure that all the girls were happy with their lot and that things ran smoothly.

There was a discernible change in Flora. She was, noted Augusta a little anxiously, walking with a decided spring in her step instead of her more usual heavy tread. She knew that it must have originated in the two hours she was left alone, most improperly, with Mr Jonathan Frost. Something had clearly passed between them, and she could tell that Flora was in a state of euphoria and nothing would be allowed to interfere with it. She didn't know whether to be sorry or glad that her sister had finally found something to smile about, such that even sitting with Aunt Euphemia for an entire afternoon was not enough to dampen her spirits.

Augusta was very much afraid that Mr Frost, although apparently a charming, bluff sort of fellow, was merely trifling with Flora and could not possibly be sincere about his interest in her. It was Flora after all! She may be the prettiest of them all, but she was horridly inclined to speak her mind with no thought for what people thought of her, and when she frowned — well, it was like watching a thunderstorm raging and one could not possibly find that attractive — unless one had no intention of honouring one's promises. She suspected that as both Mr Frost and Sir Marcus had spent most of their time in London or, worse, Paris — that they were accomplished flirts and their words actually meant nothing.

Augusta could not help then dwelling on Sir Marcus's very engaging smile and laughing eyes and with a small sigh, she wondered just how much of what he had said to her was true. Thinking in particular about him wanting to watch her sleep for a third time! She shook her head. No! That could only be taken as a most unscrupulous thing to suggest! It was most unseemly — even though it gave her a strange feeling in her stomach! He was shameless and was obviously only rusticating to escape yet another dreadful scandal in London and was merely hoping to pass the time in the country making fools of the naive provincial females before returning to the kind of sophisticated women he was probably partial to! Well, she would not fall prey to his worldly wiles! There was a small part of her that rued this decision because of the moment when she had looked up and seen him entering the sickroom. Her heart had lurched despite it being in a wearied state and she had been unable for a moment to hide her joy in seeing him. She blamed her extreme tiredness for the weakness of her mind and tried to forget how she had felt when he had told her of his scandalous past. She didn't want to think of how she had longed to save him, to cradle his head to her bosom and make everything better. Nor did she want to admit to her own imperfections when she had realised that some unhinged part of her was actually *jealous* of those dreadful women who had stolen his innocence! She was so deeply ashamed of the thought that she was barely able to look anyone in the eye in case they might recognise the wickedness in her.

Her confusion on the matter only increased when, on the following Sunday afternoon, Beecher arrived at the door bearing a large parcel addressed to Dora.

That young lady, having never, in her life received even a letter, never mind an actual parcel, could not help letting out a squeal of joy and falling upon Beecher and the unexpected package like a starving wolf upon a stray lamb!

Beecher who had been assigned to deliver the parcel and had been exceedingly dubious about being asked to undertake such a menial task, was in the end delighted to have witnessed Miss Dora's unbounded joy and found himself being so profusely thanked he was forced to keep reiterating that the package was not actually from him! Miss Dora seemed to be convinced that the bringer of such delight should be treated to a hero's welcome. And so he was offered tea and cake and all manner of treats and although he politely refused saying he had to get back to his duties, such a great fuss was made of him that he smiled to himself all the way back to the Manor.

Dora, who was flaunting the box before her sisters as though she were the Queen of Sheba herself, was eventually brought back to earth by Flora, who told her if she didn't stop capering about like a demented goat, that she'd take the parcel away from her.

Brought swiftly to her senses, Dora sank into a chair and stared at the package on her knees, "It must be from Sir Marcus, I suppose! I wonder what can be in it?"

"If you open the wretched thing, we shall all have our curiosity satisfied," snapped Flora.

"Well, there's no need to be so — oh, all right! Don't look so cross, your face might stay like that!"

"*Children!*" admonished Augusta wearily.

Dora undid the beautiful blue satin bow and slid the ribbon from the box. She took a deep breath and lifted the lid.

Inside was a note written on gilt-edged card and she picked it up with a shaking hand and read it aloud.

Dear Miss Dora,

I hope this will be suitable for your next outing. I took advice from an expert on the subject of gowns! It is in the way of a thank you for rescuing Quince and bringing him home and for being such a good friend to Imogen.

Yours etc
Sir Marcus Denby

Dora laid the note down on the table beside her chair with exaggerated care and began to push back the delicate rustling paper in the box.

She gasped.

Flora and Augusta moved closer so they could see.

Dora stood up and put the box on the chair and lifted out the contents for everyone to admire.

"Good gracious!" exclaimed Augusta.

"'Pon my soul!" said Flora.

Dora held the *robe a la Polonaise* gown against her. The pale pink reflected in her ecstatic face.

"*Titania!*" breathed Dora, her eyes filling with tears of joy. "He remembered! Oh! It's perfectly *magical!* I think I might cry!"

"You *are* crying, you wet goose!" said Flora.

"I can't help it! It's the best thing anyone has *ever* done for me! It must have been Imogen who helped him choose! She knows just what one should wear."

Augusta was eyeing the apple blossom strewn gown with admiration but also wondering how on earth she could tell Sir Marcus that Dora couldn't accept such an extravagant gift. She may not wear stylish gowns herself, but Augusta knew an expensively wrought garment when she saw one. It was exquisitely fashioned — the blooms looked as though they were real and the silk, which was the palest pearly pink, would have graced any of the highest born ladies at the Palace. The flounces on the sleeves looked to be of finest Brussels lace and there were tiny seed pearls stitched along the edge of the neckline.

Dora held it lovingly to her flushed cheek, "It looks as though it's been made by the fairies in A Midsummer Night's Dream!"

"All we need now is for Bottom to turn up!" declared Flora shaking her head.

Augusta was rehearsing a speech to Sir Marcus in her head, trying to impress upon him that to give into a child's every wish was not good for their character. She supposed that as he'd never had anyone to say no to him, he might not understand. She watched Dora's face as she spread out the voluminous skirts and apart from being astonished that the gown looked as though it was going to fit perfectly, she was thinking about the amount of thought that must have gone into procuring such a garment. She knew he was wealthy but even Croesus himself would have found it a thorny business acquiring a gown in the right size and to such particular specifications! Sir Marcus must be some sort of miracle worker.

Dora suddenly stopped admiring the gown and looked at Augusta, who had an expression on her face that bode ill for her present state of bliss.

"*May* I keep it, Gussie? Or shall I have to return it to Sir Marcus because it's not respectable to accept gifts from gentlemen?"

Flora, who had been wondering exactly the same thing, turned to her elder sister with an enquiring expression.

Augusta, who had been quite ready to brave Dora's disappointment by insisting the gown was returned forthwith to the sender, felt as though she were being assailed by a starving puppy and had in her hand the wherewithal for its salvation.

She closed her eyes and cursed Sir Marcus and his hatefully meddlesome ways.

"Of course, you may keep it," she heard herself say, "But I must ask you to promise to never mention again anything you might want in front of him!"

"Oh, I *promise*, Gussie!" vowed Dora. "I didn't *mean* for him to buy me anything — I was only *remarking!*"

"I know dear, but you have to understand that Sir Marcus is obviously a bit weak-minded when it comes to feminine wiles and does not know that he cannot just go around buying things for people!"

"Well, I think it's very nice of him and shows what a kind man he is!"

"You must write to him straight away and thank him," said Augusta firmly.

"Can I not go to the Manor and thank him personally?"

"I don't think that would be a good idea."

"I cannot think why not! He has been so kind, and he even sent Mrs Garth to help us, and you said yourself that she's a blessing!"

"Yes, and I wrote him a note to thank him for his — kindness."

"It doesn't seem enough," said Dora frowning, "Look at the blossoms and the pearls! It's so *very* beautiful!"

"It's a ridiculous extravagance," said Flora, "When will there ever be a suitable occasion to wear such a frivolous thing? It's not as though we move in fashionable circles out here in the countryside. Will she wear it to visit the poor?"

"I shall wear it when next Sir Marcus asks me to go out with him in his carriage," replied Dora with awful dignity.

"You are so sure he will ask you?"

"Oh, yes! Even though he doesn't seem to like Augusta much — "

"What makes you say that?" asked that lady rather too urgently.

"You and he argue, and I notice that he frowns when you are together and sometimes he looks as though he'd like to seize you and strangle you!"

Flora let out a snort and put a hand to her mouth to silence it, her eyes brimming with laughter, "*Seize* you and *strangle* you! I may be naive, but I think I know what *that* means!"

"Yes, she vexes him a good deal!" said Dora with the absolute certainty of youth, "Although there are other times when he just stares at you. Like this," and she made a creditable attempt to mimic Sir Marcus's abstracted air.

"Dear God," muttered Flora, "It's worse than I thought! Mr Frost was convinced there was something, but I wouldn't believe him."

"Believe what exactly?"

"That the Wicked Sir Marcus Denby would like to *seize* Miss Goody Two-Shoes!" said Flora, smirking.

"Well, *I* like him a great deal, but I *really* don't think we should allow him to *seize* Gussie!" declared Dora resolutely.

Flora went off into peals of laughter and had to mop her eyes with her petticoat, as she couldn't very well pull out the handkerchief Mr Frost had given her and she was treasuring, without causing comment.

"I don't see why you're laughing!" said Dora indignantly.

Augusta put an arm around her youngest sister and over her head sent Flora a warning glare, "Flora's not been quite herself recently. She's been a trifle distracted. Is that not so, Flora?"

Flora tossed her head, "I have absolutely no idea what you mean!" she said crossly.

Augusta changed the subject, "Dora, take that lovely gown upstairs and hang it up so that the creases drop out and then you must write a thank you letter, and we shall take it up to the Manor this afternoon."

Dora happily agreed and raced off holding the gown tenderly in her arms.

Augusta looked at Flora.

"Don't tease her so. She's just a child. Being an innocent, she doesn't understand that there are things that she cannot possibly comprehend. She doesn't know that Sir Marcus has a troubled past or that you have formed an attachment to Mr Frost."

"I have *not!*"

"Oh, my dearest Flora! If you only could see how much your demeanour has altered since his last visit! It is very revealing. You have never been able to disguise your feelings."

"I have no particular inclination towards Mr Frost, Augusta. He just — made me laugh. That is all."

"Of course."

Flora bridled at her knowing tone, "Well, what about you and Sir Marcus then! I have seen you with him and I have the distinct impression that you would very much like for him to *seize* you!"

"That is absolute nonsense. For a start, he has never shown any interest in me, and he is far too old, and his scandalous past is insurmountable! Not that I've ever even thought about him in that way!" she added a little lamely.

"Oh, that's priceless!" crowed Flora, "What a pair we are! We are so provincial that we only need two worldly gentlemen to arrive, like foxes in a henhouse and we are all at sixes and sevens! How gauche we must seem to them! They're probably laughing at us behind our backs."

Augusta, who had several times, thought the very same thing, looked aghast. "I am sure they are not. I believe Sir Marcus to be honourable in his dealings with us. He may have once been in danger of succumbing to the basest instincts known to Man, but I am convinced that he is trying to redeem himself and anyway, he is not to blame for what happened."

Flora eyed her sister with suspicion, "Have you fallen in love with him?" she asked in her usual blunt manner.

There came no answer for a long moment and then Augusta sighed, "I suppose I have. I wish it were not so because no good can come of it. We are not just from different worlds and are unalike in temperament, but I have heard that his former wife is a Great Beauty."

"What has that to do with anything, you ninnyhammer!"

"I should have thought it perfectly obvious," said Augusta gesturing to her own face, "I am *not* a Great Beauty!"

Flora considered her for a moment, "No, you are not!" she said not unkindly, "You have very fine eyes and beautiful hair though, if it's any consolation."

"It's not really," said Augusta a little forlornly and wishing she was a Great Beauty so that she could sweep Sir Marcus off his feet.

"And you do have the Beauchamp nose!"

Augusta smiled and stroked the offending feature thoughtfully, "It is a sad curse. Still, one does not need to be handsome in order to be a lifelong schoolmistress!"

"Oh, Lord, what a depressing thought!" said Flora.

"Talking of depressing thoughts — what are we going to do about Reverend Cheadle? You *cannot* marry him, Flora! It would be dreadful for you, especially if your heart belongs elsewhere and it would not be fair on him, poor man."

Flora took an impatient turn about the room, "I must have been mad! I only accepted him because Aunt Euphemia had been so unkind! Now, I am stuck with him forever and shall have to sit opposite him at the dining table while he picks half-heartedly at his food and reads me his dreary sermons! What am I to do? Would it not be a breach of promise to jilt him?"

"Oh, I hardly think so. There were no witnesses to your troth being plighted! I suspect that we would only have to show Reverend Cheadle just how truly revolting you are, and he will conveniently forget he ever proposed! It's possible, I suppose, that he might bring the Church into it, but I think once he discovers that you are not the perfect buxom wench of his dreams, he will gladly let you go!"

"Buxom wench, indeed! It's all he can do not to stare me in the bosom when he addresses me! His eyes very rarely rise above my décolletage!"

Augusta laughed, but she realised that the subject of breaking off an engagement, however casual it may have seemed at the time, could be a tricky business and she wished she had someone she could confide in and perhaps ask their advice. She didn't want to worry Aunt Ida with such tiresome things.

The door flew open, banging back against the wall and Dora skipped in, triumphantly brandishing a sheet of paper covered in cramped script, "I have written to Sir Marcus! It's a *first-rate* letter! I think he will be *very* pleased with it. Come on, Gussie! Let us go now! Fetch your hat! Are you coming with us Flora?"

Flora considered for a moment and decided against it. She had so enjoyed being flirted with, even if Mr Frost's notion of flirting was to expound upon the merits of whether it was better to add jam to bread and butter or not! She had found it charming and not at all embarrassing as she had imagined it might be. But she had the small matter of her betrothed to consider and she was still not entirely convinced that Jonathan Frost had been sincere in his attentions. She decided to be cautious and wait and see.

So, it was only Augusta and Dora who set out for the Manor that afternoon. Dora, skipping as though she were indeed a demented goat and Augusta, with a measured tread and her mind filled with all the reasons why she shouldn't go. They were all outweighed by the reason she wanted to go. She hadn't seen Sir Marcus since that telling morning in the sickroom and although she had already written to thank him for sending Mrs Garth, she wanted to make him aware of the very great favour he had done them and assure him, to his face, that she would forever be in his debt.

She practiced telling him this in various ways, using a variety of different facial expressions and was still not satisfied with the result as they arrived at the front door of the Manor.

A footman, recognising regular visitors, promptly let them into the hall and then ushered them straight to the withdrawing room, where he informed them Sir Marcus and his guests were at present.

"Thank you," murmured Augusta politely and stepped into the room, her heart secretly pummelling her ribs.

The gentle hum of conversation ceased abruptly, and she looked about her in some alarm. Dora, impatiently stepped around her and bounced merrily into the room, waving the carefully crafted letter.

She stopped, suddenly becoming aware of curious eyes upon her and dropped an unexpectedly graceful curtsy.

Sir Marcus rose to greet them, "Good day to you, Miss Dora, Miss Pennington — what a charming surprise! Come in and allow me to introduce you to my stepmother, Lady Denby and my former wife Lady Birch."

Without faltering in the slightest, Augusta stepped forward and made the necessary salutations, whilst her brain was making immediate plans to turn tail and flee.

She was immediately aware of the disdainful eyes taking in the dowdiness of her gown and the patent disapproval at the inexcusable interruption. She had time to note the pale and empty prettiness of Lady Denby and the exotic, dangerous beauty of Lady Birch. She wished a hole would open in the floor and swallow her up. She wished she hadn't been so easily persuaded by Dora to visit. She wished that she had had the sense to ask the footman if Sir Marcus were entertaining. She wished she'd thought to put on her Sunday best gown. She wished she could scream out loud in vexation. But instead, she allowed herself to be shown to the chair that Charles Denby quickly relinquished for her, and she smiled at him gratefully, surprising a look of silent apology on his face. Dora went to sit with Imogen, who was hiding on their usual window seat on the far side of the room. They exchanged speaking glances and Imogen's hand crept into Dora's and they stayed like that, silently watching the proceedings from wide eyes.

Augusta sat stiffly, her hands folded neatly in her lap, and tried not to show her abject terror.

Mr Frost was there, looking a bit like a cornered rabbit. He managed to nod at Augusta but seemed otherwise transfixed by fright.

Sir Marcus was explaining that Augusta was from the Ladies Seminary and that Dora had been keeping Imogen company. He quite deliberately left out the part about Imogen attending the school to learn to read and write. He had no wish to bring the elaborately decorated ceiling down upon Augusta's head.

"So, you are a schoolmistress, Miss Pennington?" enquired Lady Denby in a querulous voice.

"I am, my lady," responded Augusta, raising her chin just a little.

"How unusual. You seem quite — " she allowed her words to drift away.

"I expect it was unforeseen circumstances that brought you to such a parlous state," suggested Lady Birch as though an excuse were required.

"No, my lady, I chose to become a teacher quite freely."

She felt Sir Marcus's quizzical gaze upon her and ignored it.

"Merciful Heavens! How very peculiar. Who did you say your father was?"

"I haven't mentioned him, my lady."

"I must assume he is no longer with us as you have been forced into servitude."

"He was killed in an unfortunate hunting accident, and I was not *forced* into teaching."

"I understand that your aunts own the school? The Beauchamps?"

"Yes, they have run it for many years now."

"Perhaps I know them?" said Lady Denby hopefully trying to find something she might understand and be able to expand upon.

"I very much doubt it. They lived in Cheltenham before they moved here and are both unmarried and not part of the *Beau Monde* in any sense."

"I feel sure that I've heard the name before," said Lady Denby, pensively. "Beauchamp," she mused almost to herself, "It has a familiar ring to it. I just cannot recall — it'll come back to me I expect."

Augusta swallowed apprehensively and hoped she wouldn't remember.

Sir Marcus, seeing her face turn even paler, decided that it was high time he stepped in.

"Miss Pennington, did you have something particular you wanted to discuss? Is everything all right at the school? Young Master Duncan is well I hope?"

She looked at him with such relief he very nearly laughed out loud.

"Oh, yes, indeed, James is doing splendidly — he looks quite robust now. I did so want to thank you personally for procuring Mrs Garth — I know I wrote — but it's not the same! It was so kind of you to think of that. She's an absolute treasure!"

"I'm delighted to hear it. She was highly recommended."

"Marcus! Tell me you're not hiring servants yourself!" demanded Lady Birch in disgusted tones.

"Good God no!" he replied, "I asked Beecher to do it." He turned back to Augusta, "Was that all?" and his eyes were gleaming.

"Dora has something important to say to you."

Dora jumped up and went to stand in front of him, "I *do*, Sir Marcus," she held out the letter to him, "I have written you this, but it nowhere *near* manages to convey how I *truly* feel about the Titania gown that you sent! I shall *never* in my whole life be able to explain to you just how grateful — how *deeply* indebted I am — I have never seen anything as beautiful — it took my breath away and left me speechless!"

Sir Marcus's mouth twitched, "I'm delighted that you liked it."

"*Liked* it! It is the best thing that's *ever* happened to me!"

"I am most gratified."

"There is just one thing however that I thought I might mention — I was wondering if you might possibly be thinking of giving a ball here at the Manor — perhaps a Summer Masquerade? And I could wear my new gown!"

"Dora!" gasped Augusta in utter dismay.

Sir Marcus laughed, "Well, I must admit it had not occurred to me, but now you have broached the subject I can see what a splendid notion that would be. Would it not, Miss Pennington?"

Augusta found she was having trouble forming words and sent him a beseeching look.

"It seems your sister is in agreement! You and Imogen had better start making plans!"

Fifteen

Augusta was forced, in order to demonstrate her good manners, to sit and converse stiffly with the two visitors, each word being dragged from her like a tooth being drawn. It was agony and, if it hadn't been for his kindness to Dora, she would have fled, without a qualm. But he had been so thoughtful and generous that she felt obliged to stay and exchange meaningless remarks with two people she would be happy never to meet again.

She already despised Lady Denby for being so ineffectual and complaisant and within seconds she had learnt to hate Lady Birch, with her lavish clothes and jewellery and her insincere smile, fluttering eyelashes and hatefully pert nose! Augusta's nails dug into her palms, and she clenched her jaw. She listened to the refined, sultry tones of her voice and wondered how Sir Marcus could have fallen in love with such an *obvious* woman. Every movement she made was calculated to ensnare a man, every silky sound that came from between her perfect lips was to caress the ears of a gentleman. She had been created, like Eve, to tempt and she needed no juicy red apple to do it.

Augusta had seldom been so outraged and was sitting so rigidly she feared she was in danger of breaking a bone. She dared not meet Sir Marcus's eye in case he saw how exasperated she was and the moment the stilted conversation waned, she jumped to her feet, signalled imperiously to Dora and they made their excuses, smiled kindly upon Mr Denby and Jonathan Frost and went to the door.

"I shall see you out," said Sir Marcus obligingly. She glared at him.

"And I shall come too," squeaked Imogen, glad of any excuse to be away from her mother.

A grinning Sir Marcus pulled the door closed behind them and leant upon it for a moment, keeping his eyes firmly fixed on Augusta, who practically had steam coming from her ears.

"Imogen why don't you run on ahead with Dora? We shall follow in a moment."

The girls needed no second bidding and raced to the front door and out into the sunshine.

Augusta made an enraged choking sound and headed to the door.

"I am so sorry," murmured Sir Marcus, "I should have warned you to stay away. Now, I'm afraid, the cat really is amongst the pigeons."

She turned back to him, "What do you mean!"

"Miranda's got a whiff of intrigue and will be on the lookout for any signs of me showing an interest in — anyone."

"Why should it concern her? You are divorced."

"She could take Imogen away from me if she had reason to think I was back to my old ways," he said with an oddly twisted smile.

"Well, you're not, are you! So, there's no need to worry. Honestly what an absolutely ghastly shower! I've never met two such utterly vacuous and at the same time poisonous females! How you could ever have — "

He moved slowly towards her, and she backed away reaching behind her for the door.

"How could I ever have been in love with Miranda? That is certainly something that makes me question my own judgment sometimes. I truly thought I had more sense. It's surprising how stupid one can be when one thinks there may be a child involved."

"Oh, of course! You had a sound reason, but — "

"I know. There's no need to say it. You know, when you're angry your eyes are magnificent — like celestial bodies!"

Choosing to ignore this rather silly remark, she stood with her back against the door and frowned up at him, "It's really none of my business what you do."

"Isn't it? I could make it your business."

"I must be going. Dora will be getting impatient."

"Coward."

At that she bridled, "I'm not afraid of you!"

"Well, you should be," said Sir Marcus so softly she barely heard him.

She quickly turned to leave but found she was held fast, his hands on her shoulders.

Letting out a startled gasp, she tried to wrest herself free, but he just laughed and pulled her to him.

"Be still," he advised her and taking her face in his hands, he kissed her hard on her protesting mouth. She struggled for just one valiant moment insisting that he stop because someone might hear and then all the fight went out of her, and she softened into his arms and allowed him to continue expertly exploring her face with his lips. He kissed her until she felt quite faint, and it was only when Beecher cleared his throat apologetically behind them, that she tore herself away, and with her cheeks flaming, wrenched open the door and fled into the garden.

Sir Marcus watched her go and then turned to face his butler, "Just in the nick of time, Beecher." He rubbed his eyes with the heels of his hands, "Have you ever been tempted to do something that you knew you were going to rue almost immediately but damn well gone ahead with it anyway because life is too short, and you don't want to die old and alone with nothing but regrets to keep you company?"

"Yes, Sir, I have. I agreed to come and work for you," said Beecher solemnly.

* * *

Augusta said a brisk farewell to Imogen, grabbed Dora by the hand and dragged her off down the drive. She just wanted to get away from the Manor, from those detestable women and from Sir Marcus and his perfidious and yet so very enticing lips!

She would not think about him ever again! How could he treat her as though she were no better than one of his light-o'-loves! He had abused her trust and assaulted her person! She should have slapped him or called out so that someone could have stopped him! Thank God Beecher arrived at that moment before — before she had completely lost all sense of propriety.

"*Gussie!* Why are you walking so *fast!* These slippers are pinching my feet, slow down! What on *earth* has got into you?"

Augusta slowed her frantic pace and took a shaky breath, "I'm sorry, Dora. Those women — they were so — disagreeable! I could not bear to be near them a moment longer!"

"Oh, is *that* all? I thought you and Sir Marcus must have argued again and he tried to seize you!"

Augusta choked and nearly tripped over own feet. "No, it had nothing to do with him. There was no *seizing!* I'm afraid I just allowed my temper to get the better of me."

"Is that why you're so red in the face?"

"Oh, *Dora!*"

* * *

For the next week all Dora could talk about was the gown and the possibility of a Summer Ball at the Manor. She drove everyone to distraction. Flora declared that until she had rid herself of Reverend Cheadle a ball was of no use to her because she didn't want to spend a whole evening being forced to dance a dreary minuet with him and some fusty old matrons from the village. And Augusta said a ball of any kind hosted by Sir Marcus was likely to be a complete disaster as no one would want to attend any function given by someone with such an appalling reputation. Dora unfortunately overheard this and demanded to know precisely what she meant. Augusta had hedged for as long as she could, but in the end due to her sister's ruthless persistence was pressured into giving her an expurgated version of the least offensive part of Sir Marcus's history. Dora was singularly unimpressed and said anyone who refused to attend a ball because of what was obviously only a slight misunderstanding, *deserved* to miss out on all the excitement.

Flora, who had been allowed to know a little more of the awful truth, including her recent seizure at the Manor, because Augusta needed an ally and a confidant, had informed her elder sister that by trying to protect Dora from the harsh reality of Sir Marcus's iniquities, she had only succeeded in fixing her unwavering belief in him. The young innocent thought him to have been unfairly treated and she would now be ever more determined to shield him from persecution. After all, he had given her a gown fit for the Queen of the Faeries! She would never now believe that he was culpable even if he murdered someone! He had a devoted champion for life!

Augusta said they certainly couldn't tell Dora what had really happened to him because she was too young and frankly, she added, she thought Sir Marcus could do with a champion because he was presently trapped with those two hateful females and would be suffering a good deal. On the other hand, she continued crossly, he deserved to suffer!

Flora laughed, "You are too funny, the way you sway back and forth between wanting to rescue him and wanting to kill him! I have never seen you so indecisive and yet so murderous."

"He is absolutely infuriating, and he had no business treating me in such a cavalier fashion! As though I were one of his — doxies!"

"Augusta! You can't *say* that! Someone might hear! And anyway, he only kissed you, which is perfectly understandable. You cannot say that he mistreated you. You wanted him to kiss you."

"I did *not!*" protested Augusta, "And — it was not just a kiss, it was — it was something really quite vulgar! He nuzzled my neck and kissed my eyelids and — well, it was not some chaste kiss given by some innocent young swain to his beloved — it was — *practiced!* His hands! I cannot even begin to tell you! It was shaming!"

"As I understand it, a gentleman is supposed to be proficient in such matters. A lady cannot be, of course. Are you telling me that you in no way enjoyed the experience?"

"I most certainly did *not* enjoy being mauled in such a rough manner!"

Flora just smiled, "It sounds rather splendid to me. Not at all like one is warned it will be — he sounds quite passionate and dangerous!"

"I have no desire for someone to be passionate with me, thank you very much!"

"So, you would prefer the attentions of Mr Bacon!"

Augusta checked herself mid rant and the image of Cornelius becoming passionate filled her mind's eye and she snorted with laughter, "Cornelius in a passion? It's not possible! He's far too fastidious. I doubt he could even bring himself to press his lips against someone else's without feeling complete revulsion. Oh, I wish you had not made me imagine such a thing!"

"Do you not *yearn* to be kissed by Sir Marcus again?"

Augusta closed her eyes and remembered how she had felt being pressed to his broad chest and feeling the warmth of his mouth on hers.

"Not in the slightest," she lied.

* * *

At some point during an exceedingly tiresome week, Sir Marcus, having disposed of his guests to their various bedchambers and hobbies, went for a long ride across country to clear his head and burn off his growing frustration.

He had callously abandoned his daughter to the ministrations of her mother despite her sending him pathetically pleading looks. He had refused Jonathan's kind offer to accompany him, saying he just wanted a bit of peace and quiet, so that his cousin had nodded sympathetically, understanding his need for respite from their carping visitors.

He set out at great speed, allowing the horse to have its head and galloped for several fields, jumping the ditches and low hedges without much care or attention. It was only when he realised that Quince had followed him and was valiantly running alongside that he slowed to allow the stupid dog to catch his breath.

"Did I say you could join me, you ridiculous hound?" he demanded furiously. "What makes you think that I need your protection?"

The dog loped alongside his master, his tongue lolling and his ears flying, a happy grin on his face, just pleased to be in such good company.

"I suppose you've noticed that you are not much appreciated by our guests. They fear you might jump up at them and dirty their gowns. God, I wish I could just go to sleep in their presence like you do. Mind this ditch now, don't — never mind, too late. I'm sure Beecher will be delighted to clean you up when we get back! Poor Beecher. His face, when he came upon us in the hall. God, what was I thinking!" He paused to negotiate a tricky patch of briars and then continued, "She just looked so very exasperated, and it made her eyes sparkle so fiercely! I know! Do not look at me like that! I realise that it was a mistake. Although, I have to say I do not really regret having kissed her. I regret how she will now feel about me — and knowing her, she will be too indignant to ever forgive me." He slowed his horse to a walk and slumped a little in the saddle, "What is it that makes me want to goad her? Why do I feel this need to see if she will abandon me at the first hurdle? I think it's because I cannot believe anyone could really be as good as she seems. Which makes me ask why I should be bothering with such a virtuous creature! Do I just want to see how far she will be prepared to go? Am I punishing her for demolishing my hard-won peace of mind?" He looked down at Quince who was wondering whether to chase after a rabbit he had just spied and taking no notice of what his master was saying, "You do not answer my questions you useless beast. What *is* it about her? She is strait-laced and dowdy and critical and then when one least expects it, she is forgiving or laughing until she cries and then she has the temerity to look at me as though she wants to rescue me like a stray puppy! It's infuriating."

They walked on in silence for a while, Quince and master both lost in their own confused thoughts.

"The worst thing is, I think, when she doesn't come to me for help! I find that, for some reason, quite hurtful. There, I've said it! She has the ability to wound me! That is not easy to acknowledge. Why should she have such power over me? I do not care for anyone. I have never cared what people think of me and yet, suddenly I worry that she may no longer wish to be my — my what? My *friend?* God, am I eight years old! My companion? Someone who looks at me as though she'd like to box my ears and send me to bed with no supper? Am I, in truth, missing my mother?"

He laughed bitterly at this, and the noise startled his horse, which sidled and made Quince leap out of the way and let out a surprised yelp.

"Consequences," mused Sir Marcus, "Everything I do will have consequences."

Quince had quite forgotten the rabbit having stumbled upon a promising looking branch, which he was now dragging along behind him in a hopeful fashion.

By following a desperately circuitous route, Sir Marcus was able to accidentally return to the Manor by way of the village and as he happened to be passing the school, he thought he might just call in and see how Miss Beauchamp was as he hadn't seen her for a while and wished to pay his respects.

He could make no one hear at the front door and so let himself in, it being a school and open to the public in a way. He wandered through the rooms but found the place to be quite empty. Puzzled, he made his way through to the kitchens where he found Cook and Hannah busily making something that was giving off an enticing aroma of rosemary. Cook informed him that Miss Augusta and Miss Flora had taken the girls on a nature ramble through the woods and that Mrs Garth was with the tinker child.

Sir Marcus, momentarily forgot his flimsy reason for visiting and wondered if he should sit down and wait for their return but suddenly recalling the ostensible reason for dropping in, asked solicitously where Miss Ida Beauchamp might be.

Cook said that she too was out with the ramblers as it was such a lovely day, and she was so very partial to wildflowers.

"The woods, you say? Ridgewell Woods?" said Sir Marcus idly.

"No, Sir, up your way. They go along the track past Cuckoospit Grove."

Sir Marcus frowned, "But I told Miss Dora that the gamekeeper might be out shooting in those woods at any time! Miss Augusta must know that! Of course she would not listen, the little fool!"

Cook eyed him with interest, "She's stubborn that one," she remarked but she might as well have saved her breath because he had already left the kitchen at speed.

Cursing profusely, he mounted his horse and with Quince racing alongside, he set off in the direction of the woods which bordered his land. He knew them to be generously filled with vermin that his gamekeeper was keen to shoot.

Quince sensing his master's urgency, kept pace and wasn't tempted to become distracted, although he regretted leaving his newly acquired branch behind in his haste.

Sir Marcus, suffering from fury and fear, in slightly unequal measures, used all his considerable horsemanship to urge his horse along the tortuous tracks up the hill towards the woods, whilst listening out for and dreading the sound of gunfire.

He heard the girls before he saw them, the fluting sound of their voices carrying quite clearly on the gentle breeze. He reached the edge of the grove and spied the thoughtless wretches making their merry way along the ferny path as though they were walking to Sunday school! He rode a little recklessly through the wood until he reached them and saw Augusta at the head of the column turn and look to see who was approaching so speedily. He saw her face register surprise and then freeze into a mask of contempt. He dismounted and, abandoning his horse to wander as it liked and Quince to be petted by the girls, he came alongside his quarry and after greeting Miss Beauchamp as politely as he could and nodding at Miss Flora, he turned on Augusta, his eyes glittering dangerously, a grim white line around his mouth.

"Sir Marcus," said Augusta coldly, "Are we trespassing? We always come this way as it has the best flowers and wildlife."

Sir Marcus took a steadying breath but still managed to sound maddened with rage, "Wildlife! You don't say! Did I not warn Dora that there may be poachers in the woods who are not averse to shooting at anything that moves? And my gamekeeper could be hunting squirrels or rabbits! You should know better than to wander around with your head in the clouds! You could have been shot!"

Augusta, her eyes kindling with indignation, favoured him with a look of such profound loathing that he hesitated for a second.

"*Shot?* Is your gamekeeper so poorly trained then?"

Miss Beauchamp sensing an escalation of hostilities stepped into the ring and placed her small person between them, "I do think that this is perhaps not the place for a public skirmish. The girls are within earshot and are all looking quite curious. Shall Flora and I take them back to school?"

"That is a very good notion, Aunt Ida," said Augusta, tight-lipped and she watched as her puzzled aunt and vastly amused sister herded the pupils back along the path towards the edge of the grove. When they were out of sight she turned back to Sir Marcus, "You really should know better than to allow your temper to best you in front of the children!"

"Damn the children!" ground out Sir Marcus, every line of his towering figure, tense with fury, "I told Dora! The woods are dangerous! You could have been wounded or killed by a stray shot! And there are poachers who would think nothing of getting rid of a witness to their crimes!"

"Could you please stop shouting at me!"

"I'm not damn well shouting!" bellowed Sir Marcus.

"It's not seemly for us to be alone in the woods!" said Augusta suddenly realising the impropriety of their situation, "Someone might see us."

"I don't give a damn who sees us."

"Stop cursing!"

"I thought — I called in to see — Miss Beauchamp and found you gone. Cook told me where you were. I thought — "

"You thought you might find us all lying dead, shot by poachers?"

"To be perfectly frank, I was only concerned that *you* might have been hurt," said Sir Marcus, scowling down at her.

"Well, that's utterly absurd! If a poacher needed to be rid of any witness, he would have to shoot all of us, surely?"

"Augusta, do not — "

"Imagine how long it would have taken one man to shoot eight girls and three chaperones! I would think he might quickly grow weary of shooting so many do you not? And it's also very likely that some of the girls may have had enough sense to run away so he would have to follow each one until he had hunted them down! It could take all day! And the noise of the shots would bring curious folk from the village to see what was happening. I fear he would be in a dreadful temper long before he could be sure we would tell no tales." She fixed him with an innocent look, "But I can see why you should have wound yourself up into such a state! Only think of all the bodies to dispose of! You'd need a large wagon."

He shook his head and clenched his teeth, "I could quite cheerfully wring your wretched neck," he muttered darkly.

"Well, go ahead, if you think it will make you feel any better!" offered Augusta generously.

Sir Marcus eyed her neck, the neck he had not so long ago pressed his lips to, and smiled in such a suggestive way that it caused her to turn a becoming shade of pink and scowl at him.

"If you are going to try to affect the ways of a gentleman, I think you could start by not reminding a lady of a traumatic incident she would rather forget!"

"Do you want to forget it? I certainly do not," said he with a sad lack of good breeding.

"I shall be hard-pressed to forget being so ill-used! However, I expect you were just overwrought because you had been ambushed by your delightful stepmother and wife! I cannot quite see why you should take out your ire upon me though, but I realise that gentlemen sometimes have odd ways of expressing themselves. I shall forgive you, but I cannot forget."

Sir Marcus leant a little closer, "Good. I don't want you to forget. Perhaps I should just remind you — "

"Don't you dare touch me, Sir!"

"I shall not touch you again until you beg me!" said Sir Marcus scornfully.

"As that will *never* happen, I am safe from being mauled ever again! By the bye, your horse is escaping!"

With yet another volley of curses, he strode away after the animal and Augusta watched him round up the creature and return to her, followed by Quince, who was rapidly tiring of standing in a wood waiting for his master to take notice of him.

"I will see you home," he told her.

"Thank you but there is no need now, as I am in no danger of either being shot or molested!"

He ignored her snide comment and they walked back to the school mostly in silence apart from Augusta's attempts at a polite exchange of comments upon the weather and the abundance of wildflowers. She received little more than a few grunts of acknowledgement and when they reached the gates of the school, he bid her an icy good day, mounted his horse and rode away.

Augusta stood in the drive for some while and contemplated a long and miserable life with no more kissing and when she met Flora in the hallway, her sister asked in a concerned fashion if she'd been crying to which Augusta explained that some dust had flown into her eyes as Sir Marcus had ridden away.

Flora nodded wisely, "Dust can be a great nuisance. Perhaps I can suggest an excellent water for curing red eyes, made from eyebright, calamine and distilled water from rotten apples?"

Augusta couldn't help laughing, "No, you may not! I am perfectly fine, thank you."

"Did Sir Marcus continue to show just how much he minded you being accidentally killed by poachers?"

Augusta looked askance at her sister, "He was concerned for everyone."

"*There are none so blind as those who will not see*," intoned Flora.

"He was *fearfully* angry!" admitted Augusta, grimacing, "He said he wanted to wring my neck."

"He doesn't want anyone else to kill you but will happily to do it himself? He is a very confused man, I think."

"Where are the girls?" asked Augusta suddenly recalling her duties.

"They're pressing flowers in the parlour. Aunt Ida is with them, showing them how."

"I must go up and see Mrs Garth and little James. You know, I can't help thinking that James is a very grown-up name for such small fellow, perhaps we should call him Jim or Jamie?"

"Excellent change of subject, dearest," said Flora.

Sixteen

Flora was torn. She and Hannah had just changed the linen on Aunt Euphemia's bed and were about to gently lift her out of the chair, knowing full-well that she could easily move herself if she had a mind to. The old lady was complaining bitterly about their treatment and Hannah had shot Flora such a look that she had wondered for the hundredth time why on earth they all put up with such a tyrant. She imagined a lifetime of caring for her aunt and pictured herself slowly withering away to a dried-up old husk while Aunt Euphemia never aged one day and continued to taunt her for being fat and childless.

She suddenly straightened her aching back and stood up, looking down at her aunt with a slight frown.

"What is it, you silly goose?" asked Euphemia peevishly, "Why are you not lifting me?"

"Well, dear Aunt Euphemia, it just occurred to me that, as there is nothing actually wrong with you, you could jolly well make your own way back to your bed. There is no need for Hannah and me to strain our backs to lift you when with a little effort you could do it for yourself."

"Have you taken leave of your senses?" demanded Miss Beauchamp, her pale eyes bulging with indignation.

"No, I think I have just *regained* my senses!" responded Flora. "For an age we have been pandering to your whims and tiptoeing around you in the hopes that you won't notice us and single us out with your spiteful comments, but I have only just realised that we are in fact doing you a great disservice because by allowing you to think that you're an invalid, you have in fact become one and you have wasted both your own life and ours too. I cannot believe it's taken me so long to appreciate this. You will have to forgive me for being rather slow to understand that one can do as much damage by helping someone as by not helping them. Now, Hannah and I will walk beside you while you return to bed. Obviously, your legs will be a little weak after not using them for so long but with some daily use I think they will soon regain their strength and we'll have you skipping around the garden in no time!"

Miss Euphemia Beauchamp opened her petulant mouth to speak, closed it, thought for a moment and then began to weep piteously, the tears springing histrionically from her eyes and cascading down her cheeks, to great effect.

Flora looked at her dispassionately, "You should have gone on the stage, Aunt! You would have made your fortune being able to cry on demand like that."

The tears dried up immediately and were replaced with an expression of pure loathing.

"Ah," said Flora, "*There* you are. The Aunt Euphemia we all adore. Now then, we can help if you like — Hannah and I will make sure that you don't fall. It's only a few steps to the bed and I think you'll manage it very well and once you see what you can do, there will be no stopping you."

Miss Beauchamp looked her niece in the eye and realised that she had finally met her match. With an incensed sigh, she put her hands on the arms of the chair, hauled herself to her feet and took a few unsteady steps back to her bed without any assistance.

"That was *splendid!*" declared Flora, tucking her aunt back into bed. She caught Hannah's astonished look and grinned, "Now, what would you like for your dinner? You deserve a treat!"

Miss Euphemia Beauchamp settled back against the mound of pillows and fixed her niece with a baleful glare, "You'll not get a penny of my money now!" she hissed, "You're going to be an old maid, unloved and unwanted and impoverished. You'll rue the day you treated me so cruelly!"

Flora lifted up the much-despised lapdog Bonny and dropped her onto her aunt's lap, "I wouldn't want your money even if you really had any and I *won't* be an old maid because I am going to marry Mr Frost and we shall eat bread and butter every day and have dozens of fat little children!"

Hannah snatched up the large pile of dirty linen and backed towards the door, her face a picture of suppressed mirth and wonderment, "If you don't need me anymore, Miss Flora — I'll just — take this down to the laundry room."

"Yes, thank you for your help, Hannah. Would you be so kind to tell Cook that Miss Euphemia will have the usual for her dinner?"

"Yes, Miss," gulped Hannah and fled.

Smiling warmly, Flora perched on the edge of the bed and despite the threatening growls from Bonny, she patted her aunt's knee, "You know there's absolutely no need to fall into a fit of the sullens. You will find that life has a great deal to offer if you choose to acknowledge it. I know this to my cost. I have also realised, from your inspiring example, that one must be on one's guard against burning the house down to fright the mouse away! Do you see that one can become a victim of one's own anxiety and before you know it, you are trapped being someone you were never meant to be! I am in danger of becoming precisely what you think me — a fat, unloveable crosspatch. I am beginning to see that all one needs is a little encouragement and one can conquer one's fears! In my case, all I need is the courage to jilt the parson and somehow persuade Mr Frost that despite my numerous flaws I am the girl for him!"

"Good luck with that!" said Miss Beauchamp scornfully.

Flora leant forward and squeezed her aunt's delicate hand, "Do you know? I do believe I *shall* have some luck! In fact, I am feeling really rather optimistic. One day, when you are in a more receptive mood, I shall introduce you to Mr Frost. Perhaps, when you are strong enough to venture downstairs again, we could have tea. He's *such* a nice man. If you could stop being so bitter for a time, I think you'd quite like him."

"But if you marry — who will look after *me?*" demanded the old lady in quavering accents.

Flora looked upon her selfish, hard-to-please aunt with a kindly expression on her pretty face, "Well, if you're exceedingly well-behaved Mr Frost and I might have you to live with us but, I must warn you, at the first sign of dissent I shall have no hesitation in taking you to the poorhouse!"

"You are the most unfeeling and unnatural girl!"

"If I am, then we know who I inherited it from!" said Flora candidly. "Right, let us get you ready because Hannah will be here soon with your baked egg!"

* * *

"Papa? *Papa!*" hissed Imogen, tugging on his sleeve, "Do not leave me alone with her! You're not *listening* to me! Papa!"

Her father was gazing out of the bay window at the rose garden where his former wife and stepmother perambulated along the paths, shielded from the sun's heat by dainty parasols and he was thinking that Augusta never carried a parasol, which was obviously why she had that dusting of freckles across her splendid nose. She just wore a battered old straw sunhat. He glanced down at his daughter abstractedly, his mind occupied by freckles.

"Imogen. Yes. I am so sorry — I did not mean to abandon you. She will not stay forever. She must at some point return to Lord Birch."

"I think they have argued. I heard her say something to Lady Denby — Grandmama — *step-grandmama?*" whispered Imogen, terrified of being overheard, even though the enemy was a good distance away on the other side of the garden. "She said that unless he bought her the matching greys for her new white landau, that she would banish him, and he would not be allowed his usual privileges! I expect he will not get his cake at tea!"

Sir Marcus made a stifled sound and Imogen looked up at him enquiringly, "He's very fond of cake! I heard Mama telling him that he would end up looking like a suet dumpling, but he told her quite crossly that she had driven him to it!"

"I am very sorry that you have had to bear with their peculiar ways. I should never have left you. You know, I did try to keep you with me — when you were a baby — "

"Oh, I *know*, Papa! I heard Mama telling Lady — Grandmama — what a great trial you had been to her and that she determined to keep me from you just for spite! I must say it made me exceedingly happy to know you had tried and even more determined that one day I should return to you!"

Taken aback by this admission of unexpected filial affection, Sir Marcus was overcome enough to suddenly embrace his daughter, who returned his show of devotion by weeping onto his shoulder. "I am so glad she sent me to you, Papa! Please don't let her take me back!"

"You have my word, my child, that I will fight tooth and nail to keep you," said Sir Marcus, in a strained voice.

"When can I go back to school? I long to see Dora and Miss Pennington. Don't you?"

He started, "Yes, of course, we *all* miss them. We will arrange it as soon as possible, but I fear while your mother is with us, we should probably not mention it because she doesn't approve of schools for ladies, and it may convince her that I'm not a suitable parent for you. It may sound a little — deceitful, but until she leaves, we cannot be too careful."

"Oh, I understand, Papa! Perhaps, we should pretend that my staying with you will only make you utterly miserable! That would certainly persuade her to leave me here!"

Sir Marcus smiled at his devious daughter and flicked the tip of her pointed little nose, "Ah, what have I done! I have turned my innocent daughter into a delinquent."

* * *

Lady Denby contemplated the gravel path that led around the smoothly scythed lawn, with a pettish expression, "The stones will ruin my sandals," she complained.

Her companion, Lady Birch, looked about them disdainfully, "That is the trouble with the countryside. There is so much foul matter that one has to contend with. It beggars belief how anyone who is the least refined can stay clean in such primitive conditions. Fabian insists that we spend time at Birch House. He says it's expected of him, but he is accustomed to the life, although he refuses to hunt of course because his breeches and boots might get splattered with mud. He is excessively particular about such things."

"Leopold hunted. He enjoyed the violence of it all. I could never abide it. He would come in waving some bleeding dead beast and shake it at me as though I should be delighted to see such a gruesome sight! It made me sick to my stomach and my maid frequently had to revive me with hartshorn. He thought me a poor creature to not share in his triumph. I will admit that every time he was thrown from his horse, I could not but feel that it was the animals getting their revenge! He beat his horses and his dogs and had I not kept myself out of his reach as much as possible, he would probably have beaten me too!"

"Fabian would never even *consider* striking me! He is too feeble, and I must tell you that if he weren't so very wealthy I would have left him a long time ago. I think he has tendencies, you know?"

Lady Denby looked much intrigued, "No, I do not. Tendencies?"

"Oh, you must understand my meaning dear Gertrude! You cannot be that innocent!"

Lady Denby blinked at her, "I do not follow."

"*Tendencies!*" repeated Lady Birch as if she said it louder it would be easier to understand. "His clothes are unusually elaborate. He favours over-adornment in a way that must alert one to his leanings. His vanity is quite shocking, and I have the greatest fear that he is become a Maccaroni! I know, 'tis hardly credible. His pedigree is sound and his ancestors notable. I cannot think how it should have happened."

Lady Denby's mouth had dropped open, "Are you telling me — no, surely not! He could be pilloried — or worse!" She put a uselessly limp hand to her rosebud mouth, "Oh, dear God! He could be executed!" she whispered, her eyes on stalks.

"Don't be ridiculous! He's not precisely Lord Hervey! He is discreet and probably at most, merely foppish. Although I do think he is strangely drawn to elder statesmen! Oh, don't have a seizure! He is not brave enough to act upon his fancies. He says any flaws he may have are entirely my fault. He says I have driven him to it."

"And have you?"

Lady Birch shrugged her exquisite shoulders carelessly, "How would I know and why would I care? As long as he doesn't bring his tendencies home with him or end up at the Old Bailey, I do not object to his — increasingly effeminate behaviour. He is so ineffectual anyway that I have taken the purse strings and can quite easily manage without his help. If he should die unexpectedly that might cause me a little inconvenience but my future is quite settled — I have seen to that."

"I am glad to hear it, Miranda. My husband left me in dire straits, and I was forced to ask Sir Marcus for assistance — which was humiliating. Although, I will say that he did not make a great fuss about it, and he could have kicked up a very unpleasant stink if he had wished — there was a dreadful amount of debt owing. He said, rather curiously, that it was the least he could do considering his father's behaviour."

Miranda Birch twirled her parasol and pursed her lips thoughtfully, "He said that, did he? I always knew there must be more to the story! I pressed him to tell me, but no amount of feminine persuasion would induce him to share his secrets with me. It was infuriating. I soon realised that there was more to his history than met the eye and once I began to delve into his past, I came upon some very interesting tales! I was able to use that knowledge to win custody of Imogen — of course, it helped that Fabian is well acquainted with several high court judges. That taught Marcus a salutary lesson, but I made sure that he never knew the information came from me, in case I might have need of him in the future." She watched the spinning pink silk above her head as though quite mesmerised. "And now we have his change of heart over Imogen and the entrance of Miss Augusta Pennington onto the stage! Not at all in his usual style. Such a church mouse! And a *schoolmistress* as well. It couldn't be better, frankly." She gave her friend a calculating look, "What were you saying about the Beauchamps? You said you recalled something about them?"

Lady Denby shook her head, "There *was* something, I am quite sure of it, but I cannot now remember what it was. There was some sort of scandal — it'll come back to me. What are you planning, Miranda? Something deliciously naughty?"

"You know me, Gertrude! Never one to allow a chance for revenge escape me!"

Lady Denby giggled, "It feels a little unjust when Marcus has been so generous to me."

"He was certainly always open-handed — it was his best attribute. But he still deserves to be punished. Did you see his face when we turned up unannounced? It was worth the frightful journey just to see him so discomfited. And Imogen! I quite thought she would burst into tears! So amusing. I do so hate being bored. This will be vastly entertaining. I feel thoroughly reinvigorated! I may even suggest that I am longing to have Imogen back with me — which, of course, I could not possibly tolerate! It is so much easier without her at Birch House. She's always been such a disappointment. So, lacklustre and colourless!"

Lady Denby glanced up at her tall, strikingly beautiful friend with her dark colouring and flashing eyes and she wondered, "I have often wondered — 'tis such an aberration for you and Sir Marcus to produce such a pale little dab of a child. Both of you have such strong features and colouring. She must be an ancestral throwback. It's a great pity because you would have appeared to great advantage next to a daughter with exactly your looks. It would have been quite a sight! You would have been taken for sisters."

Pondering this appalling thought, Lady Birch's perfect mouth tightened, and her eyes narrowed, "Sisters? What a revolting notion! I must be glad that Imogen is so unlike me in that case — I had not considered the comparisons — what a fortunate escape! At least when standing next to Imogen no one will believe us to even be related let alone mother and daughter."

Lady Denby appeared to be deep in thought for a moment, "It suddenly occurs to me, having not seen her for a while, that Imogen reminds me of someone! When *precisely* did you meet Fabian?"

Her friend span around to face her, her expression wrathful, "Be quiet! Do not even suggest such a thing here! If Marcus should ever suspect — all my plans will come to nothing! She is the only leverage I have over him!"

"Do you mean to tell me that you think — ?"

Lady Birch tossed her head and walked away along the path a few steps before pausing and turning back, her temper quickly under control, "How should I know? I had to persuade Marcus into marriage somehow and at the time Fabian had not come into his inheritance, so I was at *point non plus* and disastrously short of options. Of course, as luck would have it, I lost the child very early and so Imogen was in fact conceived after the wedding."

"After the wedding — but there is still a possibility — ? It would explain her odd looks. Those pale eyes!"

"Do keep your voice down, Gertrude! Anyone might hear!" snapped Lady Birch, "There is a *distinct* possibility that she is not Marcus's child. There! Now you know! But he has never suspected, which considering her looks is a small miracle in itself! He fought like a lion to take her away from me, which only a father would do, and I realised then that it was surely the best way to hurt him! To keep his precious child. It's been a great trial, but it was worth the pain and inconvenience."

"So, what are your plans? Just to make him rue the day he left you?"

Lady Birch laughed, "He shall certainly be sorry for that and for dragging us through the Courts and holding us up to ridicule just to try to win Imogen back. Fortunately, Fabian is exceedingly well connected and was able to use his family's influence to sway the judge. It made quite a scandal at the time, but it worked out very well in the end, apart from having to bear the tedium of having Imogen remain at Birch House. I was glad to be rid of her but now — "

"You propose to make him suffer for something that happened so long ago? It seems a trifle — desperate, Miranda."

Lady Birch curled her exquisite lip, "Desperate? Perhaps I am a little. Money, it turns out, isn't everything. Fabian brought me a life of opulence and security and entry to the *Beau Monde*, which has been very entertaining, but I find that something is missing. I find I am not as happy as I thought I would be." She stared out across the garden, a tiny frown marring her perfect forehead, "I find that I want more."

Lady Denby, who had been listening rather vacantly, suddenly started and looked at her companion in complete astonishment, "Oh, my God! Miranda Birch! I cannot credit it!"

"What are you wittering about, Gertrude!"

A nervous giggle escaped Lady Denby, "Why, I have just realised that you still love Marcus! It is just too delicious!"

When she saw the look on her friend's face, she took an involuntary step backwards.

Lady Birch's demeanour had subtly altered and become icy, "I should be careful what you say, Gertrude."

"Yes, indeed, I am very s-sorry — I did not mean it — of course you could not possibly be in love with him still — not after all these years — it would be — I c-cannot think why I said it!"

Lady Birch sneered, "You were ever a bird-witted creature. I do not know why I made you my bosom friend in the first place."

"Well, it has only just occurred to me that you thought I would be a useful connection to Marcus — I see it quite clearly now," replied Lady Denby with an unexpected show of perspicacity and pluck.

"You had better tread carefully, Gertrude — do not forget that if I should get what I want I shall have influence over how he spends his fortune!"

Lady Denby blenched, recoiling in horror, "You would not stop him from *funding* me! You could not be so *cruel!*"

"Oh, I could, and I would," said Lady Birch through clenched teeth, "You will learn very quickly not to be disloyal."

Lady Denby was rendered speechless and stood frozen to the spot, her woefully inferior mind whirling helplessly.

"I have had enough of this perambulating — it is too warm. Let us go in," said Lady Birch, just as though they had been chatting about the dangers of freckling in the sunshine.

Together they strolled back along the path towards the house.

* * *

Behind the gazebo, which was so perfectly placed for gazing out across the grounds, Imogen stood very still, her heart pounding and her limbs refusing to move.

She stood as though turned to stone until she could no longer hear the sound of her mother's voice and the crunch of their footsteps on the gravel path. She stood there, hidden by the dense shrubs, until her knees stopped trembling and she was able to breathe easily again.

Her thoughts were in a tangle. She had no notion why she had decided to creep up and spy on her mother and step-grandmother. She had, she supposed, thought it might make something to tell Dora. She had wanted to appear a little daring and more like her friend. Once she had so foolishly concealed herself without them noticing, she was unable to move for fear of being discovered. She had already heard far too much, and it would have been perfectly obvious to them that she had been eavesdropping and she knew from experience that it was considered to be some kind of dreadful crime. She had been caught once before at Birch House for listening at doors and was severely punished for being no better than a cutpurse. The worst thing was that her modest transgression was referred to at every opportunity and she had never been allowed to forget that she was a busybody and never to be trusted. If she appeared just to bid everyone a polite goodnight, the guests were always informed of her crime. She had hung her head in shame, quite certain that she could be taken away by the authorities and incarcerated in the Tower.

Now, she had not only repeated her misdeed, but she had overheard something that changed everything. There would be no escape from the worst kind of punishment and a future where she was not wanted by anyone. She would be an orphan. She frowned. Well, as good as an orphan, anyway! In a way it would be far more serious. Neither of her parents would claim her as their own. Her mother hated her and her father — except he was *not* her father — would disown her and her *real* father — that ridiculous and hateful popinjay would be revolted by the discovery that she was actually his daughter.

Imogen had not understood much of the overheard conversation, but the tone of their voices had told her a good deal and she had gleaned enough to know that even if they never found out that she had been eavesdropping, she was about to be used as a pawn in a game she understood as little as chess. Her father, Sir Marcus, would no longer want to keep her at the Manor and her mother would be forced to take her back to live with her real father, Lord Birch, and she would never see Dora again and would once again shut her away in the nursery until she was an old, old lady and they'd find her mummified corpse there decades later, like when the shrieking maid had discovered the emaciated corpse of the dead cat that had become trapped and died in the attic.

Finally able to move her legs, Imogen eased herself out from behind the pretty stone structure and pushed through the branches until she was back on the grass path that led around the house.

She stood for a moment uncertainly. She looked up at the house and then back at the gazebo. Then, biting her lip anxiously, she came to a momentous decision.

Seventeen

Dora followed the other pupils out into the sunshine and stood blinking into the brightness. It was nearly time for tea, thankfully, and Cook said there would be Banbury Cakes. Augusta had been teaching basic arithmetic, much to Dora's disgust, as she had no head for figures and found the whole lesson a dead bore. She was missing her friend Imogen, who had been forbidden to attend classes while her mother was staying at the Manor. Having met Lady Birch, Dora was in no doubt that this was both a necessary evil, in order that the reading lessons were not discovered, and a case of unfair torture, as poor Imogen was trapped with her mother and had no one to champion her cause. It really was too bad, and she had been wondering how she might be able to ameliorate the situation. She had asked Augusta if they could visit Imogen and Sir Marcus, but her sister had been wholly against the notion and when pressed had afforded what Dora considered poor excuses for not making an attempt to rescue Imogen from her dreadful relations.

"It is not our business, Dora," explained Augusta, "She must spend time with Lady Birch, or it might cause problems."

"It's causing problems *now!*" said Dora crossly.

"It cannot last forever. Soon Imogen will be free to come back to classes and you can resume your friendship. You must be careful, my dear, when it comes to Lady Birch and Lady Denby — they are not as nice as they seem."

"They don't seem very nice at *all!* They seem perfectly *beastly!*"

Augusta sighed as it was hard to argue with her sister when she had found the two ladies to be quite horrid as well and was, in her heart, all for rescuing poor little Imogen, who must be having the most trying time imaginable.

"Yes, I know my dear, but I have a feeling that we should not anger them because it will be Imogen who suffers the most from their wrath. I am sure that Sir Marcus will be taking very good care of her — he would not allow her to be ill-treated in any way."

Dora considered this for a moment and nodded, "You're right, Gussie, he's an honourable gentleman and would stop them if they tried to bully her."

Augusta thought about the 'honourable gentleman' and felt her heart quicken but nonetheless managed to agree with her sister, reassuring her that Imogen was quite safe and not in danger of ill-use. She reminded her that there were also two other stout-hearted protectors on hand in the shapes of Mr Frost and Mr Denby. They would never allow their young relation to be subjected to any sort of unfair treatment.

Dora had to agree and felt a little less anxious about her friend.

She watched the other pupils wandering aimlessly across the lawn, chattering like sparrows and she thought they would no doubt be discussing the Ball that everyone was now hoping would be held at Cuckoopen Manor in the Summer. They had all seen her Titania gown and had been gratifyingly envious but, being good-natured girls and well brought up, they had been pleased for her and told her that she would look enchanting in it.

She had to admit that she was a little bored with the talk of the Ball now but, having made such a fuss about it, she could hardly reveal that their endless speculation about who might attend and what they'd be wearing and who would dance with whom, had grown rather wearisome. She decided that she'd rather go around to the stables and visit with Mr Sippence than join in their speculation; he always made her laugh, and she was fairly certain that he would not mention the Ball.

She was just skirting around the side of the house, past a thick hedge of laurel, when she thought she heard a hissing sound. She stopped and listened, wondering if it was a snake or a nest of fledglings. Hearing no more, she continued but was once more arrested by the same insistent sound.

"Who's there?" she called.

"Sssshhh!" came the reply.

Dora stepped closer to the hedge, "Who *is* it?"

"It's *me*," hissed a voice.

"Who is *me*?"

"I cannot say for fear of discovery!"

"Oh, for heaven's sake, Imogen! I know it's you! Why are you hiding in a bush?"

"How did you know it was me? I disguised my voice!"

"Nobody else would hiss at me like a goose — a *silly* goose! Why are you in a bush?"

"I cannot say. But needless to say, it is life or death!"

Dora rolled her eyes, "Has your mother been mean to you again?"

"Not exactly. In fact, she's doing her best to be very nice. It's terrifying."

"I cannot stand here talking to a hedge, Imogen, you'd best come out!"

"If I do, I may be discovered and then all will be up with me."

"Well, if you are determined to stay hidden, make your way to the end of the hedge and go through the little gate, where you will find the hut where Mr Sippence stores the hay. I shall meet you in there in just a moment."

"Oh, you are so good at this Dora!" came the effusive response.

Dora heard her friend patter away down the path and then the creak of the gate; she glanced around at the other girls and saw they were all occupied on the other side of the garden and then she walked very casually indeed along the length of the hedge and through into the stable yard and pushed open the door to the hay store. There she found a wide-eyed Imogen, perched upon a bale, wearing her white velvet cloak and

Sunday best hat, which was enormous and hardly suitable for sitting on a bale of hay.

"What a remarkably silly hat to choose if you want to be inconspicuous!" she couldn't help but remark.

"Oh, do you think so? I hadn't considered it until I tried to get through the gap in the hedge in the lane — I very nearly got stuck on a branch! It was almost a disaster, I thought I'd have to shout for help, which would have ruined all my plans."

"And what *are* your plans, Imogen?"

The girl's face was pale and frightened under the over-sized hat. She shook her head, so that the offending object dipped over her eyes, and she had to push it back so that she could see, "I'm not quite sure. I just had to get away before they found out."

"Found out what?" demanded Dora, a little impatiently.

"Oh, don't be cross! I'm not as good as you at this sort of thing! It's the first time I've ever done anything so daring!"

"What is it that you're doing, apart from wearing the wrong hat?"

"I'm running away, of course!" said Imogen confidingly.

Dora sat down on the bale next to her and gaped at her friend, "Running away? Why would you run away? And where are you running *to?* Do you have any money with you? A change of clothes? Where are your belongings? Did you leave your bag in the lane? You are wearing *sandals!*"

Imogen studied her delicate little shoes with the pretty ribbons and tears began to slide down her face, "I had not thought — you see, I've never run away before — I didn't know how to go about it!"

Dora patted her hand absentmindedly, "Well, why should you? Don't cry! I'm sorry. It's just that if I were going to run away, I'd make sure that I was properly dressed, and I'd have borrowed some money in case I had to take the Stagecoach and stay in coaching inns along the way. I would have worn boots and carried my slippers in a bag. I certainly would not have worn a hat the size of a bee skep that could easily be seen from the next county!"

Imogen sniffled forlornly, "But you are so clever! I was horribly afraid and couldn't think clearly! I was sure that Mama would discover me and drag me back! Oh, what am I to *do?*"

Dora sat and stared into space for a while, tapping a finger on her chin, "Are you really determined to run away?"

Imogen nodded and wiped her nose on her sleeve.

"Well, in that case, I suppose I cannot make you go back to the Manor and have no choice but to aid you in your venture."

"*Thank* you!" breathed a worshipful Imogen.

"But, you must do exactly as I say!"

"I'll do *anything!*"

"The first thing to do is take off that dreadful hat!" commanded Dora, taking charge.

* * *

Sir Marcus Denby was tying his neckcloth with so little care that Hodge, his elderly and devoted valet, winced as though in physical pain. He refrained from saying anything because all the staff at the Manor knew that Sir Marcus was under an immense amount of pressure and his temper was unsteady at the best of times. They were all tiptoeing around him, careful not to make any sudden noises that might attract his attention or make careless mistakes while tending to his needs. Beecher had had the great misfortune to clatter a wine bottle against a glass and had suffered such a roasting that one would have been prepared to believe that he'd committed murder and not just a breach of etiquette. Beecher had not been able to speak for the rest of the evening he was so shocked and even the next day was still a little shaky.

Hodge, visibly shaken by the state of the neckcloth, handed Sir Marcus his diamond pin and watched as he carelessly fixed it in place as though it were made of the cheapest tin. He drew a shuddering breath and took a step back.

"Hodge? Are you quite all right?"

"Yes, Sir, thank you, Sir."

Sir Marcus cast him a concerned glance, "I hope you are not ailing."

"I can assure Sir that I am not in the least unwell. Is it to be the green velvet or the claret satin, Sir?"

"God, must I choose? I really don't mind. You pick one."

Hodge somehow held his tongue and trod with the utmost caution across the room, picked up the claret satin coat and carried it to Sir Marcus. He held it for him so that he could shrug his broad shoulders into it, then tweaked it into position and smoothed out the creases with an expert hand.

"There, Sir, you look very fine in that. Too warm for velvet, I'd say."

"Right, as always, Hodge. I would have overheated and become irritable."

"Quite, Sir, quite."

Sir Marcus's lips twitched but he managed to suppress the smile, "You think I am irritable?"

"I would never say so, even if I did, Sir," said Hodge with awful dignity.

"You may speak your mind. I promise I won't show my displeasure."

Hodge, lulled into a false sense of security, allowed himself the luxury of telling Sir Marcus that it was suspected that he was not quite himself and that everyone was a little on edge in the servant's quarters.

"Is that so?" asked the gentleman with deceptive calm.

"It's perfectly understandable in the present circumstances, Sir," allowed Hodge kindly.

Sir Marcus adjusted his cuffs and flicked an imaginary speck from his sleeve.

Hodge swallowed nervously and quickly gathering up the soiled linen, he backed towards the door, his eyes never leaving the floor because he'd been warned never to look a mad creature in the eye.

Only when he was back in the servant's hall, did he begin to breathe easily again.

Beecher fixed him with a knowing look, "Said too much again, Hodge? I suppose it's too late to teach an old dog new tricks!"

"He promised he wouldn't lose his temper!"

"He's not been himself since they arrived." Beecher thought for a moment, "Actually, now I come to think on it, he's not been himself since he rescued Miss Dora from the stocks. Perhaps she made him think of Miss Imogen. Whenever he's left alone for a while he sinks into melancholy, and I expect him to call for the brandy and Quince sensibly makes himself scarce fearing the toe of his master's boot!"

"That damn dog's got more gumption than we have! Why on earth do we stay around to be abused?"

"He pays well," said Beecher candidly, "On the whole he's as good a master as you could wish for. His temper might be a trifle stormy when he's castaway, but he's always sorry in the morning and swears never to touch another drop!"

"We've been with him since before his marriage, unlike the others here. We've seen the changes in him. Being his valet before Miss Imogen was born, I saw how he was then, when his father was still alive. It wasn't good. He rallied when the child came along and he had some hope and then when it all went awry, it was back to his old ways with a vengeance."

"It must have been ugly," murmured Beecher sympathetically.

"It was for a while. He kept company with the Black Dog, and they were seldom parted. When we were in Paris, it was all-or-nothing, and I thought we would never come about. Then, his father died suddenly, and we came here and gradually things have begun to change for the better. At first it was just being free of his father and being away from those who knew him and then it was having something to do, to refurbish the house and conquer the grounds, which were in a sorry state. But now, he's changed again and it's like living with a belligerent bear. A bear with a thorn in its paw. And yet, on other days, he's full of the Joys of Spring! There's just no telling how he will be from one minute to the next or what may cause his next bout of wretchedness."

"I think I may have an idea what has disturbed his peace of mind," said Beecher, almost to himself, "And I fear it will not end well."

Hodge looked at the butler with interest, "Oh? Why do you say that?"

"Because many things happen between the cup and the lip, Hodge, that's why."

"You're being very mysterious."

"Where females are involved it's best to keep one's own counsel. One can never be sure how they will behave. They nearly always take one by surprise."

"You mean Lady Denby and Lady Birch?"

"Partly, although I think we all have a fair notion of how *they* will behave! They do not have Sir Marcus's best interests at heart, I fear."

"So, you are alluding to the *other* female then?"

"I am, indeed. Having been an accidental witness to — to a rather *embarrassing* incident, which I firmly believe indicates there is some feeling of warmth between them — I am convinced that his present mood stems from his understandable confusion."

"Why is he so confused?"

"The heroine of the story is, shall we say, not in his usual line — you only have to take a look at Lady Birch, to see that. Our heroine is a bird of another feather altogether and I feel quite certain that because of his past he will fight against becoming embroiled with such a *virtuous* young lady. He cannot but be wary of allowing her to become mired in his problems. She is, by all accounts, *a good woman.* He will know that by associating with him she'd risk losing her good reputation."

"They have it hard, the Quality, don't they! They have all that money, but because they have to keep up appearances, they can't really enjoy their wealth. It's a double-edged sword."

"I'm not sure that Sir Marcus cares one jot about his own reputation, but I do think that he's conflicted about our heroine. I must say that she looked outraged by his ungentlemanly behaviour the other day, although it was obvious to me that she was not entirely averse to his attentions at the time! I think he was irresponsible, and she may well now turn tail because of her modesty and virtue. That is why he is so bad-tempered at the moment — he's blaming himself and, being usually so confident, he is now all at sea. It must be disconcerting for him."

"It makes our jobs even more difficult," said Hodge gloomily.

"It's always the working man who suffers in the end," agreed Beecher.

* * *

Sir Marcus had managed to avoid his former wife for most of the day and congratulated himself on his success in keeping the inevitable arguments at bay. It wasn't precisely that they argued — there was just something in the air, like a strong perfume. It lingered and annoyed and put one off one's dinner. His stepmother was another kind of trial altogether. She was unbearably sycophantic; whining and wheedling at him constantly in order to make sure of his continued financial support. He wanted to reassure her that there was no need for it as he was so riven with guilt for his perceived part in endorsing his father's unspeakable behaviour and consequently had a deep need to make reparation. His rescuing her from his father's enormous debt was, in a way, atonement. However, she seemed to be under the impression that he would stop being her benefactor on the merest whim and she'd be left to fend for herself. It made his relations with her unnecessarily awkward, and he had taken to creeping about his own house like a thief, to avoid meeting her or Miranda and it was making him even more irascible.

When he finally managed to find some time to just sit in his study and stare into the distance, his mind's eye was entirely taken up with an image he was finding it hard to banish — a certain young lady, sprawled on a rug, in a meadow, the sun glinting on her tumbled chestnut curls, her bare feet curled together like a child's and one hand pressed against her flushed cheek. For some reason it haunted both his sleeping and waking moments.

On reflection, he thought it was because it was the very antithesis of his life up until that moment; like a window into another world that he could see but was not allowed to touch for fear of defiling its innocence. A world that offered him so much but with such mockery in its tone that he knew it could never become a reality. He then spent several nights in a row persuading himself that no one could possibly be that perfect and without a single stain on their soul. Everyone had their price and anyway, she was not at all to his tastes. He was then shattered by the resulting lack of sleep, and it made him testy, and he cruelly took it out on Beecher, who assumed a martyred air and trudged about the place as though on his way to the gibbet.

Sir Marcus was inclined, in his less reasonable moments, to lay the blame directly at Augusta's door. He reasoned that had it not been for her unnecessary and constant encroaching upon his life — his *ordered* life — he would not be in such a deplorable state. Thanks to her incessant meddling, he had lost sight of his direction and for a short while had allowed himself to become fatally distracted. He would not allow it to go any further though, he had to put a stop to it before he found himself doing something irrational.

Jonathan and Charles gently but forcibly coaxed him out of his sanctuary in an attempt to prevent him sinking yet further into despondency. They had both had to suffer his frequent bad moods and although they knew the reasons for them, they realised that he had fallen into this particular depression because of his inability to trust in anyone. The lack of trust had been established early on in his life and was stubbornly ingrained. They discussed it and came to the conclusion that he needed to go for long rides to get away from the house and its unwelcome visitors. Charles had tried, in his usual carefree manner, to find out how long his mother might be staying, but as she always deferred to Lady Birch, it made discovering the truth quite a ticklish business. His mother, although unreasonably devoted to her only son, was in awe of Lady Birch and it could be frustrating trying to winkle information out of her because her loyalties were very much divided.

"But, my dear," she said placatingly, "It cannot matter how long we stay! It is such a long and tedious journey across country, and we hardly want to set out again so soon. Are you not happy to have us here?"

Well, what could he answer! He was at a standstill either way. He had murmured something inaudible and wished he were braver. He had heard Jonathan doing his best to extract information out of her over a glass of Ratafia with just the same result, and they were no further forward. Behind the scenes the two gentlemen debated trying a different approach, but they knew that the stumbling block was Lady Birch, and she was unassailable and downright terrifying! It would take a brave fellow indeed to question her. It seemed to them that it would be best for the truth to come out naturally and they left it at that.

Meanwhile, Sir Marcus continued to torment his butler and valet and anyone who strayed unwarily into his path, and they prayed for the day that he would finally see sense, but until that day they tried to keep their heads beneath the parapet and stay out of the line of fire.

* * *

Because everyone thought someone else was in charge of Imogen and because she was such an inconspicuous little thing, no one noticed her absence until breakfast the day after her escape. Her maid, Faith was in bed with a bad stomach, and no one had told Beecher, so the usual chain of command broke down and chaos ensued.

* * *

In the end it was Faith, from her sickbed, who demanded to know how her charge was doing and, finding no one knew, she sent a housemaid to ask Mrs Primrose how the child was. When the news finally reached her that there was no sign of Miss Imogen, and her cloak and best Sunday hat were missing, Faith dragged herself shakily from her bed, washed and dressed and staggered weakly downstairs to speak to Sir Marcus. She supposed she should have gone to Imogen's mother, Lady Birch, but she loathed the woman, so scratched on the study door instead and when Sir Marcus barked for her to enter, she stepped into the room ready to do battle.

He looked up and seeing his daughter's abigail, glowered at her in an unwelcoming fashion, "Yes? What do you want?"

"Sir, it's Miss Imogen," said Faith, sensibly coming straight to the point, "She's gone."

Sir Marcus put down his pen and leant back in his chair "Gone? What on earth do you mean, girl?"

"I'm very much afraid that she may have run away, Sir. Her cloak and hat have gone, and she hasn't been seen by anyone since yesterday."

Dark brows knit, Sir Marcus rose to his feet, "Why the hell weren't you watching her?"

"I've been ill, Sir, sorry, Sir."

"Well, that's obviously not your fault. Have the house and grounds been searched?"

"I've only just found out, Sir." She wondered how much she could safely say but, seeing that he was obviously disturbed by the news, she continued, "She was unusually upset yesterday but wouldn't say why. I reckon something bad must have happened to make her so distressed."

Sir Marcus strode across the room, opened the door into the hall and bellowed unceremoniously for Beecher. He then turned back to Faith, "Anything else you can think of that might help find her?"

Faith swallowed nervously, "I don't like to say but she was scared that you'd send her back with her mother to Birch House, Sir."

"I told her I'd do everything in my power to keep her! No, there must be something else. Ah, Beecher, there you are! I need the house and grounds searched. Miss Imogen has gone missing. I shall alert Mr Frost and Mr Denby and get them to join in. Well, don't just stand there! Get moving!"

Beecher, who was still trying to grasp exactly what the situation was, bowed stiffly and removed himself from the room.

"You had better go back to your bed, Faith, you look ill. Someone will keep you informed so don't worry. Go on, off you go — and thank you for coming straight to me."

Faith, feeling quite unsteady, did as she was told.

* * *

Sir Marcus, Charles and Jonathan left the indoor staff to search the house and they mounted up and joined the search of the grounds. They spent two hours checking and rechecking the distant acres, the meadows and river, the lake and the stables and all the dozens of small and large outbuildings around the estate. They called her name over and over and even tried to give Quince the scent from her gloves, but he mistook their meaning, believing it was some game that required him to run in circles with his tongue hanging out and his ears flapping. Anytime someone tried to get near to him, he swiftly changed direction and barking madly, evaded capture. Eventually tiring of being the centre of attention and realising that his master was sounding angry, he went for a long noisy drink out of the fountain.

* * *

After a lonely night spent shivering in the hay store, on a prickly and itchy bed, with only the spare blanket from Dora's bed to cover her and her cloak as a pillow, Imogen was ready to give up her quest for freedom. Dora had managed to steal her a candle from the kitchen cupboard, but it had not been enough to stop her being awake for most of the night fearing that mice or worse might be sharing her bed with her. When she had tentatively suggested to Dora that she might share her bed in her nice warm clean bedchamber, Dora had had to remind her that Hannah was in and out of her room all day long and her sisters never left her alone for a minute!

Imogen had to reluctantly agree that being comfortable sounded fraught with danger and had to be content when Dora managed to save some of her own supper for her. Imogen had not thought to bring supplies of food with her and had missed dinner, so was consequently ravenous! She devoured the bread and cheese and a handful of pickled walnuts, which she found utterly distasteful, and a small lump of Caraway Cake, which Dora had selflessly resisted so that her friend wouldn't starve.

Imogen, who had just spent the worst night of her life, fearing death by rodent, or violent discovery and imminent return to her mother was forced to contemplate a life of loneliness in the nursery at Birch House, and had wept desperate tears into her makeshift pillow and wished she'd thought things through before trying to so recklessly emulate Dora.

The following day was even worse because Imogen, trapped in the dusty little shed, with no one to talk with for most of the morning because Dora was in her lessons, thought by the time she was found she might have gone quite mad. When Dora finally arrived with her breakfast stuffed into her pockets, Imogen was on the verge of giving herself up to the authorities and throwing herself on their mercy. She planned to beg pitiably for forgiveness and hopefully be returned to her nice mouse-free bed at the Manor.

But then Dora brought her a hard-boiled egg, a warm bread roll, a thick slice of ham and a cup of cold tea and she started to feel braver and as though she might survive after all.

"I think," said Dora after a good deal of consideration, "That you should stay here for another night, if you can bear it and then we shall find you passage on the Stagecoach. Do you have anyone who will give you shelter?"

Imogen thought hard for a moment and then shook her head, "Well, not really. You see I am escaping from my relations and there is no one else — unless you count my nanny at Birch House, but I didn't like her very much."

"That's unfortunate. I do think that if one is running away that one should have a destination in mind otherwise it's a little pointless. What about an aunt or uncle?"

"I cannot think of anyone, Dora, I am truly sorry!"

"It's not really your fault! But it would have been very helpful if you'd had a nice aunt or grandmother living nearby!"

"I only know you and your sisters."

"Yes, it's very vexing and I am struggling to think of somewhere you will be safe but not easily discovered. I cannot ask anyone like Mr Sippence to help because he'd lose his position and I had thought that perhaps Mrs Inwood might take you in out of the kindness of her heart, for she is known to be very kind but then Dr Inwood would find himself in an intolerable situation and his reputation might suffer — it really is impossible! Everyone has something to lose!"

Imogen looked as though she might burst into tears again so Dora tried to gently reassure her that she would find a solution although she was starting to wonder how on earth they would pay for Imogen's ticket on the Stagecoach when they had no money at all and could not borrow any without arousing suspicion.

She sat with her head in her hands for a while, thinking of every possibility.

Then it came to her in, what she would later describe as, a blinding flash of light!

Eighteen

Sir Marcus gathered his troops together in the hall and standing on the stairs, he addressed them, his face giving away nothing of his anxiety, but he sounded even more terse than usual.

"Thank you everyone for taking part in the search, even though it has so far proved fruitless. I think we must now look further afield, and I shall alert the constable to see if he can muster some more men. I shall give everyone a direction and we shall spread out and see if we can find clues to her destination. Jonathan and I will go to the school to see if the Penningtons have heard anything, and I think a chat with Miss Dora might be beneficial as she and Miss Imogen are such great friends. We shall continue to look for her until it gets dark and then meet back here. Does anyone have any questions?"

There was a general murmuring while the plan was agreed and then orders were issued, and everyone set forth to see to their allotted tasks.

Sir Marcus watched them go and then he and his cousin made their way to the stables and rode to the school to talk with the Penningtons.

They found the pupils were having an outdoor painting class with Miss Ida and Augusta and were sitting in the garden applying themselves studiously to their watercolours.

Augusta, hearing the approaching horses, glanced up and seeing the visitors wished she had put on a better hat that morning. She raised her hand in greeting and gave the girls instructions to be going on with before walking across the lawn to join Sir Marcus and Jonathan in front of the house.

"Good morning! What brings you here on a school day? I wish it were to bring Imogen back, we miss her dreadfully!" she said.

The gentlemen dismounted and Sir Marcus fixed Augusta with a penetrating look, "It's about Imogen that we've come. Have you by any chance seen her recently?"

Augusta shook her head, still smiling slightly, "We haven't seen her since her mother and step-grandmother arrived." She looked from Sir Marcus to Mr Frost, "Why? What has happened? You both look — so serious!"

"She's missing," said Sir Marcus bluntly. "She hasn't been seen since yesterday. There is a search party — the constable is being informed — I just thought that as you have been such good friends to her that she may have come here. Or perhaps she has shared her intentions with Dora?"

Augusta looking very much startled and anxious, glanced across the lawn to where her sister was frozen in the act of rinsing her brush, her eyes upon the visitors.

Augusta gestured to her and saw her thin frame stiffen with alarm.

She approached them, made a dainty curtsy and then stood trying to remain calm and appear untroubled.

"Dora, my dear, have you seen Imogen since yesterday?" asked her sister in a deceptively mild voice.

Dora shook her head, unwilling to actually voice the lies she would have to tell.

"This is important. She's disappeared. Everyone is out looking for her."

Dora felt as though she were back in the stocks again.

"I am so sorry, Sir Marcus. I don't know where she is at the moment," she said with absolute truth as it was very possible that Imogen had left the shed and gone for a walk.

"Has she said anything to you — hinted that she might be unhappy enough to run away?"

Ah, this was better, easily evaded. "No, she said nothing. Although, I *do* know that she wasn't very happy about not being allowed to come to school."

Sir Marcus exchanged a glance with Augusta, "I will not be angry with her — or you — if you've seen her or spoken to her. I just need to know that she's safe."

Dora looked him straight in the eye without blinking or blushing, "I have no notion where she might be, Sir Marcus. I hope that she is not in any trouble."

He regarded her steadily, "She's in no trouble whatsoever. Her flight is completely unnecessary. All she had to do was talk to me about what was troubling her, and we could have sorted it all out. I think she panicked and acted on impulse and is probably, knowing her, already regretting her hasty reaction."

Dora nodded, thinking just how well he knew his daughter.

Augusta was watching her sister and wondering, "This is serious, Dora. It's not some Shakespearian comedy! She's very young and not as resourceful as you are and could be in great danger."

Dora frowned at Augusta indignantly, "Yes, I understand Gussie! I would *never* do anything to harm her — she's my *dearest* friend!"

"All right, there's no need to become agitated, dearest. I have every confidence that Sir Marcus will find her."

Only Jonathan saw the fleeting expression on his cousin's face.

Augusta told Dora to return to her painting and Sir Marcus said that they had better start combing the village and outlying area. Augusta watched them leave and turned to see that Dora was also observing their departure anxiously. Their eyes met and Dora was the first to look away.

* * *

Dora knew they had to act that very evening if Imogen was to get away from Lady Birch. She was also aware that she was under suspicion in some way just because she and Imogen were such good friends. She supposed that it was only logical — she would have suspected her herself! She hoped that she had made a good job of reassuring them. She had not liked the expression in her sister's golden eyes, or the appraising look Sir Marcus had given her.

As soon as she was able, she gathered together some items for Imogen, a clean petticoat and a warm shawl, a comb and a more suitable hat, which was an old one of hers and a little too small but plain enough not to draw too much attention. She managed to acquire a little more bread and cheese from the kitchen and a stale Breakfast Cake that had been left on the side.

As soon as everyone had gone to make themselves ready for dinner and the coast was clear, Dora ducked out of the back door and ran around to the stable yard, and then through to the shed at the rear of the house, and, keeping an eye over her shoulder, she tiptoed up to it and let herself in.

"Oh, there you are Dora!" cried Imogen with no thought for being overheard.

"Sssshh!" hissed Dora, "We must go at *once!* I fear we may be discovered at any moment! Your father came looking for you and is *determined* to find you. He was *very* angry and upset. And Augusta was looking at me with one of her *looks!*"

Imogen's face lost what little colour it had left, and she crumpled down onto her bale-bed, all the stuffing knocked out of her.

"Papa came? What did he say?" she asked in a quavering voice.

"He said you should have told him you were worried, and he would have sorted it out. He said that you have no need to run away, and he wouldn't be angry with you anyway."

Imogen rubbed her eyes, "Perhaps I should just go back?" Then she dissolved into tears, "But I *cannot!* I *call* him Papa, but he isn't my father! Not my *real* father!"

"What on earth do you mean?"

Imogen buried her face in her hands and made soft sobbing sounds and Dora sat beside her and put her arm about her shoulders.

"I didn't tell you because it's too dreadful! I overheard Mama talking with my — oh, *whatever* she is! She said that

Lord Birch is my real father and not Papa — *Sir Marcus!* She said that he doesn't know yet. She said that he has a terrible past! She said that he tried to keep me, but she made sure that he failed. She said that — she said that she's not trying to take me *away* — she's trying to *win him back* so that I will have to live with her forever! She'll make him really unhappy, Dora! Don't you *see?* It's even worse than I thought! She's determined to get her own way and make him miserable, and she hates me!"

Dora was dumbfounded. For once she barely knew what to think.

"*Not your father!* But he *acts* like your father! He treats you like his daughter."

"Only because he doesn't know that I'm Lord Birch's daughter, not *his!* Imagine how he'll feel when he finds out! He'll cast me out!"

Dora considered this for a minute, "No, I don't believe he will, you know! Augusta thinks he's an honourable man. She practically said so. I *like* him. He's very fair. I wonder if we should go to him?"

"No, *no!* He is in Mama's *thrall!*"

Dora smiled, "Do you even know what that means?"

"No," said Imogen sadly, "I just overheard Lord Birch say it to Mama once when they were talking about Papa — he didn't sound too pleased about it so I thought it must be a bad thing."

"Do you always listen at doors?"

Imogen blushed, "Well, yes I do because otherwise I'd never know what they were planning to do with me! I like to be prepared!"

"I suppose I can't blame you! I must say that I think that Sir Marcus would be kind if you explained that you had heard Lady Birch saying such a thing and he would, I think, side with you."

"But we cannot be sure, can we? I want to leave, I am quite decided," sniffed Imogen.

"In that case, we shall go."

Dora packed up Imogen's meagre belongings and the food into the bag she'd found in a laundry cupboard and wrapped the shawl about Imogen's thin shoulders and arranged the more modest hat on her friend's rather dishevelled hair. Dora peered furtively out of the crack in the door to make sure no one was around, told Imogen to blow out the candle and be ready. Then they crept stealthily out and along the far side of the hedge that led to the boundary of the property and quickly made their way across the fields towards the woods.

"Where are we going?" whispered Imogen trying to keep up with Dora's much longer stride and already out of breath.

"Don't stop! They could be coming after us right now!" Dora grabbed Imogen's hand and pulled her along ruthlessly.

After a good twenty minutes running and walking and complaining, they reached the last field before the lane and had to push through the hedge, much to Imogen's disgust, "This is — *ouch*, that's so prickly — this is not how I imagined — running away would be!"

Dora laughed and held back a branch for Imogen to duck underneath, "I expect you thought it was going to be romantic! Under a silvery moon, with someone playing a violin or perhaps with a handsome highwayman — "

Imogen let out a horrified shriek, "Oh, *please* do not mention highwaymen Dora! I have a very great fear of them!"

They came out in a damp, nettle-filled ditch and scrambled up onto the lane.

Dora then made Imogen trudge wearily for about a mile and had a dreadful job keeping her spirits up, having unnerved her by carelessly mentioning highwaymen.

Then they could smell woodsmoke and hear voices and Imogen hung back anxiously, but Dora was relentless, "We're nearly there, come on!"

Around the corner, the tinker's encampment came into view; a glowing fire with its column of sparkling grey smoke, the wagons, the tethered horses and scrawny dogs wandering aimlessly. Dora, who had been filled with bravado, suddenly questioned her actions and wondered if this was such a good idea. Her pace slowed a little.

"Dora?"

"I know! It'll be all right. They're *really* nice. I know Mr Duncan."

"They look a bit — frightening. I'm not sure this is such a splendid notion after all!"

The dogs began to bark a warning and were commanded to be quiet. An elderly woman came forward to meet the two girls. She wasn't smiling.

"What are you doin' out at this time? You askin' for trouble?" she demanded in a gruff voice.

"We were looking for Mr Duncan? I need to speak to him urgently."

The old woman frowned, her face folding into deep creases, "What d'you want him for? Eh? Wait, you're that girl — the one who took James!"

Dora stood very still, "I didn't *take* him! I just — borrowed him."

The woman came closer and peered at Dora closely, "You'd better come by the fire, Missy. Who's this, then, this pale little ghost?"

"This is Imogen. She's my friend. I need to speak to Mr Duncan please."

She turned and bellowed, "Robbie? You'd better get out here!"

From one of the dome-shaped tents, a figure emerged. He stood and looked at them and then beckoned them into the camp.

Dora took a hesitating Imogen by the elbow and tugged her forward.

"Mr Duncan, oh, I am so *very* glad to see you! We have *desperate* need of your help!"

Robert Duncan's eyes slid from Dora to Imogen, who despite her unbecoming hat and a rather bedraggled and grubby appearance, was otherwise quite clearly fashionably dressed.

"You're Sir Marcus's child. What do you want with me?"

Imogen looked helplessly at Dora, "I — I have run away f-from my — mother and have nowhere to go! I can't go b-back!"

The old lady muttered something under her breath.

"Can't let 'em stay, Robbie! It'd mean prison if they was found here."

"Aye, I know. They lookin' for you girl?"

Dora nodded.

"That means trouble. Why you runnin'?"

"Imogen's mother wants to lock her away. And her father — he doesn't understand — it turns out that he's not *actually* her father and Lord Birch is instead and Lord Birch — he doesn't want her and her mother, Lady Birch — well, she's going to persuade Sir Marcus to marry her and then poor Imogen will have to live with her awful mother for *ever!*"

"Isn't Lady Birch already married then?" asked Robert Duncan, trying to make sense of what she said.

Dora seeing that this might be considered a flaw in her theory tried to explain, "Lady Birch is still married to Lord Birch at the moment, but she still loves Sir Marcus and will stop at *nothing* to get him. It's life or death, you see?"

"Yes, I see."

Dora wondered if he really did, "I'm so glad that little James is on the mend, by the bye. How's your wife, Mr Duncan? I do hope she is recovering!"

Mr Duncan smiled, recognising the blatant attempt to win him over, "Both doing much better, although Mrs Duncan is still not well enough to come home."

"Oh, I *am* sorry to hear that!"

"You were brave, Miss Pennington. I'll never forget what you did. And because of that you can stay here for now. Ma will give you some food, I expect you're both hungry."

"Yes, we are, I could only manage to take some bread and cheese and had to borrow two shillings from the maid and will have to pay her back somehow because she told me she only earns eight pounds yearly. I feel *very* bad indeed about borrowing it, but I really had no choice! I think Hannah can keep a secret though. Some food would be *exceedingly* welcome, I must say. I am really quite hungry because I missed dinner and we had to walk quite a long way, you see!"

Robert Duncan shook his head and smiled, "Go and sit on the log beside the fire and Ma'll give you something to eat."

Thanking him profusely, they did as they were told, looking around at the other members of the group, with interest on Dora's part and ill-disguised terror on Imogen's.

Old Mrs Duncan cast her son a dark look, "What are you thinkin', you fool? You know they can't stay!"

"I know that. But, if I'd said they couldn't stay, they'd have made off like a pair of scared rabbits! Can't have that. That girl saved James. Her sister — she's nursed him, day and night! Never left his side. And, Sir Marcus, he's always been fair with us. Lets us camp on his land — and doesn't mind if we poach a bit. Never given us any trouble." He stared at the two girls who were whispering to each other, "When they've gone to sleep, I'll go up to the Manor and speak with himself."

His mother scowled at him, "You be careful, my lad! They may turn on you and you'll never see your bairn again or your wife! They can't be trusted, none of them!"

"I know, I know. Give them plenty of food, they both look like they could do with fattening up. It'll help them sleep too. Best they are asleep — can't get into mischief then!"

"I'll give them a bit of cider with honey in it! That'll knock them out!"

Robert Duncan gave a short laugh but was in no mood for merriment. This was a serious and dangerous business, and he had no wish to bring the authorities down on his family. They had had enough trouble recently and were tired of constantly being on guard because of the relentless persecution. At least here they were left alone, as long as no one stepped out of line; as long as they did their work and obeyed the laws, all was well. It was always a brief respite from the dangers of their usual life on the road and now it seemed that even this rare place of safety was under threat.

He waited until the children had been fed and plied with diluted and sweetened cider and were put to bed in one of the tents and then he told the others his plans. There was some argument, as he'd known there would be. His family were not the most amenable folk even at the best of times. His uncle argued loudest and longest, saying belligerently that if they all ended up in gaol that it'd be his fault for being such a bleeding heart. Robert heard him out, letting him blow off steam until he'd calmed down a little and then he explained once more what he was going to do and saddled up one of the piebald ponies and rode away down the track as night was drawing in and bats swooped over his head.

* * *

As sun sank towards the horizon, Cuckoopen Manor was still alive with activity, the last few straggling searchers were coming in, tired and footsore, all with nothing to report. There had been one or two sightings of a likely young girl on the other side of the village, but it turned out to be the goose girl from East Mill Farm in the end. Everyone gathered once more in the hall and Sir Marcus thanked them and said they would have to rely upon the constable on the morrow, but if anyone was willing to give up another day, he'd pay well for their services. Most of the men agreed to come back in the morning to help again.

"There's a table laid out over there with drinks and some pasties, if anyone's hungry — or thirsty!" announced Sir Marcus and was pleased to see they were delighted to partake of this small reward for their sterling efforts. He glanced up, sensing that someone was trying to attract his attention and saw Robert Duncan, standing by the door of the hall, hat in hand and looking uncertain. He nodded to him and beckoned him in. As the young man made his way through the throng, there were a few remarks and pointed glances, but they all knew better than to make a fuss under the haughty scrutiny of the lord of the manor.

He approached Sir Marcus and stood awkwardly before him, chewing his cheek.

"Robert, what can I do for you? Did you join the search parties?"

Robert Duncan shook his head, "No, Sir, we didn't hear about Miss Imogen until just now. We're a bit out of the way up in the woods."

"Of course. So, how can I help? It's not your little boy, I hope?"

"No, he's fine. It's — it's just that I have something to tell you and I — I'm not sure — " he faltered and looked about him at the other men, milling about.

Sir Marcus nodded and with a jerk of his head he led Robert Duncan across the hall and into his study, closing the door behind him.

"Now, is that better? Please take a seat and tell me what's on your mind."

Mr Duncan said he'd rather stand and so Sir Marcus leant against the edge of his desk and waited patiently.

The tinker cleared this throat, "It's hard to know exactly how to tell you this but — I have your daughter!" declared Robert Duncan all in a rush. He saw the look on Sir Marcus's face and held out a staying hand, "Oh, no Sir! I do not mean — I meant to say that she is at our camp, in the woods! She and Miss Pennington came this evening — looking for sanctuary."

"Sanctuary! What the hell do you mean by that?"

"Miss Imogen is apparently running away from her mother and Miss Pennington is aiding her. I didn't know what to do for the best but thought it best not to scare them away so I told them they could stay the night. Ma's looking after them." He shrugged nervously, "They've been fed and are safely asleep in Ma's bender at the moment. They'll come to no harm there."

"Of that I am confident," said Sir Marcus quietly, whilst pondering the larger problem. "Wait here one moment, Robert. I must inform the men that she's been found," and he went out into the hall and Robert Duncan heard him addressing those men still lingering there.

He then returned and went straight to the tinker and warmly shook him by the hand, "I cannot thank you enough for taking my daughter in. I realise that it must have caused considerable concern, but I will make absolutely sure that there will be no consequences from this. I think that it would be unfair to wake them now, so I'll collect them in the morning, if that is suitable?"

"Perfectly, Sir. They looked to be enjoying their adventure!"

"Were they indeed! I shall be giving them a good deal to think about in the coming weeks that they certainly will *not* enjoy!"

He stopped and looked up as the door was violently flung open and Beecher appeared looking greatly alarmed, his face ashen.

"Sir Marcus! You'd better come quick!" he gasped, "The school — it's on fire!"

Nineteen

The eerie glow was visible above the trees. A strange shimmering golden light, as though the sun were setting in the south.

Sir Marcus checked on the steps for the briefest moment, taking in the disturbing sight and then he turned to Beecher, "Gather all the men still here and send them to the school — get the carriages sent down at once and plenty of buckets and blankets. Charles! Jonathan! You're with me!"

And he ran down the steps to where some of the searchers had left their horses and he and his brother and cousin mounted up the borrowed steeds with all haste and galloped away into the darkness, shadowed by Robert Duncan on his piebald pony. They were followed by some of the others on horse and some on foot. Beecher went away to organise things and a deadly hush fell upon the suddenly deserted house.

When they arrived at the school it was as though they had arrived at the Gates of Hell, and they were all stunned by the noise the fire was making and the shocking sight of at least half the building being already alight.

Sir Marcus barked orders and handed his horse to a youth who was standing by the gate looking afraid, "You're in charge of them, take any that come, away from the fire — into the lane!" The boy did as he was told.

Charles, shouting above the roaring sound, demanded instructions and was told quite sternly by his elder brother not to do anything rash. Sir Marcus had spotted Mr Sippence and a stable lad carrying buckets around the end of the house that was still unaffected by the flames. He sprinted to them and taking a bucket, doused himself liberally with water and Jonathan and Charles immediately did the same.

He issued orders over his shoulder and dashed back to the front door.

"The girls are at the back of the building. In two dormitories. I shall go to the baby first. If you can, dampen their clothes. Leave the old ladies to me. Go! And for God's sake, stay safe!"

The front hall was filled with smoke but as yet no fire. The three men raced up the stairs and set off to search for survivors. It was dark and as they made their way further into the house, the smoke became like a physical barrier. Sir Marcus tied his dampened neckcloth about his mouth and nose and leaving his companions to do the same he edged his way along the corridor towards the sickroom where he knew he'd find little James Duncan.

The smoke was disorientating and so thick in places that he had to go by feel rather than sight. The place was partly lit by the conflagration, which had just taken hold of the roof and he had to be grateful for that because as he came to each casement, he was, at least, able to see where he was.

After what seemed an age, he came to the sickroom and cautiously opened the door. The room was clear of smoke but also empty. He quickly searched but there was no sign of the child or any nursemaid.

Without pause, he made his way back along the corridor and up the short flight of stairs to the next floor where the smoke was even denser and there were already signs of flames eagerly flickering at the gaps in the doors and here and there the curtains were aflame. He had heard Augusta say that her aunts slept on this side of the house.

The fire was pounding in the walls, as though it were some kind of monstrous beast and as he reached the first door, there was a deafening crashing sound and from somewhere, a high-pitched scream.

He pushed the door open and found the bedchamber filling with smoke. Someone was coughing and a dog was whining pitifully.

"Anyone here?"

A movement by the curtained fourposter bed.

"Marcus!"

A ghostly face appeared between the drapes.

"Augusta!" he breathed, having not dared even to hope, "Are you hurt?" He pulled back the curtains to reveal some kind of miraculous Ark.

There were both the Misses Beauchamp, Mrs Garth and Flora, holding the vile dog, and Augusta clutching the baby to her bosom.

"Good God!" he said.

"I *know!* I couldn't move Aunt Euphemia by myself, so I thought it best if we were all here in one place, I threw water on the curtains," she explained, her voice faint with terror.

"Good girl."

"I knew you'd come," she said.

He gave her a searching look, but continued, "Let's get everyone out of here then. If you wrap the baby in a damp cloth — and Flora? You can take that damned dog. Mrs Garth you can lead Miss Ida and I shall carry Miss Euphemia."

"Marcus, I could not find Dora!"

"She is perfectly safe — you need have no fears for her."

He helped them get out of the bed and wrap themselves in petticoats dampened with water from the basin on the sideboard. Bonny was shaking and whimpering, and Flora held her tightly, while Augusta carried little James wrapped in a moist shawl. Mrs Garth, a determined and powerfully built female, took charge of Aunt Ida, Marcus gently scooped up Miss Euphemia, who squealed in fright and clung to his neck, and they all gathered by the door.

Marcus warned them, "Do not stop for anything! If we come across fire, it's best to go straight through if you can. You must keep moving. Stay close to me. If you get separated, call out!"

And with that he pulled open the door and they filed out into a corridor blanketed in thick woolly smoke and were all soon choking even through their makeshift masks. They reached the first landing, where the fire had greedily established itself, one wall entirely consumed by flames, and Marcus glanced back at his little troop and, catching Augusta's eye, tried to give her strength through the suffocating smoke. She nodded at him over the baby's head, and he hitched up his frail burden and pressed on down the stairs to the next landing.

Augusta, at that point, felt she would willingly have followed him into Hades if he'd asked and told the baby in her arms that they were in safe hands.

The heat was almost more than she could bear. It scorched her face and she felt it was sure to blister. She put every bit of herself she could between the flames and the baby. She then put all her faith in God and Marcus and keeping her head down she followed him into the fire.

She could hear Flora telling Bonny to stop struggling in exasperated tones and Mrs Garth encouraging Miss Ida to keep going and knew her aunt would be rolling her eyes.

She could hear the growling and thumping coming from the walls of the doomed house.

And she could hear herself promising that if they all got out of this alive that she'd tell Marcus how she felt about him and hang the consequences.

As they came to the main staircase, they met some shadowy figures coming down from the other direction, accompanied by the sound of sobbing.

"Jonathan! Is everyone all right?"

A smoke-streaked face emerged from the infernal red glow of the corridor, he was carrying Mabel Latimer and Charles had a weeping Fidelia Hill in his arms and behind them came Robert Duncan with Patience Farryer. The others were holding hands and being marched along.

"All here! A few slight burns and a little understandable hysteria, but otherwise all fine."

"Good, then get them all downstairs before the roof comes down!"

As Jonathan awaited his turn to file downstairs, he caught sight of Flora and she cast a disparaging look at the dog in her arms and then made a face at Jonathan and he found himself laughing in the midst of a burning house. Flora went first with Jonathan not far behind while, ahead of them, all the girls were soon safely out.

Marcus told Augusta to follow him down and set off carrying Miss Euphemia; Augusta tucked the baby under her chin and went after him, with Mrs Garth and Aunt Ida and Flora on her heels.

Robert Duncan, having handed Patience over to a lady from the village, met Augusta in the hall and held out his arms for his son and Augusta thankfully handed the child to him. As soon as she did, her legs crumpled underneath her and she had to hold onto the wall to remain upright. She found her way out into the garden and went immediately to usher the girls away from the house and to check on their wellbeing. She heard Jonathan and Charles urging them into the waiting carriages and handing out blankets to keep them warm. She saw Mr Duncan cradling his son and watched as a line of men scooped water from the pond into their buckets and threw it hopelessly at the fire.

She watched their school burning, the fierce light illumined the garden and the despairing upturned faces of those watching. Each explosive noise coming from the building made her jump, every groan of breaking timbers and crack of glass made her want to cry, but she was numb and unable to do anything other than stare blankly.

The carriages rumbled away with their precious cargo, and she saw Aunt Ida being helped into the penultimate one and sighed in relief.

Jennet was helping poor old Mr Sippence away, her muscular arm holding him up.

Eventually the men stopped filling the buckets, realising that it was futile and stood in respectful silence before the devastated building, dark shadows against the rippling orange inferno.

A kind of mournful air fell upon those watching as bit by bit the house collapsed in on itself.

Augusta thought she should probably get into the last carriage but couldn't seem to tear herself away.

Jonathan Frost had taken it upon himself to see Flora and Bonny into their vehicle and it might have been noted by some keen observers, had anyone not been so preoccupied with the fire, that his hand lingered a little too long on hers.

Looking around those still there, Augusta suddenly thought that she hadn't seen Hannah amongst the crowd of helpers. Frowning, she searched for the maid's face and not finding any sign of her, she went to find the young stable lad she'd seen earlier helping with the buckets. She found him standing with some villagers, their faces glowing red from the fire.

"Has anyone seen Hannah Tully?"

They all apologised and shook their heads and the stable lad shrugged. She surveyed the straggle of people and realised Hannah wasn't there.

She immediately looked around for Marcus.

And not finding his beloved face, she began to panic in earnest.

Had he noticed that Hannah was missing and gone back into the building unnoticed?

Had he become trapped by smoke and flames or had a burning beam fallen upon him?

Augusta didn't stop to think.

She picked up her skirts and flew towards the house, scrambled up the steps and plunged through the front door.

A terrifying sight greeted her, the hall was barely recognisable, the stairs had partly collapsed, and the heat was a physical blow. She felt confused and frightened but knew only one thing for certain, that if Marcus were to die, that she would not want to live.

She was sure that he would have gone to the servant's quarters to find Hannah, so she pressed herself against the wall and edged her way past what was left of the staircase. The wall was hot to the touch, and she was finding it hard to breathe, coughing and wheezing like a pair of broken bellows. Glancing up through the swirling smoke, she saw the roof ablaze, the night sky visible between the rafters but she resolutely continued through the showers of gilded sparks, which she frantically brushed from her hair and batted away from her clothes.

"Please God — please don't let him die! If you let him live, I promise that I will stop loving him! I swear I'll never think of him again! Just do this one thing for me!"

Augusta reached the kitchen door and as she pushed through it, the warping wood making it hard to move, there was a stupefyingly loud crash behind her, as the first-floor landing and the top half of the staircase exploded and descended to the ground floor in a thundering eruption.

Once in the corridor that led to the kitchen she stopped and looked into the servant's hall but there was only smoke and an ominous pounding noise from the wall that backed onto the stairs. There was no one there. The place was empty.

Where was Marcus? Had he found Hannah and left by the stable yard door?

Augusta, realising her folly, decided to try to escape through the kitchen and the scullery.

When she found that the heavily beamed ceiling in the kitchen was ablaze, she changed her mind and thought she'd better see if she could escape through a window in the buttery.

The buttery, with its cold tiled floor and marble shelves was an oasis of calm in the collapsing house but Augusta didn't pause to take a breath, she raced to the window and tried to open it. But it wouldn't budge. She beat on it with her fists until she realised that she needed something to break it and began, by the light of the fire filtering faintly through the dusty panes, to look for an implement to smash the glass.

She heard another crashing sound and thought it was probably the kitchen ceiling coming down. She had no choice but to escape through the window now. Feeling along the shelves, her feverish hands came upon something metal, and she grabbed the milk ladle and returned to the window and smashed it into the leaded glass panes. They bent but didn't break. She tried again and again.

The blood was rushing in her ears, and she was breathless and coughing with the effort of wielding her weapon. Smoke was sneaking under the door. She was starting to feel lightheaded, and her legs gave way under her and she slid down onto the floor in a heap.

She didn't have the energy to call out or even weep at her own stupidity. She could only hope that Marcus was all right and that Hannah had somehow escaped.

Augusta closed her eyes and decided that she felt quite sleepy.

The fire must have reached the door to the corridor; she could hear it pounding on the wooden panels. It sounded like an angry bear.

She wondered idly how the fire had started and hoped no one had been seriously hurt.

Her head dipped and her chin rested on her chest.

There was a blast of hot air and a voice in her dream said, "Oh, no you don't, you damned fool!"

And she felt herself being lifted and that was the last thing she remembered.

* * *

Augusta struggled to open her sore eyes and coughed feebly. Her chest hurt and she had a headache. She was being manhandled into a carriage. She could smell smoke and for a moment wondered why.

On suddenly recalling what had happened she tried to sit up but the arms that held her tightened and she gave up her weak endeavours and collapsed back again.

She coughed and groaned softly.

"It serves you right," said a familiar voice in chilling accents.

She managed to hold her eyelids open long enough to focus on the face above her, "Oh, it's you," she whispered, "I thought — I thought — "

"Stop talking. It doesn't matter what you thought. I'm taking you back to the Manor. Everyone else has been taken there for now. There's plenty of room to accommodate them, so they will all have somewhere to sleep at least. No, don't *say* anything! The smoke and heat — it can be very damaging, and you just need to rest. Here, have a sip of this," and he held a cup to her lips, and she drank the cold water thankfully. He wiped her chin with his fingers and handed the cup to someone just behind him. "Let me just get her settled and then we can go."

He adjusted himself on the seat and she realised that she was lying in his arms, like a limp rag doll and again tried to free herself.

"For the love of God, will you stop that! Just keep still and do as you're damn well told, just this once! It's not for long."

She mumbled something inaudible, and Sir Marcus stared down at her in the dim light from the still-burning school.

"Dr Inwood has gone up to the house to check on everyone. The baby was miraculously uninjured and seems mostly unaffected. Everyone is having a little trouble breathing but I am hopeful that will subside, given time and plenty of fresh air. Your aunts are doing well, and all the girls escaped without being hurt. Jonathan has a few minor burns and Charles had a tussle with a burning door and suffered some blistering, but they are otherwise quite well."

"Hannah?"

"Robert Duncan got all the servants, including Hannah, to safety through the back door before he came to help us in the main house. He has a badly burnt hand. Mr Sippence is a little overcome by the trauma but has been taken to the Inwood's cottage hospital," he frowned at her, "The school, I'm afraid, is beyond saving. I'm so sorry."

Augusta was sad about the school but found that in the end it was people who mattered, not stone and mortar. The house was nothing in comparison to her sisters and aunts and the girls and baby being safe.

And this man.

He was safe. But he was angry as well; she could feel it between them like an impenetrable barrier.

"You are not — hurt?"

He shook his head, "No, apart from some bruising and a slight gash from the glass panes — I am perfectly well. With Robert's assistance we escaped through the window in the buttery."

His voice was so constrained that Augusta began to truly despair. "I'm sorry — " she faltered.

"Don't! There's no need — you must have been momentarily out of your mind because of the stress. Otherwise, I cannot think why you should — "

Augusta closed her eyes wearily and debated.

"You could have been killed," said Marcus dispassionately.

"I didn't think — "

"That was obvious. Such a reckless thing to do — I could not believe it when I heard from one of the men — "

"I thought — "

"I don't care what you thought! You acted selfishly and someone could have been hurt — *you* could have been hurt."

His rage was so icily controlled that it was somehow worse than full-blown fury.

Her chest constricted and it made her cough, her eyes watered and then she found they wouldn't stop streaming, "I thought you'd gone — back in — to find Hannah," she whispered.

He stiffened, "You thought I — what are you *saying?* You went in because you thought *I* was in there!" His face was blank with shock, "Are you completely deranged? Why in God's name would you do anything so stupid?" He gave her a shake as though unable to stop himself, "Stop crying! Hell and damnation! Will you just stop?"

Augusta sniffed the tears back and turned her face away into his chest as there was nowhere else to hide.

"Augusta! Are you trying to tell me that you went into that burning building to find *me?*"

She nodded into his shirt, which was stiff with soot, and gave herself up to childish sobbing. She could hear him swearing and grinding his teeth but could not stop the deluge of tears that overwhelmed her, and it was all she could do not to howl like a baby.

Despite her agonising despair she felt his arms wrap around her as though trying to prevent her shattering into tiny pieces.

She cried and coughed, and her body shook with horror, as she suddenly understood just what she'd done — how idiotic she'd been. She'd been blinded by panic and had allowed it to guide her actions and in so doing could have endangered others. In fact, it was *because* of her that Marcus had been put in more jeopardy!

She began to cry even harder and Marcus, listening to the storm of sobbing, began to worry. She sounded as though she were close to having some kind of seizure.

He took her by the shoulders and gently shook her again, but it didn't arrest the weeping. He pulled her to him and held her tightly against his chest trying to still the trembling and hysterical keening.

He wished Dr Inwood were there so that he could give her a sleeping draught.

"Augusta, you must stop this! You're going to make yourself ill!"

Through the hiccupping wailing she whimpered, "I *thought* you were dead!"

"Well, I'm not. But — why should that have made you act so foolishly? You could have asked the men to help!"

"I wasn't — *thinking!* I realised that — that if you perished — that I would have to die too! I — I couldn't live — "

"Augusta. *Augusta!* Oh, for God's sake! You're making no sense," said Sir Marcus grimly.

"I *am!*" snapped Augusta, determined to get her point across, "I've known — for a while now — you see?"

"No, I don't," replied Marcus, just grateful that she seemed to be calming down a little even if she was now rambling incoherently.

Augusta made an impatient growling sound, "When you told me about — your father — I wanted to save you!"

"I don't need saving."

"The little boy in you — I wanted to save him — when you were a little boy!" She reached out a hand to him but let it fall, "It broke my heart — " she whispered.

Marcus was silent as he looked down into her face, which was soot-stained, with pale rivers of tears trailing down her cheeks. She was clearly suffering from shock, and he knew he must tread warily. If she wasn't in her right mind there was no telling what she might do.

"Marcus," said Augusta, quite clearly, "You said to me — in the woods — that day — when you were so cross with me — you said — "

"Yes? *What* did I say, Miss Pennington?"

She wriggled in his arms, trying to see his face, "You said — that I would have to beg — if you were to ever touch me again."

"You were very averse to being — er, mauled again, I seem to recall."

There was a muffled response and then a moment's silence.

"I would like to — inform you, Sir Marcus, that I have changed my mind."

"Changed your mind about being *mauled!*"

She gave a watery chuckle, "Well, as I have very little experience of being so ill-used, apart from with you, I am not able to say for certain — however, you did say that I would have to beg — if I wanted you — to touch me again."

In the dark of the carriage, it was hard to see his expression but when he spoke his voice held a smile, "Are you begging me, Miss Pennington?"

Augusta sniffed in an unladylike fashion, "I am, Sir Marcus, very politely, *begging* you."

"Let me get this straight, before I risk being slapped for misconduct! You want me to — touch you again?"

Augusta sighed, "You are depressingly slow-witted! Yes, please, I would like that very much although I am perfectly aware that it is not at all seemly."

"I am beginning to suspect that I may have misjudged you, Augusta. Perhaps you are not the little prude I had suspected you to be, after all."

"Oh, no, I *am!* I am such a dreadful old maid, but it seems that you bring out the worst in me!"

He laughed softly, "Or the best."

She would tell Flora much later, that it was the laugh that did it.

Augusta reached up and putting a trembling hand behind his neck, she pulled his head down to hers and with her heart and stomach doing over-excited somersaults, she kissed him on the mouth.

And that's all it took.

Something broke inside him and in that moment, he completely forgot himself and all that he had promised, and he kissed her back with such vehemence that it even startled him.

He felt her soften and melt into his embrace and knew that if he wanted to he could, in that moment of ardour and euphoria, have easily reverted to his old ways. He could feel her capitulation, her complete giving of herself to him and he knew that he could take her if he wanted to. And by God, he wanted to. She had been pestering his peace of mind for weeks and in some way, he wanted to punish her for that. And after the evening's traumatic events, he knew that if he pushed her weakened defences, she would surrender.

Her lips were cool under his and she opened them willingly, eager to learn and he was more than happy to be the one to teach her. His fingers stroked the swell of her breasts, as with her position and the compression of her stays, they were overflowing, and he buried his head into their enticing softness and a stifled groan escaped him.

"No," he managed to say, his lips to the silvery whiteness of her skin.

She pressed her mouth harder against his to silence him and allowed her fingers to stray down his torso to his waist, where her searching touch found bare skin beneath the much-soiled shirt. He felt her sudden intake of breath and couldn't help smiling into her mouth, her innocence was showing.

"No," he said again, with a little more conviction.

She arched her body against his and he quickly pulled away, knowing that, if he didn't, he would bitterly regret it.

"Augusta, I can't — will not — you don't know what you're doing!"

"Oh, yes I do," came the husky reply and that very nearly broke his resolve.

He put his hands around her waist and lifted her way from him onto the seat. "Stay *there*," he commanded, somewhat shakily. "Do not look at me or move towards me! Keep away, you witch!"

She giggled and even in the flickering gloom, he could see her pouting.

"But Marcus, we had only just begun — "

"And that's where we end — before you corrupt me completely!"

Her delicious little laugh, rough with smoke from the fire, made him drag her to him again and forcefully cover her mouth with his. She gasped a delighted protest and wrapped her arms about his neck, which just as quickly he reached up and firmly removed. Then, before he could change his mind, he thumped a fist on the side of the carriage and shouted to the coach driver, who, being thoroughly fed up after waiting so long for the signal and listening to the suggestively murmured conversation inside his coach, whipped the horses a little too eagerly, so that the vehicle lurched suddenly, causing Augusta to almost slide from her seat. Sir Marcus prevented her from landing on the floor in a graceless heap, by holding her back against the squabs, but when he saw the shamelessly provocative look she gave him, he swore under his breath and put her firmly away from him and removed himself to the furthest reaches of the coach.

"No, Miss Pennington. I must insist that you stay in that corner until we reach the Manor."

"Oh," said Augusta much disappointed, "Why? Do you not like me?"

He laughed a little dryly at that, "I think the problem is that I find I like you too much. One of us has to be sensible and as you have clearly lost all sense of propriety — it must be me — although, I must tell you that it very much goes against the grain."

"Well, if you don't mind me saying, it seems a trifle high-handed of you to make that decision without consulting me."

"You are far too young to know what you're about and besides, you are suffering from the trauma of what has just occurred — such a catastrophe is bound to affect your reasoning — and I cannot take advantage of that."

"Even if I *beg* you?"

"Good God, Augusta! Do not tempt me! I'm only human!"

Augusta lapsed into silence.

"Do not fall into a fit of the sullens! I cannot in all good conscience allow you to throw away your hard-earned reputation just because you are feeling momentarily imprudent. It would be unfair in me and hardly the behaviour of a gentleman."

"I am not feeling imprudent. I am feeling — curious."

"I think it was Saint Augustine who said that 'God fashioned Hell for the inquisitive.'"

Augusta shuffled along the seat towards him, "When you came to rescue us — I thought that I would *gladly* follow you into Hell."

"You were just suffering from an excess of fear and gratitude — a lethal combination. But if you add into that your youth and inexperience, it makes for a disastrous."

"I would have thought, Sir, knowing how I have suffered today, that you might take pity upon me!"

"I am. I am saving you from inevitable ignominy. One day you'll thank me. I, on the other hand shall have a hard time understanding how I could, without warning, suddenly become so damned chivalrous. It beggars belief and will do *my* hard-earned reputation no end of harm!"

"Oh, very funny!"

Twenty

Even though it was nearly midnight by the time the carriage was trundling between the tall dark hedges that bordered the drive, they could see the myriad lights of the Manor; it seemed that, expecting an inundation, Beecher had surpassed himself and there were lanterns everywhere guiding the refugees to safety.

As they approached the front of the house, neither occupant of the carriage said anything. The silence was charged with repressed emotions and important things left unspoken.

Augusta was smarting from the perceived rejection, thinking that if a man who was supposedly as unprincipled as Marcus could not bring himself to be tempted by her, then there really was no hope at all. She was destined for a lonely spinsterhood. Not, she reminded herself furiously, that she'd been angling for anything other than a moment to be closer to him — certainly not anything more permanent. She completely understood that they were worlds apart. She had merely hoped to have something to remember him by. With the school destroyed and no means to rebuild it, she was already trying to make some kind of plan to keep her family safe and secure. The idea was daunting, with so many souls to provide for and all the responsibility resting on her shoulders. In the wake of the fire and its drama, she had, for a briefly glorious moment, thought of ignoring all her inhibitions and prudish notions and behaving in a manner so far removed from her usual restrained conduct that her reputation would be forever compromised. In all the stress of the disaster and the panic of thinking Marcus might be dead, she had fleetingly lost her mind. That was her only excuse. But Marcus had put a stop to her longings in a ruthless fashion and she had to admit that it had hurt her. She had never openly revealed her feelings to anyone before and to have them so summarily dismissed was humiliating. Of course, she knew that he was right to put her in her place, but that somehow made it even worse. She felt like a small child who'd been reprimanded.

The carriage drew to a standstill and the coach driver jumped down and went to the horses and a footman opened the door and let down the steps.

Sir Marcus handed Augusta out onto the drive and still holding her hand, led her up the steps. Beecher, looking more harassed than Marcus had ever seen him, greeted them in a voice that suggested that his resignation was imminent.

"Beecher! Has it been purgatory for you? You look utterly wretched. I can only apologise but there was nothing else to be done. Give me one minute while I hand Miss Pennington over to Hannah, whom I see is just coming and then I shall be happy to consult with you in the study."

Beecher bowed, unable to form words to express just how he had suffered in the last few hours.

Sir Marcus beckoned to Hannah and was not in the least surprised when Augusta embraced the maid with obvious relief, although Hannah looked a little startled.

"Hannah! I thought you'd been caught in the fire! I am so glad to see you safe and sound. How dreadful it's been! Is everyone all right? Cook? Jennet?"

Hannah, always a steadfast girl, gave her mistress a brisk squeeze and then led her away, telling her in subdued tones about what had happened to her and the rest of the staff.

Marcus watched them go and for a moment wanted to call out after Augusta but bit back the words, knowing they would only complicate matters. He clenched his jaw and thought about the lucky escape they'd had. He gave himself a shake — he didn't have time to think about it now, there were many things to organise and Beecher to mollify. His regrets would have to wait.

* * *

Hannah, immediately on arriving at the Manor, had busied herself helping to prepare the bedchambers. She had fretted about the fact that no one had managed to salvage anything from the fire and what on earth they would do without their possessions. Miss Euphemia had been particularly forthcoming about what she had lost. Miss Ida had tried to soothe her, but her sister had been so grievously disturbed by what she had been forced to endure that her fragile mind seemed to have frayed a little more at the edges.

Lady Denby and Lady Birch were politely asked to give up some items for the survivors of the fire, which they did most reluctantly, picking out their least favourite things to donate to the cause. A petticoat with a small tear, a shawl with a tangled fringe and a nightcap with a large and unbecoming frill.

Mrs Inwood had on hearing the news, as always, leapt into action and had provided all kinds of clothing gathered from ladies in the village, and a constant stream of sleepy servants arrived with bundles and baskets of useful and undamaged garments as well as combs and brushes, ribands and handkerchiefs, underclothes and gowns. It brought a tear to Flora's eye as she unpacked and distributed the things to the girls and her aunts.

Dr Inwood was still there dosing the hysterical and dressing wounds with salves. He was as pragmatic as ever and only had any real concerns for Miss Euphemia's state of mind and a bad burn on Robert Duncan's hand. There was some singed hair, which had caused some consternation in Miss Fidelia Hill because she declared that she would never get a husband with frizzled hair! Dr Inwood had calmly reminded her that by the time that she was old enough to wed, her hair would have grown out. She stopped wailing and was further appeased when Flora said that if she used a concoction of eggs, castor oil and eau de cologne it would have a miraculous effect on her damaged hair. She was then reminded, rather tersely, by Flora, who had had enough adventure and weeping to last a lifetime, that both Mr Denby and Mr Frost had been burned in the rescue attempt and would be very sore for a long time and that Mr Duncan was, at that very moment, having a serious burn bandaged by Dr Inwood!

The Manor staff were at their wits' end and were to be seen everywhere scurrying about carrying piles of bedlinen, pitchers of hot water and cups of tea. Mrs Garth was being an absolute Trojan and had not only taken on the care of little James Duncan but had in her spare moments made an effort to calm Miss Euphemia and had thought to take Bonny and Quince for a quick walk and had chatted cheerily to the girls who were at that moment looking as though they might never manage to get to sleep that night, so very excited and upset were they.

Miss Ida had immediately found a desk and been provided with paper and ink and despite the chaos around her had penned letters to all the parents and hoped that Sir Marcus wouldn't mind having to deal with so many missives on the following morning when he would already have so much to contend with.

Miss Ida had not much enjoyed the catastrophe itself, but the aftermath was proving to be vastly entertaining. There was so much to occupy her, she hardly knew which way to turn. She had heard from someone who had been a witness that her niece had rushed back into the house and had been valiantly rescued by Sir Marcus. She noted with some satisfaction that they had still not returned to the Manor! She was optimistic that there might now be a satisfactory conclusion, killing two birds with one stone — she had seen how they looked at each other — if only they would just talk to each other! She had also been happily watching Flora blossoming before her eyes and Mr Frost clearly enjoying her unexpected renaissance, a warm expression upon his pleasant young face. There was one good thing in all of this, that Dora and Miss Imogen had not been in the school at the time of the fire; it was one less worry, although where they were at that moment, was another matter entirely. Mr Duncan had intimated that he knew where they could be found, and Sir Marcus had quite clearly told Augusta that they were safe. It was all very intriguing.

And there, at last, was Augusta herself! Streaked with soot, her hair wildly unpinned and falling about her shoulders as though she'd been living under a hedge for a fortnight and the expression in her eyes, hard to read. Miss Ida Beauchamp was both disappointed and anxious about her niece. She could see the pale streaks left in the sooty smudges on her cheeks and knew that tears had been shed, which, in the circumstances, was hardly surprising, but it was the look in her eyes that was disturbing. Augusta had always been a safe harbour in a storm for her family and although she was averse to every kind of altercation, finding them too hard to bear after coping with her father's uncontrollable rages, she would do anything to protect those she loved, they had all come to rely upon her. Ida Beauchamp frowned uneasily and after a murmured word to Flora, who was also regarding her sister with a speculative eye, she went to help Hannah guide Augusta to her allotted bedchamber.

By this time Augusta was able to do little more than stare blankly at the commotion around her from reddened eyes. Her mind seemed to have gone to sleep. It was as though the calamity of their school burning to the ground, the dreadful fear that she might have lost Marcus and the ensuing humiliation in the carriage had driven her brain into a dormant state. No coherent thought passed through it. No light illumined it. There was only a persistent grey fog that seemed determined to deaden any reasoning.

Flora had somehow managed to get all the girls into their beds and a truckle bed had been found for Hannah, who had bravely volunteered to watch over them for the night. The redoubtable housekeeper, Mrs Primrose, seemed to be everywhere at once, organising and cajoling, finding suitable night attire and providing warm milk and honey to calm their nerves and hot bricks for those who were still in shock, to stop them from shivering. She had a kind word for everyone and seemed to know just what needed to be done and arranged it with the least disturbance to all concerned.

After the girls were at last sleeping, the baby was safely in Mrs Garth's care and sound asleep despite the upheaval, and Miss Euphemia, finally running out of irrational complaints, had settled back against her pillows and was singing a nonsensical song to herself, Flora had a moment to go and see Augusta and was not reassured by what she found.

* * *

Sir Marcus Denby heard Beecher out and sympathised, praised his heroic efforts and made some helpful suggestions. He told his butler that, without him at the helm, Cuckoopen Manor would have sunk beneath the waves a long time ago. Beecher couldn't help but agree after the evening he'd had.

Beecher left the study feeling much revived. His employer had been understanding and had listened with interest and concern. It had been a very rewarding interview and Beecher trod away to the kitchen with a lighter step.

If he could have seen his employer at that precise moment, he might not have been quite so pleased with himself.

Sir Marcus was sitting with his head in his hands, shoulders hunched and feeling as though he'd been wrung out like a dishrag. He hadn't yet had time to wash the soot away and knew he reeked. His head was filled with the destruction of the school, the roaring sounds from the fire, the smell of the smoke and the wholly unaccustomed sense of panic he had felt when he realised that Augusta had gone back into the burning house.

Until that moment he had thought himself immune to strong feelings of any kind. He had learned during his early years to control emotion, to never show weakness and never, on any account, to love anything or anyone, in case that might be used as a weapon against him. His father had taught him well. The time he had spent learning how to be someone Sir Leopold Denby could admire had, he thought, erased any remnant of the boy he had once been. Even his own mother would not have recognised him. He had become used to being inured to pain and had, from an early age, tried to regard the suffering of others without a care. He had found that it suited him to be impervious to sentiment and protected from harm. In those days he had no great desire to feel anything apart from pleasure and had thought that was how he would end his days. Everything was on course for a life of self-indulgence.

Then, somehow a puritanical woman had managed to slip under his carefully erected barricades and worm her way into his once secure fortress. She had opened him up to suffering again and he was not the least bit happy about it.

In the carriage, he had been sorely tempted; it would have been so easy just to give in to his baser instincts and then forget about her. He had done it so many times. He had never suffered from remorse. Until now.

He knew that by refusing Augusta's tentative advances he had hurt her and because she was young and inexperienced, she would take his rejection badly. He shook his head, there was nothing he could do. He could not possibly have allowed himself to take such a detrimental step and be the cause of her ruin. He had already ruined too many and had at the time been careless of the consternation and damage he had occasioned. It had brought him no pleasure, but he now realised it had left behind scars that until now he had been able to ignore.

He must have groaned out loud because Quince, who had been sound asleep after a trying day, slowly sat up and looked at him enquiringly. It was very late, and the house had been filled to the rafters with noise and commotion and he'd found it disturbing. A stranger had taken him out for a walk in the garden along with another small beast that he hadn't taken to at all and his beloved master now seemed very much out of sorts. He cocked his head and stared at that gentleman hoping that they would soon be on their way to bed.

His master however had other ideas and left without exchanging a word with his faithful hound.

Sir Marcus patrolled the house and grounds to make sure that everything was in order and stood for a while at the highest point and observed the diminishing glow in the sky, over where the school had once been. His thoughts naturally returned to earlier in the evening and his first sight of a seemingly lifeless Augusta in the buttery and the agonising moment when he'd thought he was too late — that was something he was desperately keen to forget. He'd made his way through the collapsing house, searching through every room he could and finding no signs of life, had begun to despair of finding her but then the sound of the metal ladle beating on the window had penetrated his hopelessness and coming upon the buttery had found the door to be warping and stuck fast. It had taken all his considerable strength to batter it down to reach her. Never in his entire life had he been so determined or, he was now forced to admit, so anguished. He knew that moment, when he had seen her unconscious on the floor, would haunt him all his days.

He took a last look around the grounds and saw the footmen bringing in the last of the lanterns and turned on his heel and went in.

Beecher was coming out of the servant's quarters when he saw his master come in and his previous good mood evaporated immediately. He knew that look and he always dreaded it and the inevitable consequences. For a brief moment he considered standing up to him and refusing to do his bidding. Why on earth did he insist on the brandy being locked away if he was just going to demand to have it released the minute he felt a little low? It didn't make any sense to a logical man such as he. Beecher for a moment imagined himself resisting Sir Marcus's terse orders but then he thought about being unemployed, without references. It wasn't much of a choice. The brandy bottle was removed from the locked cabinet and relinquished with nothing more than a disapproving sigh.

Sir Marcus said nothing, he just strode away to his study and slammed the door behind him.

Beecher wondered if he should call Mr Frost, who had retired to bed some while before but decided that even that persuasive young gentleman would not be able to dissuade Sir Marcus from dulling his senses, after all he'd been through. The butler retired gloomily to his bedchamber and sat on the edge of his bed contemplating one of the few downsides of receiving his magnificent salary and working for such a volatile employer. When he finally climbed into his bed and tried to sleep, he found he was keeping an ear out for the sound of the bell, or his name being bellowed thunderously through the house.

Unable to sleep, he lay in the dark and waited for the summons.

*   *   *

Flora had sat beside her sister's bed and wished she had a reliable mother to turn to, or someone who would be able to advise her what to do about Augusta.

Usually so full of life, her eyes sparkling with laughter, this shadow that lay in the bed staring at the canopy over her head, was unknown to Flora and scared her a little.

"Augusta? Gussie? You must try to sleep. Shall I send for some warm milk? Try closing your eyes and just thinking of something pleasant. All the girls are safely tucked up in their beds and the aunts are already sound asleep. And apparently, according to Mrs Primrose, who was just off to her bed, Sir Marcus is still shut in his study and will no doubt, as she said, make a night of it, as is his habit apparently. It's a little disappointing don't you think? I don't mind if a gentleman likes a glass of wine or even a brandy occasionally, but I would never have thought Sir Marcus was a drunkard, would you!"

She waited, hoping a mention of Sir Marcus might bestir her sister, but when there was no sign of her either waking or giving in to blissful sleep, Flora decided that she would stay with her and got changed into some borrowed nightclothes and slid into the bed beside Augusta, who still did not show any indication that she was aware of what was going on.

An hour or so later, Flora continued to sleep peacefully, as her elder sister pulled back the counterpane and swung her feet to the floor, and without hesitation, rose and crossed the room, making no sound and went out, closing the door quietly behind her.

She made her way down the corridor as though moving in her sleep, the bare boards cold beneath her feet but she wasn't aware of anything. Her eyes were glazed and her movements dreamlike.

An overlong nightgown trailed behind her as did her long chestnut hair, which Flora had brushed but not managed to subdue before she got her into bed. She looked like a ghost, pale and unearthly, drifting along the corridors and down the stairs to the hall, not even a board creaked as she floated through the house.

The moon had come up and its cold light was sneaking into all the rooms at the front of the building. It made long blue rectangles across the floors and caught on spiders' webs and illumined the corners where the dust had settled and been forgotten.

Augusta saw none of this.

She crossed the hall and without pausing entered the study, closing the door and turning the key.

The candles burned low, and the room was silent. As she went in, Quince raised his head and looked at her, his tail wagged rather feebly and then he let his bony head fall back onto his paws; the visitor was a favourite, but it didn't look promising for him, and anyway he was tired and needed his sleep.

The visitant made her way across the room and only stopped when she reached the sofa.

She looked down at the figure lying there and didn't see the overturned empty bottle, or the discarded neckcloth and top boots, thrown carelessly to the floor.

Marcus was lying on his back, one arm flung out over the edge of the sofa and still wearing his soiled once-white shirt; his chin was dark with soot and stubble and his hair had fallen across his face in loose strands. His eyes were closed, and his thin lips pressed tightly together as though his dreams were trying.

Augusta hitched her nightgown up and daintily stepped over the sleeping giant.

He didn't move but his breathing altered subtly.

She eased herself down in the narrow space between the back of the sofa and his long, still form, stretching out beside him, like a cat would, wriggling to make herself comfortable and then once settled, she slid one arm across his chest and hooked her left leg over his thigh.

His warmth seeped through her nightgown, and she nestled her head above his heart and felt the steady thump beneath her cheek. Then, with a shuddering sigh, she closed her eyes.

She awoke some time later. It was still dark and there was only one candle left burning. She sighed and moved her arm, which was cold and cramped from being in the same position for so long. She looked around and saw where she was.

For a moment Augusta fought for breath, a wild sense of panic rising up in her chest and threatening to overwhelm her. Her heart was fluttering like a trapped and frantic bird, and she opened her mouth to scream.

A firm, cool hand pressed softly to that mouth, prevented any sound from escaping and she swiftly swallowed the urge and blinked up at the face above her. It was seamed with fatigue, the hollows shadowed and still streaked with smoke. There was a strong smell of brandy and soot.

She reached up and removed his hand.

He stared down at her through the gloom.

Augusta stared right back.

He stroked her forehead with one long finger and traced an imaginary line to her eyebrows and then on down the long nose with its high bridge, his finger rounded the tip and slid down onto her upper lip, followed the contours of her mouth and ended up on her determined chin.

He gently pulled down her bottom lip and leaning over her, just rested his mouth on hers, their warmth mingling.

She felt his lips on her neck, leaving warm kisses under her ear. She found she could barely breathe. Her insides were beginning to behave in a very peculiar fashion, and she wasn't sure that it was beneficial to her health; she felt as though she were going to melt and explode and cry and laugh all at the same time. It was thoroughly baffling.

Augusta made a soft moaning sound, which startled her, and her eyes widened in shock. She wasn't inclined to make wanton noises as a rule, having never, even at the grand age of twenty-five, been kissed by anyone but Marcus and never having had the opportunity to be in such an intimate situation before.

As his mouth returned to hers, she felt his smile against her lips and she stiffened indignantly, but he altered his position so that she was pleasantly pinned beneath him, which immediately took her mind off the chagrin she'd felt and she looked up at him with sleepy interest.

With his mouth on hers, he whispered, "I'm still — a trifle disguised. I'm sorry, I must reek of smoke — and brandy."

"I don't mind at all," she replied candidly, her voice still husky from the smoke.

"I think you've been walking in your sleep."

She nodded, "I don't remember how I got here."

"I was partly awake as you arrived but was, in my defence, a little too castaway to send you back to your own bed."

"Oh? Earlier you were *very* keen to keep me at a distance."

His eyes gleamed, "Ah, but I hadn't seen you in such an alluring state of deshabille then! I have to say it is putting a great strain upon my self-control."

"I had not thought! I must look such a sight!"

"You look enchanting, if a little as though you have spent the night nefariously."

"Well, at least I have washed thoroughly whereas you still wear the remnants of the school upon you, Sir! And, as yet, we have done nothing — *nefarious!*"

"That can be promptly rectified ma'am," murmured Marcus into her hair.

"I would very much like that. Although, I'm afraid you will have to instruct me because I am untutored in this particular area."

"Oh, good God!" said Marcus, in a strangled voice.

"What is it? Have I said something I oughtn't?"

"Augusta!"

"But you have so much worldly experience! I have kissed only my aunts and my sisters!"

He laughed softly, "Is that so? And did they kiss you like this?" he asked with a touch of menace and demonstrated what he meant by pulling her roughly to him and shocking the breath out of her once more. When he had finished, he buried his head in her neck and stayed like that until she decided that he was wasting time. She began to wriggle under him in order to get more comfortable.

"For God's sake, stop that!"

She peeped up at him, "Stop what, Marcus?"

"Moving. Wriggling. Enticing. Seducing."

She chuckled, "Is that what I'm doing? I had thought I was merely trying to get a little closer to you!"

He emitted a sound somewhere between a groan and a laugh and Augusta felt a delightful surge of something like dominance and thought it to be rather intoxicating.

She had come to think of herself as lacking in the kind of appeal that, for instance, Flora had with her voluptuous figure and pretty face. Augusta felt she had been cursed with the Beauchamp nose and a solidly ordinary face. No man wanted solidly ordinary. Aunt Euphemia was fond of remarking upon her looks, saying "What a shame! It's no wonder you're not married. To have inherited Ida's ordinary features is most unfortunate. Still, at least you will always have an occupation as a teacher." It was so very damning, and she had learnt not to spend any length of time studying her face in the glass in order to prevent certain misery. She had concentrated on what she was good at and stopped longing to be someone she could never be.

Now, she was happily lying under this colossal man, and he seemed to be showing signs of being aroused by her. She wanted to laugh out loud. It was hardly believable. She had to admit that she was enjoying herself, having been terrified that she'd find any kind of intimacy humiliating. She thought of Cornelius and realised that she had been afraid that if she were to end up marrying him, neither of them would ever have been comfortable being close; she knew that he thought her below his precise standards and would never have allowed her to forget that he was being charitable in choosing her for his bride.

For some reason best known to him, Marcus was responding to her in a way that she had not imagined possible, and it was making her feel omnipotent. She felt in that moment that she was capable of anything.

He was leaning on one elbow and watching her.

"Tell me what you're thinking," he said softly.

"No," she replied, laughing.

He studied her face, "I think I can hazard a guess anyway. I can see it in your eyes. You have very revealing eyes, you know?"

"Oh, dear," said Augusta.

"When I first saw you, I dismissed you as a prim and proper schoolmistress. I was a fool. When we next met, in the lane, you were feeling a little faint, but not too faint to pull caps with me! What a temper you were in, lying there on the side of the lane, those beautiful golden eyes smouldering with rage! It was already too late for me then, had I but known it. However, it was on our outing to see the blossom, when you fell asleep like a hoydenish shepherdess in the meadow, hair tumbled and face flushed pink. Although I denied it to myself, I was a fair way to being lost right then and had we not had two annoying chaperones, I may well have brought more dishonour upon myself and given into some very ignoble desires."

"Oh, really?" enquired Augusta pertly, "What *kind* of desires precisely?"

"Miss Pennington, you are being deliberately provocative, and I must remind you that I am suffering from the effects of too much brandy. Be kind."

"But, Marcus, I only want to know what you would have done had we been alone? It's only natural curiosity!"

"Your curiosity will get you into a deal of trouble, young lady, if you're not careful."

She chuckled, "I find that I do not wish to be careful though. I have been careful all my life and look where it's got me!"

"Yes, I can see. In a compromising position beneath a known degenerate, wearing only a flimsy nightgown and with very little hope of rescue."

"That sounds most promising. I don't *want* to be rescued, thank you!" said Augusta, and deciding it was time to take control of the situation in some way, she reached for his hand, which to her delight, was slightly unsteady, and very deliberately slid it inside the neckline of her nightgown and pressed it against her breast. She gave a little shiver but still not satisfied, with her other hand she pulled his head down to hers, "Kiss me again," she commanded him.

"No sooner said than done, my lady," murmured Sir Marcus obeying her orders to the letter and Augusta wasn't able to say anything more for quite a while. When she was at last able to speak, she just said, "*Oh!*" in outraged tones.

"Not to your satisfaction, ma'am?"

"Oh, yes indeed! I was just thinking of all the time I've wasted being virtuous!"

He gave a crack of laughter, quickly stifled, "Hussy!" he breathed, then something seemed to occur to him, and he pulled away.

"Oh, no, what is it?"

"It just crossed my mind that if I had had the good fortune to meet you earlier — my life might have been very different."

"What an awful thing to say!"

"Good God, why?"

"Because now I feel as though I should have found *you* sooner. I feel that I've let you down!"

For this she was once more thoroughly silenced.

"If you're going to be nonsensical, I shall send you back to your own bed."

"But I want to stay with you." She very nearly added, *for always*, but just managed to stop herself.

"How very fortunate as I'm rather keen you should stay although the brandy must take part of the blame because if I were in my right mind, I would want to preserve your reputation and innocence."

"Oh, pooh!" said Augusta succinctly, "I find I care naught for my reputation and as for innocence, that is just an annoying imperfection that can easily be remedied! Just show me what to do!"

Laughing, he took her at her word and putting any regrets to one side, he gave her a gentle lesson in the art of lovemaking and found that, not only was she an enthusiastic pupil but she somehow helped restore a little of his lost faith in himself. He felt that if such a woman could see beyond his past, there might be something worth saving in him. Her trusting response to his touch made him hold himself back for the first time in his life and all his concentration was on making it an experience that wouldn't frighten her. He resolutely put aside all thoughts of the other worldly-wise females who had gone before her and how each one had left a stain upon his soul, and he showed Augusta just how tender he was capable of being; it awoke in him an unexpected and rather startling desire to make someone else happy.

There was a moment when she told him to kindly remove her nightgown because she was far too hot and had decided that she might like the touch of his skin against hers, when he very nearly gave in and sent her to her bedchamber despairing of his own sadly depraved nature. But sensing his quandary, she had, in a totally unprincipled fashion, wrapped herself around him and clung on like a particularly tenacious limpet. He had no choice but to let her stay.

She murmured things, which he disregarded. He knew what ardour could do to a person and he didn't believe that she really knew her own mind in that moment. Females were apt to talk nonsense when in the throes of passion. Never before had he wanted the whispered words to be true.

As he trailed his hand up the inside of her thigh, she let out a small squeal of surprise and then dissolved into giggles, holding his hand at bay for a while until she recovered her composure.

"Ticklish," she explained.

Having never been halted in his intentions before, he was hard-pressed to continue without laughing. When he hesitated, she took his hand and guided it with all the self-assurance of a seasoned courtesan, but as he could feel her trembling from head to toe, he knew her actions were complicated by that innocence he wanted to both savour and safeguard.

Augusta gazed up at him languidly, through half-closed eyes and smiled, "I think you're being very generous — for which I'm deeply, *deeply* grateful — but is there anything you would like me to do for you?"

Sir Marcus Denby choked and for a brief moment wished he were a better man.

Twenty-One

The faint grey light of dawn silvered Augusta's disordered curls and Marcus, watching her sleep for the fourth time since he'd first met her, thought he was in deep trouble.

He had an urge to wake her and tell her that they had to begin again, knowing full well that she would comply with laughing enthusiasm. He had another urge to just hold her in his arms like this until they were old and grey, and it was this notion that made him come to his senses and kiss her until she slowly awoke, stretching and moaning like a small child. She opened her eyes and smiled at him.

"Beecher will be along soon to see if I am still alive," said he and kissed the end of the Beauchamp nose.

She put her hand to his face and held it tenderly, "I had better go then, or risk shocking poor Beecher again."

"I would much rather keep you here but with the house so full, I cannot expose you to censure and dishonour. I may be entirely without morals and lost to all hope of salvation but even I could not be that careless of your good name."

Augusta struggled to sit up, so he lifted her with ease and perched her on his lap, her legs dangling over the edge of the sofa. Even though he was exhausted from his exertions in the fire, too much brandy and a night of corrupting an innocent, he felt vague inconvenient stirrings and pushed her off his thighs and onto the edge of the sofa.

Augusta, who had learnt a great deal during the night, turned and grinned at him, "I could stay if you still have need of me!" She was pulling her errant nightgown down and then trying to make some sense of her hair, trying but failing to twist it into a coil.

"Get away from me, you witch."

She leant over and kissed him lingeringly, "I hadn't quite realised how gentlemen are such martyrs to their — members!"

"Dear God, Augusta! Will you please go!"

She rose and as she was standing in front of the window and the curtains were not drawn, the outline of her form was plain to see against the morning light. He covered his eyes and a stifled groan escaped him, she laughed and span away across the room, her overlong nightgown trailing behind her.

"What have I done?" asked Sir Marcus as the door closed behind her.

* * *

Beecher arrived just fifteen minutes later and found his master in unusually good spirits for someone who had drunk an entire bottle of brandy and spent the night on the sofa. He glanced around and began to tidy up, replacing cushions and picking up the discarded empty bottle. Quince opened one bleary eye and watched his efforts.

"Good morning, Sir. May I suggest that it might be a good idea to have a wash, Sir, and a change of clothes before the guests see you."

"You're quite right as always, Beecher. I shall go up immediately. I have important business to attend to this morning and at the top of the list is to retrieve my daughter and Miss Dora from the tinker's encampment. Could you ask for the carriage to be brought round after breakfast and ask Hannah to take hot water straight away to Miss Augusta's bedchamber. And can you inform M. Boudin that I am famished and will need an early repast? And tell Hodge I'll need a shave as soon as I've bathed. And I should very much like to give you a raise, dear Beecher!"

Beecher, suspecting his master was still a trifle foxed, nodded wisely and said, "I see, Sir."

Sir Marcus laughed, which Beecher took to be a very bad sign indeed.

"Oh, I really don't think that you do!" said his employer, "I'm not at all sure that I even see, and I was right here."

"I shall go and order some strong coffee, at once, Sir," said the butler and he bent and picked something up from the rug. He examined it and a knowing smile altered his stony expression for a second, "I believe that I am *beginning* to see, Sir Marcus," he said and handed him the little tortoiseshell hairpin.

Marcus looked at it and the memories flooded back. "God, Beecher, I may well have ruined everything."

"Oh, I sincerely doubt that, Sir. Things have a way of working out for the best."

Sir Marcus looked taken aback, "I never thought you to be an optimist!"

"I am speaking of the vagaries of love, Sir Marcus. So much depends upon good fortune and making the right choice. One slip and you are tied to the wrong person for the rest of your days. It doesn't bear thinking about."

Marcus eyed his butler with interest, "You're talking about yourself."

"I am. I wouldn't want you to commit the same folly that I did. A life ruined. A lucky escape. A change of name. A move across country. A new career. It wouldn't do for you at all, Sir."

"Beecher, this is quite the revelation. I am all astonishment."

"Yes, Sir. It astonishes me too, sometimes." He trod across the study to the door, "I shall go and prepare everything, Sir Marcus. May I suggest that you swiftly make your way to your bedchamber before Lady Birch or Lady Denby see you? There might be questions asked."

"I am on my way. And Beecher? I meant what I said about the raise. You deserve it."

"I am most gratified," said the butler and went out.

Marcus sat for a moment and stared at the hairpin in the palm of his hand. He then got up, pulled on his shirt, picked up his boots and stealthily made his way upstairs feeling like a disreputable schoolboy returning to his dormitory after a night of illicit debauchery in the local town.

* * *

Flora was sitting up in their bed and looking at her sister in open-mouthed disapproval, "Are you saying, Augusta Pennington, that you have been capering about the house in your nightgown like a — like a *strumpet?*"

Augusta flushed a delicate pink, "Well, not precisely a strumpet but perhaps in a manner not becoming a schoolmistress!"

"Did anyone *see* you like this?"

"No, I was exceedingly careful and tiptoed along the corridors. No one saw me — apart from Marcus, of course!"

"Well, thank God for that!" she frowned, "We have lost the school, it would not do to lose our reputations too, all in the same night!"

Augusta climbed onto the bed next to her and pulled the covers over her and sat hugging her knees, "Oh, please do not be cross with me Flora! I didn't know what I was doing, I swear. I only wanted to be with him for one night, just to see what it would be like — otherwise I would never know. I hope for your sake that if you and Mr Frost ever — well, I fervently hope that things like this are inherited!"

"Oh, gracious! I think the shock of the fire has unhinged you. I cannot blame you because it was dreadful and I feared for you, dearest sister, because you seemed so — lifeless. It was terrifying to see you like that — far worse than seizures or hysterics!"

Augusta leant against her sister's shoulder and closed her eyes, "I think that for a while I was unable to think clearly. At first, I felt elated — perhaps because we had survived — and the danger and excitement — and I was so frightened that Marcus had been hurt or killed — but then he wasn't, and he was there with me. I knew, you know, when we were all in Aunt Euphemia's bedchamber — that he would come for us. I just knew inside. I have never felt so certain of anything before. Then, in the carriage, afterwards, it was as though I was someone else entirely! I seemed to have no control over my thoughts or actions. And last night, I don't remember going to his study. I woke up with him lying beside me and very nearly screamed the house down!"

"Oh, Gussie! Imagine! The shame of being discovered in such a compromising position!" she regarded her sister with an anxious frown, "What if Lady Birch had found you? The scandal would have ruined us!"

Augusta hugged her, "At the time I wouldn't have cared if Reverend Cheadle had discovered us and held me up before the congregation as a fallen woman! Do you not feel the same way about Jonathan?"

Flora considered, "He makes me laugh. I feel he understands me because we are alike in some ways — although, of course, he is relentlessly cheerful. He doesn't seem to be aware of my — more annoying foibles. But, even so, I don't think I could risk everything like you have. He makes me feel comfortable about myself and that in itself is a glorious feeling. I *have* imagined kissing him though!"

"So I should hope!"

"Oh, now you are become the great expert on all things to do with love, I suppose!"

Augusta threw herself back on the pillows and stretched out her arms above her head, sighing in satisfaction, "Honestly Flora, I would never have believed it if someone had told me! It's just as well that most females go into marriage knowing nothing about what they will be expected to do because human beings would probably be no more!"

"Gracious Gussie! Is it really that frightful?"

Augusta pulled a pillow over her face to hide her feelings, "Frightful? It is certainly surprising! But also — it's hard to explain really — it's not what I expected at all, but I don't know what I expected as no one ever explained anything! He was — so very kind and considerate and never once made me feel foolish or inexperienced. I had wondered if, being so supposedly debauched, if he might not be tempted to mock me a little but he was all encouragement and praise and not once did I feel inadequate or coerced in any way."

Flora lifted the pillow, which was muffling her sister's words, "So, has he proposed? He must surely have offered for you!"

Augusta sat up in a rush, "He has not, nor will he. And, more importantly, I do not want him to. Imagine if I forced him into marriage, for that's what it would be. I pushed myself upon him after he had rejected me — I wouldn't take no for an answer. Poor man. What a marriage that would be! No, I neither expect it nor wish it."

"Have you considered that you may — you know, be — well — in a compromised state!"

"Are you trying to suggest that I might be with child?" laughed Augusta, "I am not."

"You cannot be certain! Not yet."

"I can. He explained that he would be careful, and he was. I trust him in that."

"I am so glad you are such an expert when it comes to these things, Gussie. It's a great comfort to me," said Flora tartly.

"Don't be silly. He is bound to be an authority on such things. And although his early years were not a truly happy time in his life, he somehow survived and is now in a position to teach me."

"How generous," remarked Flora with a slight sneer.

"You know, he told me that by the time we met in the lane when I was so cross with him about Mrs Crouch winking at me, that it was already too late for him! He said that, when we were in the meadow, he very nearly lost his self-control, but the girls were with us, so he had to be restrained."

"It sounds as though he's a veritable saint," retorted Flora, rolling her eyes.

"No, he's never going to be a saint. He is too much affected by his past and that will always be there no matter what he does, but I do think that he can be saved."

"I fear he needs saving from *you*."

Augusta smiled rather wistfully, "Very likely. However, he will not have to put up with me for very long. I am not going to hang around his neck. I will not be that kind of female who dotes on him and makes a nuisance of herself, pining away and having the vapours — although I may want to! I love him too much for that."

"*Why* do you love him? He seems such an odd choice for you."

"I have no notion at all. But I think I first truly suspected that my feelings had altered when we were in the meadow, by the river when he told me about his past — and there was a moment when he came into the sickroom and I was just so relieved to see him, it was like a physical blow and alerted me to the danger I was in. I tried so hard to deny it but to no avail."

"And then he kissed you."

"Yes. That was utterly unprincipled of him. He is shameless. You wait until Jonathan kisses you, you'll understand then."

Flora shook her head in mock despair.

There was a scratch on the door and Hannah came in bearing a pitcher of hot water.

"Sir Marcus's orders, Miss Augusta," she said.

Augusta and Flora exchanged a speaking glance.

"The perfect host," said Augusta.

"High-handed," said Flora.

* * *

Robert Duncan called out a greeting as Sir Marcus jumped down from the carriage and waved away the thanks he received for his part in the rescue and for looking after the two runaways.

"I was only too glad to help, Sir Marcus, after my boy was so well cared for by those ladies. Your daughter and Miss Dora have been no trouble. I don't think Miss Imogen will be wanting to join us for another night though! Miss Dora is a different matter altogether. I'd keep an eye on her if I were you, in case she decides living in the open is the life for her. She has a wild streak, that young lady!"

"Oh, I know it, Robert, to my cost! Being involved in all these adventures came about because she got herself into an impressive scrape. Are they hiding?"

"They heard the carriage coming!"

Sir Marcus called their names and they appeared in the mouth of the bender, and he very nearly laughed out loud. The sight of Dora and Imogen looking desperately uncomfortable and clinging to each other like shipwrecked survivors awaiting the imminent arrival of the sharks was almost too much for him.

He schooled his features into a mask and beckoned to them. They came dragging their feet, wide-eyed and pale.

"Good morning, I trust you both slept well. Please say your farewells and let us be going."

They obediently said all the right things in subdued little voices and followed Sir Marcus to the carriage.

He turned to Robert Duncan and shook him by the hand, "Come and see me in a day or two, when I will hopefully have everything under control once more. Although, I doubt that things will ever be quite the same again."

"No, they will not, Sir. All our lives have taken a turn and we don't yet know if it's for good or bad."

"I have a suspicion that in my case it's going to be a true test of my patience and strength of mind."

Robert Duncan laughed, "Women, Sir Marcus — they change everything whether you want it or not."

Sir Marcus emphatically agreed and joined the two quaking girls in the carriage.

The short journey back to the Manor was endured in silence, with Dora and Imogen holding hands tightly.

Sir Marcus thought dispassionately that although they looked scared and a little dishevelled and grubby, they otherwise looked well so he felt justified in making them suffer a little for their sins. It was well-deserved.

When they reached the Manor, he told them to clean themselves up and change their clothes and return immediately to his study.

They rushed upstairs, glad to be away from his brooding presence and went to find Augusta.

She had just finished having her hair brushed by Flora and was wearing a gown that Dora didn't recognise, in a pretty sage green, with cream lacing and with dark green bows on the stomacher.

Augusta and Flora looked up and for a long moment they all stared at each other and then Augusta rose and held out her arms and Dora flew into them, sobbing.

Flora crossed the room and gathered the shaking Imogen to her comforting bosom.

"I'm so sorry, Gussie! I didn't think — it was my fault — I should have come to you straight away. Mr Duncan told us what happened at the school! It must have been awful!"

"Never mind that, Dora. Everyone escaped mostly unscathed and that's the important thing — not the building, which was admittedly useful but only stone and mortar. I'm glad that you and Imogen weren't there. I'm afraid everything was destroyed though. I do not know how we shall manage but everyone has been so very kind. This gown belongs to Lady Birch — it's a little short and tight as she's so tiny! And Flora is wearing one of Mrs Inwood's castoffs, who fortunately is also buxom!"

The remarks about gowns made Dora's eyes fill with tears, but she bit her lip and said nothing, realising that it was not the time for self-pity.

"We have to wash and tidy ourselves and then go back to see Sir Marcus in his study," she said miserably.

The mention of the study made Augusta become a little heated, but she hugged Dora even more tightly, "Well, if you thought that you were going to escape without a dressing down, you're sadly mistaken, my dear girl. But after all, no real harm came from your escapade and hopefully you have both learnt a valuable lesson. You will think twice before you do anything so dangerous again."

"Yes, Augusta," murmured Dora meekly.

"I will come with you," said her elder sister, "But don't expect me to defend you because I cannot."

"No, Augusta."

*   *   *

When they entered the study, the air was charged with so many heated emotions, Augusta thought it might easily catch fire. She exchanged a swift glance with Marcus, which made her stomach lurch and then noted that both Dr Inwood and the local constable, Mr Shawe were there too. She looked anxiously at Sir Marcus, and he looked so serious that she started to feel quite faint.

"Miss Pennington, please take a seat," he said, and she obeyed.

He then addressed the two terrified girls, "Imogen, Miss Dora — I'm afraid Constable Shawe has come to talk to you both. Constable Shawe, do please continue with what you were saying."

Constable Shawe was a kindly man and he had daughters of his own, so he felt some sympathy for these two young ladies, but his job was often difficult, and he was always keen to do his duty to the best of his ability.

"I regret to inform you Miss Denby-Birch, Miss Pennington, that some important particulars have come to light, and I am required to talk to all those involved in the case." He cleared his throat and managed to look both apologetic and stern, "There has been a discovery made at the school, which leads me to believe that the fire might have been started deliberately," he paused to see how his words were affecting the girls.

They were standing quite still, as pale as moonlight, their eyes fixed upon him.

"It appears that the fire started in the hay store beside the house."

A gasp was wrought from between Imogen's colourless lips.

He pressed on, "It seems that there was an illegal occupant in the hay store, and they must have set light to the hay. The sparks carried to the house — "

"*Oh, no, no, no!*" cried Imogen.

"I'm afraid it's true. The fire was a malicious act."

Imogen had pressed a trembling hand to her mouth, and she looked as though she were about to fall to the floor or be very sick.

Dora stepped out of her sister's embrace and stood before the constable, "I did it," she said quite steadily, "I left the candle burning and it must have burned down and caught the hay."

"*Dora!*" wept her friend, utterly distraught, "You *mustn't* — !"

"It's all right Imogen. Prison will be an adventure. You know I like an adventure." She suppressed her accomplice with a fierce frown.

Imogen was trying to catch her breath, but the sobs were stifling her. She held out a hand and Dora took it and squeezed it in a meaningful way.

Imogen shook her head, "No, you — sh-shall not go alone! We will be — t-together!" She looked to the constable fearfully, "I — I left the candle! I was supposed to b-blow it out, but I forgot, in all the excitement of having to leave so hastily! I'm very s-sorry. I should be the one going to prison, not Dora!"

Constable Shawe held up a commanding hand, "This is all very interesting, I must say. It puts a different slant upon the sorry tale. If you two could just stop being such heroic martyrs for a moment, we may be able to find the truth! It seems, if what you say is true, that the whole thing wasn't deliberate after all — it was a tragic accident. This changes everything. You can stop looking like two gloomy Joan of Arcs! No one is going to prison. Although, Sir Marcus, I would strongly recommend they have nothing but bread and water for at least a month and I hear you may be planning a ball — they should certainly not be allowed to attend that as punishment!"

"*Not go to prison?*" whispered Dora, shaking from head to toe.

"No, indeed, Miss, as though we'd send little girls to prison and for an accident too! We're not completely heartless, you know!" He chuckled and winked conspiratorially at Augusta, who was glad that she was sitting down because her knees were behaving quite oddly.

Imogen and Dora threw their arms around each other and wept lustily.

Augusta put her face in her hands and sat very still.

Twenty-Two

Sir Marcus Denby saw Constable Shawe out to his carriage, and they shared a few words on the consequences of the fire and the constable enjoyed another chuckle at the thought of the two miscreants being so certain they would be incarcerated for their crimes.

Sir Marcus watched him drive away and returned to his study to find Dr Inwood had gone to check on his patients and Augusta was sitting on their sofa with her arms around the girls. She glanced at him over their heads and for a moment it was as though time stood still. Then Dora sniffed loudly, and Augusta had to rummage in her pocket to find her handkerchief to give her.

"It's all my fault," declared Dora, determined to take the blame, "If I hadn't rushed into helping Imogen run away and come to you instead, none of this would have happened!"

"Yes, you're quite right, my dear. If you had stopped to think that all adults are not ogres but quite eager to help where they can — then it would be a very different story."

"On the other hand," said Marcus unhelpfully, "One could say that the fire has changed the course of our lives in ways that we can't even fathom yet. Perhaps even for the good. Sometimes a catastrophic event can set people on a new path and just one night can make all the difference."

"Thank you so much for clarifying!"

"I'm just explaining that it's interesting how one night can be both enlightening and very — revealing, in fact — "

"I think, Sir Marcus that you have helped quite enough!" interrupted Augusta crossly, "I shall take the girls up to see Aunt Ida and Aunt Euphemia before breakfast."

"Are we to have bread and water for breakfast?" asked Imogen piteously.

"Oh, good gracious, no! Constable Shawe was just joking! Come along you two mopey creatures! You can help with the chores and make yourselves useful. There is much to do because all our things were destroyed. We have no clothes —"

"That is not a problem as far as I can see," murmured Marcus, his laughing eyes on Augusta.

She shot him one of her most infamously quelling looks and shooed the girls quickly out of the room, slamming the door on his outrageous laughter.

* * *

Lady Birch was careful to show just the right amount of concern as she listened to her daughter relating the story of their night spent with the tinkers. They had skipped over the possible reasons for Imogen's precipitous flight and made the whole into a madcap quest for adventure. Her mother, however, was absolutely certain that she was the cause of the sudden disappearance of her only child, and she was more than happy to go along with the pretence. After all, pretence was her greatest stratagem. Combined with a ruthless streak, it always proved lethal to her enemies. They would keep faith with her, believing every silken word, right up until it was too late for them. She had decided, upon hearing about the fire from Jonathan, that Miss Pennington was very definitely her latest enemy. He regaled them at the breakfast table, in vivid detail, about the fire and their exciting rescue of the girls and the Misses Beauchamp and he had then, unfortunately, gone on to describe Marcus plunging back into the raging flames, with the house falling about his ears. Her interest piqued, she had asked, in a casual manner, why he should have done such a foolish thing and Jonathan had answered blithely that his cousin had risked his life in order to rescue Augusta.

Anyone who knew Lady Birch well, would have recognised the wintry smile that followed this diverting piece of information and, whilst feeling profound sympathy for the recipient of her rancour, they would have been grateful that it was not directed at them.

She still smiled, her perfect lips curved so beautifully, her almond-shaped eyes alive with apparent interest, but the smile was reminiscent of a fox patrolling the henhouse looking for an easy way in.

Flora was a little concerned that dear Jonathan might be drawing too much attention to her sister's exploits and Sir Marcus's derring-do and was anxious on Augusta's behalf. It pointed a finger at them in a way that would surely make people begin to wonder about their relationship.

"I must say Sir Marcus was magnificent!" declared Flora a trifle too brightly, "He came to find us all and carried Miss Euphemia out of the burning building with such ease! And, of course, Mr Frost and Charles brought the girls out safely, which was not an easy task with Fidelia Hill wailing so loudly! Some of them suffered burns and singed hair but poor Mr Duncan came off worse with very bad blistering on his hand but was thankfully still able to help lift Augusta out of the buttery window."

"Mr Duncan? The *tinker?*" asked Lady Birch silkily.

"Oh, yes! He was so very brave! Not only did he have to put up with Dora for a night in his camp — which must have been extremely tedious for him because she asks endless questions — but he came immediately to help with the rescue. A splendid fellow indeed!"

"How fascinating. It certainly is lively here in the country, is it not? And one is required to mix with all kinds of diverting people. It is so very different to being in town or even at Birch House. Ah, here is Miss Pennington herself!"

Augusta came in, a little flustered because she had spent the last hour dealing with Dora and Imogen, trying to sort out some problems the pupils had with lack of underclothes and calming Aunt Euphemia, who had worked herself up into a spectacular fit of the vapours and couldn't find smelling salts of any kind in this "Godforsaken den of iniquity!"

Having smoothed her aunt's ruffled feathers and found some petticoats for the girls and assured Dora and Imogen that they would eventually be forgiven for setting the school alight, she recalled that she should really be at breakfast in case anything untoward should happen when Lady Birch and Lady Denby were appraised of the night's events. She would have to do her best to ameliorate the situation.

She entered the breakfast room in some haste and on seeing Flora's flushed face and Lady Birch's venomous smile, slithered to an ungainly halt, "Good morning! I'm sorry that I am so late. There's so much to do because of last night. I can't seem to catch up." She found her place and sank into the chair with everyone staring at her.

"I see that my gown is unfortunately far too small for you, Miss Pennington. I am sorry that I am not closer to your generous proportions, but I have always been very slight. I am dainty and you are more in the country style. Fresh air and plenty of cream and butter, I suppose — it makes one so much heartier. Robust, one could say, no?"

Augusta was no fool and she could hear the dangerous edge in Lady Birch's soft voice; she was deft at making insults sound like compliments.

"You make me sound like an ox, my lady! In fact, we have spent most of our lives in Cheltenham and only moved to the wilds of the countryside two years ago."

"Cheltenham? Oh, 'tis hardly worthy of being called a town! Did you not find it very provincial?"

"Not at all. We found it most agreeable. I must thank you Lady Birch for lending me this gown, it is so pretty. Such a lovely shade of green."

Lady Birch eyed the gown disparagingly, "It was never a favourite. That particular green does not suit my exotic colouring and it was always far too big for me! My maid included it by mistake."

Augusta tried hard not to laugh, "As I am so short of anything to wear, I do not care that it is hard to breathe once laced into it! I am grateful and for all the other donations —

without a brush Mabel Latimer's hair would have very quickly run wild and we'd have had to cut it off!"

"I was only too glad to help," said Lady Birch agreeably.

"I hope you have not suffered any ill effects from the fire, Miss Augusta?" asked Jonathan.

"I coughed a good deal last night, because of the smoke I suppose."

"I trust that it didn't keep you awake?"

Flora made a half laughing, half choking sound and buried her face in her napkin.

"Not for long, Jonathan, I will admit to being exceedingly tired after all the excitement and in the end slept soundly."

"I fell asleep the second my head touched the pillow!" said he cheerfully, "Although I had some rather disturbing dreams," and he cast a not-very furtive glance at Flora, who studiously ignored him, concentrating very hard upon re-folding her napkin.

Lady Denby, who had been keeping her head beneath the parapet, sensing that Miranda was feeling confrontational and keen to avoid her eye because she was as dangerous as a cobra in that sort of mood, looked up nervously from her plate, "I am so glad my dear Charles did not get too badly hurt. He's been inclined, ever since a child, to act first and think later! It's just like him to charge into a fire to rescue fair maidens! Silly boy."

"Well, hardly silly, my lady! They were exceedingly brave," said Augusta.

As the very brave boy walked in at that moment, his doting mother was able to turn her attention to him and embarrass him by heaping praise upon him until he had to beg her to stop. He then seated himself and with youthful self-assurance tucked into an enormous breakfast, consisting of anything within arm's reach. He took no notice of the undercurrents in the room but happily chatted away, sometimes with his mouth full, which earned him a sound ticking off from his mother.

Lady Birch was able to sit and pleasurably contemplate her revenge. She only had to look at Augusta to know. She knew the effect could have on a young and virtuous girl like Miss Pennington. She would, naturally, be insensible to any danger being such an innocent. It was clear to her that Marcus still had a penchant for causing havoc, but she couldn't quite believe that he had chosen such an ill-favoured creature considering his usual exotic tastes, but he obviously had a plan to find some entertainment there because it could be very dull in the country. Lady Birch had never been in the least troubled by his wandering eye as it absolved her of any feeling of guilt when she had found herself straying to Fabian. Not that she was much prey to feelings of guilt. She had thought, on meeting Marcus, that she had finally met her match but found, after a while, that there was something missing, something she had in abundance: the killer instinct. The notion that once you have your prey by the throat, you do not let go, until their eyes become dull, was the code she chose to live by. She glanced at her prey in her ill-fitting, borrowed gown and almost felt sorry for her — just one in a long line of insecure and vulnerable females who needed someone to validate them and cherish them. It had made her laugh to see them fall by the wayside, discarded like so much dross and anyway, he had always returned to her because of the child. The child had pinned him to her side and in order to get what she wanted she was prepared to use the same strategy again. Once she had secured him, she would think about ridding herself of Fabian and sending Imogen away to school.

Augusta glanced up and found Lady Birch's eyes on her and it sent a chill down her spine, even though the calculating look she'd briefly seen turned instantly to a condescending smile.

"What will you do about the school, Miss Pennington? Can you afford to rebuild?"

Augusta, who was trying hard not to envisage their future in any way in case she broke down, shook her head, "No, indeed, I'm afraid not. We shall perhaps be able to sell the land, but it will not fetch much. It's not a large plot nor is its aspect particularly enticing. I must say the house was not the prettiest building and the garden is small with too many elderly trees crowding it. It was part of an inheritance from my grandmother. Nobody else wanted the house, you see? So, my aunts decided to turn it into a school. It was very successful for a while."

God, thought Lady Birch, what a dead bore she is! The sooner she rescued Marcus from this tedious female, the better.

She suppressed a yawn and took a sip of her coffee, making a face as though she found it distasteful.

"Shall I send for another pot of coffee, my lady?"

"No, thank you, I have finished now. I very rarely eat breakfast. I eat very little as a rule. One must not allow oneself to become corpulent."

Flora, seething with wrath, deliberately stabbed a large piece of ham with her fork and thumped it down onto her plate, making Mr Frost look at her with the deepest respect.

Charles, not paying much attention to what was going on around him and still happily eating, looked up, "Dash it all, Miss Flora, was that the last slice of ham!"

"I certainly hope not," she replied, "I'm still absolutely famished!"

* * *

Flora was stamping in small circles on the lawn as she watched their pupils being collected by a stream of parents and guardians, some visibly distressed and others, uncaring. The grand carriages rattled up the long drive most of the afternoon, disgorging elegantly dressed couples who then interviewed poor Augusta with endless questions and examined their offspring for any signs of damage. On hearing all about the daring rescue from their wide-eyed child, they then thanked Augusta rather ungraciously and departed, bearing away their precious daughters to safety.

"You're making the gardeners exceedingly nervous," said Jonathan Frost as he came upon Flora pacing furiously and muttering to herself. "Is there anything I can say to calm you?"

Flora stopped and scowled at him, her pretty face almost unrecognisable as rage overwhelmed her, "Calm me! *Calm me!* I am not some child to be mollified with a rusk or a noisy coral rattle! I cannot be soothed with warm milk either before you ask! Just three days ago I watched our school go up in flames! I am now watching our dear girls being taken away, never to return! I am watching Aunt Ida's dream of her own establishment be destroyed! I had to listen this morning to Aunt Euphemia going on and on about how we are all come to ruin and how that now her gold — her *gold*, if you please — no doubt a pirate's hoard in a treasure chest — has been lost — we are all destined for the workhouse! And then there's poor dear Augusta being interrogated all day by those awful parents, unspeakably doting mothers who are quite happy to send their daughters away the first chance they get, to get them out of their perfectly arranged hair! And Augusta is become quite unhinged, you see! I hardly know her anymore! She's being so reckless — we shall be undone! Then there's that *woman!* Lady Birch. I just know that she's scheming. I can see it in her face. Oh, it's all too much to bear! It is all disaster wherever I turn." She took another turn about the garden, looking, if she but knew it, absolutely magnificent with the afternoon sunshine gilding her glorious hair and her lovely face quite pink from her exertions and the heat of the day.

Mr Frost observed her progress with amusement and several other emotions crowding his chest, "I do not scruple to tell you, Flora that you look exceedingly beautiful like this! Fury becomes you!"

She came to a sudden standstill and stared at him, "Is that all you have to say? When I am at my wit's end! Oh, isn't that just like a man! Here am I pouring my woes out to you and all you can think of is yourself!"

"I can assure you that I am thinking wholly of you, Flora my dear."

She put her hands on her ample hips and fixed him with a contemptuous look that usually had the effect of dampening any pretensions and kept people at a safe distance. Mr Frost did not seem to understand the power of her expressions and instead of moving away from her, he was advancing towards her, in a rather purposeful fashion and even had the temerity to be smiling at her!

"Kindly do not come any closer!" she snapped.

He paid no heed to her.

"Mr Frost! I am not in jest! I have no notion why you should be grinning at me like a fool!"

"Possibly because you look absolutely adorable when you're in a passion and so very agitated!" said Jonathan.

Her eyes flashed, "If you think that you can *calm* me with meaningless blandishments, let me tell you, sir, that you are *very* much mistaken! I am not so easily won! Honeyed words hold no sway over me! Stay *there!* Do not take another step or I shall scream!"

Mr Frost came to a halt a few feet from her and sighed, "Well, if you are quite sure? I was hoping to help."

She looked at him with withering contempt, "And I suppose that you think that all a female needs is a few insincere compliments to be brought to her senses!"

"No, indeed, I did not think that at all! I assure you that it never crossed my mind. I was just momentarily distracted from the issue by your beauty and spirit. I am so used to ladies who show very little genuine emotion. They simper and flap their fans about and say very little of any consequence and expect one to dance attendance upon them, to fall at their dainty feet in adoration and beg for their hand!"

"What has that to do with anything?" she demanded crossly.

"You would never do that. You certainly don't simper!"

"And I suppose that I don't have dainty feet either!" said Flora in dangerously quiet tones.

Jonathan, sensing a trap, carefully sidestepped it, "Your feet are perfect, and I would happily worship at them!"

"Oh, for heaven's sake! You are being utterly idiotic. I beg you to stop!"

Mr Frost considered this for a moment, "I really don't think that I can, Flora. I am become quite obsessed with you and want only to take you in my arms and kiss you!"

She stared at him open-mouthed, her eyes kindling, "You can't say that! You can't go around telling females that you want to kiss them!"

"Well, I must confess, I wouldn't normally be tempted to but seeing you in such a taking has stirred me in ways I had not thought possible! I considered myself resistant to such feelings, having become disillusioned with the fairer sex."

"What a horrid thing to say! If you knew what women are forced to endure at the hands of men just to be considered as human, let alone as equals! And here you are suggesting that we are all desperately searching for a husband and will stop at nothing to get one! I think it's unjust and does not make me think well of you Mr Frost!"

"But you accepted Reverend Cheadle not out of love but for reasons of security!"

Outraged at the truth in this, Flora glared at him, "How *dare* you mention that!"

"I thought I ought to say something, as if I am to beg you to marry me, we would have to be rid of the Reverend, which has been preying upon my mind since the fire."

Her interest caught, Flora asked, "Why since the fire?"

He looked down at her, his usually good-natured face suddenly solemn, "I was so afraid that you — that you might have been injured, or worse and I could not contemplate a life without seeing your lovely, exasperated face every day."

She gazed up at him in disbelief, "You are sadly deranged."

"Possibly," said Mr Frost candidly, "But, did you hear what I said?"

Flora blushed and looked away, "I don't know what you mean."

"I cannot, in all good conscience, ask you to be mine yet, but I want you to know that I am standing impatiently in the queue."

At this Flora couldn't help but emit a reluctant little laugh, "Queue, indeed! You are being extremely silly." She paused and studied the grass at her feet idly, "I am easily vexed," she said carefully.

"I know."

"And I fret about the silliest things."

"I know."

"And I feel I must point out that — I am overly buxom," she muttered bleakly.

"I have to admit I noticed that immediately. An alluring armful."

She glanced up at him swiftly, "You don't mean that!"

He took a step closer, "Flora Pennington, what you see as imperfections, I see as assets to be treasured."

"Deranged," said Flora in a resigned tone.

Jonathan took another step until he was standing right in front of her. Some of her indignation had abated and, as she seemed to be a little calmer, he felt there was less chance of actual damage to his person.

"If I told you that I loved you, would that help?" he asked diffidently.

"No. Yes. I don't know. This cannot be happening."

"Ever since first setting eyes on you at the church — when you snatched your hand away and thought me "oafish", I thought you were so unlike any other female I had ever come across. And then, you accepted Reverend Cheadle's hand! You could have beat me down with a feather! I've never been so at a loss for words. Perhaps, you should know some of *my* flaws, of which I have many. I am apparently far too garrulous — or so Marcus tells me. I have a reputation for being a little unimaginative and I eat too much, according to — well, everyone I know! I do like food very much, you know!"

She nodded and contemplated his rather dear, amiable face.

"Well, we have that in common, at least," she reflected.

Sensing a weakening in her splendid defences, Mr Frost took the last step.

"Flora, my dearest love, may I beg your kind permission to demonstrate my adoration for you?"

"Well, I suppose — if you must! Although, am I to assume that you mean to kiss me?"

"Indeed I do. I have been wanting to do it from that first day."

Flora rolled her eyes, "Oh, well — go on then!"

Mr Jonathan Frost tentatively tilted her chin up with one cautious finger, as though fearing injury, and pressed his lips to hers in, what could only be described as, a thoroughly decorous fashion.

He released her chin and stood back.

She looked at him.

She raised her eyebrows, "Well, what a fuss about nothing."

"I beg your pardon?" faltered a startled Mr Frost.

"Do you believe me to be shy — a timid creature? I hate to disappoint you, but I come from a family of remarkably resolute women! Frankly, that just will not do! If I am to relinquish my betrothed, it must be for a jolly good reason because telling him that I no longer wish to marry him is likely to be a most uncomfortable interview!"

Before Jonathan could reply, Flora, leaning towards him with confidence, reached up and flung her arms about his neck and to his astonishment and delight, kissed him in a manner which greatly pleased him and, it has to be said, slightly shook him.

"There!" pronounced Flora with satisfaction, "That was more how I imagined it."

Jonathan needed no further prompting and seized his beloved in his arms and proved that he had perfectly understood the lesson.

It was perhaps unfortunate that at that precise moment a small and rather battered old gig came rattling up the drive and stopped in front of the house.

Jonathan heard the cart arrive and opened one eye to see who it was. On witnessing the very Reverend Cheadle climb down from it and look in their direction, he lifted Flora off her feet and with renewed vigour put a great deal of effort into making sure she would have no more complaints and that the clergyman had a clear view of them.

Reverend Cheadle stood frozen to the spot, his eyes bulging, his mouth working and as Augusta came down the steps to greet him, thinking it to be yet another disgruntled parent, she followed the direction of his gaze and saw to her dismay, her sister being ruthlessly embraced by Mr Frost, right in the middle of the lawn, in full view of everyone!

Regarding the Reverend anxiously she thought he might be going to have strong convulsions unless she did something swiftly.

"Reverend Cheadle! How very kind of you to come to see us! Will you come in and take tea with us?"

The gentleman in question had been rendered speechless and was beyond refusing the polite offer so, with his eyes still on the dreadful spectacle on the lawn, he followed Augusta into the house.

Mr Frost, seeing that his work was done, finally released Flora, who by that time was thoroughly overcome and thoroughly dishevelled, her face pinkly glowing.

She put a shaky hand to her hair, found it to be in disarray and was rather pleased.

Jonathan, gazing down at her lovingly, felt bound to tell her that she looked absolutely glorious and that they had been seen by Reverend Cheadle.

Her adorable response was to laugh uproariously, "How fortuitous! Well, hopefully he won't want to marry me now! He will think I am a loose woman and will not want to be associated with me."

Jonathan smiled and smoothed a tendril of hair from her forehead, "Then you'll just have to marry me won't you and I shall do my utmost to rescue your tattered reputation!" he said happily.

She frowned at him, "*You* are the one who has ruined me!"

"Indeed, I have, and I take great pride in my success because it means I get what I want! You!"

She giggled, sounding remarkably carefree for one so thoroughly disgraced, "I cannot conceive why you should want me, but I am exceedingly glad that you do! You see, although I once thought you oafish — I also thought that you were rather lovely — but far too good for me so I dismissed you from my thoughts — or tried to at least."

She was once again lifted off her feet and rewarded with more kissing and then he made his way slowly across the lawn carrying her like that, her feet dangling.

"Oh, put me down! You'll damage your back! Don't be such a fool!"

He hitched her up a bit and carried her the rest of the way, pressed to his broad chest, only releasing her when they reached the steps, where he kissed her soundly once more.

"I love you, Mr Frost," she laughed.

* * *

The Very Reverend Cheadle was in a profound state of shock. He had come to the Manor, despite all his many and varied misgivings, in order to fulfil his duty as parish priest. Having heard about the fire and heroic rescues, he felt that he would naturally be expected to visit the survivors and share his infinite wisdom with them. Much against his better judgement he was risking a meeting with Sir Marcus, who was a known libertine. And for his troubles he was rewarded with the sight of his betrothed being ravished by one of Sir Marcus's depraved relations. He was trying to convince himself that Miss Flora had been showing resistance, but it had been quite clear to him that she had actually been encouraging and thoroughly enjoying Mr Frost's corrupting advances.

He had never felt so shaken or so disillusioned.

Miss Pennington was trying her very best to make up for her sister's shameful behaviour, but he was having trouble concentrating on what she was saying and then there, coming into the parlour, were the sinners themselves and neither were looking the least bit apologetic or penitent! He'd never seen Miss Flora so in looks! Why she looked positively radiant! It was a *disgrace!*

Augusta, who had been desperately floundering, greeted them with a confused mixture of relief and terror. "Mr Frost! Flora! There you are! Reverend Cheadle is here! As you can probably see. Is it not kind in him to come to pay his respects?"

There was an awkward moment while they stared at the Reverend, and he looked anywhere but at them.

"I — I have come — " he said rather too loudly and then correcting his tone, continued in a more subdued voice, "I have come — to ask Miss Flora to release me from my rather rash offer of marriage. I hope that she will forgive me if I say that I have realised that she is not quite the person I thought she was and as a dedicated Man of God, I cannot afford to be associated with a person of such dubious moral fibre."

"Confound it! You cannot talk about Flora like that! I've a good mind to draw your cork!" exclaimed Jonathan indignantly. "If you weren't a dashed priest, I would!"

Flora put a steadying hand on Jonathan's arm, "Reverend Cheadle, it is I who should be thanking you for your kind offer and begging your forgiveness for having deceived you. I am, I have just discovered, not really fit to be the wife of a clergyman. I would have made a most unsuitable spouse, I'm afraid. I should never have accepted your obliging offer. I swear, I never meant to hurt anyone by doing so. It was impulsive and very wrong. I beg you to please forgive me!"

Reverend Cheadle's vision of resting his tired head upon Flora's magnificent bosom was gradually fading and he knew that now it would never be.

He inclined his head and, casting a nervous glance at Mr Frost who was certainly a very brawny fellow, he addressed himself solely to Augusta, "I accept your sister's apology and officially withdraw my offer. It was made in haste, and I must now repent at leisure."

"Good God!" said Mr Frost, much aggrieved, but the hand on his arm squeezed a little harder and he swallowed his angry words and unclenched his huge fists.

Reverend Cheadle, somehow sensing that he was tempting Fate by continuing to be in the same room as such a barbarian, quickly said a fawning farewell to Augusta and favouring the others with just a nod and a poorly executed smile, he hastened from the room.

Moments later they heard the gig dashing away and exchanged looks of suppressed mirth and some concern.

"You two should be thoroughly ashamed of yourselves! Behaving like that in public! Poor Reverend Cheadle," said Augusta, in admonishing tones.

Flora leant against Jonathan's side and his arm slid around her and she had never felt so comfortable and then, to everyone's consternation, she promptly burst into tears.

"*Flora!*" cried Augusta in dismay.

Sniffing loudly and speaking into Jonathan's chest, Flora announced in stifled accents, "I'm so *happy!*"

Twenty-Three

Sir Marcus had an audience with Robert Duncan that evening and was able to tell the young man that he would like to offer his family a permanent place to stay, should they wish to return to the district. He explained that he would like to set aside a small parcel of land on the other side of the woods, which had two stone cottages with sound roofs, a decent barn and a walled yard for the animals. There was plenty of timber available and they would have permission to hunt on his land and nearby there was a lake, rich in trout, fed by a very reliable stream.

Robert Duncan looked at him with deep suspicion, "Why?" he asked.

"I would have thought it obvious. In gratitude for your help."

"I don't want your gratitude. *Sir*," he added quickly. "I didn't ask for anything. I wanted only to repay Miss Pennington and Miss Dora for taking in my boy and caring for him."

"Well, you have repaid them. And now I wish to repay you for helping me rescue Miss Pennington from the fire. I cannot even begin to explain what that means to me."

Mr Duncan regarded Sir Marcus for a moment and made a slight shrug, "I wondered, Sir. To risk one's life like that — twice. It made me think."

"It made me think too," admitted Sir Marcus dryly, "I could not have borne it had she been hurt, or worse — she has become hugely important to me and I find that everything I do now is to hopefully please her and make her think well of me — which I realise does not reflect well on me! I should be trying to be a better man because I want to gain entry into Heaven, or some such nonsense, but instead I just want her to trust me and not cast me out. Do you think that is too much to ask?"

Robert Duncan smiled, "No, I don't. My wife and my wee lad, they mean everything to me, so I do understand. Best you secure her quickly then, Sir."

"I plan to, but I have a few loose ends to tie up first. So, what are your thoughts on the land? Will you agree to it? Or is it too much of a commitment?"

His companion was silent for a long moment, then he nodded briskly, "I'll take it — for the boy. I don't want him to have no choices like the rest of us. This would give him a chance — if he wanted it."

"Excellent, then I shall have my lawyer draw up the proper papers so that it's all legal and above board. No, don't look like that! It won't tie you down, you'll still be free to roam if that's what you wish."

They shook hands and as the young man was leaving, he turned to Sir Marcus and said, "I'll not forget, Sir. They say my wife can come home next week and I'll be able to tell her then that she can settle if she likes. You know women, Sir!"

Marcus shook his head, "I certainly once thought I did — I'm not so sure anymore!"

* * *

Charles Denby was grinning from ear to ear, his eyes dancing, and Quince, who sensed excitement in the air, got out of his basket, stretched his long back and limbs, wagged his tail ingratiatingly and looked optimistically at Charles, who ignored all these telling signs and only when a cold, wet and very insistent nose was pushed into his hand was he forced to take notice, "Yes, Quince, yes! We will go out later! There are important things afoot here though — so you must be patient!" He turned back to his brother, "I think it's a small miracle, do you not?"

"It seems that way. There is an abundance of miracles at the Manor at the moment. It seems they have all come at once, but this one I will admit is somewhat unbelievable."

"Ah, I hear them coming at last! I say, Marcus! What a time we're having! Who knew the country could be so dashed exciting! It's one thing after another! Just when you think things are quieting down — off they go again! I might just move down here, you know!"

"Not if I have any say in the matter," said Marcus without rancour.

The door opened and Beecher ushered in Augusta and Dora looking anxious.

"Do not look so worried. I can immediately allay your fears. You are not, for a change, in any trouble Dora!" said Sir Marcus.

Dora's expression relaxed and she managed a smile, "Oh, thank goodness! I was cudgelling my brains to think what I had done but couldn't remember anything apart from — but I shan't tell you that!"

Augusta was watching Charles's eager young face, "I think something has happened and that Mr Denby is bursting to tell us! You would never be a good spy!"

Mr Denby chuckled, "No, indeed, I would be hopeless! Come in! Make yourselves comfortable."

The girls found themselves hastily guided into chairs and they both sat very upright, their faces filled with curiosity and amusement.

With a quick glance at his brother for permission Charles took the floor, "Miss Dora! I have something for you, and I hope that you will see that although — well, I think I'll just show you! Words are not my forte."

He reached behind the deep armchair next to him and pulled out a large box, blackened with soot and much singed.

Dora's face froze.

He carefully removed the lid and pulled out her Titania gown, which was, apart from some staining from the smoke and a few small burns, otherwise still miraculously intact.

Dora said nothing but held out her arms and received it as though it were something infinitely precious and yet broken, her eyes were filled with unshed tears and her bottom lip caught between her prominent front teeth.

Augusta came and knelt beside her, "But it's impossible, Charles. How could anything survive the fire?"

"It appears that the girls' side of the house is the only part left standing and the blanket chest, where the box had been placed, was made of oak so solid that it bravely withstood the flames for most of the time. The smoke, I'm afraid could not be excluded and has damaged the gown but only a little," explained Charles in triumph.

"It's beyond belief! It may smell a bit of soot but if we put it out in the sunshine that will fade, and a little essence of lavender will help. The smoke stains can be removed, and the scorches patched and mended and covered with additional blossom! It will barely show Dora!" exclaimed Augusta.

Dora looked at her sister but could not find a smile, "I am so very glad that the gown is safe, Gussie but — I cannot feel entirely happy because everyone else has lost everything they own and I am the only one who has been fortunate, which is so unfair because after all, the fire was my fault!"

"Oh, Dora, my dearest ninnyhammer! You cannot go on blaming yourself — it was not your fault and although you certainly might have been more rational in your thinking, the fire was no more than an unhappy accident and you know, good things have come from it, which might otherwise not have happened. There is a reason the gown has survived as there is a reason that no one was seriously hurt. You've seen how oddly happy Flora is? That is due to the fire. She and Mr Frost are betrothed because of it."

"Flora's still very disagreeable," said Dora moodily.

"Yes, and she always will be. A leopard cannot change its spots. But she is, on the whole, a much more contented person and I believe that she and Mr Frost will make each other very happy. You see, when something serious like that happens it often brings to light other things, which have been waiting in the shadows for someone to take notice of them."

"And it was a very ugly old building," said Marcus amiably.

"That is quite beside the point!" responded Augusta tartly, "It was our home and shielded us from the weather and provided us with a means of earning a living. It may not have been much to look at, but it was all we had. Dora and Imogen are not to blame but we are nevertheless now homeless."

"Dora, why don't you take the gown to Mrs Primrose, she's an authority on repairing things and will know what to do," suggested Marcus.

Dora, a little overcome, made her curtsy and left cradling the gown in search of the indomitable housekeeper, who always had an answer for everything.

Charles shook his head, "That girl!"

Augusta hardly knew what to say but was kind enough to point out to him that Quince had not yet given up hope of some exercise. The hound was sitting just in front of Charles staring up at him from soulful eyes as though all hope would be lost if Charles continued to ignore him and life would be, from then on, without meaning.

The young man ruffled the animal's drooping ears and laughing, gave in and they both bounced out of the door, one declaring that there was much fun to be had in the woods and the other yelping in high-pitched anticipation.

"As bad as each other," remarked Marcus.

Augusta jumped to her feet, suddenly realising that they had been left alone, "Well, I must be getting on. There is still so much to do," and she made haste to reach the door before he could say anything.

"Are you avoiding me Augusta?"

She didn't turn around but instead addressed the door, "Of course not! Why should I! I am just very, very busy."

She suddenly felt his closeness and reached for the door handle as though it were a lifeline.

"There's no need to turn tail when you see me. I may be a degenerate, but I think I am still gentleman enough to know when my attentions are not wanted."

At this Augusta drew in a sharp breath and turned to face him, "Do not describe yourself so! You are *not* a degenerate! I do wish you wouldn't set so much store by what other people think. They do not count."

He considered her indignant face, "I find that I do not care what anyone thinks — apart from you. I hold your good opinion of me very dear. Something however is making you keep your distance — ever since the night of the fire."

He watched with surprisingly intense pleasure as her face flushed pink and she lowered her eyes, "I cannot — we should not — it must have been the fear and dread — it made me lose my faculties for a while. A sort of madness came over me. You must have suffered it too!"

"I see," said Marcus carefully, "I must tell you that despite the brandy, and being overcome by the very real fear of losing you, I was in my right mind that night. I have never been more so."

He observed the confused array of expressions crossing her face but made no move to touch her.

She didn't dare look into his eyes in case he could see the longing in hers so she continued to stare at a button on his waistcoat with frowning determination, "It can never be. You don't understand. We are so far removed from each other — there is so much that stands between us. So different, so very different."

"Any problem can be disentangled. Any differences can be easily ironed out. There is nothing that cannot be made wholly insignificant with a little judicious thought."

"You make it sound so simple, but it isn't. I really must go."

"Then go," he said curtly, his temper suddenly getting the better of his good intentions.

She cast him a hurt look and he put out his hand to stay her, but she was gone.

*   *   *

It seemed to Augusta that their odd life at Cuckoopen Manor was becoming too agreeable and even with the unwanted presence of Lady Birch and Lady Denby, she was finding that she had settled into the rhythms of the house with far too much ease. She saw that Dora and Imogen had formed an unbreakable bond and were seldom seen without the other and Aunt Ida was enjoying the unusual peace and quiet after decades living in a cacophonous school environment, where noise was just part of the fabric of being a teacher. She was able to spend her days wandering the gardens, pulling out weeds and pruning rose bushes or sitting quietly in the library with a book in her lap.

Aunt Euphemia had taken to her bed once more and refused to be coaxed out of it. She had taken the news of Flora's betrothal as a personal slight and for several days would not reply to anything her niece said, sticking her chin in the air and staring off into the distance. Whenever Flora suggested that her aunt might make an effort to go downstairs and enjoy some kind of normal life, all she received was a furious puff of air blown through the smallest of the Beauchamp noses and then a cold shoulder.

Flora was so blissfully happy that nothing Miss Euphemia could do was able to prick her bubble of joy. She was no less ill-humoured than usual, but criticism and insults could not hurt her. When Aunt Euphemia eventually deigned to speak to her and told her bluntly that she was the worst niece to ever live and that besides that she looked like a puffed up hen, Flora, who was perched on the edge of the bed, had rested her chin in her hands and said dreamily, "Jonathan likes to rest his head on my puffed up bosom — he says it's his favourite place to be."

Miss Euphemia Beauchamp was utterly revolted and immediately demanded her vinaigrette in outraged accents. Bonny, hearing her mistress in distress had growled at Flora but she took no notice of the bared teeth, flapping at the dog's nose with her aunt's fan in an absent-minded fashion.

"He also told me that I look like Botticelli's Venus! So ridiculous. I fear his attics are to let! But do you know? I just cannot seem to care. I love him so much. I wish you could be happy for me, Aunt Euphemia! It seems I am not destined to be an old maid after all."

Augusta had too little to do even though she kept telling herself that she was giving Marcus a wide berth because she had endless tasks to perform. With the girls gone and no teachers to organise, little James Duncan having been returned to his family just after the fire and in good health, Flora being so bewitched by Jonathan and Dora behaving herself for once, she was very much left to her own devices.

She walked to the village and visited Mr Sippence who had been returned to his home in fine fettle and was keen to hear all her gossip. She had called in on Robert Duncan and his family in their camp in the woods and been invited to stay for a tin cup of some delicious concoction made from elderflowers and a biscuit baked hard in the embers of the fire, but nonetheless surprisingly tasty. She had poked her head into the bender to meet Mrs Duncan, who had been released from the cottage hospital but still had regular visits from Dr Inwood, and Mrs Inwood had let slip that Sir Marcus was footing the bill. Mrs Duncan was still too thin and seemed a little unfocused at times but seemed otherwise quite healthy and seeing her son's cross little face had helped her recover. Augusta was happy to be able to hold the little boy in her arms and see that his face was pink and his cheeks filling out nicely, but she hadn't had him for many moments when Mrs Duncan held out her arms for his return.

She smiled at Augusta in apology, "It's been so long. I thought he was lost, and it was more than I could bear. You've been so kind — "

"The wife wanted me to say to you that we cannot thank you enough — " began Robert Duncan in explanation.

"Oh, goodness gracious, you must stop thanking me, Robert! We shall be forever thanking one another every time we meet! Let us just say that what is done is done and that's what friends do."

Robert Duncan looked thoughtful, "After what Sir Marcus has done, I must say that it won't matter how many pots I mend, it'll never be enough!"

"Oh? And what exactly has he done?" asked Augusta desperately keen to hear anything about Marcus.

Of course, when she'd been told about his offer of the land and cottages, she was filled with such a feeling of certainty that she wanted to run all the way back to the Manor and fling herself into his arms.

"He's a good man, you know. Whatever the rumours say his past may have been, you can be sure of him," remarked Mr Duncan casually.

She started, "Oh, how did you guess — ?"

"He talked to me about you, Miss. If you'll pardon the presumption, he said he just wanted to be a better man for you."

"What a dolt! I don't need him to be any better! He's perfect as he is. Did he say anything else?" she demanded, not even bothering to seem unconcerned.

"Yes," said Robert, grinning, "He said he didn't understand women!"

Augusta laughed, "That doesn't surprise me at all! Knowing the sort of women he has chosen to fraternise with."

"The past is past, Miss Pennington."

"Is it? I wish someone would remind Lady Birch of that!"

Robert Duncan narrowed his eyes, "There are ways of ridding oneself of pests, Miss. Just say the word!"

"No! Dear oh dear! However much I may think of dropping her headfirst down a deep well, I could *never* — oh, you are *joking!*"

The young man shrugged, "I might be — I might not. But remember that we have ways and means — "

Augusta clapped her hands over her ears, "Don't tempt me! It's a very appealing notion, but I shall have to find some other *legal* method of ridding myself of the pestilence we have at the Manor." She looked about her at the tidy little camp, the fire and the ponies, the black hound scratching behind its pointed ear, "I was wondering how you are received here by the locals? Are they unfriendly?"

"Aye, you always get some — but since the fire I've noticed things have changed a bit for the better. We've had a few more people asking for mending and for the carved spoons and such."

"I heard Sir Marcus telling some local dignitaries, who called at the house, about your bravery and how you helped rescue the girls, some of whom are from this area. He will have spread the word, so hopefully there will not be so much ill-feeling."

Robert eyed her with a knowing look, "A good man, that man of yours," he observed.

When she left the camp, Robert Duncan shook her hand and reminded her that he knew where a deep and isolated well could be found.

* * *

Flora wasn't really listening. She'd just had an argument with Aunt Euphemia and had somehow missed her breakfast. Her stomach was grumbling, and she was thinking about M. Boudin's baked ham and was not in the mood for frivolity. She glanced up at Jonathan as she rolled the blue thread onto its wooden spool, "That's nice. Did you have any breakfast? I didn't and I'm famished! I wonder if M. Boudin could spare a bread roll and some butter. You'd think there might be some lying around in the kitchen — unguarded!"

"Flora!" said Jonathan in despair, "I'll fetch you something to eat in a minute! Did you hear what I just said?"

"That you'd fetch me something to eat."

"Were you not listening to what I was saying before that?"

"Probably not. I am so *very* hungry. I was thinking of baked ham and trying to remember which colour went on this spool. I didn't mean to be rude."

He rolled his eyes, "I'd like you to pay attention to me just for a moment please!"

"Well, there's no need to get on your high horse! I'm listening, so do please continue!"

He took the spool from her and set it on the drum-table beside her and then he possessed himself of her hands, "Flora, I have something to tell you — "

Her eyes flew anxiously to his, suddenly alert, "You don't want to marry me anymore!"

"No," he said very patiently, "Far from it. Please be quiet while I try to tell you. I have been meaning to say for some time — you see — I love you so very much — "

"Oh, dear God!"

"Flora! *Do* shut up! I have been wanting to tell you for a while, but you are so very determined to be in charge! I wanted to explain that there will be no need for you to take in sewing or teach in a school like you've been planning — you see, and I'm sorry to disappoint you, but I am wealthy and have a very nice house with grounds — so you can stop worrying about our finances after we are wed!"

She stared at him for a second and then thumped his arm, "You utter blockhead! I thought you wanted to retract your offer of marriage — I *thought* — oh, I could *throttle* you! That's nice that you have a house. I'm very happy for you. Does it have a nursery? I'd like to have lots of children, if you wouldn't mind. Well, unless they turn out like Dora or Aunt Euphemia of course! I'm not sure I could cope with that. But at least we won't be homeless."

Mr Frost pulled her to her feet and kissed her quiet.

* * *

Augusta watched Quince digging frantically at the mouth of a rabbit burrow, a cascade of dirt and stones spraying out behind him. Every so often he stopped to snort loudly at the entrance to the tunnel and then continued with his futile excavation. He issued forth little barks of joy when he thought he'd sniffed out his quarry and then when no rabbits appeared, he remained cheerfully undaunted and continued his frenetic tunnelling with renewed vigour.

The sun was high in the sky and warm on her skin. There was a slight breeze, which she found a relief; she took her battered straw hat off and discarded it on the grass. She really didn't care if she got freckles, or her hair became disordered. Nothing seemed to matter anymore. It was as though she had been living in permanent expectation of a thunderstorm or an earthquake. She had been happy at the Manor, but she knew it couldn't last. Eventually Flora would marry and leave with Jonathan, and Dora would need to go to school again. Her aunts had to be found a home of their own, but she had no notion how that might be achieved; it kept her awake at night. She knew that what little looks she possessed were suffering, the dark shadows under her eyes a clear sign of her unrest.

But none of it mattered because she could not seem to have a sensible conversation with Marcus without angering him or finding herself near to tears, so although she had stopped trying to avoid him, she became, when face to face with him, unreasonably exuberant and she had to force herself to look him in his smouldering grey eyes, without revealing how she felt inside because to do that would mean to expose herself to ridicule or disappointment. And now, she'd had to come to terms with how stupid she had been and somehow find a way to rectify her mistakes. He had once thought her prim and proper and she realised to her dismay that she possessed a wide seam of prudery that occasionally startled her with its magnitude. That extraordinary night after the fire had, she decided, been caused by the extreme stress they'd been under and the relief of just being alive. There could be no other explanation for her shocking behaviour.

* * *

Earlier that day, Flora had informed her in her habitually blunt manner that she was being a ninnyhammer and that she was cutting off her splendid Beauchamp nose to be revenged upon her face!

"What are you afraid of, Gussie?"

"I don't *know!* Of being wrong, I suppose. Of not being good enough. Of being compared to the others."

"The *others!* You mean all those frippery females he probably never even cared a jot about?"

"Why is his awful wife still here?"

"*Former* wife! You're being a silly goose! Anyone can see that she's driving him to distraction!"

"Then why doesn't he ask her to leave?"

"Because of Imogen, of course."

Augusta fell into a deep abstraction.

Flora heaved an irritated sigh, "You are supposed to be the sensible one out of the three of us! You know, Jonathan sees this milkmaid face and the comfortable bosom and for some reason thinks me beautiful and loves me, but he is not dazzled by my attributes because he also sees the shrew and thankfully is not in the least daunted — he merely finds a way to make me feel safe and to make me laugh. You have become locked into being a spinster schoolmistress and cannot see beyond that. There is a valuable lesson to be learnt in this — that we are sometimes harder on ourselves than is necessary and that you can find love in the most surprising places. In Sir Marcus you have found someone who, for some unfathomable reason, has decided that you are the one. I cannot think why! He has shown you in every possible way that he loves you and yet still you run away from him. Is it because of his past? Is the idea that he had a life before he met you too much for you to countenance? Or is it because that life he had was so dissolute that you cannot forgive him?"

Augusta shook her head, "I don't know. I don't blame him for what happened to him — how could I? He was too young to have any say in the matter! If I blame anyone, it's his father, of course. I know that Marcus feels something for me — I've seen it for myself. But a man can be consumed by unreasonable lust for any female — it does not have to be love. He is so imbued with the depravity he grew up in, how can I ever be certain that I am not just a passing fancy or that he will not quickly tire of me once the novelty has worn off? I am despoiled now. Perhaps he is already regretting his actions."

"*Despoiled!* Merciful heavens! You were not *despoiled* Augusta — you went to *him* of your own free will! You *stayed* because you wanted to be with him. If anyone was the despoiler, it was *you!* He had already said a resounding no to you in the carriage and fended you off quite *heroically*. He was being honourable at an intensely emotional time. And then after he had drunk an *entire* bottle of brandy and was easily led astray, you took advantage of him."

Augusta couldn't help laughing a little reluctantly, "I suppose you could say that, but it didn't seem that way at the time. It just seemed — right."

"There, that's all you need to know then! It seemed *right*. What a ridiculous creature you are! Making mountains out of molehills. You just need to think things through, and you will see. Jonathan says — "

"Oh, is that to become your new refrain — 'Jonathan says'!"

Flora giggled, "Well, I must own that he does say some exceedingly sensible things! He *said* — that he'd never seen his cousin like this before, that Sir Marcus's temper is frayed to tatters and yet he appears to be happier than he's ever seen him!"

"Really?" gasped Augusta.

"Jonathan says — that Marcus talks of little else but you. In fact, he's becoming a dead bore! It's Augusta this and Augusta that! Although apparently he does not always put it so politely!"

"He *is* rather inclined to use poor language when he's sorely tried but I expect that he learnt it in those — gaming hells!"

"Gussie! You cannot say such things! What if Aunt Ida should hear you? Or Lady Denby!"

"Oh, pooh to Lady Denby — what a widgeon! I cannot understand why a man like Sir Leopold would marry such a hen-witted creature!"

"Precisely because she *is* hen-witted, and he could ignore and abuse her as he pleased. It's a wonder they managed to have such a lovely boy as Charles — he's like a human version of Quince! Needs lots of exercise and plenty of food!"

"Oh, Flora! I shall not be able to look him in the eye now!"

"Who? Quince?" asked Flora, grinning.

Dora burst in a moment later to find her elder sisters convulsed in fits of giggles.

She stood and looked at them in despair, "Honestly, it's jolly lucky that I am so sensible! Augusta, Mr Bacon is here to see you, I bumped into him in the drive and thought I'd warn — let you know of his arrival. He looked horribly serious."

Flora looked at Augusta, who was suddenly soberly unsmiling, "You'd better tidy your hair, it's looking a little windblown. What shall you say to him?"

"I have no notion!" muttered Augusta crossly, trying to smooth her hair into some semblance of order. "Whatever he wants, it can only be bad news. He has obviously heard about the fire and has come to offer his ponderous condolences."

"I'll come with you as chaperone," said Flora selflessly.

"You only want to hear what he has to say and anyway you never mind leaving Marcus alone with me!"

"True but then the worst has already happened where you and he are concerned! Any efforts to keep him out of your dastardly clutches seem a little pointless now."

Augusta cast her a withering look and they went out to meet Mr Bacon.

Twenty-Four

Mr Cornelius Bacon was feeling exceedingly high-minded as he waited in the parlour. He had overcome his extreme reluctance to cross the threshold of this house of ill-repute, concluding that as an English gentleman of some note, he had an obligation to the honour of his family name and to his own laudable reputation, and as someone with the noblest instincts, he realised that he had a solemn duty to perform that could only enhance his standing in the eyes of the people who mattered.

The door opened and he turned to greet Miss Pennington and Miss Flora with his usual stiffly formal bow and, bearing in mind the significance of his visit, he remained in an attitude of obsequious genuflection for several moments longer than was entirely necessary.

"Cornelius! Again, you have surprised us! What brings you to the Manor? I would have thought you would have given it a wide berth after previously hearing your opinions on Sir Marcus and his relations."

Mr Bacon advanced towards her and kissed her hand with just a touch of reverence, "Miss Pennington, I am happy to see you although I must say that you do not look at your most radiant."

"How kind of you to mention it, Cornelius. I think I have a good excuse for looking a little tired — the fire, you know? Do pray be seated and tell me what has brought you here."

Mr Bacon bowed again and then went through his ritual of finding and preparing a place to sit. Augusta exchanged a speaking glance with Flora as they sat down and waited for him to make himself comfortable.

As every movement he made was as though he were trapped in aspic and in no particular hurry to be free, the wait seemed interminable.

In an attempt to speed things along Augusta began talking before he was sufficiently composed and nevertheless had to wait, with her words floating impatiently in the air, until he had arranged the skirts of his coat and taken out his quizzing glass to polish it, by which time Augusta was seething.

"In answer to your question, Augusta, I have been to see the family lawyer once more — he resides nearby, as I believe I have already told you and would have thought you might remember. I often have business with him. His practice is conveniently close by." He carefully crossed his thin legs, smoothing the creases from his breeches with an air of someone who has all the time in the world to arrange his clothing to his exacting requirements. "It is a mere two miles from there to Cuckoopen Manor. Although it is some ten miles from my home to here and the roads are, in places, suffering from this unpleasant spell of warm weather. The going is quite hard. We passed two overturned vehicles on the way. My groom was good enough to check each carriage for injured persons but found that they had been abandoned, so on we went. Risking life and limb. The purpose of my visit today will, naturally, be no surprise to you." He gave Augusta his best and most condescending smile, "I heard the dreadful news from our parson, who had heard it from one of his parishioners in church. He bethought himself of me and my connection with the school and with you, of course and felt I should know of your predicament as soon as possible. He rode straight over to us and enlightened us as to the shocking result of the fire."

As he was forced to take a breath Augusta quickly interrupted, "It was an unfortunate accident. It began with a small fire in the hay store and quickly spread. We were sad to lose the school, of course, but thankful that no one was seriously hurt or killed."

"Ah, you mistake my meaning, Augusta! The destruction of the school was not my primary concern. In fact, all things considered, it was probably for the best."

Augusta opened her mouth to utter her outraged thoughts, but he continued unabated.

"As I have already told you, the idea of you teaching in a ladies seminary did not sit well with my father and his opinion is of prime importance to me. He thinks females are best taught only the genteel things of life — sewing and painting, music and dancing. All the requirements they will need for marriage. To try to teach them more is to tempt them to become dissatisfied with their lives. My father believes that if that were to happen, the very essence of English life would be in great peril!"

Augusta, quite overcome with a desire to throw the fire irons at her guest, jumped to her feet, her face suffused with high colour, "Your father sounds like a complete gudgeon, and I have to say that although I feel desperately sorry for your mother — she must have been utterly shatter-brained to marry such a fossil in the first place! Would you please come to the point of your visit, Cornelius before I lose my temper!"

Mr Bacon regarded her in some confusion, "I have no notion why you should have become so agitated, Augusta! I must say it is not very becoming behaviour. But, as you say, I am on a mission and must tell you how I came to be here today."

"I do wish you would!"

He cast her a wounded look, "You seem to be particularly prickly today, Augusta. I find your hostile attitude hard to understand when the compromised position you are in, is entirely your own fault. To be in this house, of all houses! It is the most shocking state of affairs. You must be sensible to the whispers — even my own clergyman was scandalised by your predicament! You must realise that by putting yourself into the hands of Sir Marcus Denby that you have sullied your name. Your poor aunts and your sisters, innocents who will suffer because of your choice to bring them here to this — this house of vice and shame! And the Misses Beauchamp — to end their lives under such a cloud of ignominy, it's a wonder it can be borne at all."

"So, you have come here to insult me and to defame our kind host, whose benevolence has saved us from being homeless and hungry?" said Augusta in dangerous tones.

Mr Bacon, not recognising the warning signs, blundered on, "I had heard that it was due to his efforts that you were rescued from the fire, which is commendable, but I must remind you that we are all tied to our pasts and shaped by them. Sir Marcus is renowned for his life of debauchery and even more, for his lack of remorse. But, even taking all this into account, I have come to offer you a way out of your shameful predicament. I have discussed it at length with my father and we are agreed that my offer of marriage still stands and that, with certain caveats, we may be wed. As soon as possible, in order to quell the scandalmongers. We shall start our married life together in my father's house, but he insists that, as soon as we have issue, we should remove to the very substantial Lodge, in the grounds. So, we will be on hand if they need you to help them and the children will not bother my father's sensitive hearing. It will be mutually beneficial. We are far enough away from any neighbours to not be bothered by their gossiping and curiosity and you need not go out into society."

Augusta sank back into the chair and put her head in her hands, "Flora, I fear I am about to commit murder," she muttered.

"I will protest your innocence to my last breath!" declared Flora.

Mr Bacon looked from one to the other, "I do not understand."

"No, of course you don't! All you can see is that by taking in my aunts, my sisters, my staff and seven of my girls, that Sir Marcus is some kind of fiend! Which, of course, is utter nonsense! By rescuing me *twice*, I might add, through no fault of his own, he is, according to you, acting only as one would expect a libertine to act! I think that you have got your moral rectitude in a tangle, Mr Bacon! You *dare* to stand there — or rather sit there — and pronounce Sir Marcus beyond salvation and denounce him as a degenerate when just a week ago he risked his life to rescue a dozen people he barely knows — as well as a sickly baby! And a perfectly *beastly* dog. He is, frankly, the bravest, kindest, wittiest, most *provoking* man I have ever had the misfortune to meet! You, on the other hand, have done nothing heroic or useful and as far as I can see you do not have any merit at all! If you think that I am going to leave the shelter of a *gentleman* — and I use the word deliberately — of the calibre of Sir Marcus Denby, in order to marry a good-for-nothing dandiprat like you — you must be unhinged. Now, I have things to do so I would be exceedingly grateful if you would please leave before I call Sir Marcus and his very large relatives and have you forcibly removed!"

Augusta marched to the door and wrenched it open in a fury, "And kindly tell your father that the very notion of having to live in close proximity with him has driven me willingly into the arms of Sir Marcus, a known seducer and drunkard! Perhaps he'd care to say a prayer for me when he's next in church! I bid you good day, sir!"

Shocked and utterly bewildered, Mr Bacon picked up his hat and gloves and made his way unsteadily across the parlour and quite forgetting to bow or say farewell, he staggered into the hall and out to his carriage with no idea in his head about what had just happened. His father would later tell him that he'd had a lucky escape and he might have ended up wed to a female so lacking in morals that the Bacon family name would have been dragged through the mire and never recovered its social standing. He said darkly that Miss Pennington and Sir Marcus deserved each other and would come to bitterly regret their unnatural union.

Flora stared at her elder sister with deepest respect, "I had no *notion* — if I *ever* had any doubts about your feelings — that little performance was enough to convince me that Sir Marcus has not only won your heart but also your mind. I can see no reason for you to hesitate any longer, Gussie!"

Augusta was still shaking from her encounter with Cornelius Bacon and having a little difficulty breathing in a normal fashion. She felt very hot and suddenly had a strong desire to be outside in the fresh air.

"I shall take Quince out for a walk in the grounds," she told Flora. "I need time to think."

Flora suddenly hugged her and said, "Well, be quick about it! Time and tide wait for no man — or woman! You know what is right so don't try to talk yourself out of making the most rational decision."

* * *

And so, Augusta found herself sitting in the Far Meadow watching Quince joyously ruin a perfectly nice grassy bank in his quest for a rabbit to chase. She had ostensibly just wanted some fresh air and time to think but her thoughts were muddled, and she seemed to be going round in circles.

Quince let out a muffled snort of indignation and backed out of the hole he'd made and looking utterly ridiculous with a small hill of dirt balanced on his nose, he ambled wearily over to where Augusta was sitting and threw himself onto the grass beside her, panting expressively. He rolled his eyes at her, flopped back and promptly fell asleep, exhausted and disillusioned. Augusta, unable to marshal her thoughts into any order that pleased her or just made any sense, lay down with her head on Quince's shoulder and squinted up at the few feathery clouds gathering above her head, the brightness of the harebell blue sky making her close her eyes, and within minutes she was asleep.

It was the first few large drops of rain hitting her face that woke her.

Startled she began to scramble up, in the process, waking Quince from his pleasant dreams and as he tried valiantly to get to his feet, he became all legs and knees like newborn foal, and slithered desperately on the wet grass trying to get a foothold and making an impressive job of distributing mud all over Augusta. She felt it splatter onto her face and tried to smear it away, only managing to make it worse.

"You thoughtless creature! Look at what you've done! Oh, it's raining so hard! We shall be drenched by the time we get back to the house. Why did you let me sleep, you abominable hound!"

Augusta snatched up her sodden hat, lifted her skirts and ran.

Quince, thinking this was purely for his amusement, yelped with delight and danced along beside her, jumping up at intervals and unhelpfully getting tangled in her petticoats. She had quite a job just staying on her feet and her progress was hampered by the heavy rain loosening her hair so that wet tendrils flew into her eyes, blinding her.

As she ran, she had just one thought in her head; she had to find Marcus.

Flora was right. She'd been a fool. Her life as a schoolmistress had not prepared her for the onslaught that was Sir Marcus Denby and everything that came with him, all the darkness from his past that leeched into the present and the damage it had done to him or, in the end, the surprising strength of her feelings for him.

She had been left confounded by the unaccustomed deluge of emotions and sensations over which she had no control and, in the beginning, had desperately tried to resist her feelings, but to no avail as he had stolen her heart anyway. To have such a wicked person take an interest in her when she thought she was so very commonplace had been both alarming and intoxicating. Being blessed with one volatile and yet remarkably pretty sister and another who was so wild and amusing that she drew the attention in a very natural way, it was hard not to make unfavourable comparisons.

She slowed her momentum as she reached the lawn at the side of the house and thinking that her shoes and gown were now ruined past repair, she laughed at her own folly.

The rain was running in rivulets down her neck and her saturated tippet was sticking to her skin; she would have to tidy herself before seeing anyone or they would think she had lost her mind.

She decided to go in by the side door, which led to a corridor by which she could access the back staircase and reach the first floor without being seen.

She had to pass by the withdrawing room windows and prayed that it was unoccupied so that she could sneak past without notice.

As she approached them, she heard the unmistakeable sound of exasperated voices and without thinking, stopped to listen. The noise of the rain made it hard to discern what was being said to start with, but she could tell it was Lady Birch, her voice was all too clear and throbbing with emotion. The other voice, having a deeper tone, could barely be heard but Augusta could tell that Sir Marcus sounded as though he were controlling himself with the greatest difficulty.

She flattened herself against the wall, half-hidden in the creeper that framed the window. Quince, fearing he was expected to stand there in the rain, rolled his eyes and made off around the house to the stables, in the hopes of finding someone to give him a rub down and a bone to gnaw upon.

The tense voices drifted out through the half-open casement and Augusta strained to hear what they were saying, at the same time as scolding herself for being an unprincipled eavesdropper.

"But Marcus, we all make mistakes! You must surely be able to forgive mine just as I forgave yours! Mine was so small and insignificant in comparison."

"Leaving me for Fabian? Insignificant? I think you mistook the gravity of the situation."

"I cannot be blamed for a momentary lapse in judgement. I wanted to punish you for being so thoughtless. You only really cared for Imogen."

"That, taking everything into consideration, is hardly surprising."

"I wanted you to fight for me. To prove your love. But you just gave up. And for all these years I have suffered because of that cruel decision. I have been caught like a fly in a web. Fabian does not love me — he loves only himself! He thinks only of his clothes and which club he should frequent, and I have to tell you that I believe he — has tendencies!"

A bitter laugh was heard, "Who can blame him if he has? Although, I do not believe the talk in the clubs. I'm sorry for him, he means no harm, apart from being a trifle self-regarding. He is merely a popinjay who also had the misfortune to fall under a malevolent spell. But perhaps you were dazzled by his prodigious wealth?"

"Well, despite that wealth, he is nonetheless callously penny-pinching, which you never were."

"I was unfortunately influenced by my father's ostentatious manner and look where that got him. He left Gertrude nothing but debts and a step-son who despises her."

"I don't know why you despise her. She is my dearest friend."

There came no reply.

Augusta shivered, the warmth she had felt before had dissipated and the rain continued unabated, relentlessly dripping from the vines and soaking her down to her skin.

She thought they'd finished speaking and made a move to leave her hiding place.

"Oh, Marcus, my darling, can you not forgive me? I cannot bear to be with Fabian any longer. I find him tedious and so very weak. Would it not be better if I came here to be with you and Imogen and we could be a family again."

"We were never a family, Miranda."

"But we could be! I am sure we could make it work this time."

"Do you really think you could be faithful? And live with Imogen? Put up with my ill temper, my blue devils? You would not be so keen I think once you had weighed up your options and found that you cannot live without unlimited riches and the fashionable society you love so much."

"You are not precisely pockets to let though!"

"No, indeed, I am very comfortable, thank you. And Imogen? What would we do with our daughter?"

"Well, I was thinking that she could go to that very good boarding school in Bath. Gertrude says it's highly regarded amongst the *ton*."

"I don't think Imogen would like that — and nor would I."

"What has Imogen to do with anything! She will not want to be here if I am here. She does not care for my company at all!"

"You only have yourself to blame for that."

"You would not want to send her back to Birch House! Fabian is not at all keen on children. He thinks them noisy, dirty things. I had to keep her locked away in the nursery so that he didn't complain all the time."

"Locked away in the nursery? Yes, she mentioned that."

"What would you have me do with her, for God's sake?"

There was a slight pause, "Love her, perhaps."

"I tried, Marcus, *I tried!* But she never favoured my company and when you and I divorced — how *hard* it is to utter that dreadful word! — she was left entirely in my care —"

"And the nursemaid's."

"Well, as to that — the nursemaid is old and not much use —"

"And yet you consigned Imogen to her custody."

"We led such a busy life, I had no choice," said Lady Birch sulkily. "Oh, do not be so cross with me! You know how it upsets me!"

"You insisted on the divorce — it was not of my making, although in the end I was forced to obtain one because of the scandal you embroiled us in — not that I give a damn about such things."

"No, you would have stayed because of Imogen though! But not for me!"

"God, Miranda, you were desperate to have Fabian. You can hardly accuse me of duplicity or favouritism when the whole shambles was of your making," his voice was deep with emotion and Augusta closed her eyes on the tears that welled up.

"But Marcus, I have only ever loved you! Fabian was a terrible mistake because I wanted to make you jealous. You always seemed so distant — so unapproachable. I couldn't reach that part of you that you keep buried — you kept me at arm's length."

Augusta heard a movement from inside the withdrawing room.

"*Look* at me! Am I not still beautiful and desirable? Do you not want me? We were so perfect together. I looked ravishing next to you. We could have that again. Oh, Marcus! You cannot possibly prefer that insipid church mouse to me!"

A silence fell and Augusta felt a wave of nausea but could not help inching forward and peering around the window mullion.

Through the rain-streaked glass she could see Lady Birch had her arms about his neck.

Her heart shattered into pieces.

"Marcus, my love!" said Lady Birch in sultry tones.

Augusta bit her lip so hard it began to bleed.

"Marcus!"

She dug her fingernails into her palms to stop herself from crying out.

"What do you mean by this?" demanded Lady Birch petulantly.

"You will see, if you care to read it. It is from my attorney. I think you will find everything is in order. To sum it up for you as simply as I can, I am taking Imogen away from you and your so dear husband forthwith. You shall not have her again."

"I — I don't understand — you *cannot* — I will not allow it!"

"Do you know Lord Latimer? He is the magistrate who has kindly taken charge of our case. He has explained that the father always has the right to take their child. It matters not about his reputation — they simply do not take that into account. The father holds all the cards, which in this particular case, is a good thing."

"Lord Latimer? But — "

"Yes, it seems that his daughter Mabel attended the school, and he was rather pleased to have her returned to them unscathed after the fire, Jonathan having carried her out of the building to safety. Lord Latimer was also most grateful that we had given her shelter. It turns out, that not only is he a very reasonable fellow, but he also wields a good deal of influence. The fire has brought unexpected benefits in many ways, you see — one of them being my little church mouse."

"That's very clever of you. You have certainly thought it all through. There is, however, one thing that must have a bearing on the case and you haven't taken into consideration, Marcus, my dear — and that is, Imogen is not in fact your daughter!" Lady Birch sounded triumphant.

There was a sudden crashing of something that sounded like furniture being knocked over and Marcus said in menacing tones, "Do you think I am stupid, Miranda? I have *always* known. The poor child has it written all over her face. Also, I had finally come to understand you and how you like to manipulate people. I have always known the truth and it makes no odds to me. She will be happy here with me. I wouldn't put Quince into your care let alone my child!"

Lady Birch let out an eldritch screech and from the sound of it must have launched herself at Marcus.

Augusta took off running, skidding across the slippery lawn, up the steps and into the hall before she had had time for a coherent thought, and she burst into the withdrawing room at the same time as Jonathan who had also arrived having heard the scream.

Augusta stood on the threshold of the room, her chest heaving, hair hanging in dripping coils, gown and shoes soaked and muddy, her face smeared with dirt and tears mingling with the rain on her cheeks.

Jonathan immediately leapt into action and gently but forcibly guided Lady Birch into the nearest armchair and held her flailing arms so that she could do no one any damage.

Marcus turned and looked at Augusta.

His face was pale and haggard. She made a move towards him but saw him flinch, so she stopped and waited.

Lady Birch, seeing Augusta and the state she was in, just laughed. It was a spiteful sound, "Oh, dear me! So, this is the glorious siren that keeps you here? I had thought you'd lost your mind over a church mouse, my dear — but *this?* This is the best you can do? I pity you!"

Marcus said nothing.

The disturbance had brought the others from all parts of the house. Augusta found an arm circling her waist and looked down to see Dora beside her and behind her was Flora looking warlike, then came Imogen, looking terrified, and tottering in after her, Aunt Ida, keen not to miss the excitement. Then, arriving in a scrabbling of claws, and excited panting, Quince, newly washed and brushed and looking very pleased with himself and Charles, trailing after him, looking decidedly wet and spattered with mud.

"What on earth — ?" he exclaimed, seeing the peculiar scene before him, "Have I missed something?" His astonished gaze took in his brother's stony expression, Augusta's sorry state, the rain dripping from her clothes and making small puddles on the floor at her very wet feet, and Jonathan apparently restraining Lady Birch. "I had to put Quince in the horse trough to get him clean," he explained, but no one heard.

Lady Birch shook off Jonathan's hands and rubbed her wrists, "It seems you have missed the truth coming out! It seems that you have missed your stepbrother hoodwinking me at the last moment. I am not to be allowed to keep my daughter!"

"Papa!" cried Imogen, her hand to her mouth, eyes wide.

A gleeful laugh greeted this, "Oh, my poor dear child — of course, you don't know do you — !"

"Miranda! Don't!" snarled Marcus.

"Imogen, it turns out your *darling* Papa is not actually your father!"

There were gasps all around the room.

Imogen regarded her mother with contempt, "I know, and I don't care," she replied quite clearly.

A stunned silence fell, broken only by the sound of Quince licking his leg.

"You know?" said Marcus, holding out his hand to her.

She ran lightly across the room and took the proffered hand and leant against him, "I overheard Mama and Lady Denby talking in the garden — I didn't mean to — not *really* — you see, she said you didn't know — and that's why I ran away! Mama said she didn't want to keep me — and I was afraid that if you found out that you would make me leave —"

Her father pulled her to him and kissed the top of her mousy head, "That will never happen, Imogen. You see, I have always known from the very beginning, and it changed nothing and now I have made sure that you will be able to stay here with me. You will always be my daughter so there's no need to be afraid anymore — or to run away again!"

She buried her head into his coat and muffled sounds of sobbing could be heard. Marcus looked up and met Augusta's watery gaze — she was trying hard not to cry too.

Miss Ida, unable to stand up any longer, found a chair and sank into it, "If someone would care to explain — "

Twenty-Five

Lady Birch stood up, her face a shade less beautiful than it usually was, "I shall not keep you any longer. Gertrude and I shall remove to an inn for the night and leave for Birch House in the morning."

"There's absolutely no need for that Miranda. You may as well stay and leave in good order tomorrow. I don't suppose Gertrude would relish the notion of sleeping at The Wheatsheaf and I doubt she would find Mrs Crouch, the landlady, at all agreeable."

"You think I want to stay under your roof a moment longer than I have to — !"

Jonathan interrupted her, "If Marcus says it's all right, for God's sake just be grateful and accept the offer! Surely we've had enough of all of this nonsense now!"

Augusta was watching Marcus, trying to read his expression, but his face might as well have been carved from stone. Dora was holding onto her for dear life and Flora could be heard muttering darkly under breath.

Charles, who had been leaning against the door jamb, arms folded across his chest, suddenly said, "If anyone's interested, I can hear a carriage approaching!"

"Oh, Heaven forfend! It's probably Mr Bacon come back to try again!" complained Flora.

"To try what again?" asked Marcus.

"To get Gussie to marry him. She threw him out on his ear last time! You should have heard her — like a veritable virago! Or do I mean Valkyrie? I'm never quite sure which is which."

"Oh? And why was she so — violent?"

"Defending your honour, of course! Apparently, you're not far off becoming a *bona fide* saint! You should have *heard* her!" laughed Flora.

"I wish I had," said Sir Marcus quietly.

Augusta cast her sister a fulminating glance which Flora ignored.

The cacophonous sound of wheels and horses' hooves on the gravel drive could be heard, the shouts of the driver and grooms and a good deal of unnecessary bellowing.

"This Mr Bacon — " began Marcus but never finished the sentence because the hall erupted into chaos as Beecher opened the front door. Quince, sensing an invasion by persons unknown, leapt to his feet barking furiously and flew out of the room to attend to the intruders. There could be heard shouts of rage and dismay, growling and Beecher's voice raised in a commanding fashion, "Quince! *Sit!* Sit down! Let go of the gentleman! I am so sorry, sir!"

Marcus handed Imogen to Miss Ida to comfort and strode out into the hall to see what was going on.

There followed a shout of laughter.

He returned dragging the unrepentant dog, hackles still standing to attention and teeth bared, and was followed, at a more leisurely pace, by a vision in periwinkle blue satin, face delicately painted, with a towering wig, such falls of lace that would have made even Royalty envious, jewels glinting fiercely, and bearing an embroidered parasol in pleated pale blue silk.

He was met by stunned silence and several mouths falling open in a combination of consternation and poorly suppressed amusement. Charles was heard to snort gracelessly and received a warning frown from his elder brother.

The visitor lifted his quizzing glass and observed the occupants of the room, his eye finally falling upon a shocked Lady Birch.

"My good wife, Lady Birch. There you are. I am come to fetch you. You will gather your belongings at once and be ready to leave in half an hour. Do not keep me waiting. It's raining so I do not want to be kept kicking my heels in the damp air, it is not good for my chest. Come along! Do not just stand there gawping!"

Everyone then looked at Lady Birch, who was frozen with one hand in the air as though she had meant to catch something and then forgotten what she was doing. Her beautiful mouth was forming a perfect O and she was clearly shaken by the sudden arrival of her husband.

"This is like a Shakespearean comedy," whispered Dora but loud enough for everyone to hear.

Lady Birch still didn't move.

"I will give you this one last warning, Madam! Either you do as I say, or I shall enlist my servants to remove you by force."

"Oh, my word," said Miss Ida, in thrilled accents.

Lady Birch's face flushed becomingly, "Well, there's absolutely no need for this ridiculous demonstration of manliness, Fabian! I will come when I am quite ready and not before."

"You will come right *now!*" bellowed Lord Birch waving his parasol at her in a menacing manner and taking a threatening step towards her.

Lady Birch laughed nervously and tripped daintily across the room to him, "There's no need to shout in such a vulgar fashion!" she hissed at him, as she went out into the hall.

He followed her, but at the door he turned back to his stupefied audience, "I do beg your pardon! I am quite sure that she has been a great trial to you all and it is most unfortunate, but she cannot seem to help it. She just needs a firm hand. Sir Marcus, as ever, your servant!" he made a florid bow, waving his glass in their general direction and then nodding briefly at everyone else, he went out.

Charles closed the door behind him and leant against it, his eyes dancing, "That was *most* unexpected! I thought Quince would eat him, but he bravely fended him off with his parasol, if you please!" He shook his head in wonderment, "What in God's name *was* that, Marcus!"

"That, my dear boy, was Lord Fabian Birch, who, by some miracle, seems to have found a backbone just in the nick of time!"

Jonathan let out his breath as though he'd been holding it in, "I have never seen him so incensed before! I quite thought he would burst his stays!"

Marcus smiled at Imogen and held out his arms again and she flew into them, resting her head against his waistcoat, "Papa!"

"Yes, my daughter!"

Miss Ida looked at her elder niece and said softly, "Augusta, you'll catch your death in those wet clothes! You really should go and change, my dear."

Flora suddenly bestirred herself, as though she'd been in a daze. She made an expressive face at Jonathan who immediately went to her side and looked down at her enquiringly, she put a hand on his arm to steady herself, "Would you be so kind as to tell Lady Denby that there will be tea in a moment and call Beecher and ask him to bring tea to the withdrawing room. I think Aunt Ida might like some refreshment after all the excitement and Dora and Imogen would certainly appreciate some cake, I am sure! And Charles, perhaps you might like to — oh, I don't know — walk the dog?"

"But *Flora!*" protested that young man, "I've just bathed and dried him and it's still pouring outside! I'm dashed well not going out in this again. I'm going to change my clothes — he covered me in filthy water when he shook himself!"

"Then, I expect you will want to take Quince with you and shut him away where he can do no more harm and talking of harm, 'tis a pity that we shall still have Lady Denby here — it is certainly not ideal but I'm sure I can find some purpose for her. Off you go then, Charles."

Charles made a face at her but obediently left, dragging the bewildered hound with him. Jonathan blew Flora a kiss and left, thinking what a magnificent creature she was.

Flora gently pushed Dora and Imogen into chairs at the beautifully polished table and guided Aunt Ida to a deep wing chair by the fire, "Tea won't be long," she told them.

She then took Augusta by the hand and led her out and across the hall to the study, "There's a nice fire in there and it's very cosy," she said firmly and propelled her in. She frowned back at Sir Marcus who was standing quite still, and she gestured towards her sister, "It's time," she said imperiously, "Try not to make a mess of it."

He found himself being encouraged across the hall and into the study. Flora shut the door emphatically behind him.

* * *

Aunt Ida smiled at the girls, "It's been quite a day has it not! I don't believe it could have been much more exciting, do you?"

Dora rolled her eyes, "No, it's been very odd. Why has Flora taken Gussie and Sir Marcus away, Aunt Ida? Gussie looks like she's fallen in the lake! What a *sight!* I wonder what they're doing. Will they come to tea do you think? There will be cake!"

"I don't think so, dear, not just yet at least."

Imogen was staring into the fire and looking thoughtful, "I think there's not enough cake in the world to entice them," she mused.

"What do you *mean?*" asked Dora.

"I have the strangest feeling in my middle. Like when you jump off something very high."

"But what does that *mean?*"

"I think — and I do hope I'm right — I think that we may be going to be sisters."

Dora shook her head in bewilderment, "But *how?*"

"Oh, Dora! Do you not see? Papa and Miss Augusta — always fighting! But really, all along, they were just in love."

"In love! *Gussie!* With *Sir Marcus!* That can't be!" She stopped and frowned at Aunt Ida, "*Can* it? *Are* they in love?"

Miss Ida Beauchamp smiled wisely, "It would certainly seem so — although neither seem able to agree upon it at the moment. Sometimes there are barriers between people — invisible barriers — that they put up to defend themselves and sometimes those barriers can, if they're not careful, prevent them from being happy."

"Why do they not just knock the barriers down? *I* would!" declared Dora.

"That is a very good question, my love. I think, on the whole, they cannot see those impediments and because they are frightened of making a mistake or being embarrassed — they become stuck fast and cannot seem to disentangle themselves. Let us hope that Augusta and Sir Marcus can find a way to overcome their differences."

"I could help them! I could tell them that if they don't then Imogen and I will never be real sisters! That *must* persuade them! They would not want to ruin our lives!"

Miss Beauchamp nodded, "Yes, indeed that should do the trick! However, I think it's best left to them to decide because that is all part of falling in love. There are obstacles and tribulations, and they must learn to talk to each other and to listen to the other. You see, your lovely sister is used to being a very independent woman, she's used to running things as she likes them. It can be exceedingly difficult to then have to take into account someone else's opinions and wishes. I am sure they will find a way though. They are really quite sensible people underneath all the misunderstandings. It's just that high emotions have a way of complicating quite simple matters. You will see one day, when it happens to you, Dora."

Dora looked quite revolted, "I do hope not! I do not think I could bear to behave in such a childish fashion! It would be too awful."

"We shall see, my dearest, we shall see."

* * *

Flora was being held in an enthusiastic embrace in the darkest corner of the hall. Her earlobe was being nibbled and kissed with great dedication, but she was busily bemoaning people's inordinate stupidity and was, therefore, a trifle distracted, "I shall give them half an hour to work things out and if there is no settlement by then I shall go in and knock their stupid heads together!" The kissing stopped, "No, *don't* stop! I like it!"

"Well, you could stop complaining and show your appreciation a little more conspicuously so that I don't feel that I am wasting my time!"

She looked up at him and smiled, "You could never do that. Carry on, do! I must own that it is a most pleasurable sensation!"

"Flora, my love! You make it sound as though I am reading you poetry! I do wish you would pay more attention!"

"I am so sorry but there are important matters taking place just behind that door over there. My sister's happiness depends entirely upon the outcome."

"I feel it necessary to point out, in a somewhat selfish manner, that *my* happiness depends upon you showing some interest in my loving attentions!" declared Jonathan indignantly amused.

Flora took a moment to convince him that he was very much appreciated and then continued to complain and worry while Jonathan gazed at her adoringly but with a wry smile lighting his kindly eyes.

* * *

In the quiet of the study, it could not yet be said that there was a meeting of minds. The warm, applewood scented air throbbed with an unusual intensity. The rain gently pummelled the leaded windowpanes — a very persistent summer downpour. The fire crackled lethargically, but the occupants of the room made no sound.

Augusta found that breathing was all she could manage. She seemed to have been stunned into some kind of trance-like state, where she could hear and see but all other senses had been rendered useless. Her sodden skirts leant heavily against her legs, weighed down with rain and mud and her hair stuck to her forehead in lank curls. The silk of her shoes was shrinking and pinching her toes and the ribbon on one stocking had come undone so that it was sliding uncomfortably down her leg. The mud on her face was starting to dry and felt tight and itchy and she was covered in gooseflesh and shivering. It was not the best of circumstances.

She couldn't look at Marcus, who was still standing in the shadows on the far side of the study. Her eyes were firmly fixed upon the fire as it was the only animated thing in the room, but she didn't see it.

"You should get out of those wet clothes," said her companion gravely.

She looked up at him, startled out of her daze.

He shook his head, "No, I was not implying anything other than you will catch cold if you do not change into dry clothes."

She returned to studying the flames.

"I am surmising from your bedraggled state and your precipitous arrival in the withdrawing room that you overheard my conversation with Miranda."

Augusta, at once ashamed of being caught eavesdropping but also too confused by events to be able to think clearly, was caught in a no man's land where she didn't dare say or do anything. She was overcome by too many terrible possibilities and could not even begin to fathom what she wanted, or what she should do.

"If you were listening, you hopefully heard that I want nothing to do with her." He was watching Augusta's face for any signs of a reaction, "And you know that I am to keep Imogen. I always knew that Miranda had lied about the real father and now the child is grown I can recognise Fabian in her face. When she was just a baby and life was already becoming untenable, I came to the conclusion that I could not abandon her to their tender mercies, whomever the father might be, but it was taken out of my hands. Seeing her again has only confirmed that feeling. So, now, I officially have a daughter. And, as you saw, Miranda is leaving — with her poor husband who, I am forced to admit, has rather impressed me. Imogen will be happy here, I shall make damn sure of that, but she would be even happier still if she had a mother who could love her."

At this Augusta turned her head to regard him blankly.

"Damn it, just say something Augusta! Anything. Say you hate me. Say you want to leave but please talk to me."

"You let her embrace you," said Augusta bleakly.

He made an impatient sound, "No, I did not, I stopped her from trying to embrace me and handed her the papers. The whole argument was about trying to be rid of her but to hold onto Imogen and somehow win you. That's all I want. Since that moment when you were so ferocious with me about Mrs Crouch and then when you fell into whoops over the goose in the chimney. That's when I began to realise that I had carelessly stumbled into a bear-pit!"

"Thank you," she said, flinching slightly.

"It's true. I have never had any desire to shoulder responsibilities or to allow anything to shackle me again. I had had more than enough of that and just wanted an easy life without complications. Then along you came, and you were nothing but complications. And the more I saw of you, the more I had this urgent need to be with you. I fought it as best I could — ask Beecher if you don't believe me — he had to deal with the unsavoury aftermath. He was not at all pleased with me and I think was on the verge of quitting again, which would have been extremely inconvenient because he has always taken good care of me when I am blue devilled. I feel I should say, in my defence, that you are enough to try the patience of a saint, and we all know that I am not, nor ever shall be, a saint. I own that I was content with my previous life of dissipation — I knew very little else. And I make no excuses — I was old enough and wise enough by then to make different decisions about the way I conducted my life. I just felt it was a little too late to change. I suppose I had no reason to change — until one day when I had the misfortune to meet a prim and proper schoolmistress, who captured my heart and scattered my wits."

He rubbed his tired eyes with the heel of his hand and moved a few steps further into the room.

"I have something of yours. You left your shawl at the Manor after the cricket match — and I assured Jonathan that I would return it to you, but I kept it. It retains your scent, and I could not give it up. Will you not say anything?"

"What is there to say?" said Augusta woodenly, whilst her pulse raced wildly at the thought of him keeping her shawl because it seemed so intimate.

"Tell me what you're thinking."

"Why — why *me?* I am just a church mouse. I see Lady Birch and I cannot believe you."

"*Hear my soul speak: The very instant that I saw you, did my heart fly to your service; there resides, to make me slave to it.*"

She glared at him, "Do not *dare* to quote Shakespeare at a time like this!"

"What better time is there? I am prepared to use any weapon in my arsenal."

"It's wholly unfair."

"*All advantages are fair in love and war.*"

"Stop it."

"You said, when I came to find you in the fire, that you knew that I'd come. Why did you say that?"

"I have no idea. I was out of my mind with fear."

"Stop fighting, Augusta. We both know that there was something that bound us together right from the beginning. When I saw you were unhurt and that you had placed your faith in me — it made me realise that you believed in me in a way no one else had ever done. It made me want to protect you for the rest of my life, if you'd allow it," he said and searched her face for any hopeful signs of acquiescence.

"I was so certain in my heart that you would come — "

"And the look you gave me when you were caring for the baby — you had no time to disguise your feelings and I dared to hope."

"I was *very* tired," said Augusta weakly.

He smiled at her, "And then you threw yourself at me in the carriage — "

"I did not *throw* myself at you! I had been under a *great* deal of stress and then you rejected me!" she snapped.

"I could not possibly have taken advantage of you after such a traumatic experience. I can assure you that it was very much worse for me!"

She regarded him curiously, "I was in complete turmoil, and I see that I may not have been thinking very clearly at the time."

"If you only knew how difficult it was to say no to you! Much to Beecher's disappointment I then buried my woes in a bottle of brandy. But you came to me in your sleep, and it would have been churlish to refuse such a sweet offering!"

Augusta felt the guilty heat rise in her face and turned away, "Flora says I took advantage of you when you were insensible. She said you were easily led astray."

"Seeing you, curled up beside me in just your nightgown? It was like stumbling into Heaven. I was utterly lost. You were quite enchanting and so very willing to learn — "

Augusta covered her flaming cheeks with trembling hands, "Oh, please do not *speak* of it! I am so ashamed!"

"Ashamed! Don't be ridiculous. If you knew what it meant to me for you to show such trust in me — I have never felt like that before."

"It seems I am always to be covered in soot or mud when near you," said Augusta mournfully.

"At least you don't reek of brandy! I think you look perfectly delightful."

"You must have taken leave of your senses," she told him with gentle reproach. She bit her bottom lip and found the wound she had made earlier when listening through the casement and was reminded of her headlong race to reach him, "I was coming find you — to tell you — I finally understood and I needed to tell you immediately and then I overheard you talking to Lady Birch and I thought at first — but she attacked you — " she faltered.

"And you flew to my rescue like an avenging angel even though I know you cannot abide altercations — I suspect because of your father's poor behaviour, but you certainly made a spectacular entrance in order to defend me! I've never been so glad to see anyone in my life! Although the look in your eyes told me that you'd overheard and probably come to the wrong conclusion as you are rather inclined to."

There were sudden noises in the hall, servants talking, and trunks being manhandled and doors banging. Amongst it all, Lady Birch's imperious instructions could be heard. Then there was the sound of carriage doors being slammed in temper and eventually the crunching of wheels on the gravel and then blissful silence.

"They've gone, thank God," said Marcus with feeling.

"She is so very beautiful."

"Yes, she is beautiful, but it is an empty beauty, and she does not have the Beauchamp nose!"

Augusta's hand flew to cover the offending feature, "Oh, such a dreadful affliction!"

"Thankfully, you have no idea just how lovely you are, Augusta. When your golden eyes flash like a wildcat and when you laugh — helpless laughter, tears streaming down your face — God, there is no one more beautiful!"

"Oh, Marcus — you cannot mean it!"

"*Doubt that the stars are fire, doubt that the sun doth move his aides, doubt truth be a liar, but never doubt I love.*"

Augusta held out a hand to arrest him, "Don't! *Odious* man!"

Then she stopped, suddenly hearing his words.

"You *love*?"

"I do."

"Oh," murmured Augusta.

"*I would not wish any companion in the world but you.*"

"But — "

"I have waited a long time for you, Miss Pennington. I think I must have known in my heart that one day I might meet the perfect woman for me and was waiting patiently for you to arrive."

"I am not perfect. I am a prim church mouse."

"I am sorry you heard that, but I find that a prim church mouse is precisely what I've been looking for all these years and I will happily spend the rest of my days proving it to you if you will allow me."

"Oh," said Augusta again, her eyes shining with tears.

"Have you finally run out of nonsensical arguments?"

She gave him a tremulous smile, "I can think of no more — apart from the need to confess that I too have kept something — I still treasure the daisy chain you made for me that day by the river."

"I wish I had known that earlier — I would have had more reason to dare hope. I should perhaps tell you Augusta, that if you are truly not ready to take me on with all my imperfections, I am perfectly prepared to wait for you, for however long it takes to persuade you to change your mind," said Marcus, in a voice charged with emotion.

Augusta laughed at this, "You *idiot!* You'd only have to wait a minute!"

And seeing the expression on her face, he crossed the room in two strides and seized her in his arms so that he could cover her muddy, tearstained face in feverish kisses, quite taking her breath away with the ferocity of his embrace.

She was eventually forced to protest, whilst still clinging to him and nearly fainting from joy, "Marcus! I must catch my breath!"

A stifled moan burst from him, and he lifted his head and slightly relaxed his violent hold on her, *"I humbly do beseech of your pardon, for too much loving you!"*

She giggled into his neck, "Well, I must own that although it is exceedingly pleasurable, I was thinking that someone might hear!"

"I don't give a damn if they do!"

"I warned you that I am prim and proper! You had better learn to behave with a little consideration for my schoolmistressy ways."

"I will do anything you say."

"Really?" queried Augusta, an unholy glint in her eye.

"Anything," he promised, once more kissing her with very little restraint.

"Perhaps I should bathe first," she gasped.

"Oh, my God, Augusta! Do not tempt me with such images — ! When we are married I shall — "

"Married? Are we to be *married?* I had no notion! It is the first I've heard of it."

Sir Marcus Denby, exercising a good deal of self-control, put her away from him and with a stormy look, he lowered his considerable bulk down onto one knee in front of her.

She let out a horrified squeal, "Oh, no! What are you *doing!* Not when I look like *this!* You cannot!"

"I will do just as I please, Miss Pennington and this is how a knight should propose to his intended bride! Will you, for the love of God, consent to be my wife as quickly as possible so that you can make an honourable man of me at last and I can cease being jealous of the handsome Mr Bacon — whom we will need to talk more about in due course!"

Augusta threw herself down onto her knees and took his hands in hers, "Marcus, you utter dolt! You are the most honourable man I have ever known, and I love you more than I am able to express using mere words!"

And at this tender moment the door opened and in tumbled Flora followed by the rest of the family, who had all gathered impatiently in the hall to eavesdrop, and Quince, who quite lost his mind due to the noise and excitement in the study and leapt from one person to the next trying eagerly to convey the depth of his feelings.

Dora stood in the doorway and surveyed the chaotic scene before her, her arm around Imogen's waist, and said in a voice suppressed by tears, "*No sooner met but they looked, no sooner looked but they loved, no sooner loved, but they sighed, no sooner sighed but they asked one another the reason, no sooner knew the reason but they sought the remedy."*

The End

Epilogue

Mr Sippence was puzzled. He looked over his shoulder at the strange item in the back of the cart, which was causing him such concern and told the groom to stop dawdling, they had to get to the Manor as soon as possible. The groom, excited to be taking part in some kind of wild dash, whipped the rather plodding workhorse into an unsteady trot and they made their way slowly up the long hill to Cuckoopen Manor.

Miss Ida, Augusta and Flora were in the withdrawing room when Beecher ushered in Mr Sippence and the groom carrying a large object that obviously weighed almost more than he could comfortably bear.

"Mr Sippence!" cried Augusta, delighted to see him looking so well, "What on earth brings you all this way?"

Mr Sippence, being quite elderly and a little out of breath from his exertions, took a moment before replying, "Miss Augusta! I had to see you!"

"Oh, do come in and sit down! And, young man, put down that dreadfully heavy looking thing, you'll hurt your back!"

They both did as they were told and Augusta exchanged a puzzled look with Flora, who shook her head in confusion.

"Why did you have to come, Mr Sippence?"

"Well, we been clearing up, you know — around the school? There was a bit of a collapse two days ago and the final walls came down — quite a noise it made too, bringin' with it the dormitories and the attics above! It was lucky none of the men were in that area at the time, Miss! Anyway, all sorts came down — beams and chimneys and beds and chairs — and *this!*" He gestured towards the item they had brought with them, "This chest. We found it in the rubble."

Augusta got up and took a closer look.

She rubbed away the soot from the lid, revealing some gilded initials, topped by a crown.

"Oh, goodness gracious!" she breathed.

The door opened and Sir Marcus came in, followed by Jonathan.

Her eyes met those of her beloved and for a moment nothing else mattered as they smiled at each other.

Recalling herself, she gestured to the trunk, which was bound with brass straps and covered in brass studs and was mostly undamaged by the fire or its dramatic fall from the attics.

Puzzled, but realising what his task was to be, Marcus knelt and prised open the metal buckles and with some effort lifted the slightly warped lid.

Everyone gathered round the trunk.

Marcus grinned up at Augusta, shaking his head in wonderment.

Flora suddenly started laughing and leant against Jonathan, helplessly overcome.

"What is it my love?" he asked anxiously.

Flora mopped her eyes and tried to gather herself, "I cannot really believe it, but I think Mr Sippence has discovered Aunt Euphemia's famous but much doubted treasure chest of gold! The monogram! The Crown! It seems that everything she told me was true!"

Everyone looked at her in astonishment and then back at the laden strongbox and there was total silence apart from the sound of Quince scratching behind his ear with complete indifference.

Historical Romance

by Caroline Elkington

Set in the years shown

A Very Civil War (1645)
Dark Lantern (1755)
The House on the Hill (1765)
Three Sisters (1772)
The Widow (1782)
Out of the Shadows (1792)

A VERY CIVIL WAR
1645

Con's life in the small Cotswold village, where she spent an idyllic childhood, is nothing out of the ordinary, which is good because she likes ordinary. She likes safe.

Her three boisterous nephews have come to stay for the summer holidays, and she's determined to show them that life in the countryside can be fun — she has no idea just how exciting it's about to get.

Whilst out exploring with them in the fields near the village, they find themselves face to face with a Roundhead colonel from the English Civil Wars and, due to some glitching twenty-first century technology, Con is transported back to 1645 and into a world she only recognises from books and historical dramas on television and finds hard to understand. She reluctantly falls for the gruff officer, who is recovering from injuries sustained in recent hostilities with Royalists but must battle archaic attitudes and unexpected violence in order to survive.

With no way of getting back to her family and her nice secure real life and unable to reveal who she really is, for fear of being thought a witch, she struggles to acclimatise to her new life and must fight her growing feelings for Colonel Sir Lucas Deverell and deal with the daily problems of life in the seventeenth century and the encroaching war. When she intervenes to save a dying man, suspicions are raised and she begins to fear for her life, with enemies on all sides.

Constance Harcourt discovers a love that crosses centuries and all barriers, but which could potentially end in heartbreak. Can the power of True Love overcome the power of the Universe?

This is a time-slip story filled with passionate romance, the very real threat of persecution and war, the charm of the Cotswolds and touches of Beauty and the Beast.

Dark Lantern
1755

An unexpected funeral, a new life with unwelcoming relations and a mysterious stranger who is destined to change her life forever. Martha Pentreath has been thrust into a bewildering and perilous adventure.

Set in 1755, on the wild coast between Cornwall and Devon, this swashbuckling tale of high society and secretive seafarers follows Martha as she valiantly juggles her conflicting roles, one moment hard at work in the kitchens of Polgrey Hall and the next elbow to elbow with the local gentry.

Then as dragoons scour the coast for smugglers, she finds herself beholden to the captain of a lugger tellingly built for speed. Unsure whom to trust, Martha soon realises that everything she thought she knew was a lie and people are not what they seem.

With undercurrents of The Scarlet Pimpernel, Cinderella and Jamaica Inn, this is a story of windswept cliffs, wreckers, betrayal, secrets, murder and passionate romance.

Martha fights back against those who would relish her downfall and discovers the shocking truth about her own family. But she will find loyalty and friendship and a love that will surprise her but also bring her heartache.

THE HOUSE on the HILL
1765

After falling on hard times due to a family scandal, Henrietta Swift lives with her grandfather in a dilapidated farmhouse and is quite content to live without luxury or even basic comforts.

However, she's being watched.

Someone has plans for her and despite suffering misgivings she has no real choice but to accept their surprising proposition in order to give her beloved grandfather a better life.

It leads her to Galdre Knap, a darkly mysterious house, where her enigmatic employer, Torquhil Guivre, requires a companion for his seriously ill sister, Eirwen, who is being brought home to convalesce.

With her habitual optimism, Henrietta believes all will be well — until the other-worldly Eirwen arrives in a snowstorm. The house then begins to reveal its long-buried secrets and Henrietta must battle to save those she loves from the sinister forces that threaten their safety and her happiness.

In the process, she unexpectedly finds true love and discovers that the world is filled with real magic and that she is capable of far more than she ever thought possible.

Here be Dragons and Enchantment and Happy Ever Afters.

THREE SISTERS
1772

The prim and proper Augusta Pennington has taken over the management of a failing Ladies' Seminary with her two sisters, grumpy Flora and wild Pandora. Their elderly aunts, Ida and Euphemia Beauchamp, can no longer run the school and have been forced to hand over the reins. They are losing pupils, as they lag the fashions in female education, and are struggling financially.

Their scandalous and irascible neighbour, Sir Marcus Denby, is reluctantly drawn into their ventures by the younger sister, Pandora, who tumbles from one scrape into another, without any concern for her safety or her family's reputation.

With the help of Quince, a delinquent hound, Pandora befriends Sir Marcus's estranged daughter, Imogen, who has been much neglected by her beautiful but venomous mother.

Augusta, initially repelled by Sir Marcus's notoriety, tries desperately to resist the growing attraction between them. It takes a series of mishaps and the arrival of some unwanted guests to finally make Augusta understand that not everything is as it seems and love really can conquer all.

THE WIDOW
1782

Nathaniel Heywood arrived at Winterborne Place with no intention of remaining there for longer than it took to conclude a business proposition on behalf of his impulsive friend Emery Talmarch.

Impecunious, cynical and world-weary, he is reluctant to shoulder any kind of responsibility. Nathaniel was just looking for an easy way to make some money to save Emery from debtor's prison and possibly worse. He had no idea that he would be offered such an outrageous proposal by his host, Lord Winterborne, and find himself swiftly drawn into a web of intrigue and danger. He wants nothing more than to escape and be trouble-free again.

Above anything else he wanted his freedom.

And then he meets Grace.

OUT of the SHADOWS
1792

In this deeply romantic thriller, an inebriated and perhaps foolhardy visit to London's Bartholomew Fair begins with an eye to some light-hearted entertainment and ends with a tragic accident.

Theo Rokewode and his close friends find themselves unexpectedly encumbered with two young girls in desperate need of rescue. As a result, their usually ordered lives are turned upside down as danger stalks the girls into the hallowed halls of refined Georgian London and beyond to Rokewode Abbey in Gloucestershire.

Sephie and Biddy are hugely relieved to be rescued from the brutal life they had been forced to endure but know that they are still not truly safe. Only they know what could be coming and as Sephie loses her heart to Theo, she dreads the truth about her past being revealed and determines to somehow repay her new-found friends for their gallantry and unquestioning hospitality, but vows to leave before the man she loves so desperately sees her for what she really is.

Her carefully laid plans bring both delight and disaster as her past finally catches up with her and mayhem ensues, as Theo, his eccentric friends and family valiantly attempt to put the lid back on the Pandora's Box they'd unwittingly opened that fateful night at the fair.

ABOUT CAROLINE ELKINGTON

When not writing novels, Caroline's reading them - every few days a knock on the door brings more. She has always preferred the feel — and smell — of a real book.

She began reading out of boredom as she was tucked up in bed by her mother, herself an avid reader, at a ridiculously early hour.

In the winter months she read by moving her book sideways back and forth to catch a slither of light that shone through the crack between the hinges of her bedroom door.

Fast forward sixty years and she's someone who knows what she wants from a book: to be immersed in history (preferably Georgian), to be captivated by a romantic hero, to be thrilled by the story, and to feel uplifted at the end.

After a long career that began with fashion design and morphed into painting ornately costumed portraits and teaching art, she has a strong eye for the kind of detail that draws the reader into a scene.

Review This Novel and See More by Caroline

Point your phone's camera at the code.
A banner will appear on your screen.
Tap it to see Caroline's novels on Amazon.

Printed in Great Britain
by Amazon